A TREASURE WORTH SEEKING

Carolina looked up at him, her face flushed and expectant, and Drake's heart began a wild pounding against his ribs. How could he make her understand that he had loved her when he no longer believed in love, that he had wanted her when he had felt cursed with that desire? How could he tell her that she had healed wounds he had believed too deep to cure and that having her in his arms, knowing she belonged to him alone, was a treasure more precious than gold?

He stroked her cheek with trembling fingers, tracing the line of her brow, the curve of her jaw, the satin line of her lips. His voice was a throbbing whisper. "This is only the beginnin', darlin'. There are so many ways to say I love you."

Then gently, expertly, lovingly, he began to show her every one.

ELAINE BARBIERI

MORE PRECIOUS THAN GOLD

ZEBRA BOOKS
KENSINGTON PUBLISHING CORP.

ZEBRA BOOKS

are published by

Kensington Publishing Corp.
475 Park Avenue South
New York, NY 10016

First printing: September, 1992

Printed in the United States of America

Prologue

A leaden sky hung threateningly over the denuded hillside as Carolina braced herself against the biting wind. The muddy ground tugged at the hem of her gown as she walked between the uneven rows of grave markers and finally dropped to her knees beside the one she sought. Tears blurred her vision as she stared at the roughly carved name.

Bittersweet memories swept over her. She remembered the first time this man had held her in his arms. She recalled the tremor in his voice, the promise in his eyes, and the taste of his lips. She remembered that he had trembled as well as she in that ecstatic moment when their eager flesh had met, and that she had loved him so.

The wind whipped harder, flaying her with loosened strands of pale hair. Covering her face with her hands, Carolina sobbed. Her memories of him were so keen that they were almost debilitating. But somehow lost amid the joys, sorrows, and regrets was the most crucial detail of all — that exact moment when everything changed, and the beginning became the beginning of the end.

One

1876
Black Hills, South Dakota

The ground trembled under the thunder of approaching horses as gunfire from the circled wagons grew heavier. Savage war whoops echoed above shouted commands from within the grouped wagons, drowning out sharp cries of pain signifying another of the wagon train party had fallen.

Covering her ears against sounds of the lethal scene, a terrified young woman burrowed lower between boxes stacked beneath her wagon. She slid out a hand to adjust the canvas sheeting shielding her from sight just as a heavy body thudded to the ground nearby and a painted face loomed suddenly above her. Yanked viciously to her feet by her hair, she looked up, frozen with horror, to see a war ax swiftly descending.

Shattering pain was simultaneous with the sound of a gunshot and a piercing scream that she did not recognize as her own.

Darkness.

The smell of smoke penetrated the young woman's unconsciousness and she coughed, then coughed again. It was so hot. She struggled against her discomfort, fighting to overcome the throbbing in her head that robbed her of lucid thought as she forced her eyes open.

Fire!

Managing to drag herself out from under the burning wagon, the young woman collapsed a few yards away. Uncertain how much time had elapsed, she opened her eyes again to a twilight that was strangely without sound. The pounding in her head continued as she touched a shaky hand to her temple. She drew it back sticky with blood and a desperate urgency invaded her senses. Forcing herself to her feet, she took one wobbling step, then two. A keening wail started within her mind as she surveyed the carnage around her.

Bloodied bodies, grotesquely mutilated, littered the ground against a backdrop of charred and burning wagons. Staggering among the debris, she shook one grisly form and then another, to no avail. They were all dead. . . .

Turning, the stunned young woman saw another body illuminated by the flames of the wagon under which she had been lying, and a new sobbing began inside her. Fighting the heat of the blaze, she inched closer, crawling on her hands and knees, until she stared down into the smoke-blackened face of a young man. Blank, lifeless eyes stared back at her and she screamed aloud.

Not him! He couldn't be dead!

The heat of the blaze grew more intense, driving her back. Swaying to her feet, she fled blindly. Breathless, the hammering in her head growing more intense with every step, she stumbled, then picked herself up to run again. She was still running as daylight waned and darkness closed around her.

The call of a bird penetrated the young woman's confused dreams, and she awoke with a start. Her eyes snapped open, renewing the pain in her head which had been with her through the dark hours of the night. She looked at the unfamiliar wilderness surrounding her, at the slope of heavily foliated hills and great natural walls of stone illuminated by the first light of morning, and her panic grew. She was cold. Her throat was parched and sore and the drumming in her head was unrelenting. Fear and a strange panic assailed her as another misery which had struck her during the night grew stronger. Dragging herself to her feet, she stumbled on.

The sun was high when the young woman was unable to walk any longer. The throbbing in her head was intense, but it could not compete with the pains that knifed through her body, doubling her up, bringing her to her knees.

Collapsing, she writhed in agony. The sun blazed a brilliant red against her closed eyelids as she cried out aloud. She was being torn in two, to die alone in the wilderness. It wasn't supposed to be this way. . . .

A sound in the brush, and the young woman caught her breath. A vision of the painted face of death returned and her eyes snapped open once more to see a horse and rider had drawn up a few feet away. The heavily bearded man was on his knees beside her in a moment. She was caught by the intensity of green eyes shot with gold as he studied her, and by the unexpected resentment she glimpsed there as his dark brows furrowed and he questioned her sharply.

"You're havin' that baby now, aren't you?"

Another pain, more severe than the last convulsed her. Unable to speak, the startled young woman clutched her distended stomach. Her eyes widened in sudden realization.

Oh, God . . . she was having a baby. . . .

His forehead beaded with sweat although the morning was chilled, Drake McNeil stared at the wild-eyed young woman lying on the ground. He swore under his breath as he crouched beside her. He looked at her head wound, then at her small, white hands where they clasped her bulging stomach. No one had had to tell him that the smoke he had seen on the horizon a day earlier marked the spot where Indians had caught up with another party of gold seekers, and no one had to tell him that this woman was probably the lone survivor of that train.

With an angry sound of disapproval, Drake turned to his horse and retrieved his canteen. Kneeling back beside the young woman, he supported her shoulders carefully and held the canteen to her lips. She drank greedily, her light eyes closing a moment later as she drew back sharply with a small, incoherent sound.

Another thing no one had to tell him was that this woman's time was near.

The woman's face contorted with pain. She cried out, and Drake's heart began a slow pounding. He swore again under his breath, then addressed her flatly.

"I'll do the best I can for you, lady."

His bearded face stiff, Drake raised her skirt.

There was no present, only pain. Floating in a nether world beyond consciousness, the young woman heard the bearded man's voice, but it was not his words that gave her ease. The tone of his voice was reminiscent of one she had heard before. It teased her pain-filled mind.

Reaching out, she grasped his hand. He looked up at her and she saw that he was angry . . . resentful, but she also saw—

A breathtaking pain shattered her thoughts and the young woman cried out aloud. Another pain followed, and another until her confused mind whirled in an agony without end.

Then a sudden, momentous thrust . . . sweet release . . . a baby's cry.

Darkness.

Two

Keenly aware of the unnatural silence of his cabin, Drake stooped to add another log to the already blazing fire. His expression dark, he glanced around him, scrutinizing the hasty shelter he had erected a few months earlier to protect himself from the rigors of winter in the Black Hills wilderness. He had made the furnishings himself—a rough table and chair and a cot that spared him the dampness of the dirt floor. They had been sufficient for his needs, but it had not been until that particular moment that he had become fully aware of the crudeness of his surroundings, of the dank smell of mildew, and of the chilling dampness that the fire did not dispel.

Drake glanced at the woman who lay sleeping on the cot nearby and his discomfiture increased. The woman's shuddering had intensified and he knew her condition was not good. Her head wound was severe and she had suffered from exposure to the severe dip in temperature the night before he had found her. She had also lost a lot of blood.

His concern deepening, Drake strode to the corner of the room and picked up a fur robe lying there. Back at the woman's side, he adjusted it across the blanket that covered her, but he knew it would do little good. Beneath the dirt and bloodstains that marked her face, he could see her color growing hotter. Her temperature was rising.

Taking an anxious breath, Drake looked toward the small wooden crate on the table a few feet away. His stomach clenched as he assessed the infant resting quietly within.

Wrapped in the remains of her mother's petticoat, the grime of birth washed from her fair skin as well as his awkward hands had been able to manage it, the little girl was motionless except for the occasional pursing of her incredibly dainty lips.

As he watched, the infant's fine features wrinkled into the preface of a wail, and panic rose anew in Drake's mind. With a soft string of oaths that he knew was unfit for her dainty ears, he picked up a small, knotted cloth lying beside her and dipped it into a nearby cup. He lifted the infant into his arms and touched the moistened cloth lightly against her lips.

There it was again . . . that tightening in his stomach in the moment before the baby seized upon it and began sucking. Still holding the infant a short time later as her almost translucent lids drifted closed, Drake was momentarily incredulous. Damn it all, how had this happened? How had he come to be standing here, in a cabin in the wilderness, pacifying a baby with a sugar teat? How had he become responsible for a sick woman whose name he didn't even know—a woman who would probably not survive another week in her present condition? And what in hell would he do with this baby if she didn't?

His frustration building, Drake lowered the infant back into the wooden crate, more acutely aware than ever before that he was in the middle of hostile Indian territory, several days from the nearest town. He hadn't minded the isolation when he had first arrived. He had actually anticipated the eventual arrival of other prospectors with distaste, although he had known it was inevitable. General Custer's announcement that the sacred Black Hills of the Sioux were rich in gold had started a determined influx of gold seekers, despite the illegality of any claims they might attempt to stake. The first to arrive the previous year had been driven from the hills by the army and their gold had been confiscated. Others had managed to avoid army patrols only to suffer the same fate as this woman's wagon train. But others, like him, had proved that no one could keep them from going where they wanted to go.

Drake's huge hands balled unconsciously into fists. He had settled into this ravine while snow was still on the ground and fierce storms had guaranteed that the Indians had gone to winter on the reservation. He had taken only enough time to erect this simple cabin before setting up a crude placer mining operation in the nearby stream, and in the months since that time, his work had netted him enough color to make the effort more than worthwhile. His small sack of gold dust was growing. Everything had been progressing according to plan, until now.

Drake controlled the urge to curse again. He was still uncertain what had prompted him to start over the hill to investigate the sounds that had echoed down to him as he had worked. His present predicament was his reward.

An unexpected whimper from the woman who lay on his cot a few feet away interrupted Drake's frustrated thoughts. The woman jumped with a start, in the throes of a vicious dream if he were to judge by her thrashing about and the look of terror on her face. He walked instinctively toward her and stood looking down at her twitching face. It was strange . . . He had just delivered this woman's child. He had touched her intimately, in ways he was certain no other man had ever touched her before. He knew she was in pain and that her life lay in his hands, but he felt more contempt than sympathy for her. She was an adult, responsible for her own actions and for the stupidity and greed that had brought her to her present state of affairs. He told himself that although they had both come to the hills in search of gold, his decision had been carefully weighed. Before making it, he had assessed the risks, knowing he could expect no help or protection from the army on land that had been legally ceded to the Indians years earlier. He had then accepted full responsibility for his actions, knowing he had no one to blame but himself should anything happen. Most important of all—the only life he had put at risk had been his *own*.

Drake unconsciously turned toward the sleeping infant. For all intents and purposes, this woman had signed her unborn child's death warrant with the first step she had taken

13

onto Indian ground. She had needed only to wait for it to be served. She had not waited long.

The young woman's thrashing increased, and Drake raised his bearded chin in an unconscious gesture of defiance. The painful truth was obvious. The baby's survival depended on the survival of the mother. He'd do his best for the woman just as he had said he would, but the contempt remained.

Seating himself on the edge of the cot, Drake withdrew a cloth from the pan of water lying on the floor nearby. The young woman regained consciousness with a start as he attempted to clean the bloody gash on her head. She made a strange, choked sound, terror in her gaze as it met his. Her silver eyes held his stare for long moments before the terror faded abruptly and she closed her eyes.

Drake's contempt soared. She trusted him . . . without knowing who or what he was! She was even more of a fool than he had thought her to be.

Drake drew himself abruptly to his feet. He stood towering over the sleeping woman before picking up the pan beside the bed and walking to the fireplace. Returning with warm water and a bar of soap, he sat beside her again, his expression stiff. Knowing he could not put off the task any longer, he lathered the cloth, the heat of the woman's brow searing his skin as he cleansed her wound. She was mumbling incoherently when he drew back, satisfied the wound was finally clean and intensely aware that his ministrations could not stop there.

More angry by the minute, Drake began working at the buttons on the woman's dress. She was a pathetic sight. Her hair was matted with dried blood, her face scratched and blackened with smoke, and her clothes torn and bloodied, but he felt little pity. Knowing he had no choice he stripped her free of her clothes and wrapped her in a blanket without sparing her nakedness a conscious glance.

Returning from the fireplace with fresh water, Drake lathered the cloth and cautiously bathed her face. Small, unexceptional features and smooth white skin emerged from beneath the grime, revealing unexpected youth. Continuing

14

his chore, he told himself it made little difference that the narrow shoulders he scrubbed so carefully seemed hardly strong enough to support a woman's tasks, and that the small, pink-nippled breasts did not appear adequate for the task of nursing the babe. He frowned at arms that did not give the appearance of any great strength, at a rib cage and stomach that seemed remarkably flat, considering the great protrusion there only a few hours earlier, at barely curving hips . . .

Drake's hand momentarily stilled. His throat tightened as he viewed the stains of birth on this slight woman's female delta and slender thighs. Only a few hours earlier this thin, almost childlike body had brought new life into the world. He had taken the child from this woman's womb. He had heard its first cry — and he knew he would never forget it.

Drake continued his work without pausing again until the woman was spotlessly clean, redressed in his only spare shirt, and carefully wrapped to avoid further staining. Finally sitting back, he assessed her silently. Pale brown hair, dark brows, small, ordinary features, and so painfully thin. . . . She was a plain, colorless little wren, but he had learned the hard way that a young, innocent face often concealed a heart as cold as stone. Beautiful or plain, all women were the same. Some were luckier than others, that was all.

The gold band on the woman's finger caught the light and Drake thought of the young woman's husband. That fellow had already paid the price of his greed. Would she pay as well?

A violent shudder racked the woman's slender frame and Drake's jaw tightened.

The long night yielded abruptly into day in a way that Drake had come to know was typical of the Black Hills. Hardly conscious of the brilliant sunshine streaming through the small windows of the cabin, he wearily rubbed his bearded chin as he assessed his unwelcome charges.

Well, they had made it through the night.

Stretching the stiffness from his broad shoulders and

powerful arms, Drake flexed hands cramped from the delicacy of the tasks he had been performing for hours on end. All was quiet. He knew, however, that the silence was only temporary. As she had throughout the night, the infant would soon begin with a whimper that would build into a hungry wail. He would then pick her up and spend a few frantic minutes attempting to satisfy her with sugar water. She would fall off into a restless sleep afterward, only to begin crying again a short time later. That routine had established itself mercilessly throughout the night, and he knew with steadily growing apprehension that sugar water had its limitations. The babe would soon need more nourishment.

Frowning, Drake looked back at the infant's mother. The woman was temporarily quiet, but the deep flush to her skin revealed that she was not doing well. He had spent the night splitting his attentions between her and the infant while thoughts of childbed fever raised his anxiety. The woman was a fool, but he did not wish her dead.

As if in response to his thoughts, the woman cried out softly. A glistening veil of perspiration appeared on her skin and the violent shuddering he had fought during the night resumed abruptly, with a vengeance. Within moments, her eyes grew frenzied and her teeth began chattering audibly, and Drake knew the time had come for drastic measures.

Snatching up the nearby bucket, Drake walked to the door. Back from the stream a few moments later, he stripped the blanket from the woman's shaking form and plunged it into the cold water. He wrung the blanket as dry as his shaking hands could manage and taking a deep breath, covered her with it.

If he lived to be one hundred, Drake knew he would never forget the stark terror in the woman's eyes or the eerie cry that escaped her quivering lips when the cold blanket touched her heated skin. Nor would he forget the accusation in her fevered gaze. In the space of a moment, her disoriented mind had registered betrayal and declared him an enemy. She became a fragile bird, struggling in the clutch of a dark predator, panicked, wild, determined to win her freedom, even at the cost of her life.

16

Resolved that he would not let her pay that price, Drake clasped the woman's arms against her sides, restraining her with the weight of his torso. The erratic beating of her heart pounded against his chest as she continued fighting him, but she was weak. Knowing she could not survive much more, Drake cupped her thin face between his palms and forced her to look up at him.

Uncertain if she could hear him, much less comprehend his words, Drake rasped, "Stop fightin'. Listen to me! I'm tryin' to help you, not hurt you, damn it! I won't let you die, but you have to do your part! You have to relax — lie easy. I'll do the rest."

The woman's struggle continued and panic nudged his senses as he continued harshly, "You trusted me before and I helped you. I'm tryin' to help you again. Listen to me, please. . . ." Despising the plea that had entered his voice and the fact that he did not even know her name, Drake promised, "I want you to get well."

The woman's struggles slowed and Drake felt a surge of hope. Knowing the battle was not yet won, Drake drew closer to her, fixing her gaze with his as he whispered, "I'm goin' to try to get your fever down. You have to trust that I'm doin' what's best for you. Will you let me do it? Tell me you trust me."

Drake waited for her response as the woman searched his face with her wavering gaze. He stared at her lips as they struggled to form words that would not come, and his throat tightened. She could not afford to expend any more energy fighting him. He needed to regain her confidence if he hoped to save her life. He pressed, "Do you trust me?"

The woman's lips moved again and Drake leaned closer. His heart began a furious pounding as she forced a single, hissing sound.

"Y . . . yes. . . ."

Drake drew back abruptly. Forcing aside reaction to her weak response, he turned to the task before him. The ritual began . . . soaking the blanket in cold water . . . wrapping the shuddering woman until it warmed . . . soaking the blanket again . . . racing steps back and forth to the stream

. . . endless moments of uncertainty.

The sun was high as Drake returned from the stream with fresh water and walked wearily through the doorway once more. His senses suddenly acute as he approached the bed, he stopped abruptly. Something was wrong. The woman was motionless, her thin face devoid of color except for a faint tinge of blue around her still lips.

Beside her in a second, Drake grasped her arms. Her body was cold. He shook her, unwilling to accept—

A small sound, and Drake froze into motionlessness. The woman's lips moved as she whimpered again. Her eyelids fluttered and relief flushed his senses.

"You're all right. . . ."

Again a single word. "Yes."

Three

Light pressed against her closed eyelids and the young woman fought to respond. She had floated in the darkness for so long—but she had not been alone. The sounds of a deep male voice had echoed in that void, allowing the image of clear green eyes to supplant the painted face of death that had terrorized her dreams. The throbbing in her head had responded to gentle probing, and the fire that had burned under her skin had cooled just as the voice had promised. She had known it would.

The man had asked her to trust him, and she had. He had not seemed to realize that the plea was unnecessary. She trusted him because she had recognized him the moment she had seen the startling color of his eyes and heard his voice.

The woman slowly opened her eyes, struggling to focus. The pounding in her head had lessened, but her body ached and her breasts burned. Her arms were leaden weights that refused to obey her as she attempted to raise her hand. Abandoning the attempt, she looked uncertainly around the primitive cabin.

Stark log walls met her view, their sole decorations a variety of canvas bags, cooking equipment, and harnesses hanging from nails. A pot boiled over the fire in a fireplace across from her bed, and standing at the nearby table, a big man fussed over a wooden box resting there. She knew it was he, and although she was seeing him clearly for the first time, she had known he would be a big man because she had felt the strength in his touch. She remembered his dark, full beard and the thick wavy hair that touched his shoulders,

19

but his strong features had been blurred except for those angry eyes that had been so vividly clear.

His attention fixed on the wooden box, the man frowned. He was an intimidating sight, with power exuding as clearly from his unyielding expression as from his muscular proportions, but she was unafraid.

A baby's cry interrupted the woman's thoughts and the woman froze. Fragmented memories of convulsive pain assaulted her. She had wandered alone in that world of agony beyond bearing until she had heard the big man speak words that still rang in her mind.

"I'll do the best I can for you, lady."

Again the sound of a baby's cry, and as she watched, the fellow reached gingerly into the wooden box and lifted a squirming infant into his arms. She gasped aloud and the man turned toward her, but she saw nothing but the babe in his arms. It began wailing and rooting against the man's chest, and a strange, responsive sensation started in her breasts. The ache grew stronger and with a jolt of startling recognition, she knew the child was hers.

The big man approached the bed. His voice was harsh as he asked flatly, "Can you manage her?"

She swallowed thickly. "G . . . give her to me."

She thought she saw resentment in the man's face as he did, but all thought was swept away the moment the babe was in her arms. Guided by an instinct older than time, she pushed aside the rough cotton shirt she wore and unashamedly bared a small breast. The infant seized upon it, and the woman closed her eyes, indulging a singing sense of fulfillment as the infant drew from her with hungry, gulping sounds.

But her elation was short-lived as frightening, fragmented pictures flashed against her closed eyelids, destroying her brief tranquillity. She opened her eyes in an attempt to escape them and found the big man assessing her silently. In desperation, she blurted out her muddled thoughts.

"This baby is mine. . . ." She paused, weakness again assailing her. "A . . . are you the father?"

The man studied her intently before responding. "Don't

you know who the father is?"

The woman shook her head, her confusion growing as the pounding in her head increased. The man continued his scrutiny, then asked unexpectedly, "What's your name?"

She strained to recall. A name filtered through her muddled thoughts and she grasped at it.

"Carolina . . . Carolina Brand."

"Do you remember what happened to you?"

She shook her head again, regretting the action as the hammering there assumed ringing proportions. She was unable to escape it, and as consciousness drifted away, the last thing she remembered was the big man's scowl.

Aware that lack of sleep was beginning to take its toll, Drake wearily stirred the pot boiling in the fireplace. Damn, he was tired! He had barely closed his eyes in twenty-four hours, much less taken time to eat.

Raking a heavy hand through his hair, Drake glanced at the careless pile of spare prospector's trappings in the corner, knowing that his steadily growing cache of gold dust lay buried beneath. It was already May, and he was intensely aware that he was behind in the schedule he had set for himself after entering this "holy wilderness." He had considered himself relatively safe in this ravine and less likely to be visited by the Sioux because of their belief that the evil spirit held his realm in the deep gorges of the hills. He also knew, however, that with the warmer weather the Sioux would be returning in great numbers to these hills, their sacred *Paha Sapa,* to worship where the Great Spirit sat enthroned on the lofty peaks. Gathering on the prairie on their religious pilgrimage, they would camp in view of the hills to fast, sweat, and meditate. Trespassers would not be tolerated and once discovered, would not live to tell of the meeting.

His arrival during the winter when his presence was least likely to be discovered had been the first part of his careful plan. He had made as few trips to Deadwood to replenish supplies as possible and he had cautiously concealed his exact location. He wanted no part of the circus that was presently underway in that mining camp, and he had not come

21

with the thought of "striking it rich." His plans were more modest, more realistic—but he was determined to succeed. The only thing he had not taken into account was the possibility that the brilliant showing of color he had found upon his arrival might lessen as the months wore on, and that his cache of gold dust might grow at a slower pace than he had anticipated. Having planned on a limited stay, he had eventually accepted the reality that his stay might be lengthened by six months or more, and he had adjusted his schedule accordingly.

Drake's stomach voiced an appropriate growl as the aroma of salt pork and beans wafted up to his nostrils, interrupting his thoughts. The reminder of his own hunger stirred a resentment with which he had become familiar as he turned and looked again at the sleeping "Carolina Brand."

He didn't like playing nursemaid. He didn't like taking responsibility for a woman who should have had better sense than to have come to this savage wilderness in her condition. He didn't like the nagging concern he felt knowing that she had nursed her hungry daughter, and in doing so, had further weakened herself. He didn't like having been forced to plead for her trust.

Still staring at the plain little wren, Drake felt his anger turn hard. But most of all, he resented being played for a fool.

Looking up at a sack hanging from a peg directly in the woman's line of vision, Drake gave a harsh laugh and read the stamped label aloud:

"RICE • CAROLINA BRAND"

The sound of his caustic laughter was still echoing in the silent cabin when Drake realized that the situation wasn't really funny at all.

She was running again, fleeing the painted face of death. The world was dark around her, but as she raced blindly forward she saw a glimmer in the darkness. She rushed toward it, only to realize when it was within reach that the light in the darkness was the glint of a war ax descending toward her.

She screamed aloud, a piercing cry that blended pain and terror in one shattering sound. She was shivering wildly when she heard his voice. It drew her slowly back to reality, forcing her to open her eyes, and she gasped with relief at the sight of the big man crouching beside her.

"You were dreaming." The big man pressed his hand against her forehead, seeming relieved at the assessment he made there. She felt his light eyes move over her face the moment before he raised her shoulders gently and propped the fur rob behind her back. He drew himself to his feet and within minutes returned to her bedside with a metal plate in his hand.

She turned her head away, only to hear his gruff command. "You have to eat, Carolina, or you won't be able to feed the child."

Carolina. Was that her name? Yes. . . .

Carolina looked at the wooden box on the table, and the big man responded to her silent question.

"She's all right, but she'll be waking up soon. I want you to be ready for her when she does."

Carolina nodded. He was right. She must eat. This big man was always right.

The question emerged shakily from Carolina's lips.

"W . . . who are you?"

The man's blank expression flickered the moment before he responded. "My name's Drake McNeil." He held the spoon closer.

The food touched her tongue and Carolina struggled to control her stomach's wrenching spasms. She chewed determinedly as she attempted to sort out her confused thoughts. How had she arrived in this man's care? He had said his name was Drake McNeil, but who was he? Her heart jumped nervously. For that matter, who was she?

Carolina swallowed with difficulty. And why, despite his kindnesses to her, did Drake McNeil dislike her?

23

The baby's clipped cry snapped Carolina's head toward the sound only to have Drake comment sharply, "Don't worry about her. She'll be all right for a few minutes. You have to eat."

"No." Carolina closed her eyes as her head resumed a dull pounding. "I can't."

"You have to eat if you expect to be able to feed the baby."

Carolina struggled against rising tears. She didn't want to fight with this man. "I can feed her. Give her to me." Her voice broke. "Please. . . ."

She saw an almost undetectable flicker in Drake's eyes the moment before he drew himself to his feet. He returned with her child and Carolina's whirling mind stilled the moment he placed the infant in her arms. Adjusting the babe against her breast, Carolina studied her uncertainly. She was beautiful . . . a light dusting of golden fuzz on a well-shaped head, blue eyes tinged with silver, and minute, doll-like features. The infant's fair skin became flushed with the exertion of nursing and Carolina felt a flush rise to her own face as well. Was her own hair that same golden color? Were her own eyes that incredible blue? Did the child resemble her?

Carolina attempted to recall her own image, but her mind was strangely blank. She tried harder, her heart beginning a frightening pounding when the painted face of death flashed before her eyes in its stead.

At a touch on her arm, Carolina looked up to see the big man frowning. Not realizing that she was trembling, she asked, "Does she look like me?" She swallowed tightly. "What do I look like?"

The big man dismissed her anxiety with a flat response. "No, she doesn't look like you."

He held the spoon again to her lips and Carolina dutifully opened her mouth. She was grateful for the briefness of his reply. Somehow, she was not ready for more.

Four

Rosie Blake was in her element. That was obvious in the smile that played on the curve of her well-rouged lips and in the sparkle in her dark eyes as she walked briskly along Deadwood's Main Street. She passed a cluster of conversing prospectors and all heads snapped toward her. Expertly batting heavily kohled lashes, she added an inviting wiggle to the sway of her hips as she continued down the street, but she knew the effort was not truly necessary. No man who had ever seen Rosie Blake in all her finery had ever been able to tear his eyes from her until she slipped out of sight.

Rosie gave a short laugh, amused at her own thoughts as she sidestepped a shaft situated awkwardly in the middle of the street and continued on. She had been told many times that she was beautiful, and she did not need to be reminded that her womanly proportions were lush enough to make even the most reserved of men salivate. Several years earlier she had decided to accept those attributes as recompense from a fate that had not provided well for her in other areas of her life. Doing just that, she had "made use of the best and dismissed the rest," and she had not been sorry she did.

Rosie paused a moment to look around her. Well, here she was, and damned glad to be there, too! Rip-roaring Deadwood, situated at the point where the gold-laden waters of Deadwood and Whitewood Creeks came together, was her kind of town!

Rosie paused again to reconsider that thought. It really wasn't much of a town. It was more like a mining camp that had outgrown its britches. The story was that the camp had gotten its name from the dead wood that had once littered the spot as the result of a forest fire seasons earlier. It was laid out smack in the middle of sacred Indian territory, with Forest Hill on one side and the hoary crest of White Rocks on the other. The valley was hardly wide enough in spots for Deadwood's one, narrow street, and access was so bad that wagons had to be lowered one at a time with a pulley device in order to make it into town in one piece.

But she liked it here. She liked the fact that all contrasts were sharp and clear, that the sun appeared to leap from behind the mountain at the beginning of day without the need for dawn. And she liked the way the sun dispensed with purple twilights by dropping back behind the pines of Forest Hill at the end of day to abruptly usher in the night.

Rosie looked around her with amusement as she continued her rapid step. As for the town itself — two score of hastily constructed log cabins with countless tents pitched hither and yon with no regard to regularity, the hustle and din of buildings being raised on every side, the coming and going of emigrant wagons and pack trains squeezing past each other on a street that was sometimes almost impassable, and the excited babble of prospectors and fortune hunters of *another* type as they dodged in and out between the wagons in their way up or down the street — the entertainment never ceased.

As for herself, Rosie knew she could be classified as a fortune hunter of the *other type,* but she didn't care. She was a farm girl who had tired of the farm, a woman in search of the good life — and she was going to get it. For that reason, and another which she refused to acknowledge, she had readily joined a group of adventure-seeking bar girls who had left Cheyenne a few months earlier to take their chances in this illegal mining camp. She hadn't regretted her decision for a minute.

Rosie's broad smile faltered briefly as she crossed the muddy street and turned toward the Nugget Saloon. She was aware of the dangers in her kind of work. She had seen women come and go as liquor gradually became more ne-

26

cessity than fun. She had seen the most hardened of her peers make the mistake of falling for men who then loved and left them. She had seen others darting down dark alley-ways in search of an opium pipe to make their lives bearable after the gilt had tarnished from their lives. And she had seen those few who had decided that going on wasn't worth the effort.

She'd never be one of those.

Rosie raised a steady hand to the upward sweep of her hair, aware that the plumed black straw she wore atop her heavy, black locks was in perfect contrast with the brilliant red of her dress. She raised her chin proudly. She *earned* her way in this town, just as she had in every other town since she had struck out on her own. She earned it by entertaining the fun-starved, lonesome miners who came to town with bulging sacks of gold dust. In the beginning she had enter-tained in the most intimate of ways, but she was indepen-dent now, and if she brought a fellow back to her satin and lace bedroom in her cabin behind the saloon, it was because she *wanted* to. She was a businesswoman at the youthful age of twenty years, part owner of the Nugget Saloon, and if she wasn't entirely respectable, she didn't much care. She was getting rich and having a good time doing it.

Stepping up onto the brief boardwalk outside the Nugget, Rosie raised her skirt to her ankles and took a moment to stamp the mud from her bright red shoes. She noted with a raised brow that heads snapped toward her once more, and she quipped, "Like what you see, boys? There's more to see inside the Nugget than the turn of an ankle." She winked. "Come on. The first drink's on me!"

The synchronized chorus of "After you, ma'am!" was to be expected, as was the stampede to the bar the moment she was clear of the doorway, and Rosie laughed again. She was still laughing when a nattily dressed, well-built man ap-peared at her elbow. He shook his handsome head with fa-miliar tolerance and she spoke to him in a husky voice calculated to bring a twinkle to his eye.

"You got any complaints, Tag, honey? You know no prospector in these parts ever stopped at *one* drink. I'm thinkin' that some of those fellas will be sittin' down to your poker table sooner or later and you'll be able to part them from more of that pretty yellow dust that's weighin' their pockets down."

Tag Willis's trim mustache twitched with amusement as he looked warmly into her eyes. "That's why I let you buy into the business, Rosie, *honey*—because you're always thinking."

"Is that the *only* reason?"

An almost indiscernible flicker touched the honey brown of Tag's eyes as he gave a short laugh. "Well, I can think of one or two more."

Her playfulness momentarily fading, Rosie whispered earnestly, "I *like* you, Tag Willis. I really do." Her bold smile quickly returning, she touched a crimson-tipped finger to his smooth-shaven cheek. "And you're such a handsome devil."

"I'm handsome and you're beautiful." Tag's smile grew a trifle forced. "We make the perfect pair."

Unwilling to comment on that last statement, Rosie turned toward the bar, only to be stayed by Tag's touch on her arm. She looked back at him as he whispered gently, "It's been a long time, Rosie, and I've been lonely these past few nights."

Rosie hesitated, her smile faltering as she responded, "You know how I hate seein' any man feel lonely, Tag, honey." She raised her chin. "Maybelle over there's been eyein' you with a real hungry look these past few weeks. Why don't you give the girl a treat? I know she'll do her best to take care of you."

Regretting her words the moment they had left her lips, Rosie saw Tag's face still. Damn! He had been so good to her. She didn't know why she said things like that.

Oh, yes, she did. . . .

But there was no need to express her regret. Reading her thoughts, Tag slid his hand up her arm and squeezed her shoulder lightly. "Do you really want me to do that?"

Her throat suddenly too thick for words, Rosie cupped Tag's cheeks with her hands and firmly drew his mouth down to hers. Kissing him long and sweet, enjoying the familiar taste of him too much to bring the kiss to an early conclusion, she drew back only when raucous calls and appreciative whistles from the tables nearby grew too loud to ignore. Looking up into Tag's eyes, she whispered, "No. I don't. Why don't you walk me home tonight?"

Tag's response was written in his eyes, and as Rosie turned to the bar, the touch of his hand lingered.

Rosie walked straight from his arms to the bar, where old Doc Fitz stood unsteadily, and Tag felt a familiar agitation rise. He knew Rosie had a genuine affection for the old reprobate, and he knew that she would handle him as she had so many times before. That was Rosie's job, running the Nugget and smoothing over the rough spots with a wink and a smile. She was damned good at it, too, but that didn't mean he had to like it.

Tag's gaze lingered, and he was reminded of something Rosie had once said—that when a fellow first saw her, he didn't stop looking at her until she stepped out of sight. He had seen that statement proved true countless times, and he had recognized long ago that that was part of his problem. He hadn't had eyes for any woman but Rosie since the first time he had met her, years ago. He didn't think he ever would.

Turning away at last, Tag walked toward the poker table in the far corner of the room where he spent the greater part of each day. He was silently grateful that Rosie hadn't called him "Tag, honey" *after* she had kissed him. He didn't think he could have borne that.

Seating himself in his usual seat, Tag surveyed the crowded bar for potential customers. There weren't too many familiar faces there, but that, too, was the norm for Deadwood. Men came and went here, some never to be seen again after they ventured up into the hills, but he didn't give the matter much thought.

Absentmindedly picking up the cards, he shuffled them with an expert hand. If anyone had told him a year ago that

29

he would abandon his lucrative, beautifully accoutred setup in Cheyenne for a small saloon in this barely civilized mining camp, he would have called the fellow a fool. A single street littered with every manner of filth, where every yard was pockmarked with shafts running down into the bowels of the earth, where it was cheaper to buy liquor than flour, and where there was no hope of permanence—that was Deadwood. But it seemed *he* was the real fool, because here he was, and here was where he was going to stay. And the reason was simple. Rosie.

He remembered the first time he saw Rosie, almost four years ago. She had been a pretty little saloon girl, straight from the farm, but he had seen something special in her, even then. She had been popular with the men, and he had been one of her best customers. He couldn't remember when he first decided that he wanted things to change between them, but he knew he had wanted it badly. He took her under his wing and it wasn't long before the little farm girl emerged into a fabulous woman.

Tag smiled softly. Some might dispute that point, emphasizing that painted ladies were never beautiful, but Rosie was. Paint didn't hide fine, high cheekbones or creamy skin. Neither did it hide the brilliant blue of her eyes. And the truth was that Rosie's lashes were thick and black even without kohl, and that her lips were naturally a warm, red color. She was as beautiful inside as she was on the outside, too. He knew Rosie didn't think so, but she was.

You see, he knew the "true" Rosie. He knew she had believed her present life was more respectable than her former had ever been, and for a while he had been willing to accept that. But the situation had become too difficult for him. He had been determined to effect a change, and he had been succeeding—until a year ago. That was about the time Rosie had abruptly announced that she intended joining the girls who were going to take their chances in the Black Hills gold fields. He remembered the pain of Rosie's departure, and he remembered he was determined not to follow her. But he did.

As it turned out, Deadwood was the opportunity he had

been waiting for—a chance to offer Rosie a valid partnership, one that would not damage her hard-won independence. She had made it clear to him then that he had not bought her with the partnership, that she would remain her own woman, and he had accepted that. He had thought everything was going so well, until—

His distress suddenly too great, Tag halted his thoughts. His gaze slipped back to his beautiful Rosie as she gave the perspiring bartender an encouraging wink, and Tag felt a familiar swell of emotion. Oh, yes, he loved her. He had come to this godforsaken hole in the Black Hills to win his Rosie once and for all. He knew it wasn't going to be easy for her to put the past behind her, but he was going to try to see that she did.

The scraping of chairs against the hardwood floor snapped Tag from his thoughts and he nodded a welcome to two unfamiliar fellows as they sat down and slapped bulging sacks of gold dust onto the table beside them. Taking a minute to shuffle the cards, Tag dealt with a flick of the wrist that brought a smile of appreciation from the eager prospectors.

Affixing his professional mask into place, Tag awaited their first move. He was a gambler after all. He could only hope that the most important gamble of his life would be one he would win.

His bulgy eyes popping, his bald head glistening with sweat, Barney Potts snatched a nearly empty bottle of redeye off the bar and put it on the shelf behind him. He turned back to the thin, gray-haired fellow staring menacingly at him through drooping, bloodshot eyes. Other patrons of the Nugget watched with amusement as Barney repeated with a hint of panic, "I'm tellin' you, Doc, I ain't servin' you no more liquor today! I got my orders!"

"Orders! You're tellin' me you've got orders not to serve me in this damned, foul-smellin', hellhole of a place?" Dr. Jerome Fitz was getting mad. Drawing himself up unsteadily to his full, unimpressive height, he bellowed,

"Who gave you those orders?"

"I gave him those orders, Doc."

Accompanying that husky female voice behind him was a soft arm that slipped slowly around his shoulders, and as Doc turned to Rosie Blake, he could feel his belligerence melt. Damn, she was one, good-looking young woman! In his twenty-five years as a doctor, he had treated women in all shapes and sizes. He didn't give their looks much thought when he was professionally involved, but when he was out on the town . . . Doc Fitz grinned. Hell, he was a man, wasn't he?

Doc fought to hold on to the last shreds of his anger. *"You* gave Barney orders not to serve me any more liquor tonight, Rosie?"

Rosie pinched his stubbled cheek. "That's right, Doc."

"Now don't try gettin' around me, Rosie. I'm up to your tricks. My money's as good as any man's, isn't it?"

His full, black mustache twitching with annoyance, Barney responded in Rosie's stead. "I thought you was supposed to be smart, Doc. Or maybe you got a short memory, that's all. Wasn't it just last week that you got a real snoot full and started swingin' at every man in this here saloon? You did a real job on old Henry Gardner, too. It took you all of an hour to stitch him back up when you was done, and a hell of a poor job you did, too. Henry ain't never goin' to look the same!"

Doc squinted at the frowning bartender. "You're exaggeratin' as usual, and I don't mind tellin' you that I don't like it. I wasn't talkin' to you, anyway." He turned back to Rosie to focus unclearly on her flawless face. She was a beauty, all right. He cleared his throat and strove for a dignified expression. "Now, my question to you was—"

"—if your money was as good as any man's here in this saloon, and the answer is yes." Was he imagining it, or did Rosie take a step closer. In any case, Rosie stood eye to eye with him as she continued softly, "You're one of my favorite customers, Doc, and you know it. And from what the girls tell me, you're one of their favorite customers, too." She winked. "I guess there isn't any beatin' a medical man for knowin' how to please a lady."

A warm feeling started spreading in Doc's loins, and he all but groaned aloud. This was one clever lady . . . and he liked clever ladies . . . but that was something else again.

"Don't change the subject, Rosie! How come you're puttin' a cork in the bottle for me tonight?"

Rosie's expression sobered unexpectedly. She looked deeper into his eyes and Doc could feel her gaze down to his toes as she said, "Because I like you, Doc. Because I won't ever forget that time when you stayed with Pearl all day and all night when she was dyin'. And because I respect you." She winked, the old Rosie quickly returning as she continued, "And because I wouldn't ever want you sewin' *me* up like you did old Henry. Barney's right. Henry's never goin' to look the same."

A hoot of spontaneous laughter escaped Doc's lips. "Hell, old Henry never did look that good in the first place, whereas *you* . . ." Suddenly slipping his arms around Rosie's luscious young body, Doc kissed her short and hard on the lips. Drawing back with more reluctance than he cared to admit, he smiled. "But if you don't want to serve me anymore this afternoon, that's all right, Rosie, 'cause I'll take a kiss instead of a drink any day, especially if it's from you."

Drawing himself up as straight as he could manage, Doc darted a quick wink at a smiling saloon girl standing nearby. "Now don't you go gettin' jealous, Nellie. I just might come back to visit you later. But in the meantime" — Doc shifted to feast his eyes on Rosie a few minutes longer before concluding — "I think I'll take my leave for a few hours. Will that make you happy, Rosie, sweetheart?"

"Just as long as you promise to come back to see me again."

The note of sincerity that rang in Rosie's words touched Doc's heart. This little girl was truly a rose among thorns. He gave an unconscious sigh. Too bad he was too old to take the chance of getting his fingers pricked.

He responded sincerely in return. "There's no doubt about me comin' back to see you, Rosie."

Turning on his heel, aware that the room rocked as he did,

Doc started toward the doorway. He was standing unsteadily on the board platform outside the door when he realized he had never felt so good about getting kicked out of a saloon in his life.

Doc took an unsteady step and then two, his spirits rising as he consoled himself mentally. Rosie was right. He was the best doctor in this hell-raisin' town, and the people here needed him sober. Hell, he was supposed to be respectable. He was part of the committee formed to find a way to force the government in Washington to take the prospectors here seriously enough to open this land for settlement. How seriously would those fancy senators and representatives take him if they could see him now?

Doc took a moment to consider that last thought, then suddenly laughed aloud. Aw, who gave a damn what they thought! A man needed a little recreation, and for a day that had started out badly, with a poor young fella whose name he didn't even know dying in his arms, it had turned out pretty well after all. Hell, it wasn't every day that Rosie Blake whispered in a man's ear, and it wasn't—

His unsteady step coming to an abrupt halt, Doc felt his euphoria drain. An actual shiver rolled down his spine as the icy gaze of the widow Higgins met his. Steeling himself against the onslaught that was to come, he planted his feet firmly on the boardwalk, refusing to sway as the widow advanced toward him.

Halting her step within a few feet of him, the widow looked down at him from her superior height. Her tone was rank with criticism as she spoke.

"So, I see you've been overindulging yourself at the Nugget again, Jerome."

Furious at her gall, Doc was determined to sizzle that icy stare. "I sure enough did, Miriam." He rubbed his chest with a satisfied smile. "And I drank a little too much, too."

Her shocked gasp the exact reaction he had been seeking, Doc tipped his hat and turned away, his step lighter than it had a right to be.

* * *

The sounds of laughter became more raucous and the voices in the crowded saloon louder and more slurred as the night progressed. The Nugget was slowly emptying and Rosie gave the signal for the last round at the bar, then turned toward the rear of the room and the poker table where a lone patron lingered. She nodded to Tag, and within a few minutes the prospector rose and wandered toward the door.

Rosie watched Tag unconsciously as he scooped up his chips and swept them into a container. A partnership — Tag and she worked well together. It had been a deal well made, and Rosie knew her new "respectability" was just another in a long line of things for which she had to thank Tag Willis. She wondered why she—

Tag rose from the chair. He caught and held her eye in a way that brought Rosie's thoughts to an abrupt halt. Her heart began a slow pounding, just as it always did when Tag looked at her in that manner, and she marveled anew at his ability to turn her insides to molten heat with a single glance.

Rosie frowned, a moment's rebellion rising. She didn't really want it to be this way between them. She had other plans . . . other dreams. . . .

Tag walked directly toward her, ignoring the last-minute preparations being made for closing, and Rosie's thoughts drifted from nightly routine as well. He reached her side and without a word, cupped her chin to cover her mouth with his for a deep, lingering kiss. When he drew back, Rosie knew that for the next few hours, no other plans or dreams would come between them. Taking his hand, she turned toward the bar.

"Close the place up for me, will you, Barney?"

Barney gave them an assessing glance, then grinned. "Sure thing."

Tucked in the curve of Tag's arm, Rosie barely heard his reply as they proceeded toward the rear of the saloon. Managing to slip free of Tag's possessive hold, Rosie unlocked the door of her cabin moments later. She lit the lamp and had not yet blown out the match when Tag's arms closed around her. Her breathing short, her heart fluttering against

35

her breast like a captive bird, Rosie turned in his arms, welcoming the thrust of his tightly muscled body against hers. She felt him harden, a joy rising inside her with the knowledge that she would soon give him the satisfaction he sought.

Tag's mouth captured hers, and Rosie closed her eyes. Her breath caught in her throat as he slipped his hands inside the daring neckline of her dress and gradually pushed it to her waist. His mouth relinquished hers, descending lovingly down the white column of her throat to spread moist, warm kisses against the full curves of her breasts, and the molten heat inside Rosie began to churn. She felt his tongue lave her engorged nipples and she cried out aloud as he lovingly took one, then the other, into his mouth. Raising her arms high over her head to give him full access, she splayed her fingers wide, reveling in the myriad sensations coursing through her as Tag worshiped her tender flesh. His heady assault continued and Rosie held her breath, fighting the urge to pull her to him, determined that she would not be first this time to plead for release.

A familiar tumult of emotions rose inside her as Rosie remembered that it was Tag who had managed to break through the frozen, smiling façade behind which she had hidden while in the arms of other men. Her throat thickened as she remembered their first time together, years earlier. She had known immediately that he would be different from the rest. She had raised careful defenses against him, but he tore them down patiently by refusing to accept the false face and hardened routine she presented to her customers. He took her gently, generous instead of demanding. He gave to her, unsatisfied until her body sang at his touch, unsatisfied until she reached a climax that for the first time was not feigned. He treated her with more tenderness than she had ever received in her life, and when he told her that she was special, that there was no other woman in the world quite like her, she had believed him.

She loved him for that — simply for making her realize that she *could* love.

But the hunger now growing inside her was an emotion

aside from love. Unable to remain motionless under Tag's ardent ministrations a moment longer, Rosie lowered her arms to clutch Tag against her. She cried out as Tag nipped her breast, and she heard his low curse when he realized he had hurt her. Rising to tangle his hands in her hair, he held her immobile, his burning gaze touched with remorse as he searched her face. She saw the passion in his eyes in the moment before he closed his mouth again over hers, devouring her with his kiss.

She was shuddering with a desire only Tag had been able to raise inside her as Tag abruptly separated her from him. Visibly trembling he whispered hoarsely, "I don't want this to go too fast, Rosie. I want to savor you, darling. . . ."

Slipping free of her dress with a deft movement, Rosie stood for a moment in her brief underdrawers and black stockings. She knew how she looked with the smooth curves of her body bared to his gaze, inviting him. She knew his hands longed to strip away that last impediment between their hot flesh, and she knew she wanted him to. But most of all she wanted to please him. She owed him that.

Cupping his face with her hands, Rosie kissed him long and hard, drawing back with a soft, "No," when he sought to clasp her close. Instead she carefully slipped his coat from his shoulders and tossed it on the nearby chair. Holding his eyes with her burning gaze, she slid her hands to his waist and unbuckled his belt, then unbuttoned his trousers. Her trembling increasing, she slid her hand inside to caress the rock-hard proof of his passion, her own emotions rising as his eyes dropped closed and he shuddered visibly. She stripped away his shirt as he kicked away his trousers, then halted him with a shake of her head as he took an eager step toward her. She pressed his anxious arms against his sides in a silent plea for patience, feeling a jolt of elation as he waited motionless for her next move. Moving slowly, Rosie slipped free of her underdrawers and stepped out of them. Clothed only in her black silk stockings and red high-heeled shoes, she raised her arms again over her head and closed her eyes, swaying sensuously as she inched closer. Her thickly lashed lids rose slowly as her aching breasts brushed his chest, as her moist female delta pulsed warmly against him. Slipping out of his reach, she moved behind him, brushing against him, rubbing her buttocks against his, then turning to press her breasts to his skin, slipping up and down against him until he had felt her breasts brush every inch of his exposed back.

Suddenly slipping her arms around his waist from behind, Rosie clasped him close. Tag's strong body trembled like a leaf in the storm, his gasp reaching the pitch of a shout as she grasped his engorged organ. Her breasts clasped tight against his back, her body aching, she held him firmly. He was shuddering as she tortured his earlobes with her tongue and stroked him between hoarse whispers. She felt his passion rising out of control, felt him quaking. Releasing him abruptly, she slipped in front of him once more. Locking her gaze with his, she whispered, "Take what you want when you want it, Tag. And when it's done we have all night to savor . . ."

She saw it again fleetingly, that look in his eyes that had so often frightened her, but in the moment it took for him to close the distance between them, it was gone.

She was in his arms, the satin bed covering cool under her back, and Rosie raised her arms to him.

"Now, Tag. I want you inside me."

Thrusting deep, Tag filled her, and Rosie wrapped herself around him. Holding him close, she rode his wild passion to culmination, shuddering as he shuddered, aware that even as her arms had slipped weakly away from him, Tag still clutched her possessively.

Tag slipped to the bed beside her without relinquishing his hold. His breathing restored to normal, he kissed her heavy eyelids, the pulse in her temple, then brushed her lips with his. For a moment she sensed he was about to speak, but he did not and she allowed her eyes to close. She knew she was safe in Tag's arms. She trusted him. He was a friend . . . an intimate, loving friend whom she cherished. She was not *in* love with him, but she loved him. She would do anything for him, just as he would do anything for her. Yes, it was good to have a friend . . .

Secure in that knowledge, Rosie drifted off to sleep.

Tag awoke to the sound of sobbing in the musky stillness of the night and he reached automatically for Rosie beside him. The lamp had burned low, and in its dim light he could see that although she still slept, her face was streaked with the muddy tracks of kohled tears. Her sobbing increased and Tag took only a moment to wipe her cheeks clear before whispering, "Rosie, wake up. You're dreaming. Rosie . . ."

Rosie was slow to awaken and Tag faced the moment with dread. He knew what he would see in her eyes when she did. It had been during a night such as this when he had first learned that the Rosie everyone thought they knew, the farm girl who had tired of the farm, had never really existed. Instead, he had discovered a Rosie whose innocence had been lost at the hands of a drunken stepfather when she was too young to protest; a Rosie who had suffered years of his abuse while her mother denied anything was wrong, even to herself, because she was too frightened to interfere. He had uncovered a Rosie who had escaped that torment after a vicious scene in which her own mother had turned against her.

Rosie shuddered in his arms, and Tag held her closer. Those were the memories that tormented the true Rosie, and Tag knew that the woman he held in his arms had been as innocent of blame for her circumstances then as she was now. He knew that this Rosie, *his* Rosie, was a woman with much love to give, and that although she had given her body many times to many men, she had never given her heart.

Rosie stirred, her moist eyelids fluttering as she emerged from her painful dreams, and Tag vowed as he had many times before that he would dispel *all* the shadows from Rosie's past, and that she would be his alone. Because he loved her—as a friend, as a lover, and as the woman he wanted to keep with him the rest of his life.

Tag frowned, knowing he dared not reveal the full extent of his feelings for Rosie. She wasn't ready yet for that kind of commitment. One last obstacle remained between them, but he was determined that he would overcome that one as he had all the others. He had contented himself for the present in knowing that she allowed no other man but him to love her. He was resolved that no other man ever again would.

"Tag . . . ?"

That look was there again in Rosie's eyes—the fear, the uncertainty, the *shame*. Unable to bear her pain, Tag smothered her uncertainty with his kiss—and as she responded to him, grasping at the lifeline of his presence, he knew he would never let her go.

Five

The day had been excessively warm and sultry for so early in the season. Thunderclouds gathered as Drake approached the summit of the hill and looked up at the menacing gray of the sky, feeling the weight of its threat. His bay twitched nervously beneath him as he watched the play of chain lightning in the clouds hovering over the mountain peaks to the north and west. His eyes narrowed and his skin crawled eerily. In this desolate mountain wilderness it was easy to see how the Sioux could imagine the presence of an angry god who sent bolts of lightning from his home on the high crests of those dark mountains. He knew that to be untrue, but he was aware of a very valid danger of another kind.

Darting a glance at the donkey lagging placidly behind him, Drake tugged sharply at his lead. The small animal barely responded and Drake swore under his breath. Had the situation not been so desperate, he would not have ventured out in this rapidly deteriorating weather, much less left a sick woman and a newborn child alone, even for so short a time. But the situation was more than desperate. It was critical, and he knew it.

With growing discomfort, Drake recalled the few hours before he had left the cabin, his attempt to feed the young mother food that was too heavy for her stomach to tolerate in her fragile condition. He also remembered his own pitiful attempt to care for a baby with nothing more than the stained petticoat in which she was wrapped and a coarse wool blanket that was already wet through. He knew he needed supplies other than those few basic staples on which he lived if the woman and child were to survive—and he knew of only one place close by where he might find them.

Drake spurred his bay into a faster pace as he approached the crest of the rise. Even now it was difficult to believe that Carolina Brand had managed to travel so far on this difficult terrain. Despite himself, he gained new respect for the woman's seemingly frail stature.

As for the woman herself, Drake had not yet made up his mind. His early prejudices aside, he wondered why she was reluctant to relate any details about herself. His suspicions rose. Had she and her party come to the Black Hills for reasons other than prospecting? Running guns to the Indians had always reaped high profits. Their game could have backfired on them, and that would account for the reason she had lied when he asked her name. Drake's lips tightened. If so, she was deserving of exactly what she had gotten.

A voice in his mind decried his harsh judgment and called for compassion for the woman's dire circumstances, but Drake ignored it. He knew full well that pregnancy was not necessarily a badge of honor—that even the most unscrupulous of women were capable of bearing a child. He did not choose to forget it.

Thunder clapped loudly and Drake hunched his shoulders against the growing force of the wind as he tilted the brim of his hat further down on his brow and spurred his horse on. The heavens would soon open with a deluge that would complicate the already difficult task before him, and he did not care to extend this foraging campaign a minute longer than necessary.

The wind whipped through the treetops, shrieking wildly as Drake reached the crest of the hill, but Drake was immune to nature's wild display as the charred ruin of a wagon train came into view below him. Losing little time in his descent, he dismounted among the human debris, his stomach churning. Stiff, mutilated bodies still in the postures of violent death lay strewn across the ground, evidence of carnage so vicious that Drake could scarcely

42

believe one person had indeed escaped.

His stomach revolting as he moved from one putrifying corpse to another, Drake pulled himself upright with relief at last. Ten men in all—no women. Judging from tools he had discovered in the wreckage, they had come to prospect for gold, and only one man had been fool enough to bring his wife along. It was somehow ironic that the woman should be the sole survivor.

Drake glanced around him once more, wondering which one of the bodies was that of Carolina Brand's husband. He dismissed that thought a moment later, realizing he had no time to waste in speculation when each moment spent dallying was at the expense of the young mother and child.

A deafening crack of thunder reinforcing the only decision he knew he could make, Drake gritted his teeth and went to work. Feeling more scavenger than savior, he removed a basket from his pack animal's back and began collecting whatever appeared salvageable, without taking the time to examine it for suitability for his purpose. When the basket was full, he looked around once more. Another eardrum-splitting clap of thunder convincing him he had lingered long enough, he secured the basket on the donkey's back, and mounted his horse.

Lightning flashed and thunder crashed, releasing a freezing torrent of rain that within seconds had soaked him to the skin as Drake directed his mount back up the hill. Flash after flash, peal after peal followed in rapid succession, rattling the hills around him as he climbed steadily higher. A vicious wind whipped him with icy, stinging drops as he pulled his hat down lower on his forehead and slanted his head against the abusive storm. The howling rage of the elements was so complete that Drake was suddenly compelled to glance toward the far peaks that were almost invisible in the darkness of the storm.

The eye of an angry god blinked at him, and Drake's heart momentarily stopped . . .

Dismissing that thought as ridiculous a moment later, Drake continued on.

***

A deafening clap of thunder awoke Carolina with a start and she looked around her in momentary confusion. A primitive log cabin . . . a bright fire in the fireplace across from her. . . . She attempted to draw herself to a seated position, only to find herself too weak to accomplish the task. Her aching head complicated the problem of the annoying haze that clouded her mind as she tried to think.

A short whimper from the wooden box on the table nearby, and Carolina was suddenly alert. She remembered a big man who had helped her. The infant's cry grew to a wail, and Carolina's anxiety grew. Where was he?

A flash of lightning momentarily lit the crude window coverings with the lightness of day. The thunderclap that followed shook the bed in which she lay and the baby wailed louder. Again attempting to rise, Carolina searched the shadowed corners of the cabin with her unfocused gaze. Where was the big man who had soothed her baby's distress? She needed him.

More blinding flashes and resounding claps of thunder followed in rapid succession, and Carolina's fear turned to panic. The big man had abandoned her. She was alone in this cabin. There was no one to take care of her child but herself. She had to reach her baby . . . to comfort her. . . .

The supreme effort costing her dearly, Carolina slowly raised herself to a seated position. She paused, her head swimming as she supported herself on trembling arms that threatened to betray her. The babe's wail grew louder, more frantic, and Carolina felt her desperation rise. She needed to hold her daughter. Then everything would be all right.

Managing to slip one foot over the edge of the bed, and then the other, Carolina looked at the table a few feet away. The distance stretched to miles as she studied it with wavering uncertainty. Her weakness allowing her no recourse, Carolina lowered herself to the dirt floor. Lightning crackled and thunder crashed, but Carolina was deaf to nature's violent orchestration as she dragged herself toward the table and attempted to draw herself to her feet.

Leaning heavily on a chair, her fingers digging into the

44

rough wood, Carolina ignored the growing thunder within her throbbing head. Her child's cry driving her, she fought the shadows closing in on her, refusing to submit.

A sudden, deafening crack—a loss of stability—darkness.

Wet and shivering with cold, Drake drove his mount to a relentless pace in the darkening forest. Uncertain of the cause of his growing alarm but knowing that it had nothing to do with his own physical discomfort, he strained his eyes into the shadowed woods. He released a ragged breath as the vague outline of his cabin came into view. A faint light was reflected against the windows and he felt a surge of relief. The fire had not yet gone out.

A brief break between the rolling booms of thunder allowed a baby's frantic wail to sound over the drumming of the rain and Drake's relief turned to panic. Spurring his bay into a leap forward that was almost disastrous, Drake cursed his stupidity, the driving rain, and the growing fear that tied his stomach into knots as he drew his mount back and forced himself to proceed with impatient caution.

Not waiting to shelter his sodden animals, Drake leaped from his mount at the door of the cabin. Bursting inside, he slammed the door closed behind him and came to an abrupt halt. Water dripped from his soaked clothing into muddy puddles on the dirt floor as he stared at the empty cot. Where had the woman gone?

One step, then two, and he saw her lying on the floor. A choked sound escaping him, Drake rushed to her side. He touched her. She was cold. Her wound had reopened where she had obviously struck her head on the chair, but she stirred under his touch. The lump in his throat thickened as her eyes slowly opened and she looked up at him.

"The baby . . ."

Furious, Drake scooped the woman up into his arms and placed her back on the cot. Abruptly realizing that his shaking had little to do with his previous chill, he rasped, "Damn the baby! You could've killed yourself with that fall!"

Appearing confused the woman whispered hoarsely, "I

. . . I thought you had left us."

Covering her with the blanket at her feet, Drake growled, *"Don't* think! Don't move, and don't do anythin' I don't tell you to do. I'll take care of you and the baby. All you have to do is lie there. Understand?" Poking his face down closer to hers when she did not respond, Drake demanded, "Do you understand?"

The woman nodded.

Suddenly conscious of his intimidating posture, Drake drew back and turned to the table. He picked up the trembling child and her frantic wails ceased. Her delicate lips still quivering, she stared up at him with light, unfocused eyes, and Drake was struck with the thought that she had recognized him.

Realizing the absurdity of that idea, he placed the child in her mother's arms and returned to the furor of the elements awaiting him.

Carolina followed the big man with her gaze as he walked to the door and slipped out into the storm without speaking another word. Feeling none of the fear that had previously robbed her of rational thought, she reviewed the anger in the big man's gaze as he had crouched over her cot. His dripping hat shadowing eyes that were fierce pinpoints of light, his heavy black hair, beard, and clothing plastered to his body, his immense shoulders holding her in the darkness of his shadow, he had been an alarming sight . . . but she had not been frightened.

Don't think! Don't move, and don't do anythin' that I don't tell you to do. I'll take care of you and the baby. All you have to do is lie there. Understand?

His words, spoken in anger, had strangely comforted her. She didn't *want* to think . . . or act. Those simple functions were temporarily beyond her. Her mind was cloudy, uncertain, and haunted by frightening images, but on one point she was abundantly clear. Despite his anger, she was safe in this big man's shadow as she had never been safe before.

The stormy afternoon had slipped into evening. Drake sat by the fire, his brow furrowed with concentration. The furor of the storm had abated to a steady rain that held little menace, his animals were sheltered, and all was quiet within the cabin. Stretched out across a rope near the fire hung his coat and shirt, now nearly dry. Still wearing his damp pants, he glanced at his sleeping charges before returning to sort the pile of miscellaneous garments rescued from the site of the massacre. He perused them slowly. Most were torn beyond repair, but he knew even the scraps would be useful in keeping the babe dry. Digging further he found three men's shirts and britches hardly bigger than a boy's had survived intact. He considered them thoughtfully. They were far more suitable clothing for the woman than his own oversize shirt. He put them aside. Next was a pillowcase rent with several slashes and several other linens similarly abused. He squeezed the pillowcase with his hand. Soft . . . exactly what he had been looking for. The fact that there were no garments for the babe scattered in the debris was an indication that the woman's wagon was one of those which had been totally consumed by fire. He paused at that thought. The woman had lost everything, even her husband. Her way would not be easy when she was again fit enough to resume her life.

Forcing his mind from that thought, Drake looked again at the sleeping babe. The child would not be fashionably clothed but she would soon be clean and dry.

That thought in mind, Drake took a determined breath. He would warm some water and bathe the child as soon as possible. He didn't expect it would be difficult. He had handled squirming babies before without doing them any harm, even if those babies hadn't been of the human kind. The little girl couldn't be that much different and she needed to be bathed completely clean of the stains of birth. Uncleanliness, especially with this small, perfect little infant, went against his grain.

Taking a few minutes to rinse the baby's linens in the bucket beside him, Drake then stretched them across the rope he had strung by the fire. That chore accomplished, he returned to the sleeping woman's bedside. He touched his palm to her forehead. He was pleased by the normal heat there and more than satisfied at the progress of affairs since his return. His visit to the site of the massacre had netted him a few foodstuffs that had been overlooked—a package of dried apples, a portion of which he had already boiled over the fireplace and then mashed into a coarse sauce—a can of baking powder which he had used to make up surprisingly good biscuits. He had even found a few jars of preserves that had survived intact. The young woman appeared to be tolerating this lighter food well, and for the first time he felt relatively optimistic about her chances of full recovery.

Drake's frown unconsciously returned. He was more secure in regard to the young woman's health, but his uncertainty in another area had not faded. The woman had lied about her name and he intended to discover the reason.

As if on cue, the young woman awakened. Her eyes were clear and Drake took the opportunity afforded him to draw a chair to her bedside. Surprising him, she was the first to speak.

"Th . . . this isn't a dream, is it." She continued without waiting for his response. "I wish it was."

"Wishing is for children." Drake's tone was cold. "I should've thought you'd have learned that by now."

The woman looked at him strangely. "I . . . I suppose I haven't."

She glanced toward the cradle and he responded to her unspoken question, "Don't worry about her. She's all right."

"Yes . . . thank you."

"I'm not lookin' for thanks—just cooperation."

Unexpected spirit flickered in the woman's eyes. "I woke up during the storm, and the baby was crying. You weren't here. I . . . I thought I could reach her, but it was harder than I thought."

"You leaned on the chair and it toppled over on you." Drake's frown deepened. "That was a damned foolish thing to do."

"I know that now."

The young woman had started to tremble, but Drake was unaffected. He had seen similar appeals for sympathy before. What this woman didn't realize was that there was no sympathy forthcoming.

Drake's eyes narrowed. "What else do you know?" And when she appeared confused at his question, "Do you know your wagon train had no right on this land? It belongs to the Indians."

"B . . . but *you're* here. . . ."

Drake ignored her response. "Where did your train come from and where was it headin'? Was somebody expectin' you? Do you have family somewhere?"

His questions appeared to confuse the young woman. She shook her head. "I . . . I don't know."

"What do you mean, you don't know?"

A slow panic began to negate the clarity of the woman's gaze. A small pulse in her temple began pulsing visibly and her breathing became stressed. Her face whitened. "I can't remember."

"You can't remember . . ." Drake paused, appearing to consider her response. "All right, you told me what you can't remember. Now tell me what you *can* remember."

The young woman shook her head. Her shaking grew more intense. "Nothing."

"You must remember something."

"I . . . I remember fire and pain . . . and I remember a face. . . ." Her eyes closed briefly. "A terrible, painted face. It won't leave me alone."

"What else?"

"I remember you. I remember you helped me."

Drake stiffened. "What else?"

"Nothing . . . nothing. . . ."

Drake searched the woman's pale face. She looked so innocent, but she had lied about her name. That thought was foremost in his mind when he spoke again.

"All right. Now I'll tell you what *I* know." Drake fixed her gaze with his. "I found you wanderin' in the hills and brought you here. Before the storm broke today, I rode over the mountain and found a wagon train that had been attacked by Indians. . . ."

Drake studied the woman's reaction to his words. Her face whitened further but it was otherwise blank. "There were six wagons, but there wasn't much left of them. Ten men were with that train. They were all dead."

The woman swallowed spasmodically. *"All* dead?"

Drake nodded.

"Except me."

Drake did not bother to respond and the woman closed her eyes. A single tear slid down her cheek. Opening her eyes again, she said unexpectedly, "I . . . I suppose I should be thankful that my baby and I are alive . . . and that I can at least remember my name." She swallowed again. "It's Carolina Brand."

Drake stood up abruptly. Carolina Brand . . . sure . . .

Bringing their conversation to a curt end, he said caustically, "All right, *Carolina.* Go to sleep."

His frustration soaring, Drake turned away from her without another word. Their conversation had been a waste of time! He had learned long ago that most women were incapable of honesty, and it appeared he was about to be taught that same lesson again.

Looking at the sack hanging beside the fireplace, he read the bold label again under his breath:

"RICE • CAROLINA BRAND."

He gave a scoffing snort. "Well, if that's the way you want it, *Carolina . . .*"

Snatching the sack off the wall, he tossed it into the flames and walked away.

Six

Miriam Higgins leaned over her steaming washtub, unconsciously studying the clothes swirling in the rapidly darkening water. Her thin nose twitched. How fully grown men could keep the same clothes on their body until they reached this degree of filth was a mystery to her. Another mystery was how she could bear to touch the foul-smelling articles, much less wash them!

Drawing back, Miriam wiped a hand across her perspired brow before resting it on her flat hip. Suddenly conscious of a flying wisp of graying hair that had escaped the bun she wore at the nape of her neck, she tucked it back securely. She was a proud woman. If she was forced to do the work of a laundress in order to survive, she did not choose to look like one.

With more difficulty than she chose to reveal, Miriam assumed the erect, formal posture that had become her trademark in Deadwood, the glorified mining camp that had the gall to call itself a town. She rubbed palms that had once been smooth and callus free against her damp apron and adjusted her shirtwaist sleeves so they would not touch the water. She knew many were amused by her strict adherence to propriety in both dress and manner. She had been advised more times than she cared to count that she had left propriety behind her when she had accompanied her husband to the Black Hills, and that she should put it finally to rest. But she would not, and she knew why.

Jonas Higgins, her husband of twenty-five years, had

been a dear, conscientious, and reasonable man, and she had loved him with all her heart. Always a plain woman with a thin face and sharp features whom few found appealing, she had been happier than most and no little surprised when Jonas had declared his love for her and asked her to marry him. They had led a happy but unexciting life in the small Ohio town where they were both born. Their union had not been blessed with children, and she had accepted that deficiency in her life by devoting herself to her beloved nephews and nieces. She had been a contented woman, and she had thought Jonas was content, too, until that fateful day. . . .

Miriam remembered it vividly. Jonas had arrived home unexpectedly in the middle of the afternoon and she had rushed to the door of their small, comfortable home with the thought that he was ill. He had walked through the doorway quite calmly, and taking only enough time to remove his hat, adjust his glasses, and push a lock of thinning hair back from his forehead, he had stated flatly that he had made up his mind to join a wagon train that would be starting for the gold fields in the Black Hills at the end of the month.

She remembered just as vividly that she had immediately believed that her dear Jonas was indeed ill. In the hours following his announcement, she had reasoned, cajoled, pleaded, begged, and then cried, to no avail. He had been determined that he would not spend the remainder of his years mourning the adventure he had let pass him by.

Her tears then had come from the realization that although she had been content with their life, Jonas had not. Loving him as she did, she had asked him if he wanted her to accompany him. Emotion stirring anew, Miriam recalled that Jonas had taken her into his arms and cried as well as she when he had whispered that he wanted that more than anything in the world.

Miriam's small, dark eyes misted. Dear Jonas. He had been as happy as a child as they started out on their illicit quest. He had seemed to expand in front of her eyes, to grow taller, stronger, even younger as they met the test of their harrowing journey. When they had made love under the stars with the limited privacy afforded them and with potential dangers lurking in the surrounding darkness, it had never been better between them.

A tear slid from the corner of Miriam's eye. Jonas did not find the gold he sought, but during the three months they spent together in this "sacred" wilderness, she knew he was truly content for the first time in his life. During that brief period, they came to know each other more intimately than they had in all their previous years of marriage. When he was stricken with an unexpected illness and died suddenly, she had known instinctively that her dear Jonas had no regrets.

She had buried Jonas on the hillside overlooking Deadwood, beside other marked as well as unmarked graves. She had decided then that when the time came for her, she would be buried beside him.

Upon making that decision, Miriam had made another as well. Unlike others who were content to *take* from Deadwood without giving in return, and uncomfortable with the town's illegal status, she had determined to devote all her energies to legitimizing the status of Deadwood Gulch and the other mining camps that had sprung up in the Indians' "holy" wilderness. She had spent every spare minute working toward that goal in the time since, enlisting the aid of anyone and everyone who shared a similar interest. That goal had become her life's work, and she was determined to achieve it.

Wiping another straying tear from her cheek, Miriam looked self-consciously around her. It would not do to allow anyone to think that she was weak if she hoped to achieve her purpose. She strove to negate that impression with every step she took, and with every word she spoke. She had allowed no compromise in her life and had continued to conduct herself as she would in any civilized town. And if she was forced to take in laundry to support herself, an occupation she might have thought demeaning only a year earlier, she was now proud of the contribution she made and the independence she had won with her own two hands.

Miriam frowned unconsciously. She had succeeded in

putting her sorrow behind her. She had thought that no one could jar her from the course she had set — until Dr. Jerome Fitz had taken it upon himself to bring a war of a different kind into her life.

Even now, Miriam was uncertain how the smiling conflict between them had first begun. Was it due, perhaps, to the few poorly chosen words with which she had expressed her disgust with his degenerate ways? Had it been her criticism of him as she saw him stagger home from the Nugget or some such saloon on a regular basis? Had it been her openly expressed opinion that as an educated man, he should set as good an example as she strove to create, and that he should be one of those to *lead* the cause to legalize their status in the Black Hills — instead of staggering behind it?

Or had it begun with Dr. Fitz's taunting ways . . . his ridicule of her refusal to compromise with the free-and-easy way of life of the mining camp? Had it been when he was called to tend to her when she was too ill to protest and he had told her flatly that she was still a young woman and too young to bury herself in her husband's grave?

She had been incensed! She had told him to mind his own business!

He had told her to mind hers!

She had raged that unlike him, at the age of forty-one years, she was an *adult* — not an overage delinquent, that she *knew* what she wanted to do with the rest of her life, and that she was doing it!

He had looked her straight in the eye and replied that at the age of forty-nine years, he had decided what he wanted to do with his life, too — that he was doing a great job of being the best goddamned hell-raiser in Deadwood, and that was the way he liked it!

Miriam paused in her thoughts. What was the term she had heard used for the status of affairs between them? Stalemate . . . impasse . . . ? No — *Mexican standoff!* That was what some laughingly called it. The only problem was that she wasn't laughing.

Miriam turned to look at the line stretched across the backyard of her small cabin. It was filled with clothes of assorted sizes and condition, some of the most poorly abused of which belonged to Dr. Jerome Fitz.

There was no escaping him!

Restraining an unladylike urge to curse, Miriam swore to herself as she had many times before that she would turn that man around to her way of thinking if it was the last thing she ever did!

A sudden shouting on the street beyond her yard abruptly interrupted Miriam's raging frustration and she turned toward the sound. She approached the street with as dignified a step as curiosity would allow. She was accustomed to the wild ways of Deadwood and she disapproved, but in a concession she would admit only to herself, she was aware that her occupation as a voyeur was the only diversion she was allowed as a decent woman in Deadwood Gulch, and she was determined to take advantage of it.

Halting as she reached the street, Miriam perused the anxious crowd gathering around a bull train stalling traffic on the busy thoroughfare. She was aware of rising excitement as anxious prospectors within the crowd pushed and shoved and shouted to the bull whacker standing close by. Her curiosity more than she could withstand, Miriam grasped the arm of a grizzled fellow hurrying by. He turned to her with annoyance as she questioned briefly, "What's going on over there?"

"Cats."

A polite response momentarily beyond her, Miriam responded bluntly, "What?"

"Cats — I said cats! Old Harry brought a wagon load of cats up from Cheyenne with him and he's sellin' them for ten dollars each!"

Astounded, Miriam resisted the fellow's attempt to shake off her hand. "You mean those fellows are that excited about buying themselves a cat?"

"That's right, ma'am, and I'm goin' to get me one, too!"

Miriam stared at the fellow with disbelief as he dislodged her hand with a jerk of his arm and joined the pressing throng. Turning her back on the growing crowd a moment later, she shook her head with astonishment and went back

55

to her work, certain the ways of Deadwood Gulch were beyond her.

Standing on the opposite side of the street, Tag Willis paid little attention to Miriam Higgins's departing figure as he puffed at a thin, black cigar and watched the jostling crowd around the old bull whacker's wagon. He gave an amused chuckle. Leave it to Harry Whitebottom to come up with another scheme to make money from the lonesome miners who populated the hills. But then, he supposed a cat to keep on his crude hearth was the closest most of these men would get to the memory of the girl they left behind for a long time to come.

Smiling, Tag watched the surging crowd as one by one the rough, hard-bitten prospectors pushed their way free to emerge with a frightened feline cuddled in his arms. A particularly seedy-looking fellow stepped out of the crowd, and Tag's smile froze. Held gently in the prospector's dirty, oversized hands was a small white kitten.

An intimate, haunting memory returned vividly to Tag's mind. He remembered Rosie as she had been those years ago, a beautiful saloon girl with a brash personality that kept men laughing. And he remembered the first night she allowed him a glimpse of the insecure, frightened girl she concealed behind that brazen façade. She was a girl who had been denied a childhood, a sweet young victim who had been stripped of her innocence in the cruelest of ways, but who had managed to cling to a picture in her mind of the hearth where she sat only in her dreams. She had described it in detail to him one night when she was particularly vulnerable, its warm, inviting colors and the small, white cat playing beside it.

Without consciously realizing his intent, Tag grasped the old prospector's arm as he walked past. To the grizzled fellow's inquisitive gaze he commented with a forced smile, "Nice cat you have there. How much did you pay for it?"

The fellow's eyes narrowed suspiciously. "I paid twenty dollars for this here cat, and she's worth every penny of it."

56

"That so?" Tag raised a skeptical brow. "Seems to me I heard the highest price being paid was *ten* dollars."

"You asked me what I paid and I told you. What business is it of yours anyway?"

"I'll pay you thirty dollars for it."

"Thirty dollars!" The old man clutched the squirming cat tighter. "Why would you pay me thirty dollars for this cat when there's a whole wagon load of them over there that you can get for ten—I mean twenty?"

"Are there any more white cats in the wagon?"

"Don't think so. . . ."

"Then I'll buy this one from you."

The old fellow's whiskers twitched as he eyed Tag speculatively. "Yeah? Well, I ain't sellin' This here cat's the only thing that's goin' to make my life worth livin' when I'm slavin' in them hills for a few grains of dust. She's goin' to be somethin' to go home to, and I'm goin' to—"

"Forty dollars."

"Forty dollars!" The prospector's gaze narrowed into slits. "What do you want this cat for, anyway?"

"I want to buy it for a lady."

The old man laughed aloud. "Now I *know* you're crazy! There ain't no *ladies* in this here town—not under the age of forty and worth courtin' anyhow!"

Tag's smile dulled. "That's where you're wrong. Fifty! Take it or leave it."

The fellow hesitated only a moment longer. "I'll take it!"

His bleary eyes cautious, the old prospector watched carefully as Tag counted out the sum in gold coins. He then turned over the squirming cat with a gleeful smile. "You know what I'm goin' to do now? I'm goin' to hop right back into that crowd and buy me *two* cats, at *ten* dollars each, and with what's left over, I'm goin' to have me a night on the town! And for that I thank you, brother!"

Nodding, aware that the old fellow thought he had done a masterful job of snookering him, Tag held the frightened kitten gently. It didn't make much difference to him what that old boy thought.

Smiling broadly, Tag left the howling crowd in his wake.

* * *

The white kitten lay sprawled contentedly on the bed behind him as Tag stared critically at his reflection in the washstand mirror. His own quarters in Deadwood's only hotel contrasted sharply with the satin and lace of Rosie's cabin that was as much a part of her as her glorious blue eyes and flashing smile, but it was good enough for him. Unlike Rosie, he didn't need familiar possessions around him in order to feel secure. His needs were different and he had recently discovered that he could be perfectly content with the basic necessities — clean clothes, good food, a pack of cards . . . and Rosie.

A frown marred Tag's smooth brow as he viewed his image in the mottled glass. Rosie was right. He was handsome, but few realized the effort he had expended to achieve his present image. During an underprivileged youth when he had often worn clothes that were no better than rags, he had been given the nickname "Rag-Tag" Willis. A knack with cards and a will of iron had brought him up in the world an inch at a time until he now wore nothing but the best of clothes. But, like Rosie, those early years were still with him in many ways. They were as much a part of him as his easy charm and the fastidious appearance with which he would not compromise. He was keenly aware, however, that he would need to employ all of his assets most avidly before this night was over.

Thoughtfully, Tag assessed his appearance more closely. His well-tailored black frock coat stretched smoothly across the broad expanse of his shoulders and his pearl gray trousers fit to perfection because they had been cut specifically to his masculine proportions. His embroidered white shirt was of the finest available material, and his brocade vest, from which the gold chain of his pocket watch draped neatly, was in excellent taste. He did not have to examine his reflection further to see that his heavy dark hair lay clean and neatly trimmed against his neck and that the fine, dark mustache on his otherwise smooth-shaven face added just the right touch of virile appeal. Neither need anyone tell him

58

that his compact, powerful body attracted women, rarely disappointed them, and was silent warning to other men to show him the respect he was due.

The impressive diamond ring he wore on his pinkie finger winked at him in the limited light of the room and Tag gave a wry laugh. All this, and he was depending on a little white kitten to achieve his end.

A low purring sound interrupted his thoughts and Tag walked the few steps to the bed. He scooped up the kitten into his hands and held its small face up to his. His voice was soft and filled with unexpected emotion as he whispered into the animal's expressionless face. "Tonight it's going to be different, little fella. Tonight I'm going to win my Rosie once and for all."

Smiling at the kitten's purring response, Tag slipped the small feline into his coat pocket, picked up his hat, and opened the door.

Rosie glanced out her cabin window, grateful that the shadows of night signaled the end of another day. Picking up a cotton puff, she dusted a brighter color to her smooth cheeks and added a touch of color to her already well-rouged lips. She frowned at the forest green satin gown she wore. Its rich color looked good with her coloring and the dip of its daring bodice was certain to draw attention to that well-endowed portion of her anatomy, but it wasn't her favorite dress.

Turning a glance toward the corner rack where her generous wardrobe of dresses hung, Rosie looked longingly at the simple blue silk that contrasted sharply with the other, more flamboyant garments hanging beside it. She had never worn that dress, but she knew she would . . . someday.

Briefly closing her eyes, Rosie opened them again, angry with herself for the impatience that had become the bane of her existence. She had waited so long. . . . What possible difference could another few weeks . . . a month . . . even a year make? Her patience would be rewarded in the end.

Turning at a knock on the door, Rosie chased the shadows

from her thoughts and smiled.

"Come in."

The door opened slowly to reveal Tag's handsome face and Rosie's heart leaped in the way it always did when Tag stuck his head around the corner of her door. She smiled more broadly as Tag raised an arched brow.

"Do you always say 'Come in' before you know who's knocking, Rosie? You could get in trouble that way."

"Sayin' 'Come in' has brought me a lot more fun than trouble in my life, Tag, honey. I'm not about to start holdin' back now."

"Hummmm." Tag advanced to stand so close to her that she could feel his warm, sweet breath on her face. "I suppose I approve because I choose to take your comments as a personal compliment." He moved an inch closer his gaze touching her lips warmly, "But I've found out lately that I'm beginning to become a jealous man."

Rosie gave a short laugh, truly amused. *"You,* jealous? Of who? Me?"

Tag's eyes flickered momentarily with an unreadable emotion. "Yes, you. You're looking beautiful tonight, darling." He brushed her lips with a light kiss, then repeated lightly, "I'm jealous of you, all right."

A slow tightening began in Rosie's stomach as she shook her head and whispered, "Don't be jealous, Tag. We're friends, remember? Friends take each other as they are. They comfort each other and share their happiness and pain with each other . . . and they accept each other's shortcomings."

Tag's smile was soft. "What shortcomings? You don't have any."

Rosie was no longer smiling. "Don't tease me, Tag! You know better than anyone else what I am and what I — "

"Rosie . . ." Unwilling to allow her to continue, Tag cupped her cheeks with his hands. "Stop talking."

Lowering his mouth to hers, Tag kissed her lightly, his kiss deepening as her mouth accepted his warmly. Her arms moved around his neck, seeking the mutual comfort that had always existed between them, but he held her apart from him, appearing content solely to indulge her kiss. Frustrated at the distance he maintained between them and uncertain what it meant, Rosie drew back, her delicate brow furrowed.

"What's the matter, Tag?"

Tag gave a short laugh. He was obviously physically affected by their short exchange, but as his warm brown eyes searched hers, she read a hesitation there that she hadn't seen before. She heard that same hesitation in his voice as he whispered, "What's the matter . . . ? Well, the truth is that I didn't mean for things to go this way between us this evening—not yet, anyway."

Tag's unexpected words sent a chill down Rosie's spine and she took spontaneous refuge in anger. "I must be slippin'—or maybe I just misjudged that bulge I can feel movin' real warm against me."

As if in response to her comment, the bulge made a strange contortion and Rosie gave a short leap backward, her eyes widening.

"What in hell . . . ?"

Reaching into his pocket, Tag withdrew a small white kitten. He held the squirming animal up to her face and nodded. "Yes, I'd say you misjudged. . . ."

Unable to speak, Rosie took the little feline into her arms. She held it close, incredulous at the bright blue eyes looking back at her. Tearing her gaze from the kitten's sweet face, she looked up to see that Tag was no longer smiling.

"Do you like him, Rosie?"

Rosie's throat was still too filled to speak. She had recognized this cat immediately, and she knew Tag did, too. She had played with it in her dreams when her young life had been too terrible to bear. It had loved her the way she wanted to be loved, and she had escaped with it to a warm, beautiful hearth where the sound of her stepfather's voice was never heard.

A soft sob escaped Rosie's lips and she hugged the kitten closer. Tag's arms slipped around her and she felt his cheek against her hair as he whispered apologetically, "I didn't mean to make you cry, Rosie. I wanted you to be happy."

Brushing the tears from her cheeks with her free hand, Rosie forced a wobbly smile. "I *am* happy. You . . . you're too good to me, Tag."

Drawing back far enough to look directly into her eyes, Tag was suddenly intently serious. "I'd make you even happier, if you'd let me. I'd spend the rest of my life making you smile, because the truth is that I'm never happier than when you're happy. I love you, Rosie. I want to marr—"

"No, don't say any more, Tag!" Her heart suddenly pounding, Rosie closed her eyes. Snapping her eyes open a moment later, she was suddenly angry.

"Why did you say that, Tag? Why? You know how it is with us! We're *friends* . . . loving friends, and that's all we'll ever be. You're not the man by that hearth, Tag!" And at the pain that came alive in his eyes, "I never said you were, so don't look at me that way. You know how it is with me. I'm frozen inside. You brought my body to life—you're the only one who ever did—but there's a part of me that nobody can touch."

"Nobody, Rosie?"

Rosie closed her eyes. "Just one."

"He doesn't want you, Rosie."

"He will."

"You're wrong."

"No, I'm not. We're the same, him and me. We've both been forced to face the blackness of our soul, and we've lived through it."

"Rosie, honey." Tag's voice reflected her pain. "Your soul's bright and beautiful, just like you are."

"It will be."

"You're wasting your time waiting for him."

Rosie's clear eyes turned belligerent. "It's my time to waste."

"And if I'm not willing to wait to see how it all turns out?"

The pain of that thought suddenly almost more than she could bear, Rosie whispered, "I don't want you to leave me, Tag, but . . . but I'll understand if you do because there're some things we have to do because we don't have any choice."

Raising her chin, Rosie blinked back her tears. "Thank you for the kitten. It's the best present I've ever received."

Turning away from Tag the most difficult thing she had ever done, Rosie walked out of the cabin still clutching the squirming kitten. At the bar minutes later, her aching heart carefully concealed behind a stiff smile as she watched the kitten settle itself into a wooden box in a safe corner, Rosie felt a strong arm slip around her waist. She turned as Tag whispered with a smile, "A real gambler always bets against the odds."

Slipping more firmly into the curve of his arm, Rosie felt Tag's warmth close around her.

Seven

Drake moved restlessly in his sleep. He awakened slowly as the sound that had intruded into his slumber grew louder. Suddenly realizing he had been awakened by sobs coming from the nearby cot, he drew himself to his feet.

Angry with his own sleep-drugged wits, he walked to the woman's bedside in a few anxious strides. He looked down at her sleeping face, his stomach knotting at her pained expression. She was dreaming. He touched her forehead lightly and found it cool. Relieved, he ran a weary hand through his hair.

The woman cried harder and Drake crouched beside her. The woman — *Carolina* — had been having severe headaches and he had begun worrying if she was hurt more seriously than he could see with the naked eye. She sobbed again and he knew he could not let her suffer her nightmares any longer.

He shook her lightly. "It's all right, Carolina. You're having a bad dream."

Carolina jumped with a start at his touch and Drake took her hand to steady her. It trembled in his grasp like a small, captive bird. He instinctively clenched it tighter as he whispered, "Don't be afraid. Go back to sleep."

The young woman closed her eyes and Drake released her hand. Remaining by her side a few moments longer, he studied her face. The scratches and bruises on her damp cheeks had already begun to heal and the blue shadows under her eyes had lightened as well. The ravages of her ordeal were fading . . . but she was still a plain little wren.

64

That thought giving him a moment's pause, Drake speculated at the type of man who would be attracted to her . . . at the kind of man who would place his wife and unborn child in jeopardy because of his greed. He frowned, reaching the conclusion he had reached before, that if Carolina had married such a fool, she was probably a fool herself.

Suddenly uncomfortable with that judgment, Drake looked toward the babe's cradle. The child had responded to her mother's milk like a flower slowly unfurling under the sun. She appeared to be growing more content as well.

As if to refute that last thought, the babe stirred. Drake grimaced and looked at Carolina as the infant's low whimper began building in intensity. Knowing it was not yet time for her feeding, he moved to the babe's side. Sliding his hands under the child he lifted her into his arms and rocked her gently. The babe's fretting grew more intense and he looked again at the sleeping woman. Small and pale, Carolina looked like a fragile, battered doll on his oversize cot and he knew he could not disturb her sleep again.

Drake rocked the babe harder, to no avail. Desperate to pacify her as her soft cries grew to a wail, he did the first thing that came to mind. In a voice just above a whisper, he sang in time with his energetic rocking, "Oh, Suzannah, don't you cry for me . . . I come from Alabama with a banjo on my knee. . . ."

His reluctant baritone miraculously stilled the baby's quivering lips. Her eyes widened comically, her unfocused gaze becoming trained on his face as he continued his strained lullaby. He was still singing as the babe's eyelids slowly drooped closed and her small body went gradually limp.

Lowering her back into the cradle, Drake paused to study the infant's small, peaceful face. It struck him that he had been the first person in the world to see that face. He wondered at the adult woman she would one day be, then scoffed at the thought. In a few weeks he would relieve himself of responsibility for both mother and child and deliver them to Deadwood. They would probably take the first wagon train back to wherever they had come from and put the Black Hills forever behind them.

Drake drew himself to his full height, his expression hardening. In a few months he would put the Black Hills behind him, too. He had plans of his own.

The child and mother dismissed from his mind, Drake returned to his blanket on the hard floor and to harsh memories that he had thought far behind him.

Silent and unobserved, Carolina watched the big man roll himself in his blanket and close his eyes. Restless, she had stirred awake a few minutes earlier to see his broad back etched against the flickering flames of the fireplace behind him. She had raised her head, ignoring the painful throbbing the effort cost her. Nightmares and pain had become an unending circle that was broken only by the sight of his face, the comfort of his touch, and the joy of her child at her breast.

Her child . . . a daughter yet unnamed because of the impenetrable void where her memory had once been. . . .

The big man had shifted and she had seen that he held the babe in his arms. He was rocking her, singing softly. She had heard his whispered song.

"Oh, Suzannah, don't you cry for me . . ."

Her babe asleep in her cradle a short time later, she had lowered her head back to the pillow as well.

Her eyes drifting slowly closed, Carolina allowed her mind to wander. She thought about Drake McNeil, and then she thought about her babe . . . her child . . . her daughter . . . Suzannah.

Yes . . . *Suzannah.*

Drake squinted up at the brilliant morning sun overhead. He shook his head. He supposed he would never become accustomed to the vagaries of the Black Hills climate. He had passed a harsh winter in the cabin behind him . . . experiencing some of the bitterest cold of his life. Spring had been welcome but undependable as the weather had shifted from rain to snow and then rain again. An hour earlier, he had heard the rumblings of thunder in the mountaintops and had seen flashes of lightning flickering there although the day was clear.

Certain that whatever changes the seasons would bring, they would be abrupt and drastic, as evidenced by the unexpected heat of the sun now scorching his skin, Drake allowed his ax to slip to the ground. He stripped off his coat and wiped his arm against his sweated forehead. He glanced back at the cabin behind him and listened. Silence. He released a relieved breath. The woman and child had been with him for several days during which his life in this virgin wilderness could not have changed more drastically if it had been a lifetime.

Drake gave a grunt of disgust as he surveyed the long line of laundry flapping in the gentle breeze. The rope was stretched from the cabin to a nearby tree and he knew that as soon as the babe's linens had dried, there would be more waiting to take their place. He had finished that endless chore earlier in the day — *after* an early-morning trip into the surrounding hillside where he had shot a bird for the pot, *after* he had cleaned the bird and set it to boil so he might have some nourishing soup for his patient, *after* he had prepared a morning meal for her *which she had barely eaten, after* he had bathed the child and slipped her into clean wrappings. . . .

Drake picked up his ax and resumed his work. He recalled the previous morning when Carolina had awakened and asked for her child. He had placed the babe in her arms and had been startled into momentary stillness when she had whispered to the squirming infant, "Hush, Suzannah. Everything will be all right."

Drake swung the ax savagely. He didn't like knowing Carolina had heard him singing to the babe. He didn't like her acceptance of the name he had unthinkingly assigned the child. He didn't like her making his efforts out to be anything more than a necessity.

Drake frowned as he glanced in the direction of the nearby stream and the tools which lay neglected beside it. The past few days would cost him dearly in many ways. A longer period of time spent in these hills than he had anticipated would eat drastically into his profits, with flour going at almost two dollars a pound and other staples proportionately priced.

That thought in mind, Drake resumed his attack on the nearby tree. He had worked all morning long without reward, but he was determined to take time now to see to his own comfort. He did not intend to spend another night on the hard cabin floor.

A few more swings with the ax and the tree shuddered briefly before falling to the ground with an earthshaking thump. A familiar wail began inside the cabin, and Drake closed his eyes with frustration. The cry grew louder and Drake dropped his ax with a curse and turned toward the door. He pushed it open to see Carolina on her feet, swaying weakly as she attempted to walk.

"Oh, no, you don't!"

Carolina turned abruptly toward him, paling. At her side in a minute, Drake grasped her arm and lowered her back onto the bed.

"I told you to stay put!"

"B . . . but Suzannah . . ."

"I'll take care of Suzannah. Just do as I say."

Turning, Drake picked up the child, noting that she was wet to the shoulders. Grateful that he had had the foresight to leave a few previously washed linens ready on the table, he balanced the infant carefully, supporting her back in one large hand as he unwrapped her sodden garments. The babe went quiet, content to rest in his palm as he pushed aside her wet covering.

Drake turned back to Carolina's watchful gaze when Suzannah was dry once more. He put the child in her arms, noting unconsciously that her gray eyes were clearer than he had ever seen them as she said, "I . . . I want you to know that I appreciate all you've done."

"I told you I don't want your thanks."

"I'm not thanking you." She paused and raised her chin. "I want to ask a favor."

Caution prickled along Drake's spine. "What do you want?"

"I want . . ." Carolina took a steadying breath. "I want you to stop treating me as if I'm sick every time I try to get up."

"You *are* sick."

"No, I'm better. I want to walk."

"You'll walk, when you're strong enough."

"I'm strong enough now."

"No, you aren't."

"Yes, I am."

"I say you aren't!"

Carolina's eyes flashed. "My headaches are almost gone and I'm feeling stronger. I want to get up. If I do . . ." The steadiness of her gaze appeared to waver. "If I do, I know I'll start to remember. . . ."

"No."

"Drake . . . please . . ."

Drake looked at the self-named Carolina Brand. Her face was pale, but she was determined despite the quaver in her voice and the plea in her eyes. She did not know, however, that he had been subjected to this type of appeal before, from an expert. It did not move him.

"I'll let you know when I think you're ready."

About to turn away, he was stopped by the young woman's unanticipated question.

"Why do you dislike me, Drake?" She searched his face intently. "Is it something I did — something I don't remember? Do you know something about me that I don't? Is something wrong?" Her breathing quickening, Carolina paled even further. "Do you know who I am — where I came from?" She began trembling. "Did you know the father of my child? Is that it? Who was he?"

"Look, Carolina . . ." Suddenly recognizing his unintentional cruelty, Drake took her trembling hand. His gruff voice softened without conscious intent. "You don't know anythin' about me. I'm not the kind of man you think I am, but I will tell you this. I gave you my word that I'll do my best for you and Suzannah, and I'll keep it."

Carolina was unable to respond, and Drake's resentment grew. He would not allow this young woman to touch him. Nor would he let her difficulties become a part of his life. He had enough problems of his own. He had already said more than was wise, and he would not

69

let her maneuver him into saying more.

Suddenly realizing he still held Carolina's hand, Drake dropped it abruptly. Without another word, he turned to the door.

Drake pulled the cabin door closed behind him and Carolina briefly shut her eyes. He was angry. She had not been able to make him understand.

Carolina looked down at the beautiful, fair-haired babe suckling at her breast. She was this child's mother. Her name was Carolina Brand, but who was she? Where had she come from? Pausing, she searched her babe's flushed face, her anxiety rising. Had this child been conceived in love? If so, why had she felt strangely numb when Drake told her that all the men with the wagon train had been killed?

A fragmented picture flashed before Carolina's mind—a burning wagon, a young man motionless on the ground beside it, his eyes void of life . . .

The image faded as unexpectedly as it had appeared, leaving Carolina shaken. She didn't know that young man. He couldn't have been her husband, or she would've recognized him . . . wouldn't she? She stared at the plain gold band she wore. Why couldn't she remember him?

The babe moved restlessly. Suddenly realizing her arms had tightened around the child to the point of discomfort, Carolina loosened her anxious grip. A warning sounded somewhere in the back of her mind. She shouldn't become agitated when she was nursing. It wasn't good for the child. It could sour her milk . . . make the babe ill. *Someone* had told her that.

Carolina slid a shaking hand across her eyes and attempted to still her shuddering. Drake was right. She needed to rest. Her memory would return when she was well. It had to.

Forcing all other thought aside, Carolina took refuge in the only security she knew. Drake had promised to take care of them. She and Suzannah were safe while they were with him. That was her reality . . . and her consolation.

70

* * *

The flickering light of the fire played gracefully against the walls of the cabin, but the scene within was rapidly deteriorating. Drake looked at the partially constructed sleeping bench a few feet away, then at the cot where Carolina attempted to pacify her screaming infant. His agitation mounted. Night was rapidly falling, and with it came the sinking feeling that he was destined to spend another sleepless night on the cabin's dirt floor.

Drake ground his teeth with frustration. It had seemed so easy at first. He had cut and assembled the lengths of wood he needed and carried them into the cabin, knowing he need construct the oversize piece of furniture inside. He remembered thinking that with just a few nails and a few strips of rawhide webbing, a good night's sleep was ahead of him. He had been extremely satisfied with himself as he had picked up the hammer.

Then he had struck the first nail.

With an eardrum-shattering shriek that had set his hair on end, Suzannah had brought him to his feet in a flash. He had rushed to her cradle and spent a few frantic moments attempting to discover the cause of her distress. She had been quiet at last when he had placed her in her mother's arms and returned to his work.

The second strike of the hammer had raised another bloodcurdling howl. He had pounded once more, just to make certain. . . .

"I think the noise frightens her."

The sharpness of his glance had snapped Carolina's gaze back to her daughter without further comment. Determined, he had then struck the nail again.

The babe had not stopped crying since.

Drake sat back on his heels. His head was pounding harder with each shrieking wail. Damn it, he was tired! Scrubbing and cooking, running and fetching, and countless midnight hours spent rocking . . . rocking. . . . All he wanted was a good night's sleep!

A pitiful sigh came from the direction of the nearby cot and Drake felt the prick of conscience. The babe was still shud-

71

dering, but she had finally stopped crying. Unconsciously drawing himself to his feet, he found himself looking down into the infant's perspired face. Carolina looked up at him, and for the first time he realized the entire episode had taken as much out of the mother as it had the child.

The baby's quaking slowly stilled. Glancing back at the sleeping bench that begged to be completed, Drake was struck with a sudden thought. It was ridiculous, but he was desperate enough to give it a try.

Assembling the pieces once more, Drake carefully positioned a nail. He raised the hammer. Scowling darkly, he took a deep breath before singing out at the top of his lungs, "Oh, Suzannah . . ." He hit the nail a powerful shot. "Don't you cry for me . . ." Another ear-splitting whack. "I've come from Alabama with a banjo on my knee. . . ."

Another pounding blast timed to the rhythm of the song, and Drake paused to glance cautiously behind him. The child was silent — and he suspected the mother was hiding a grin.

Suddenly unreasonably angry, Drake sang more loudly than before, "Oh, Suzannah (whack), don't you cry for me (bang), I've come from Alabama (crack) with a banjo on my knee (boom). Oh, it rained all day . . ."

Hoarse, and feeling more the fool than he had ever felt in his life, Drake assessed the completed cot a short time later. All was silent behind him. He had not looked back during his enforced serenade, but he knew he could avoid it no longer. Preparing himself by affixing an expression on his bearded face that bespoke more clearly than words that *he* wasn't amused, he turned abruptly.

His mouth fell agape. They were both asleep!

Drawing himself to his feet, Drake looked down at the sleeping pair with incredulity. It occurred to him as he did that the man he had once been, might've laughed . . . but the man he was now, didn't have a laugh left in him.

Eight

Shaking his head as his door closed behind Barney Potts's disreputable figure, Doc Fitz plopped himself down behind his battered desk and yanked out the bottom drawer in one deft, well-practiced movement. Withdrawing a half-filled bottle of red-eye and a sticky glass, he poured himself a shot and swallowed it in a gulp. He belched loudly, wiped his sleeve across his mouth, and sat back with relief. He had made it through another morning of lancing boils, dispensing stomach remedies, sewing up knife wounds, cauterizing snakebites, and digging earwax out of ears that hadn't seen a speck of soap since they'd hit the Black Hills. He'd done his duty for the day. The rest of the afternoon — and night — belonged to him.

Sitting back, Doc speculated on how he would spend it. He then wondered if it really mattered, since he probably wouldn't remember much of it in the morning.

His mind drifting unexpectedly into the past, Doc remembered his younger days when he was fresh out of medical school. He had been a different man, then. An idealist, he had set his mind to saving the world. To his everlasting regret, he had also convinced an equally young, bright, energetic and eager Emma Waverly to help him.

Saving the world had not been an easy task, but Emma had worked cheerfully alongside him as his wife and helpmate for fifteen years. He had suspected her dedication to his patients was intensified by their inability to have children, and in his all-consuming conceit, he had even convinced himself that

73

they were denied progeny by a higher authority who had seen fit to set other priorities for Emma and him. He had been a pompous, self-righteous ass who had learned the sheer stupidity of his thinking only after Emma was stricken by smallpox while nursing his afflicted patients.

Doc poured himself another drink. Many of Emma's patients had recovered, but she had not. It had not taken him long afterward to recognize his vanity and to realize that if not for it, Emma might still be alive.

His dedication to his personal cause had faltered after that, and when the war between the states came along, he had offered his services to the Union Army and a cause of another kind. As it turned out, that experience became the turning point of his life.

Doc unconsciously shuddered. The blood spilled during those horrendous years of slaughter still haunted his dreams. He could not possibly remember the number of limbs he had sawed off to save lives — without saving them. He could not count the futures that had been ruined, the women widowed, the babies orphaned, all in the name of a cause. Time and again, he had wanted to cry out that there was no cause worth such a heavy toll in human life! But he had known that no one would listen.

Steadfast, having no other choice, he had followed through to the end of that terrible war, and when it was over, he had promised himself to spend the rest of his life *free* of causes of any kind. While remaining as true to his Hippocratic oath as he was able, he had determined that he would dispense his hard-won wisdom along with medication to anyone who would listen, and that he would follow his own advice when he said that life was too short not to spend every possible moment appreciating and enjoying it . . . that the only cause to which a man should dedicate himself was the determination to live it to its fullest.

Doc paused in his thoughts, recalling the moment he had first become inclined to follow the gold rush to these Black Hills. He was still uncertain if he had been lured by the delirium of the quest or by the obvious danger involved. He only knew that in following his own philosophy, life had become strangely stale in Cheyenne, as it had in so many other towns since the war, and that the excitement the rush had generated, the promise of new, young faces and light, adventurous spirits had been too much to withstand.

Squinting as he continued to look back into the past, Doc recalled his first sight of the Black Hills. He remembered the shout, "The Black Hills!" that had echoed through the wagon train when the long line of dark, shadowy hills vaguely outlined against a bright blue sky had first become visible across the plains. To the right, easily recognizable as it stood guarding the entrance into that land had been Bear Butte. His heart had begun a rapid pounding, and he had wondered unexpectedly what disappointments lay in store in this place of brilliant promise.

He had not been disappointed, and it had not taken him long to realize that in reaching Deadwood he had found the perfect spot for a man with his newly espoused philosophy of life. He had maintained strict adherence to that philosophy in the time since, and he had been enjoying every minute of it, until . . .

Miriam Higgins's thin, sharp features intruded into his thoughts just as she had intruded into his life, and Doc's mouth twisted into a grimace. The woman was a fly in his carefully prepared ointment of life. She was a specter from the past that had returned to haunt him. She was a leech that had fastened herself to him to suck his life's blood. And, damn her, she wouldn't be satisfied until she had drained him dry!

Rubbing a callused hand over his stubbled cheeks, Doc gave a low groan. He wasn't really being fair, and he knew it. Miriam Higgins couldn't help what she was. She was a product of her upbringing—a stiff-necked, moralistic, pain-in-the-tail reformer. She was a woman with a *cause*. . . .

Doc Fitz paused in his rapidly accelerating agitation. He knew he wasn't being fair for another reason, too, because it had become obvious, even to him, that the time had come for legalization of the migration into the Black Hills. The land was too rich to leave to the Indians and the elements. It held too much promise and reaped too high a reward for those willing to take the risk, and he knew the steady influx would not cease. He was not so blind that he did not see something else as well — that the land's wealth went beyond gold and that the grasslands, richer than any he had ever seen, would not go unheeded by the cattle-conscious West for long.

The only problem was that he was *done* with causes. He detested having a part of him exhumed that he had considered carefully buried.

Abruptly rising to his feet, Doc reached for his hat. To hell with it all! He'd go to the Nugget. He liked that place. He liked the way a man was treated there — fair and square, but most of all, he liked Rosie Blake. He liked her beautiful painted face, her lush warm curves, and the warmth that he sensed came from her heart. He also liked the ability of youth that she so typified, to laugh off the present with the thought that there was no end to the progression of tomorrows.

The thought of Rosie bringing a smile to his age-roughened face, Doc slapped his hat on his head, shrugged his rounded shoulders into a coat that had seen better days, and headed for the door.

Only two steps out onto the short boardwalk outside his office, and Doc groaned aloud. Standing boldly in the walkway, obstructing pedestrian traffic as she waved a sheaf of papers in her hand, and spoke loudly in a voice that was too close to shrill for him not to shudder, stood Miriam Higgins. She put him in mind of a scolding black crow in her severe black dress and matching hat decorated with a single, depressing black feather but her gaze was as keen as an eagle's.

Knowing that Miriam's oration was directed at no one more than him, Doc realized that if nothing else, he need take the opportunity to hone his wits against the formidable widow or run the risk of being cut down.

So he paused, and listened. . . .

"Times are changing in the Black Hills, gentlemen, and I implore you to recognize that change! The renowned General George Armstrong Custer instituted the first change in this virgin wilderness when he reported the vast deposits of gold, but his service to our country and to us has not stopped there. He, and brave generals such as he, even now march in the wilderness in pursuit of those savages who have taken so great a toll on our number in this untamed land. He, and brave generals such as he, even now protect us, the bastard children of this great nation, from harm. It is our duty to him and to the brave men serving in his command to demonstrate our gratitude to them by legalizing our status here so that we will be bastard children no more!"

Miriam waved the sheets in her hand emphatically. Her voice grew in volume as a natural result of her vehement belief in the crusade that she had made her life.

"Gentlemen, we must open our eyes to the future that is fast approaching. Deadwood cannot remain a sprawling mining camp populated with men serving fast fortune with no thought to tomorrow. It is too important! It is the nucleus of the future, a new frontier with endless promise! It is the hope of our great country, a dream of greatness that each one of us has cherished! It is the future generations of our loved ones. . . ."

"Is that what Deadwood is, Widow Higgins!" A bearded heckler interrupted in a slurred voice, turning the sharp-eyed widow toward him. "I'm sure glad you told me. And here I thought Deadwood was the place I come 'cause I was likin' the taste of the Nugget's red-eye and the sight of all them pretty girls lined up at the bar. I guess I was just goddamned ignorant!"

The round of snickers that moved through the growing crowd was short-lived as Miriam looked directly into the prospector's lopsided smile.

"That's right, my inebriated friend, you *were* ignorant, but I don't intend that you, or others like you, shall remain that way. Tell me, if you will"—she pinned him more closely—"how long have you been working your claim in these hills?"

The bleary-eyed fellow's smile dimmed. "I've been workin' it for nigh onto four months."

"Has it proved worthwhile?"

The fellow raised a bulging sack of gold dust proudly. "I'd say it has!"

"How would you like to have it taken away from you?"

The fellow's smile fell. "Ain't nobody goin' to take my claim away from me!"

"Not even the government of this United States?"

"Not nobody, unless they put me six feet under!"

Miriam's tight smile cut deep. "You won't be able to enjoy your gold dust from that depth, now will you?"

Another round of snickers moved through the crowd, this time at the scowling miner's expense, and Miriam pressed her point. "These papers will settle that technicality once and for all because they will help legitimize our status in these Black Hills — because they will urge Washington to take these lands back from the savages to whom they were ceded without a thought to the welfare or future of the civilized portion of our society . . . those willing to make use of the land, to build on it, to live full and rich lives in a community that will be beneficial to all!"

"How's a paper goin' to do all that, lady?"

Another voice from the crowd turned Miriam to a slender fellow who eyed her skeptically.

"Because these papers constitute a petition that will carry our voices to the seat of our government in Washington, D.C. . . . because it will tell our President that although he has made bastards of us simply because we wish to better our lives, we *will* be recognized!"

Turning abruptly, Miriam directed herself to the brightly dressed young woman who stepped into sight nearby, "Because it will tell our government that unlike *some* members of this community, we are not all here for the amusement and profit of the moment . . . that most of us are honest citizens, engaged in hard, physical work and interested in an honest living that does credit to the people of this great country."

Taking up the challenge, Rosie responded without hesitation, "Are you tryin' to tell these nice fellas here that there's somethin' that ain't honest about me, Mrs. Higgins?" Turning to slide her hand onto the shoulder of a fellow standing nearby, Rosie batted her thick, kohled lashes. "Pete, honey, have I ever cheated you out of anythin' when you came into my saloon?"

Blushing a bright red under Rosie's brilliant gaze, the fellow stammered, "No, Rosie, you ain't. As a matter of fact, I always got treated real generous at the Nugget."

Rosie's voice dropped huskily, "And did you come out feelin' better than you went in?"

"Sure enough, ma'am."

Rosie winked. "Then you all come back again, and I'll show you what it is to have a *really* good time."

Hoots and hollers sounding from the crowd did not drown out the sound of Miriam Higgins's scorn as she stared at the smiling young woman with fire in her eye.

"Only fools look at today and forget tomorrow, Miss Blake!"

"Is that what I am, Mrs. Higgins?" Rosie's cheeks flushed with revealing color and her brilliant eyes sparked with unexpected anger. "If you believe that, then you're more of a fool than you accuse me of being."

"If you are satisfied with status quo here in these Black Hills, you *are* a fool! If you would allow vicious savages to hold land that is rightfully ours, you are."

"Don't you think you have things turned around a little bit, Mrs. Higgins?" Rosie took an aggressive step forward. "It was us who took the land from those 'savages.' "

"And you would advocate that we turn it back, is that it? Or is it that you're content to take a fast profit from these men here and run when the going gets difficult because you don't have the stomach to fight for what we all have earned here?"

"Mrs. Higgins, honey," Rosie's voice became a dangerous purr, "you just keep it up, and I'll give you a firsthand demonstration of just how willin' I am to fight—anybody, anywhere. . . ."

Her thin face growing cold, Miriam turned her back on the beautiful young woman and continued with increasing ardor. "This petition will fight for you, gentlemen! It will carry our cause to the seat of our great nation. It will tell our President as well as Congress that we will not be ignored, that we will not be forced from land that we now claim as our own. It will *demand* that we be heard! This petition is your chance to play a part in history! Will you pass it by, or will you sign it and lend your strength to our cause? Who will be the first to sign? Step up here, men. I implore you. It is your duty as well as your right!"

Smiling as the first man stepped forward, Miriam handed him a pencil, her small eyes growing bright as the crowd shuffled in line behind him. Trembling with excitement, she felt the flush of success. She was exalting the generous step she had taken toward her goal when she noticed Doc Fitz moving directly toward the cheap saloon woman who had openly challenged her. Her gaze frigid, she stared him down, only to have him tip his hat politely before he smiled into the young woman's painted face and offered her his arm.

As they turned their backs and walked away together, Miriam seethed. . . .

Rosie's light skin was flushed and her brilliant eyes were filled with fire. Behind her broad smile, she seethed. . . .

"Don't let that woman get to you, Rosie." Doc Fitz squeezed her slim arm. "You're too pretty to get so upset."

"I'm more than pretty, Doc. I'm beautiful . . . but I've got a brain in my head, too, although that old biddy would like everybody to think I haven't!"

"Rosie . . . Rosie . . ." The old doc shook his head. "You know damned well it ain't your brain all the fellas come into the Nugget to see."

But Rosie did not respond to Doc's smiling banter. Instead her serious azure gaze held his. "There's more to me than a pretty face and a warm body, Doc. I thought you, more than anybody, understood that."

Suddenly as serious as she, Doc nodded. "I understand that, all right."

"Then why . . ."

"Why do I tell you to forget about the widow's nastiness? Because she's a woman who's got her priorities all mixed up, and I don't want you to mix up yours."

Rosie looked him directly in the eye. "I'd be interested in hearin' what priorities *you* think I should have, Doc."

"What priorities . . . let me see . . ." Supporting her politely as they stepped up onto the wooden platform outside the Nugget, Doc pushed open the door and stood aside to allow her to enter. His eyes were thoughtful. "Well, at any age, I'd say the first priority is to be happy . . . and that's where Miriam Higgins has gone wrong. She's forgotten how. You know, I remember what she was like the first day she and Jonas rode into Deadwood. I remember thinkin' that her eyes had the look of youth when she looked at that man of hers, even though she wasn't exactly young, and that even if she wasn't a very pretty woman, she looked downright appealin'. Then that man of hers took sick and died, and another woman took over inside her. I told her what I thought. I said she was too young a woman to bury herself beside her husband, but you can imagine what she said to that. Then I told her she should go back where she came from, so she could live out her life in comfort among family and friends. She said she wasn't going *anywhere*. And I'm telling you, Rosie, I knew right then and there that we were all in for trouble."

Appearing suddenly to realize that he had strayed from the point, Doc led Rosie to the bar. Pausing for a short, "Set them up for the lady and me, Barney." He looked back at Rosie. She could feel the thought he was putting into his response as he continued a bit more softly than before, "My point is that Miriam Higgins believes she's leading an exemplary life, and I suppose to some, she is. But not to me. You see, I've seen too much to believe that one minute spent otherwise in this world when a person could be happy, is the greatest waste of all." His gaze growing more solemn, Doc whispered, "The first priority is happiness, Rosie . . . no doubt. As for the rest, well I'd say for a beautiful woman your age it would be to look to secure her future for herself, and maybe find herself someone she'd like to spend the rest of her life with."

Doc took her hand gently and raised it to his lips. Rosie's throat choked closed as he whispered earnestly into her eyes, "If I was twenty years younger, I'd say you wouldn't have to look any farther for that man, but I've got too many years and too many memories behind me. Anyways," his lined face brightening with a slow smile, Doc added, "you need a good *young* man to give you babies . . . at least two or three, Rosie, honey, because it would be a downright waste for you not to bring a few beautiful young women into this world to brighten the hearts of fellas like me after you're gone."

Rosie raised her chin and strove for a smile. "What about joinin' the widow in her fight? You don't think I should concern myself about—"

"No *causes,* Rosie. They're a mistake!"

Rosie was momentarily taken aback by the ferocity of Doc's interjection.

"Even when it's a good cause that would benefit most everybody?"

"Causes are a threat to happiness, Rosie. When a man—or a woman—sets his mind on a cause, he loses sight of the present, he loses sight of the personal, he loses sight of the everyday things that make life worthwhile. Don't misunderstand me, honey. I'm not sayin' there's no use strivin' for anything, because that would be just as much of a waste. I'm sayin' dedicatin' your life to somethin' to the exclusion of all else, to the point where everyday life is just the time spent in between, or usin' up the hours of the day thinkin' how things should be or will be instead of appreciatin' how they are, is just plain *wrong.* If it's meant to be, it'll come to the test. There's time enough to choose sides then."

"But when you know somethin' *should* be, when you've known it all your life, when you know nothin' will never be right unless you can *make* it happen—that's a cause worth dedicatin' your life to, isn't it, Doc?"

His small eyes narrowing thoughtfully, Doc cocked his head. "Is this a hypothetical question, Rosie, or are you talkin' about something you feel real strong about yourself?"

Rosie's full lips twitched revealingly. "Just answer the question, Doc."

"I'd say I already have."

"What are you sayin'?"

"I'll repeat what I said before, that when a person sets his mind on a goal or a cause that consumes him, he loses sight of the present. And the truth is, Rosie, that each day and everything in it is too valuable to waste for somethin' that might never come to pass."

"Oh."

"Oh? That isn't what you wanted to hear, right?"

Rosie shook her head and averted her face.

"Rosie, look at me." When she did, Doc commanded softly, "Smile for me now."

Looking into Doc's face, Rosie could not resist a smile despite the expanding ache inside her. It was such a damned homely old face.

"That's right, honey. And remember, a smile sets up the good in tomorrow."

Rosie shrugged. "So, you're tellin' me that if I smile, everything will turn out all right."

"No, Rosie. I'm tellin' you that I don't want you settin' yourself up for heartbreak, 'cause by the look of you, that's just what you're doin'."

Rosie forced her smile brighter and cocked a flirting glance. "Do I look better now, Doc?"

Doc gave a short laugh. "Not better. Honey, you look downright dangerous!" He shook his hoary head with a soft groan. "Damn my old bones. . . ."

Unable to resist, Rosie leaned temptingly close, poked him gently in the ribs, and whispered in a confidential tone, "What do you think, Doc—should I sign the widow's petition?"

"Damn the widow's petition!" Snatching up his glass, Doc downed its contents in a gulp and slammed the flat of his hand onto the bar. "Fill 'er up again, Barney!"

Deliberately duplicating Doc's actions of a few days earlier, Rosie turned Doc toward her, cupped his unshaven cheeks in her palms, and kissed him hard on the mouth. Into his startled expression, she whispered, "You're a lucky man that you *aren't* twenty years younger—and a bit better lookin' maybe—'cause you'd have to beat me off with a rake, you know that?"

Doc gave a short, breathless laugh. "In my fondest dreams, Rosie."

Turning away with a broad wink, Rosie added in afterthought, "You aren't goin' to make me tell Barney to cut you off at the bar again tonight, are you, Doc?"

The cocky glint returned to his eye as Doc responded, "Well, maybe I will, and maybe I won't. Maybe I'll just take myself somewhere else, where they don't count my drinks. What would you do then?"

Rosie pinched his rough cheek. "I'll tell you what I'd do. When I saw you lyin' in the street later on, drunk as a skunk, I'd throw you a kiss as I pass by."

Leaving him with a dazzling smile and a wiggle of her shapely backside, Rosie walked toward the rear of the saloon. She didn't pause to consider the interested gazes that followed her because her smile was all on the outside. On the inside, her heart was aching.

Sitting unnoticed in his chair in the far corner of the Nugget, Tag had watched the scene between Rosie and Doc as it had transpired. He had seen the genuine warmth between them as they had entered arm and arm. He had seen Rosie's intensity as she had listened to Doc speak. He had seen the way her gaze had searched his grizzled face as she hung onto his every word. He had seen the old bastard leer back in return.

His stomach tightening into knots, Tag recalled the way Rosie had kissed the old lecher, and he had barely restrained the urge to jump to his feet and tear them apart.

That image still clear in his mind, Tag cursed under his breath and slapped the cards down on the table with a vicious thump. What in hell was the matter with him? He knew Rosie, and he knew that although she was too attached to the old fellow for him to be entirely comfortable, he had nothing to worry about on that quarter. No, his problems lay in an entirely different direction.

Abruptly rising, Tag straightened his coat and ran a hand against his smoothly combed hair, giving the room a speculative glance as he did. Business was slow this time of day. Barney and the girls could handle things if he should join Rosie in her room for a little while.

Thinking better of that idea a moment later, Tag strode to the bar. That was all he needed . . . to go to Rosie's room in this frame of mind. It would all spill out then, the nagging jealousy that gave him no rest, his helpless rage in knowing that if a certain man cocked his finger, Rosie would go to him and never look back.

But he had known that all along, hadn't he . . . almost from the first? He had known that the place where Rosie had retreated in her mind when her life was too terrible to bear had changed as the years had passed. He had known that along with that hearth and white kitten, she had come to cherish the image of a man she saw standing there. That image had grown bigger than life, and he knew that whatever else had changed for Rosie as the years had passed, that image had not.

He also knew that image had never, at any time in his and Rosie's long, loving relationship, even resembled him.

"Give me a brandy, Barney."

Emptying his glass a moment later, knowing no manner of anesthetic could dull the ache inside him, Tag turned toward the door.

Pausing on the step outside, he caught the appreciative glance of a popular bar girl from a nearby saloon. Encouraged by his hesitation, she sauntered toward him and posed artfully close, allowing him a full view of her generous bosom. She raised a hand to her golden, upswept hair, and whispered throatily, "It appears to me that you might be in the mood for a change tonight. Gettin' tired of brunettes, Tag, honey?" Her eyelids lowering seductively, she whispered, "I'm a natural blonde, I really am. I'd be happy to prove it to you, too—free of charge. Maybe I can show you what you've been missin'."

Tag smiled. He was accustomed to advances from women and he seldom gave them a second thought, but this time it was different . . . and timely. In the space of a few short moments, this sultry young woman had shown him only too clearly that despite his frustrated jealousy and his helplessness against it, there was no other woman for him but Rosie.

His dark eyes warm, Tag tipped his hat. "That's a generous offer, Ella. You'll never know how much I appreciate it, but I'm afraid I'll turn you down this time." At her genuinely crestfallen expression, he added sincerely in return, "But you can be sure that you'll be the first woman I'll tell if I should ever lose my taste for brunettes."

Tag stepped down into the street a moment later. His own words rang in his ears. ". . . if I should ever lose my taste for brunettes. . . ."

He knew he never would.

Nine

The day had dawned bright and clear with the unseasonably warm weather continuing. Drake glanced at the wooded area around him and rubbed his bearded chin. He grimaced. His beard had served its purpose during the bitter cold of winter, but its value was rapidly fading.

Drake's grimace moved into a scowl. During the winter months he had looked forward to spring when the weather would no longer be a problem and he would be able to spend every daylight hour working at the stream. He had anticipated awakening in the morning with no thought in mind but the gold dust he would add to his modestly growing cache. He had been organized, dedicated, and determined.

So, what had been his first thought when he had awakened this morning and seen a brilliant sun pop over the mountain? He had thought it would be a perfect day *to hang out laundry.*

Drake looked down at the bucket on the ground in front of him. His scowl darkened into a growl. It had been filled and emptied and filled again with Suzannah's linens. It amazed him that one small infant could soak herself so frequently. He supposed it was a good sign — that the child was getting enough nourishment — but if that were true, why did she spend the major portion of the night crying?

Even now Drake was at a loss to explain it. Carolina was not yet up to the task of handling her, despite her insistence. He had watched the previous night as she sought to pacify the babe when it refused to nurse any longer. He had seen her grow so pale at the effort that he had taken Suzannah from her, against her protests. During the endless hours that followed, he had walked a rut in the hard dirt floor of the cabin, had sung himself hoarse, and had rocked the small, squirming infant until his arms were numb.

As it had turned out, the babe had finally fallen asleep just as the sun had prepared to rise. She had been sleeping ever since.

Stretching the last of the linens out over the line, Drake turned back toward the cabin. His thoughts drifted back to Carolina. She had appeared to be recuperating well. For that reason, he had been totally unprepared when he had noticed an unnatural brightness in her eyes as she had nursed her child the previous night. He remembered the jolt of alarm he had experienced when he had touched her forehead and found her fever had returned.

With the arrival of morning, Carolina's forehead had been cool, but he had not been reassured. There were too many uncertainties in caring for this woman. Was her head wound a greater problem than he knew? Was there a sickness growing inside her because of the circumstances of Suzannah's birth? Was her loss of memory a sign of a more dangerous condition — or was it simply a lie?

Drake turned wearily back toward the cabin, disgusted with his uncertainties. It would be so easy to blame them on the fact that he was tired, but he had been tired before. He had spent days without sleep and had continued to function normally. He had worked under conditions fit only for beasts, had been treated like an animal, and had begun to behave like one. He had been exhausted, unclean, convinced that the world was a cesspool in which he was drowning, and he had been enraged — but those experiences had made him stronger, harder, more determined. He had learned a new vocabulary with that new way of life, from which the word compassion had been eliminated, just as it had been eliminated from his life.

Drake's lips tightened into a straight, hard line. Mankind was a race to which he reluctantly belonged, and *womankind* was a race to avoid, except for the most base of reasons. He had saved his life and his sanity with that philosophy and with the core of ice inside him that had left him invulnerable to appeals of any kind.

Drake ran a hand through his shoulder-length hair, disturbed by the agitation which assaulted him again when he thought of the two within the cabin. He didn't like the feelings stirring to life inside him. The man he had become was the aggregate of years of harsh experience — entirely different from the man he had once been — and he liked it that way. The man he had been was a fool who had played a fool's game. The fellow he had become had no patience for games, and seldom left anything to chance. He had become a man who accepted those things he could not change, often without grace, and then moved on. He was a man who allowed little to touch him and for whom driving ambition had become the purpose of his life. He had been untouchable. . . .

Determined to distract his mind from his discomfiting thoughts, Drake looked around him, remembering his first venture into the hills after leaving Deadwood. He had traveled up and down over rough divides, into dark canyons where the sun shone only at midday and where the silence of the heavily timbered hills was so deep that it had seemed almost unnatural. The forests of pine had been dense, almost impenetrable, with unexpected glades scattered with hemlock where the bright winter sun shone down through the branches to weave a delicate pattern on the snow-flecked ground. The clatter of his own horse's hooves and the occasional bray of complaint from his pack animal trailing behind, had been the only sounds to break that primeval silence as the echo of their progress had reverberated from hill to hill.

Drake gave a short, caustic laugh. But the silent hills were silent no longer. They rang with the wail of a fussing newborn and, at times, with his own reluctant baritone. He did not enjoy either sound, and he was equally uncomfortable with both.

His thoughts coming to an abrupt halt, Drake paused at a sound coming from inside the cabin. The woman was calling. . . .

In a few quick strides, Drake was beside the cabin door. His hand on the latch, he was about to thrust it open when he paused in realization. Carolina hadn't called him. She was singing.

Swinging the door slowly open, Drake paused. Unaware of

his entrance, Carolina was still propped in the seated position in which he had left her. The slightly disheveled brown hair streaming onto her shoulders framed her small, serious face as she looked down at the babe who lay in the crook of her arm. She was singing softly in a voice that was clear and true. The babe stared motionlessly up into her mother's face, the nameless lullaby appearing to enchant her as his own harsh baritone had not during the previous night.

Drake was strangely moved. There was a purity and innocence about the woman and child, a beauty that went beyond the conventional sense. He was reluctant to shatter the tranquillity of the moment, even as a small voice in the back of his mind called for caution.

That voice grew louder. It told him that he knew little about this woman, and that she was reluctant, possibly unable to tell him more. It told him that the only positive fact she had related to him . . . her name . . . had been a lie, and it reminded him that appearances, no matter how appealing, were often deceiving.

The voice was insistent. It drew Drake's brows into the frown with which Carolina was greeted as she looked up unexpectedly. Apparently as uncomfortable as he, Carolina attempted a smile.

"Suzannah fell asleep while I was feeding her. She started fussing again when she woke up, but she's all right now."

Noting Carolina's heightened color, Drake walked to her side. A touch to her forehead found her skin pleasantly cool. Drake was startled to hear himself comment, "I heard you singin'."

"I don't sing very well, but I taught myself to play the piano. I—"

Carolina halted abruptly, her breath catching in her throat. Appearing suddenly unable to continue, she started trembling so violently that Drake took Suzannah from her arms. He lay the child in her cradle and was back at Carolina's side in a moment to steady her with his arm.

"What's the matter, Carolina?"

Carolina strove to respond but could not. She closed her eyes, and swallowed spasmodically, then managed, "I . . . I see it every time I try to remember . . . that painted face. . . ."

Drake forced a firmness to his voice that he did not feel. "Don't be afraid. It's all right."

"The face was grinning! Then I saw the blade coming down toward my head. . . ."

The terror in Carolina's eyes was too spontaneous to be feigned. Her thin body was shuddering violently and he pulled her closer.

Unwilling to lose her moment of sharp recall, Drake pressed, "Tell me what you can remember . . . all of it."

"I can't!"

"Yes, you can."

"I'm afraid."

Drake steadied her frantic gaze with his. "You're safe here. Tell me."

Carolina searched his gaze, her hesitation so prolonged that Drake had almost given up hope of response when she began haltingly, "Th . . . the first thing I remember is waking up. My head hurt and I smelled smoke. When I looked up there was fire all around me. I got up and ran, and then . . . then I saw him. . . ."

"Who?"

"That man lying by the wagon." Carolina clung closer. "I thought he was looking at me. His eyes were wide open, but he was dead. . . ."

"What else do you remember?"

"Nothing . . . nothing. . . ."

"What else, Carolina?"

"Please, Drake . . ."

"What else?"

"I remember . . ." Carolina hesitated, finally continuing in a sudden rush. "I remember that I was *repelled*. . . ." She looked up, obviously expecting condemnation. When she saw none, tears streamed down her face. "They were all dead! All of them! There was so much blood, and I was afraid that I would die, too, so I started to run. And I kept on running . . . until I found you."

A strange sensation knotted Drake's stomach. *"I found you. . . ."*

91

"No . . ." Carolina shook her head. "It wasn't that way. All the while I was running, I knew . . . I knew . . ."

"You knew what?"

"I knew I was looking for someone. When I saw you, I knew you were the person I was looking for."

Drake shook his head. "You're confused."

"No, I'm not. I recognized you. I knew I was safe when I saw your face."

"I never saw you before that day I found you in the woods. You have me mixed up with someone else."

Carolina clung to him. "No . . . no. I didn't know your name, but I knew you."

Denying her words as much to himself as to her, Drake was adamant. "You're mixing things up."

"No. I *knew* you, but I don't know anything *about* you. Tell me about you."

"No."

"I *need* to know something about you, Drake. I need something to fill the blank spaces in my mind. I need *memories,* even if they're not my own. Please. . . ."

A dull roaring sounded in Drake's ears as Carolina's words registered deep inside him. He recognized the sound. It was the crashing of the first of his defenses as he heard himself respond, "All right. What do you want to know? Where I'm from? I'm from Texas . . . a little town in sight of the Rio Grande that nobody's ever heard of."

"That's why you talk like that." Carolina's lips wobbled with an attempt at a smile. "Almost like a purr. . . ."

Drake frowned. He hadn't "purred" to anyone in more years than he could remember.

"Did you have brothers or sisters?"

"No. My parents were older when they had me."

"Are they still alive?"

"No."

"Oh."

The distress in Carolina's single word of reply struck Drake sharply. It was absurd. She had lost everything in the world except her own life, and she was commiserating with him for the loss of his parents, something that had happened so long ago that he hardly remembered the pain. This was all wrong . . . out of step with the present. He didn't want to be drawn into this puzzling young woman's confused world. He didn't need—

"I . . . I don't think I had any brothers or sisters, either." Carolina became pensive. "I think I would feel differently than I do, if I did." She appeared momentarily puzzled by her own statement, then asked abruptly, "Are you married?"

Drake stiffened. "I was, once."

"But she's . . . gone."

"Yes."

Carolina nodded, her eyes growing strange. "My husband's gone. I can't mourn him because I can't even remember his face. . . ."

The moment was rapidly deteriorating, and Drake responded without thought. "You'll remember everything soon."

"No." Carolina surprised him with her unexpected adamancy. "I don't want to remember. I don't want to remember any of it!"

Sensing an oncoming crises for which neither of them was yet prepared, Drake responded with a confidence in his tone that he did not feel, "You may not want to remember now, but you will. When you're ready, it'll all come back. But in the time bein', you have to rest. You've done enough talkin' for a while." Bringing their conversation to an abrupt halt, he lay her back against the pillow, "Close your eyes and try to get some sleep before Suzannah decides to try her voice again."

Carolina's abrupt compliance was somehow strange. Uneasy, Drake stood over her, watching until her breathing became slow and even. Asleep, her expression was as innocent as her child's and he—

Reality returned with the sharpness of a slap.

There was no such thing as innocence.

Abruptly recognizing himself as the fool he had begun to play, Drake turned and headed for the door.

The sound of the cabin door flicked Carolina's eyes open

just as Drake's back disappeared from sight. Watching as he pulled it closed behind him, Carolina allowed the image of Drake's broad frame to remain in her mind. His strength reassured her. Consoling her even more as her eyes drifted closed was the knowledge that Drake's true power came from within him. She knew it would not fail her.

His agitation at full throttle, Drake strode toward the stream in broad, angry steps. He stood looking down at the sluice he had so carefully erected months earlier. He thought of the time lost . . . the upheaval found . . . and his distraction grew.

The sun, beating warmly on his head, increased his discomfort and Drake made a sudden decision. Back at the cabin moments later, he scanned the area for the heated water he had brought outside earlier. Finding it, he snatched up the soap and strode toward the strop and razor hanging outside the cabin door. After a few preliminary swipes, he tested the blade with his thumb. It was as sharp as an old maid's tongue.

Soaping his beard liberally, Drake applied the blade with expert care. His cheeks bared minutes later, Drake slapped the razor down on the log beside him and picked up the pail to throw the remaining water into the woods with a vicious swing. Walking too rapidly for caution as he turned back to the stream, he tripped over the drooping line of his pack animal's hobble. He stumbled forward in a few lurching steps, then turned to shoot the taciturn donkey a heated glance. Finding little satisfaction there, he continued on.

Carolina opened her eyes and looked around the cabin. Drake was not in sight. In the absence of sound, the crackle of the fireplace seemed to grow in volume, and the sound of her own babe's breathing from her resting place in the wooden crate on the table appeared to swell.

Uncertain what had awakened her, Carolina attempted to shake off her growing anxiety with little success. She looked up with relief at a sound outside the door. Drake had returned.

But Drake didn't enter. Another thump at the door, and the flesh at the back of her neck began to crawl.

"Drake, is that you?"

No response. She attempted to pull herself to a seated position as she called again, "Drake . . . ?"

The door slowly opened and a large shadow fell across the floor. She heard a sharp, animalistic cry and she screamed. The door swung wider and she screamed again. She screamed and screamed and screamed. . . .

Stripped to the waist, Drake kneeled by the stream. Venting his agitation with broad sweeping strokes, he scrubbed his neck and chest, rubbing briskly under his arms before rinsing himself with the frigid water. Snatching up the discarded top of his long underwear, he dried himself and paused only a moment longer before plunging his head into the cold, rippling water. He lathered his hair, then plunged his head into the stream again.

A brisk, unexpected breeze whipped his bare skin, but Drake ignored its chill as he stood up to dry his hair briskly. He had needed this — to clear his mind. Leaning over, he snatched up his shirt, only to come upright again with a start.

A scream? Carolina!

Snatching up a discarded hammer nearby, he ran up the sandy bank. He stumbled, righted himself and ran again, only to come to a screeching halt as he approached the cabin to the sight of his donkey's backside protruding from the open doorway.

Carolina screamed again and he charged forward. Squeezing past the stubborn animal, he burst into the cabin as Suzannah joined her mother with a hearty wail.

His bared chest heaving, Drake scanned the cabin. Carolina was shaking wildly, her hands over her eyes. As he neared, she screamed again.

"Carolina, it's all right."

On his knees beside her, Drake pried Carolina's hands from her face only to find her eyes squeezed closed. Her face was a ghastly white that contrasted vividly with the strand of soft brown hair adhering to her wet cheek. He brushed it back, ordering, "Open your eyes."

Carolina's eyes snapped open, but Drake was not prepared

for her shock as she looked at him.

"Who . . . ?" She gulped, then blinked. "It's you — Drake." She glanced toward the door in puzzlement. "Wh . . . where did he go?"

"Who? There's nobody here."

"I heard him pounding at the door. He didn't answer, but I knew who it was." She shuddered again. "I saw his face. It was painted, just like before. He was coming to finish what he started."

She darted a glance toward Suzannah's cradle, trembling more violently than before. "He wanted to kill us both."

"Look at me, Carolina." Drake grasped Carolina's shoulders firmly. "It wasn't anyone. It was just old Jack. He tries for a free meal on anythin' he can find in the cabin every time he gets loose. I tripped over his line and I must've pulled it loose. . . ."

"No . . ." Carolina shook her head. "I saw him!"

"You were dreaming."

"No . . . no . . . !"

Carolina began sobbing and knowing no other way to silence her, Drake drew her tight against his chest. He held her securely, tightening his hold when she attempted to withdraw.

"It's all right, Carolina. It's all right. . . ."

Waiting until her trembling slowed, Drake drew back, demanding softly, "Carolina, look at me. It's all right."

Carolina looked up slowly at Drake's urging. Still secure in Drake's protective embrace, she scanned the face so close to hers, momentarily uncertain. This new Drake's eyes were the same clear green, but he was younger than the bearded Drake. His features were strong, clearly cut. The skin of his cheeks was pulled tightly over sharply chiseled cheekbones, and his jaw was square, his chin deeply clefted.

A lingering tremor shook her.

"What happened to your beard?"

"I shaved it off."

"Why?"

Drake's eyes narrowed. "Because I wanted to."

"I liked your beard."

"It's gone."

"You look strange without it."

"Strange or not, that's the way things are." Drake appeared suddenly impatient. "Are you all right? Is it safe to leave you alone for a few minutes before Jack finishes up the bacon?"

Carolina glanced toward the doorway where the unconcerned donkey continued its purloined meal. She felt her face flame.

"I heard a sound, and I was so sure . . ."

Carolina's voice trailed away as Drake released her and turned toward the animal in the doorway.

Push . . . shove . . . curse . . .

Drake's colorful litany continued as he struggled with the recalcitrant donkey. The doorway finally clear once more, Drake reappeared minutes later, buttoning his shirt as he entered. He pushed back a strand of dark, damp hair, and Carolina silently assessed the clean-shaven Drake again. He was handsome . . . but he had always been handsome to her. She knew that whatever he looked like, he always would be.

"Thank you, Drake." When he did not respond, she forced herself to go on. "Thank you for not laughing at me. You must think I'm an hysterical fool for mistaking a donkey for—"

"I don't *think* anything." Carolina realized that the new Drake was no different from the old as he continued with a touch of anger, "I don't judge people, and I don't want to be judged. As long as you remember that, everything will be fine."

Carolina accepted Drake's words as he turned to the fire. She had heard what he said, and she had heard the meaning behind it. She would remember. . . .

Carolina was silent as Drake turned to the fire. Reverberating in his mind were his hypocritical words of a few moments earlier, and sounding above them was a silent accusation that would not cease.

Ten

Doc drew the door of his office closed behind him with a snap. The burning globe in the brilliant blue sky above him had delivered another balmy day, but he was unappreciative of the warmth that touched his lined face. His mind fixed on the unwelcome task ahead of him, he adjusted his dusty hat down lower on his forehead and took an aggressive step forward.

Dodging between the long line of wagons clogging the street, he frowned at the vile language of a small, wiry fellow who sought to avoid a furiously barking dog belonging to the owner of the wagon ahead of him and followed the train to its head.

He should have known. . . .

A short distance away, impervious to the traffic backing up behind them as she rested her fatigued team in the street, stood Madame Canutson. She was dressed in the cotton dress and bonnet that had become her trademark, and she carried the bullwhip that had earned her the respect of man and beast. Everyone knew that the ten yoke of oxen that pulled her wagons were as obedient as babes under her firm hand. Doc snickered in silent amusement. So was everybody else who came up against her while she held that trusty piece of leather.

Doc stopped to consider the woman in silence. The journey from Cheyenne took thirty to forty days. It followed old buffalo and Indian trails through rough, dangerous country. He knew the woman trudged beside her lumbering wagons all the way, directing her team with simple vocal commands. "Gee" turned them left and "Haw" turned them right, but it was the crack of a whip that never drew a drop of blood that kept the laboring animals moving. He had heard she left a husband and a young family at home to make these trips to the Black Hills because she was a better hand with the team than her husband. He didn't doubt it.

Doc studied the woman's coarse, weather-roughened skin, her sober, unsmiling expression, and her long, strong strides as she turned suddenly and walked toward the lead wagon. He had heard that she was tough, in some ways tougher than a man, but he knew she never abandoned a woman's garb for the comfort of a man's clothing and always demanded the respect due her sex. He supposed a man had to admire her tenacity as well as her skill and courage.

He was considering that thought as Madame Canutson raised her whip and cracked it expertly over the head of her team. She accompanied that action with a stream of colorful words that brought the weary beasts to their feet and left his jaded ears burning. It occurred to him that he'd be incapable of repeating that string of oaths, even if he was of a mind to. It also occurred to him that everything he had heard about the woman was probably true.

Continuing on, attempting to avoid the ever-present mud that sucked at his boots, Doc silently cursed and adjusted his grip on the bundle he carried under his arm. He growled an appropriate greeting as he passed the grocery store, the pharmacy, the barber shop, the baker's shop, and arrived at the end of the street. The log cabin he sought met his view. Beyond it lay tents of all shapes and sizes, a mushrooming village of canvas pitched helter-skelter without regard to pattern or device. He knew without counting that there were at least a dozen more tents in that crowded mass than there had been at the beginning of the week, and he also knew that next week, there would be even more. Shelter was at a premium in Deadwood, with more prospectors pouring in every day and no relief in sight.

A brisk wind tugged at Doc's hat and he slanted his head against it, gripping the soiled brim as he turned toward the cabin. The brisk crack of linens flapping in the breeze turned him to the lines of laundry strung across the yard, and he smiled despite himself. There was a warm familiarity to the sound. It brought back memories of earlier days, pleasant times that he thought of too seldom. He wondered what would have happened if he had—

A familiar figure emerged from the back door of the cabin, bringing Doc's musings to a halt. He gripped his bundle tighter, taking only a moment to fortify himself against the confrontation to come. The widow spotted him and Doc saw the woman's formerly pensive expression turn stiff.

Oh, damn. . . .

"So, it's you, Jerome! I guess I don't have to ask what you're doing here." She eyed the bundle under his arm with a raised brow. "Couldn't stand those clothes on your body another second, eh?"

"I didn't come here for an oration on cleanliness and purity, Miriam. I just came here to pick up my laundry and to drop off a few more pieces."

"Hummm. . . ." Miriam's narrow face grew pinched as she assessed him with a keen eye. "You're looking particularly peeked today. What happened? Couldn't make it all the way back home to your bed last night?"

"Well, maybe I did and maybe I didn't, but I don't see how where I spent the night, or in whose bed I spent it, is any business of yours!"

Miriam Higgins's expression tightened. "Neither do I care, *Doctor* Fitz! But I tell you now that I believe it's more likely you spent the night lyin' drunk in the street than in some harlot's bed!"

"Such brazen talk!" Doc regarded her with mock astonishment. "You shock me!"

"You're too numb to shock, and you know it."

Doc raised his stubbled chin. "You underestimate me,

Miriam. You always have." Realizing that he had voiced that last sentiment with more sincerity than he intended, as well as with a true trace of resentment, Doc continued, hurriedly, "Where's my laundry? I've got things to do and places to go."

"Oh, yes . . ." Miriam looked up at the position of the sun in the midday sky. "You must be at least half a pint behind by now."

Doc's jaw tightened. "My laundry, please."

Miriam turned away from him and walked to a table a few feet away where several piles of laundry lay carefully folded and tied with string. She picked up a bundle that had not been bound and motioned him toward her. Doc approached her warily.

"As you can see, I haven't quite finished preparing your laundry, but since I haven't, I do believe a few of these articles are worth comment." Whipping out a pair of underdrawers that were liberally ventilated, the widow smiled caustically. "I think you need to be reminded that a few more washings and these things won't be fit to wear."

"Well, that's easy to remedy, Miriam." Doc fixed her with his stare. "I'll just make sure I don't have them washed anymore!"

Miriam did not smile. "This shirt." She waved it at him accusingly. "There's a hole in the sleeve and the collar's threadbare."

"I bring my clothes here for you to wash, Miriam, not for you to criticize. If you don't like the condition of my laundry, I'll have somebody else do it."

"You don't scare me, Jerome. You know there isn't another decent laundress in this godforsaken town."

"There's Old Lady Leonard . . ."

"I said 'decent' laundress. When that woman does laundry, everything turns out the same color — gray!"

"Well, it just might be worth changin' to gray if I got silence along with it!"

Slapping the shirt down on the table with a loud smack, Miriam advanced toward him unexpectedly, her small dark

101

eyes snapping as she stared down into his face. "You ought to be ashamed of yourself, *Doctor* Fitz!"

"You've said that before."

"And I'll say it again! You make a good living in this place. God knows, there's enough going on at night in the saloons to keep a whole legion of doctors busy sewing up wounds and digging out bullets."

"As usual you exaggerate, Miriam."

"Oh, do I? What about that altercation in the Nugget last night? You must've seen it." She sneered. "That *is* your favorite saloon, isn't it?"

"I'd say you've been spendin' a lot of time learnin' about my extracurricular activities. I—"

"Answer the question!"

Doc drew himself up stiffly. "And if I choose not to?"

"You don't have to! Your exploits in that place are legend! They had to carry three fellows out of the Nugget last night, and not because they were drunk. Two of them were unconscious for over an hour, and the third fellow had been stabbed!"

Doc gave a low snort. "You'd have tried to slit old Jake Bellamy's throat, too, if you'd have heard him sing! He wouldn't stop, either! He just kept bellowin' at the top of his lungs until old Ted Knopp couldn't stand it anymore. He got Jake with his knife, but before he went down, Jake picked up a stool and brained him—and his partner, too, for good measure."

Miriam was not amused. "A fine state of affairs. . . ."

"Well, Jake didn't sing anymore after that."

Miriam raised her pointed chin. Standing there in her dark skirt and spotless white shirtwaist, her graying hair tightly bound and her hands resting on her flat hips as she eyed him unyieldingly, she could have been his old nanny, or his grade school teacher, or the old spinster next door who had left him no peace while he was growing up.

Strangely, Doc squirmed with the same discomfort as Miriam fixed her penetrating gaze on his face. "You're a disgrace to your position, Jerome! Look at you! Your eyes

102

are bloodshot, you need a shave and a haircut, your mustache is so long that it probably strains your food when you eat, and your clothes are downright seedy! You make a good living. You don't have to walk around in frayed shirts and drafty underdrawers."

"Miriam!"

"Well, you don't! But instead, you'd rather spend your earnings on wine, women, and song."

Doc cocked his head as he considered her words. "Well, two out of three isn't bad."

"It's that woman who draws you to the Nugget, isn't it?" Miriam's face flushed unexpectedly as she continued, "That brazen hussy, Rosie Blake."

Doc ceased to be amused. "Leave Rosie out of this, Miriam."

"Leave her out of it? Why? What is there about that cheap harlot that exempts her from criticism? That young woman is representative of far too great a portion of our community here. It's her type who will hold us back from being taken seriously here in the Black hills. She's a bad mark against every one of us. She's—"

"That's enough, Miriam!"

Suddenly more furious than he could conceal when Miriam attempted to continue, Doc took a sharp step forward and met Miriam's anger with a growing ire of his own.

"I said that's enough! I'll listen to your criticisms of me, but I won't let you condemn a young woman you don't really know at all, except from gossip. Take fair warnin', Miriam. Watch your words, because you may find yourself eatin' them someday."

Snatching his clean laundry off the table, Doc grated into Miriam's flushed face, "How much do I owe you?"

Miriam grated in return, "Five dollars for the laundry. The lecture was free of charge."

"That's a good thing." Doc reached into his pocket and withdrew the necessary sum. "Because the lecture wasn't worth a damn!" He slapped payment into her hand. "Now, do you want me to leave my dirty clothes here or not?"

"Doctor Jerome Fitz, I wouldn't miss doing your laundry for the world! It's my biggest challenge!"

Slapping his bundle down on the table, Doc glared at the feisty widow in silence for a prolonged moment before turning on his heel and making for the street. He was walking briskly back in the direction from which he had come when he asked himself, as he had so many times before, why he continued to subject himself to Miriam Higgins's harangues. Taking a tighter grip on the laundry for which he had paid so dearly, he considered the question.

Doc's smile grew slowly. He supposed it was because it was good for him once and a while to be reminded of what he had left behind him.

Doc grinned for the first time that day. *Far* behind him.

Doc was still smiling as he walked into the nearest saloon and stepped up to the bar.

Miriam Higgins stood, her hands on her hips as she watched Doc walk away with an angry, determined stride. He disappeared from sight and Miriam raised her chin and blinked back her tears. She swallowed hard against her temporary, uncharacteristic weakness as she tucked a straying wisp of hair back into her tight bun. She then started toward the nearest clothesline and began sweeping the dried garments off into her arms.

A single tear escaped her eye and she brushed it angrily away. She disliked admitting it to herself, but there were times when she didn't like herself very much. Unfortunately, this was one of them.

Returning to the table, Miriam dropped the clothes there and began sorting them. She was having a very difficult day. She supposed that was so because it had started out so poorly, with dreams of Jonas haunting her until dawn. It was strange how the image of his smooth, smiling face could cause her so much pain. She supposed she should be glad that those final months of his life were so happy, but in the dark hours of the night she realized even more vividly than before that his happiness then was proof of the previous, discontented years of their married life. The thought was difficult to bear.

She supposed those dreams of Jonas had been stirred in turn by the news that had arrived from Cheyenne the previous day and her vow to have the ground in which her dear husband lay declared legally his. Things were not going well with the illegal status of Deadwood and other mining camps like it in the Black Hills.

Miriam sighed. It had all looked to be so easy the previous year, when President Grant had called a Grand Council with the Sioux in an attempt to placate the angry savages who claimed their sacred hills had been violated. In order to appease them, the President had authorized his representative to buy or lease the land of the Black Hills, but the greedy Sioux had behaved foolishly, demanding the exorbitant price of seventy million dollars! Senator Allison, acting in behalf of the President, had turned them down. Angry at the collapse of the negotiations, President Grant had then ordered the military to withdraw from guarding the hills and had warned all citizens who entered there to arm themselves and travel at their own risk.

Miriam considered the thought that there were some who would say that the act of withdrawing the military from the hills was a flagrant violation of the Treaty of Laramie. She did not agree. Their wise President had realized that the treaty should never have been signed in the first place, and that the gold-ribbed Black Hills should be taken back from the grasp of savages who were too ignorant or too lazy to develop their potential. He knew that enterprising pioneers could develop the resources of the hills to the best interests of themselves and the country if left to their own devices.

Miriam smiled. It had been in Jonas's and her mind to do just that as they had made their way through the wilderness. Admittedly, she had traveled with more trepidation than her dear husband, but she had known from the moment the journey had started that she would have followed him into Hades if he had asked.

She had loved him that much.

Turning from thoughts that would only bring her down again, Miriam recalled that the influx to the hills had been steady since then, and that the Sioux resistance had continued. Wild marauding bands had grown in strength and number until the Commission of Indian Affairs had been forced to issue an ultimatum in December demanding that all Indians not occupying the Great Sioux Reservation by January 31, 1876 would be considered hostiles and treated as such.

Oh, the pity of plans that had gone astray! News had arrived in Deadwood only that morning that the ultimatum had been ignored, and attempts to route the hostile Sioux and Cheyenne in their winter camp in the Big Horn and Powder River regions had failed. Blizzards had bogged down General Terry's two columns and when General Crook had pushed up the Bozeman Trail in deep snows to attack the winter camp of the Sioux and Cheyenne, the Indians had forced him to retreat to Fort Fetterman.

Miriam sighed again. Spring had arrived and with it would come more battles, she was sure. She knew the result would impact directly on the status of every prospector in the Black Hills. The status of Deadwood and all other mining camps like it was becoming more uncertain every day.

Miriam paused in her thoughts, her lips tightening into a straight, hard line. Of course, that fact would be hard to ascertain from the faces of the men who traveled Deadwood's Main Street right now. They were all such fools! They could think no further than their first strike, or the amount of gold being taken from the claim next to them, or the weight of their pitiful pouches of gold dust. What difference did it make, anyway? The majority of those pathetic souls spent more in a single night on the town in Deadwood than they took from Mother Earth's bosom in a month!

Who was the greatest profiteer then?

Rosie Blake's lovely painted face came immediately to mind.

Miriam's narrow nostrils dilating, her thin lips twitching, she recalled the proprietary manner with which Jerome Fitz had taken Rosie Blake's arm, tipped his hat, and walked away from her on the street. It was a disgrace, that's what it was! Rosie Blake and her kind were the very people who, if allowed, would bring Deadwood to a dishonorable end!

Besides, Rosie Blake was young enough to be Jerome's daughter!

Miriam clipped a piece of string and tied the nearest pile of laundry with a meticulous bow. Pausing, she looked at her chapped and callused hands . . . the broken fingernails. *Rosie Blake's* hands had been soft and white . . . her nails perfectly manicured. Of course! No one could see Rosie Blake's calluses, because they surrounded her cold, black heart!

Oh, Jerome! Miriam turned to the bundle of dirty laundry he had left behind him. She picked up a threadbare shirt and shook her head. Scandalous, that's what it was! There had been a time when she had thought Jerome and she could actually be friends, but it had become all too obvious that the fellow preferred that they remain adversaries.

Looking up, Miriam caught her reflection in the small mirror which hung beside the cabin door, and she allowed her eyes to slowly close. Did she need to reason why? What man, young or old, rich or poor, would prefer friendship with a thin, colorless old woman to the company of a beautiful, vivacious . . . she sighed again . . . *young* woman. Dear Jonas, might his generous soul rest in peace, was the only man who had ever seen past her plain exterior and her admittedly occasionally sharp tongue, to the passionately loving woman who lay beneath.

Suddenly realizing that her hands were trembling, Miriam forced a businesslike mien as she scooped up the doctor's clothes and dropped them into a nearby pot. As usual, she would have to boil his shirts to get them white. As for the rest of his garments—Miriam could do no more than shudder.

Inhaling with a deliberation that forced distress aside,

Miriam drew herself firmly erect. Legalization of Deadwood's status in the Black Hills was the first priority. She would not let a man in Deadwood forget it! As for herself, she would not give up an inch of ground in Deadwood that she now considered her own—most especially that six feet of earth where her dear Jonas lay at eternal rest.

Her zeal summoned anew, Miriam was reminded again of Dr. Jerome Fitz's angry departure. Damn him! Couldn't he see the importance of her cause? Or was he too blinded by drink, and by the brilliance of Rosie Blake's brilliant blue eyes to realize it?

The answer was obvious.

Damn him!

Rosie Blake's brilliant blue eyes widened with terror. The heavy hand of Oscar at the piano and the warbling tones of Nellie's husky alto as she concluded another outrageous ditty faded from her hearing. Scattered applause sounded from the tables around her, but she was unconscious of all but the thin fellow man who had walked up to the bar a few minutes earlier. The fellow's appearance, with his dusty, stained clothing and the unkempt beard that did not fully cover the grime of the trail still marking his face, reflected a long trek through the wilderness that recently had come to an end. He had caught her attention by the way he had downed his first drink and by the look in his eye that said he had seen things he would like to forget. But like so many of the men before him, it appeared he was unable.

Callous as it appeared, Rosie had been ready to dismiss the fellow from her mind. She had seen too many men with that look since she had arrived in Deadwood. She had been too involved in her conversation with Tag as he sat opposite her and with the way his dark eyes played across her face as he spoke. Tag was so good for her. He soothed the loneliness she concealed within. He made her feel beautiful at times when the ugliness of her early years returned, and when she feared that ugliness must be reflected in her eyes.

He made her feel she was the person she pretended to be — gay, lighthearted, with not a dark thought in her mind.

Then something the slender fellow said had caught her ear. She had then listened attentively as he had spoken with the horror of his words reflected in his voice.

"I tell you, I ain't never seen nothin' like it. Half them wagons was burned and the other half had been looted. And bodies . . ." The fellow shuddered. "They was lyin' all around — ten of them in all — what was left of them. Me and the other fellas had a damned hard time buryin' 'em, I'll tell you. They stank to high heaven, and they was stiff as boards. There was this one fella, especially. Damn, he was big! With all that black hair and that beard, he looked more like a bear than a man. Me and the others worked like hell tryin' to get him . . ."

The fellow was still talking, but Rosie heard little else as she slowly rose from her chair. Not realizing her intent, she was beside the fellow in a moment, clutching his arm. He turned to her with a smile that faded quickly when he saw her expression and heard the quaking in her voice.

"That big man you were talkin' about . . ." Rosie attempted to swallow the lump that was growing larger by the moment in her throat. "The one who was dead on the trail . . . where did you see him?"

"I can't tell you the exact location, ma'am. Our wagon train wandered off the regular route a bit, and then we ran into what was left of this here other train that seemed to have done the same thing."

Rosie nodded, her heart pounding. "The big man . . . you described a big man. . . ."

"Yeah, that's right. He was kinda lyin' off to the side, a distance from the others."

"W . . . What did he look like?"

The fellow paused, noting her shuddering. He looked around for an explanation and met the eyes of the dark, well-dressed man who stepped up supportively behind the beautiful saloon girl and signaled him to respond.

"Well, ma'am, he was big . . . real big, with dark hair

and beard. That's about all I can tell you."

The woman's quaking worsened. "What did he look like? Was he handsome? Did he have strong features?"

"I can't say as I could really tell, ma'am."

"What do you mean you couldn't tell?" Rosie's eyes became wild. "You must tell me! How old was he? In his thirties? Did he have a broad smile and patient eyes? Did he—"

"Rosie, get hold of yourself!"

Tag gripped her arm, turning Rosie toward him, but Rosie ripped herself free to turn back to the startled stranger.

"Can't you tell me anythin' else? Can't you even tell me if his eyes were green?"

"Yes, ma'am."

The fellow nodded and Rosie's heart seemed to stop. A low cry rose in her throat as he continued in a rush, "I can tell you that because the fella's eyes was open—like he died surprised or somethin'." He nodded again. "Yep, that fella's eyes was black as coal."

"Black . . ." Rosie's short laugh cracked on a sob. "His eyes were black. . . ."

"Yes, ma'am. Black."

Turning to Tag, unable to see his face for the tears that blurred her vision, Rosie whispered, "His eyes were black, Tag."

Sliding his arm around her, Tag turned her toward the rear of the room. His voice was gruff as he called over his shoulder, "Tell Sheila to take over for me at the poker table, Barney. I'll be back in a little while."

The door of the saloon closed behind them and Tag scooped Rosie up into his arms. She did not protest but leaned against his chest as she vented her tears. She did not hear the door of her cabin close behind her and hardly realized the satin of her bed cover was beneath her back until Tag raised her supportively with his arm and held a glass against her lips.

"Drink."

Rosie separated her lips and allowed the burning liquid to slide down her throat. It stung all the way to her stomach. Bourbon. She didn't like bourbon. She kept it in her room only for Tag.

Tag . . .

Rosie looked up into Tag's handsome face, realizing for the first time that he was furious. Her gaze pleaded his understanding.

"You heard what that fella said, Tag. He said he found a big man—with black hair and a beard. He said the fella was dead. I thought—"

"I know what you thought!"

Rosie shook her head as if to negate Tag's anger. "Don't be angry, Tag."

"Why shouldn't I be angry? You were sitting with me, holding my hand, and I was telling you that I love you in every way but with the words when you suddenly got up and walked away from me."

"I thought—"

"I told you, I know what you thought! You thought your precious dream man had been killed. What would you have done if it was true, Rosie? Tell me!"

"It wasn't true."

"If it *were* true."

Rosie held Tag's savage gaze without flinching. Her response was a broken whisper. "I'd have died, too."

"No, you wouldn't!" Gripping her shoulders roughly, Tag shook her hard. "I wouldn't have let you, do you hear me? You have a fixation about this man in your mind."

"It's not a fixation. It's lov—"

"No, it isn't! Rosie, look at me." Tag's handsome face was creased with anxiety and Rosie's kind heart felt his pain, as he whispered, "You love me, Rosie. You don't realize it, but you do."

"No, I—"

Halting her words with a savage kiss, Tag clutched her desperately close. His kiss deepened as he drew her closer, his ferocity gradually lessening as she softened in his arms, as she parted her lips under his.

Groaning low in his throat, Tag tore his mouth from

111

hers. He drew back to assess her tear-streaked face as he questioned hoarsely, "Rosie, darling, can't you see? Even when you're thinking of another man, you go soft in my arms. You respond to me the way a flower does to light. Your petals open up for me, darling. They draw me in because unconsciously you know that we're right for each other."

Her heart breaking, Rosie responded gently, "I've tried to tell you how I feel, Tag, but you won't believe me. I can't let you think . . ." Rosie paused and started again. "I owe it to you to be truthful, so I'll say it again. If the dead man had been him . . ." Rosie's voice broke on a sob, but she forced herself to continue. "If it had been him—if he was dead, I would've died, too. I've lived all this time, since that day I ran away from home, with only one thought in mind—that I'll belong to him someday, Tag, that he'll love me, and I'll love him, and all that was dark and ugly in my life will disappear."

Her expression taking on a familiar glow, Rosie raised her hand to Tag's still face. "He'll cleanse me, Tag."

"Stop that . . . that damned foolish talk right now! Oh, Rosie . . ." Tag drew her back into his arms. Rosie could feel the heavy hammering of his heart as he whispered against her hair, "Can't you see . . ." He clutched her closer, straining her against his chest, "If you loved him, you couldn't respond to me the way you do."

Feeling his desperation, Rosie whispered in return, "The way I am with you has nothing to do with my feelings for him. Tag, with you I celebrate life. You made my life bearable when it had deteriorated into a long line of empty days of waiting. You put joy in my smile, Tag, and you gave me pride. I owe you so much."

"I don't want your gratitude. I want your lov—"

Interrupting, Rosie whispered, "I'll give you all I have to give, right now." Encircling his neck with her arms, Rosie drew back far enough so she might look into Tag's dark, sad eyes. She brushed his lips with hers, once, twice. Her voice dropped to a husky whisper, "I want to give to you.

Will you let me?" Her tone grew more earnest. "Please, Tag."

Rosie waited, her heart suddenly pounding. She saw the anger in Tag's eyes. She saw the frustration and she saw the pain. She saw the refusal that sprang to his lips and a dagger of pain pierced her heart as she waited for his response.

Before her eyes, Tag's resistance crumbled. The moment before his mouth met hers, she heard his ragged whisper.

"All right, Rosie, you win. You'll always win with me, darling. There can't be any other way."

Tag's words echoed softly in her mind as Rosie lost herself in his arms. Dear, loving Tag. . . .

But in her heart she was still waiting. . . .

Rosie's hand on his arm, Tag elbowed his way down the street through the jostling crowd of rollicking miners and noisy bull whackers as evening fell. A quick glance toward Rosie revealed that the hours they had spent together in her room earlier in the day had had their usual effect. She was smiling. Her beautiful face was flushed with excitement and her brilliant eyes were clear and quick. The fear that had robbed her of sane thought and reduced her to unaccustomed tears was gone without a trace. She was the old Rosie now, lovelier than words could express in her purple satin dress and red high-heeled shoes, and he knew he had never loved her more. The only trouble was that Rosie didn't love him.

Denying that thought a moment later, Tag squeezed the hand she rested on his arm and smiled into her shining eyes as she glanced up. The dozens of kerosene lamps that lit the street were mirrored there but he knew that glow was more than simple reflection. Rosie loved the excitement of evening in Deadwood. She loved walking down the street past brightly lit stores, saloons, and other places of amusement frequented by the lusty, fun-seeking males that sauntered past. She loved the noise, the music from antiquated pianos and cracked violins that mingled with the songs and hilarious laughter that seemed to reach the street from every quarter. She enjoyed looking at the crowds of men of all classes who lingered at the gaming tables in the different saloons, watching as if fascinated as hundreds of dollars were won and lost. She loved being watched as she walked on his arm, and she rewarded interested glances with a teasing wink and a toss of her head. But most of all, he knew she liked being on his arm, safe from the press of male attentions as she had never been safe before.

Rosie responded with a quip to a familiar greeting and Tag smiled. Rosie always made him smile—almost always. She was so clever and her enjoyment of life was so intense when she was able to put her past behind her. He was keenly aware that her smiles were often feigned and her enjoyment dulled by dark memories, but he had long ago determined that he would be the man to erase those haunting images from her mind for good. He had succeeded for the most part, too.

His mind drifting from the street around them, Tag recalled the loving they had shared a few hours earlier. He remembered that Rosie had responded passionately, returning kiss for kiss, caress for caress. With techniques she had learned during her years of working at the trade, she had pleasured his body so completely that he had thought he might expire, but he knew that there was honesty and love in her touch when they were together. It was in times like those that he was grateful for his vast experience with women, so that he might be able to gauge the feelings he read in her eyes when he pleasured her in return. It was his greatest reward, his moment of true ecstasy, when he heard Rosie's gasp of culmination, when her lush, warm body gave to him as he knew she had never given to any other man. He knew in his heart that Rosie loved him . . . that her feelings for him ran deeper than feelings she could ever have for any other man. The only problem was that Rosie didn't agree. . . .

Tag's smile faded as a familiar specter returned to stand boldly before his mind's eye. Rosie's dream man was difficult to fight. He was bigger than life. In her mind he had taken up the image of savior—and Rosie wanted so desperately to be saved.

Rosie looked up unexpectedly and he saw her hesitation the minute before she spoke.

"Tag . . . don't you think we should be back at the Nugget? Deadwood is really active tonight. The poker table is probably three deep."

"Sheila can handle things for a while."

"She has other duties to attend to."

Tag raised his dark brows. "Sheila won't miss out on anything. If I know her, she'll have the fellows waiting in line outside her door when I relieve her at the table. She's a very enterprising young woman."

Rosie's smile dimmed. "Like I was."

"No." Tag was suddenly serious. "There's no one like you, Rosie. You're one of a kind—an original."

Rosie returned his sober stare for long seconds. He felt the wonder of her gaze down to his toes as her smile slowly brightened and as she gave a slight shrug of creamy shoulders covered in a full satin wrap. "So you say."

"And I'll keep right on saying it."

"You're crazy."

"Crazy about you."

Rosie ignored his retort, obviously preferring to change the subject. "I don't really know what we're doin' walkin' the streets when we should both be workin'. You know I don't need a new dress. I'm thinkin' both our time would be better spent rakin' in some of that gold dust those good old boys seem so anxious to part with tonight."

"The Nugget can get along without us for a little while longer. Barney does a good job of watching the bar, and I feel generous tonight—generous enough to let those fellows hold on to their money a little longer—and to buy you that black dress."

"But I already have a black dress! And you know black isn't my favorite color."

"Blue is." Tag's smile momentarily dimmed. "Isn't it?"

115

Rosie wisely ignored his question. "Black doesn't do me justice."

"Rosie, this dress is different." Tag lowered his head to brush her lips lightly with his. "Trust me."

"But . . ."

"Trust me."

Dodging a swaying miner as he lurched past, Rosie gave a low giggle. "I suppose I will. I always do."

Tag drew her with him as they approached the well-lit tent that temporarily housed the newest of Deadwood's several general stores. Pausing momentarily at the entrance, suddenly sober, Tag asked, "Have you ever been sorry— that you trusted me?"

Rosie was suddenly as sober as he.

"No."

"And you never will be."

Without another word, Tag drew her inside.

Her eyes widening, Rosie stood before the cracked mirror in the canvas general store. Surrounding her was a chaotic mess of barrels, sacks, boxes of clothing and shoes, picks, shovels and other equipment. A short distance behind her stood a lone rack on which hung an array of dresses that obviously took center stage. Tag had removed a gown from that rack immediately upon entering and had pushed her behind a blanket strung across a crowded corner of the tent so she might slip the garment on.

Protesting all the while, she had struggled with the tiny buttons that secured the back of the dress and had finally emerged out into the light of the flickering lamps. The gasps of miners milling close by had momentarily set her aback. She had immediately walked to the mirror, only to find that she was as stunned as they when she saw her own reflection.

Black lace . . . she had never thought black lace could be so beautiful. She had not realized that the glow of her flaw-less ivory skin could reach new depths of radiance when reflected through the delicate fabric. She had objected strongly at first to the high neckline edged in a narrow band of lace and the long sleeves which covered her arms to the wrists. The style had seemed a poor choice considering her chosen walk of life, but she had not taken into account that beneath the fine layer of lace, the neckline plunged almost to her waist, exposing a generous swell of her full breasts and an ever-diminishing view of the clear, tight skin of her midriff as the slashed neckline gradually narrowed. The bell-shaped skirt lay smoothly against the curve of her hips and flared out above her ankles to provide a silhouette that was both daring and breathtaking. Rosie turned and shot Tag a brilliant smile. She loved it!

"How did you ever find this dress, Tag?"

Tag shrugged, obviously pleased. "The minute I saw it, I knew the gown was made for you."

"So it is. . . ." Rosie ran a hand against her gleaming, upswept hair. "I don't want to take it off."

Tag turned to the balding proprietor whose smile was just short of a leer. "The lady will wear the dress."

Stepping back out onto the street a moment later, Rosie smiled up into Tag's appreciative gaze, repeating the words she had said so many times before, and never meaning them more.

"You're too good to me, Tag."

"Seems to me I've heard those words before."

Rosie felt a wave of almost debilitating warmth sweep over her. "That's because they're true. I could've paid for this gown myself. You didn't have to—"

Her gaze slipping to a man on the street out of Tag's line of vision, Rosie halted suddenly, the color draining from her face. In a panic, she glanced left, then right, desperately seeking the best way to avoid the crowd gathering around him ahead of her. Her heart began a heavy pounding that resounded so loudly in her ears that Tag's voice was a distant whisper as he demanded, "What's wrong, Rosie?"

The crowd shifted and Rosie's face paled. She knew who the tall fellow standing on a crate in the center of the street

117

was. He was kindly looking in appearance, about fifty years old. He had dark hair and eyes and a short, neat beard. She had seen him before. He worked during the week at mining, carpentering, timber cutting, wood chopping, any manner of manual labor that would earn him enough to live on, but on Sunday he followed his calling as a minister and preached in the street to anyone who would listen. He was a "man of God" . . . and she knew what kind of man that made him.

Panicking, Rosie pulled Tag's arm. Her tone was desperate.

"I have to get away from here!"

Frowning, Tag glanced at Preacher Smith. "Why, Rosie, because of him?"

Because of him . . . because of him . . . ? Tag's words echoed in her mind as dark memories slowly assumed control. She remembered . . . yes, she remembered. . . .

The church had been filled to capacity with pale, unsmiling faces as she had stood before the pulpit. She had been trembling, just as she was now. The sun had shone through the stained-glass windows behind Reverend Martin, reflecting brilliant rainbow hues on his sweated, bald head, and she recalled thinking that the sparkling colors were the only beautiful thing in that cold, sterile church.

The reverend's nasal voice had echoed against the frame walls as he had called her forward and descended from the pulpit to stand beside her. She remembered the touch of his cold, damp palms as he turned her toward the assembled congregation so all might see her face and watch her tears fall as he flailed her with his words. She remembered those words. She was the deepest of sinners. Her beauty was a gift of the devil who would soon claim her soul for instigating "incest" with the man who had acted as her father most of her life. She need repent. She need confess her guilt to each and every one of the men and women before whom she stood. She need get down on her knees and beg them and the Lord to forgive her.

She had been shaking so badly that she could not speak

as censuring gazes met hers one by one. The chorus of condemnation had started low and grown gradually louder as she had refused to admit to a sin that she had not committed. Reverend Martin had become so enraged at her refusal that he had sent her from the church with shouts of, "Tool of the devil! You will be condemned to Hell!" That chant had been taken up by those who had witnessed her degradation as she had run down the aisle and burst through the doors out into the light. She remembered those shouted denouncements had followed her every step of the way as she had fled.

And she remembered that her mother, standing solemnly in the first row, had been the first to condemn her.

She had run wildly from the scene of her debasement, feeling more dirty, more defiled than she had ever felt before. Blinded by tears, she had been stopped in her flight by a pair of strong, comforting arms. She remembered that sweet haven, the deep voice, and the words that had restored sanity to an ordeal that she had not believed she would survive.

Green eyes shot with gold had been moist with compassion as they had looked into hers, and she had loved him then. She loved him still. She always would. . . .

"Rosie . . ."

Rosie looked up, her moment of mind-shattering panic gone as quickly as it had come. Meeting Tag's gaze, she put the dark memories behind her as she had so many times before. She forced a smile.

"Let's go back now, Tag. I've had enough of the street for a while."

Tag took her arm, his brow still dark with concern. Rosie raised her chin. Tag was her comfort, her consolation . . . but *he* was her salvation. . . .

119

Eleven

Silver shafts of moonlight shone through the window hangings of the cabin, illuminating the still darkness as Drake abruptly awakened. Suddenly alert, he glanced toward Carolina's cot a short distance away. Seeing no movement there, he looked at the makeshift cradle on the nearby table, but the babe was silent.

The howl of a wolf echoed in the distance, a lonesome sound that was followed unexpectedly by the startling screech of a wildcat. Carolina jumped revealingly and Drake realized that the prowling predators of the night had aroused her from sleep just as they had awakened him.

The wildcat called again with a sound eerily reminiscent of a baby's cry, and Carolina moved restlessly. Consoling himself that neither sound appeared close enough to present a threat to his animals tied behind the cabin, Drake maintained his silence, somehow reticent to speak.

"Drake . . . are you awake?"

Carolina's whisper was tentative, and Drake considered pretending that he was sleeping. It had been a long day . . . one of many since he had discovered his charges on the hillside a week previous. He had seen a gradual improvement in Carolina's physical condition. She was able to get out of bed for limited periods, although she still claimed no memory beyond that which she had already related.

The sounds of night grew louder and Carolina pulled herself to a seated position in her bed. He saw her look toward the table where her baby slept, then back at him. The bright light of the fire danced against her shadowed face, illuminating an expression midway between hesitation and fear.

Carolina pushed a strand of hair back from her cheek, her hand freezing there as she tried once more. "Drake . . . are you awake?"

His response was reluctant. "Yes, I'm awake."

"What was that noise?" Her voiced cracked. "Was it . . . was it —"

"It's a wildcat on the prowl. It's too far away to bother us."

"You're sure?"

Drake's response was stiff. "As sure as I can be."

Carolina lowered her hand to her lap with a grace of movement that he had discovered to be inherent in all she did. She hesitated before speaking again. "I didn't mean to doubt you but that cry sounded almost human."

"It wasn't."

Carolina paused. "I . . . I've heard that Indians make sounds like animals when they call to each other in the night . . . that they do that before they attack. . . ."

"Who told you that?"

"I . . . I don't remember."

"Then forget it. You can't believe tales from anonymous sources."

There was a moment's silence before Carolina laughed unexpectedly. "You have a strange sense of humor."

Carolina's response was unanticipated. A day or so earlier, she would have maintained her silence and deferred to his obvious preference not to talk. With the return of her strength, however, had come a tendency to challenge his detachment in a way that was more threatening than a direct assault. He wasn't sure he liked it.

His response was pointedly curt. "I don't have a sense of humor."

"So you'd have me believe."

"I don't really care what you believe."

Again that hesitation, this time allowing him opportunity to regret his churlishness. He was unprepared as Carolina challenged him once more.

"Why are you so determined to dislike me, Drake?"

"Oh, am I?"

"You know you are." Carolina paused, her voice dropping lower. "I *did* do something to you, didn't I . . . something I don't remember. Tell me if I did. I want to know."

"You're imaginin' things."

"No . . . I'm not. Drake, I—"

"Go to sleep."

"I can't sleep."

Carolina turned again toward the babe, allowing him a glimpse of her profile etched against the yellow light of the fire and he was stunned at its effect on him. He remembered a cameo his mother had worn when he was a child. It paled in comparison.

"How much longer do you think it'll be before you'll be able to take me back to civilization?"

Drake paused in response. "That's up to you. I don't expect to keep you here any longer than necessary, if that's what's worryin' you."

"No, that's not what's worrying me. Oh, Drake," Carolina's voice dropped to a whisper. He strained his eyes to see if the desperation he heard in her voice was visible on her face as she continued, "What am I going to do if . . . if I'm *never* able to remember my past?"

Drake strained to retain an emotional distance from this woman whose appeal had begun to tear at the carefully constructed armor he had placed around his feelings.

"I suppose you'll have to be satisfied with the present."

"Drake . . ."

"I wouldn't worry about it, Carolina. Your wagon train was obviously headin' for Deadwood. Considering the traffic movin' into the hills at the present time, what's left of the train must've been found and identified by now. When we get there, there'll probably be all kinds of information waitin' for you."

"Do you really think so?" Carolina glanced again toward

the table. "Suzannah needs a family. She needs to know who her people are."

"Is that the only reason you want to know who you are?"

A moment's silence met Drake's question, then a whispered response. "No . . . but it's the only one I'll allow myself to think about." Carolina's voice became barely audible over the crackle of the fire. Drake strained to hear her as she continued, "There's a whole world out there that I can't remember, but the bits and pieces that return are too difficult to bear, so I chase away the memories even as I try to recall them. I . . . it wasn't the sounds outside that awoke me tonight, Drake. I was awake long before I heard them. I was awake because as much as I struggle to remember during the daylight, when night comes, I . . . I'm afraid. The pictures that flash across my mind are so vivid when it's dark, and they're always the same."

Drake heard the unconscious appeal in Carolina's voice, and he knew she needed comforting. The problem was that during the darkness of night, his own memories returned to haunt him. He remembered other times, gentler times, and he *wanted* to comfort her. He wanted to tell her that everything would be all right, that he would take her back to Deadwood and that he wouldn't abandon her to a world of strangers. But he also knew that with the coming of dawn reality would return.

"Drake . . ."

"We all have our demons, Carolina."

"I don't want to think about demons. I want to think about better things. Tell me about Deadwood. You said you'll be taking Suzannah and me there. What's it like?"

Drake suppressed softer feelings. "Deadwood's an overgrown minin' camp. There's not much to recommend it. It's noisy, dirty, crowded, and gettin' more so every day, but you'll be able to get transportation back to wherever you want to go from there."

"If Deadwood's so bad, why does it keep growing?"

"Because it's in the middle of the richest gold deposits anybody's found so far in the hills."

Carolina hesitated again, then asked bluntly, "If there's so much gold in Deadwood, what are you doing *here?*"

Drake's voice was heavy with irony. "I like privacy."

"Oh."

The pause that followed was extended and Drake had begun to believe that he had put an end to conversation between Carolina and him for the night when her soft voice sounded again in the darkness.

"You said you were born in Texas, close to the Rio Grande, that you had no brothers or sisters, and that your parents are dead. Did you have a happy childhood?"

No response.

"Drake, please talk to me. . . ."

"I had a happy childhood."

"Tell me. . . ."

Drake briefly closed his eyes, knowing it was no use refusing her and silently cursing himself because he didn't really want to. He allowed an old memory to sweep over him.

"I remember ridin' with my father when I was about eight or ten years old, helpin' him work a herd at roundup. We had about a thousand head then—ornery steers with minds of their own. We had been in the saddle for over five hours. I was tired, hungry, and sore, and the dust was so thick that I couldn't see more than a few feet in front of me at times, but I remember thinkin' that there couldn't be anythin' better in life than havin' a herd of my own someday and bein' just like my pa."

"But you changed your mind?"

Drake's warm memory went suddenly cold. "I grew up."

"I suppose we all grow up sooner or later." Carolina's reply was thoughtful. "But I have the feeling that we all do it in our own way, and that time has very little to do with it." She paused again. "And I think, sometimes, that 'growing up' isn't always a change for the better. Maybe that's why I don't want to remember."

Puzzled by Carolina's words, Drake remained silent. He pondered their conversation, recognizing the danger of

124

words spoken in the darkness to a woman who had become a graceful shadow and a sympathetic voice. He had spoken to another woman that way, and he had lived to regret it. The memory tainted the moment.

"Drake . . ."

"Go to sleep. There's nothin' to be afraid of."

"Drake . . ."

"I said, go to sleep!"

A familiar whimper interrupted the sudden harsh turn of their exchange. The whimper grew into a fussy squall and Drake threw back his blanket at the same moment Carolina attempted to rise.

"Lie down. I'll get her."

"I can manage."

Drake was already on his feet. "I said, I'll get her."

Waiting only until Carolina relaxed back against the bed, Drake walked to the table and looked down at the squirming babe. Appearing to sense his presence, the babe turned toward him, her bright, unclear gaze searching. Strange, that with the passage of a week he could see so much more of her mother there. Drake paused at that thought suddenly uncertain if the change he had noticed had taken place in Carolina or in her daughter. Then wondering abruptly what possible difference it could make, Drake took the child to her mother.

Standing beside Carolina, Drake noted the hesitation with which she bared her small breast to offer it to the babe. He had noticed her increasing discomfort at these times over the past few days, but he was somehow reluctant to allow her the privacy she seemed to desire. He was uncertain as to the reason.

Drake was still looking down at Carolina and her babe when the answer became suddenly clear. This coming together of mother and child was one of the few truly innocent, giving acts that remained in a harsh world. He supposed, however reluctantly, he wanted to be a part of it in some way.

Reaching out unconsciously, Drake touched the soft

125

brown hair at Carolina's temple. She looked up. Her questioning gaze startled him from his thoughts. Uncomfortably aware that the intimate darkness of night was a poor time to reflect on innocence and beauty, he remarked gruffly, "Your wound is healing well."

Back in his own cot a few minutes later, Drake closed his eyes. Annoyed with himself, with the sound of the babe's soft suckling, and with the fact that his mind kept wandering back to the woman and child, Drake gritted his teeth, determined to keep those thoughts at bay.

The chirping of birds intruded into Carolina's confused dreams and she slowly stirred. Shafts of bright morning sun streamed through the window behind her, just as silver moonlight had the night before, and Carolina glanced at Drake's cot a few feet away. It was empty. She looked toward the table and listened, smiling unconsciously at the sound of her babe's even breathing. She recalled drifting off to sleep the night before with Suzannah dozing at her breast. She had opened her eyes again as her daughter was being taken from her arms. The last thing she recalled was the outline of Drake's broad shoulders leaning over the child's rough cradle as he put her to rest.

A slow warmth pervaded Carolina's senses. Dear Drake. She remembered the first time she had awakened to an empty cabin here in this mountain wilderness. She had panicked, believing herself alone and defenseless, but Drake had returned. In the time since, she had come to realize the foolishness of those moments of panic because she knew now that Drake would never abandon her—that she had been a fool to believe that even for a moment.

Their brief conversation the previous night returned and Carolina pictured the boy of eight Drake had described to her—the boy he had once been. She wondered how that contented, sensitive young fellow had turned into a gruff, cautious man who never smiled. She tried to imagine Drake's smile. It would be beautiful, she had no doubt, because Drake's lips were full and well shaped, and his teeth white and even. She remembered her shock when she had seen him clean-shaven for the first time. She had not been prepared for the perfect symmetry of his strong, masculine features. The hint of menace in his eyes and the touch of brooding in his curt personality added strangely appealing facets to a man whom she realized as the type to attract women's attention without any effort at all.

But it was not Drake's masculine beauty that drew her to him. As blunt as he sometimes was, as stern and harsh as he forced himself to be, she had seen those cold green eyes warm at unexpected moments—when he held her child, and when he looked at her as he had last night. She knew that to be the true Drake. She had responded to that part of him the first moment she had seen him. She had sensed a bond between them that somehow existed long before that first day on the hillside, and she knew that although Drake chose to deny it, he felt the tug of that bond as well as she.

That consolation firm in her mind, Carolina threw back her coverlet and slipped her legs over the edge of her bed. She drew herself upright, impatient with the brief bout of dizziness that ensued. She stood purposefully, her bare feet on the cold floor. The oversize dress, which Drake had returned to her washed clean of the stains of her ordeal, flopped down around her ankles as she steadied herself with a firm hand on the chair. She was tired of having Drake wait on her hand and foot. She had been raised to pull her own weight in life despite her slender stature. She had always been proud of her stamina, her ability to accomplish tasks that other women twice her size found difficult. She remembered . . .

Carolina gasped. Yes . . . she was remembering . . . !

Her heart beginning a ragged pounding, Carolina gripped the chair tighter as brilliant pictures and remembered sensations flashed across her mind. A bright, golden meadow filled with flowers . . . the buzzing of insects . . . the warmth of the hot morning sun on her face . . . the colors of a butterfly as it caught a current of air and was swept up into the sky . . . She remembered lying in the sweet-smelling grass with the glow of the sun bright red against her closed eyelids. The sensation of strong arms around her was suddenly vividly clear. She felt gentle kisses against her eyelids, against her lips, and she felt love that turned to a hot, molten glow inside her. The arms tightened around her, drew her closer and the kiss deepened. She remembered a hoarse, whispered plea as the man drew back and looked down at her. The man's image was a shadow etched against the brilliant light of the sun behind his back, and Carolina strained to see his face, but she could not. He kissed her again, claiming a part of her that resided deep within, and her arms slipped around his neck. Her hand slipped into his hair. It was thick, warmed by the sun's rays as she wove her fingers through it. The man drew back from her again with a whisper that was deep and throbbing. She sought to penetrate the shadows that hid his face, but it was difficult. Her serenity gradually slipping away, she struggled against the darkness surrounding him. She grew frantic at the effort, trying harder, only to realize the picture was fading. She could not see . . .

A sound at the door and Carolina turned toward Drake's entrance. He was beside her in a moment and she grasped his hand as she rasped, "I . . . I remembered a meadow filled with flowers. I was in a man's arms. I tried to see his face, Drake, but I couldn't see it."

His expression unreadable, Drake urged levelly, "Try again."

Trembling, Carolina closed her eyes. She saw the meadow, but the beauty was gone. There was no sun, no warmth, only the shadow of a man's face, an image growing gradually more dim.

"I can't. It's slipping away." Carolina's voice was ragged. "I can't see it anymore."

Drake did not respond. Instead, he slipped his arm around her, drawing her against his side in unspoken support. His strength consoled her and Carolina leaned against him, allowing it to strengthen her as well. Her past had again eluded her, but her present had not. Drake was her present, and she was secure.

The water was cold and numbing as it rushed against his boots, but Drake felt little of its discomfort. The narrow, winding stream where he had spent most of his days in recent months had become as familiar to him as his own face.

Frowning, Drake stared at the sluice he had constructed months earlier. He had built it according to the directions he had received from a patient old prospector just prior to leaving Deadwood. Because of his inexperience, it had taken him longer than he had thought to set it up, but he had finally gotten it to work efficiently, and he had quickly made up the time he had invested in building it.

The sun was hot against his head as Drake unconsciously wiped his forehead with the back of his arm. He was perspiring, but he had long ago grown immune to the discomfort of perspiration. He had earned that immunity a drop at a time during long, hard years when he had had the choice of learning to ignore it or expire. He had become calloused against the chafing of ankle chains that rubbed his flesh raw in the same way, and had learned silent acceptance of long days of backbreaking labor that made his dawn-to-dark efforts at the stream seem child's play.

Drake dismissed that dark memory as another took precedence in his mind.

I remembered a meadow filled with flowers . . . I was in a man's arms. . . .

His reaction to Carolina's words had been so intense as to startle him. He had been strangely relieved when her memory had faded, and in the time since, he had been unwilling to reason why.

Still unwilling, Drake inspected the riffles on the sluice with a practiced eye. Noting black sand was accumulating heavily on the down side, he adjusted the slant accordingly and allowed himself a simple rationalization. Carolina would be with him for another week or two—three at most.

Until then, she was under his care and he was responsible for the welfare of her and her infant. His concern was a necessary part of that responsibility. Once they reached Deadwood, however, things would be different. Then he would—

A sound of movement from within the wooded copse bordering the stream interrupted Drake's thoughts, turning him abruptly. He glanced at the bank, furious with himself that he had been so distracted that he had walked out of the cabin without his gun. Spotting the knife he had used earlier on the bank, he moved swiftly toward it. His hand curled around the handle just as another sound came from within the trees.

His heart pounding heavily, he crouched, ready to spring, when he was brought suddenly upright by the sound of a familiar voice.

"Drake, are you there?"

Carolina stepped into sight. Beside her with a few rapid strides, he grasped her arm angrily.

"What are you doin' out here?"

"I . . . I wanted to get some air."

"I told you to rest. You're not well enough yet to try walkin' this far alone. You could've fallen."

"I'm all right."

"No, damn it, you're not!"

Drake attempted to turn her back toward the cabin, but Carolina resisted with a soft plea.

"No, not yet, Drake. I . . . I wanted to talk to you for a few minutes . . . out here, where we're on a more equal level."

"What are you talkin' about, Carolina?"

"There's something I wanted to say, and I'm not sure how to say it." Obviously hesitant, Carolina continued a moment later, "No, that's not exactly right. There's something I *have* to say." Carolina's gray eyes held his. He felt their clear intensity as she continued earnestly, "I . . . I know I act strangely at times. I suppose that's because I feel so strange at times. Everything's so mixed up in my mind, but

130

there's one thing I want you to know I'm sure of—that you're my friend."

Drake stiffened. "I don't have any friends."

"You do."

"Then let me put it this way." Drake spoke with deliberate emphasis. "I don't want anybody to think of me as a friend."

Carolina's pale eyes flickered in the moment before she raised her chin with a soft response. "I'm sorry, Drake. It's too late."

Silent, Carolina held his gaze for a few moments longer. Drake saw the proud tilt of her chin and shoulders in the moment before she turned back in the direction from which she had come. He was still watching her, myriad emotions warring inside him, when her step suddenly faltered, snapping him from his bemusement. At her side in a moment, he scooped her up into his arms despite her protests and started resolutely back toward the cabin.

Twelve

"Come here, darlin'." Rosie's voice was soft and coaxing and sweet as honey. "You're a devil, do you know that?"

Her wiles falling flat as the small white kitten crawled further under the bed, determined to elude her, Rosie shook her head with annoyance. "You're gettin' to be more of a rascal every day. Come out here, you hear?"

A soft mewing her only response, Rosie tossed aside the dish linen she had been holding, dropped to her knees, and peeked under the bed. The kitten was about to make himself comfortable and it was obvious she was going to have to push him outside for a few necessary minutes before he had another accident.

Moving as quickly as a flash, Rosie was suddenly flat on her belly and scrambling under the bed after the surprised kitten. Her hand curled around the little fellow's rounded stomach just as he attempted to skitter away, and she laughed aloud as she dragged herself and the squirming kitten out into the light.

"You should know better than to try to get away from Rosie, Silky." Rosie whispered into the kitten's pleading expression. "It's time for you to go outside for a while. Don't worry. I'll let you back in again."

The kitten meowed his objections as she walked toward the door and Rosie could feel his body stiffen. She knew the reason for the small feline's hesitation to go outdoors. The noise, the excitement, the steady traffic of heavy boots, horses hooves and occasional dogs that ran wild on the street was too much for the timid animal. Sympathy welled inside Rosie. She knew what it was like to be forced out, ill-prepared, into a world that had little sympathy for youth, inexperience, or personal tragedy. Like the kitten that now squirmed in her arms, she had been timid, uncertain, afraid to take that first step. The only difference between the panicking kitten and herself was that her own fears had been carefully concealed. On the outside her mask had been perfectly drawn. That mask had not slipped in the presence of others for a single minute since that first day.

Rosie sighed and tightened the belt on her pink satin wrapper as she reached the cabin doorway. She drew the door open and stood looking out at the street for a few moments. Her cabin's position behind the Nugget allowed her some privacy from prying eyes and the occasional opportunity to watch comings and goings on the street without being observed. The feeling of being able to see without being seen was somehow stimulating and she smiled as she lowered the protesting kitten to the ground. Catching him as he attempted to scramble back inside, Rosie pulled the door closed behind her and set him down on the ground again.

"Go on, Silky. That's right, little fella. I won't let anythin' hurt you."

Rosie followed the kitten's cautious progress with a concerned gaze as he walked across the muddy ground with tentative, light-footed steps. She knew the kitten had not understood a word, but she had meant what she said. She would never abandon him as she had been abandoned.

Rosie's beautiful mouth tightened. Some would take exception to that statement. They'd say that she hadn't been abandoned—that she had run away from home—and she had. She knew, however, that she had been abandoned long before the day she had turned her back on the only family she had ever known. She had been left to shrivel up and die inside. She would've died, too, had it not been for *him*.

He had rescued her. He had discovered the wicked truth about her and he had not despised her. He had looked past it to the girl within her who was as pure as the driven snow,

133

and in his comforting arms the terrible sins had almost been washed from her soul. He had—

A sudden barking jerked Rosie's head up the moment before a large brown dog rounded the corner. Her eyes darting to the kitten, Rosie saw Silky's blue eyes widen with terror as he froze, back arched and claws bared as the dog charged toward him.

Without a thought to personal safety, Rosie jumped between them, shouting and waving her arms in an attempt to frighten off the larger animal. Dodging the canine's snapping fangs as it lunged at the kitten again and again, she was momentarily successful in grasping the dog's collar, only to lose it as the dog made another savage thrust. Frantic, Rosie swung her fist with all her might, catching the wild-eyed animal on the side with a blow that turned him unexpectedly on her. The furious beast crouched with a low growl, preparing to spring, but his attack was thwarted by an unexpected kick that sent him howling, tail between his legs, out of sight.

Taking only a moment to scoop up the kitten, Tag was beside Rosie in an instant. He grasped her arm, dragged her back into the cabin, and slammed the door behind them. Dropping the kitten onto the floor, he turned to her, rigid with fury.

"What in hell did you think you were doing out there? Damn it, that dog's already bitten several people! Don't you realize he could've torn you to bits?"

"H . . . he would've killed Silky! I had to protect him!"

"What about you? Who was supposed to protect you? If I hadn't happened along . . ."

"But you did." Rosie released a shaken breath. With an attempt to still her trembling, she forced a smile. "Thank you, Tag."

"Thank you, Tag. . . ." Tag repeated her words through stiff lips. His handsome face remained tight with anger. "I don't want you to thank me. I want you to tell me you'll never do anything that stupid again!"

Rosie paused in response, suddenly as serious as he. "I'd like to tell you I won't, but the most I can say is that I'll be

134

more careful the next time I let Silky out."

"Damn the cat! I never should've bought it for you!"

"Oh, yes, you should." Rosie took a step forward that brought her so close to Tag that she could see her own reflection in the dark mirrors of his eyes. She slid her arms around his waist and whispered a hairsbreadth from his lips, "Don't worry, Tag. It won't happen again. I told you, I'll be more careful."

"Don't let the cat out anymore."

"I have to, Tag."

"Keep him inside for a few days." Tag slipped his arms around her, drawing her closer. "I'll get someone to fence in an area beside your door."

"Tag . . ." Not quite believing the depth of his concern, Rosie whispered, "It won't happen again. Stop worryin'."

"You're damned right it won't happen again! And don't tell me to stop worrying! If I had arrived a few minutes later, that dog would've been at your throat!"

"You're exaggeratin'!"

"I'm not! Damn it, Rosie!" His grip tightening almost to the point of pain, Tag rasped, "I love you. If that dog had attacked you—"

"If the dog had bitten me, Doc Fitz would've taken care of it."

Tag paled. "Doc Fitz! You don't mean you'd actually let that butcher touch you! You saw what he did to Henry Gardner when he sewed him up! The poor fellow will never look the same!"

"Doc had a snoot full that night. Besides, he'd never do that to me."

Tag's smooth cheek twitched and Rosie knew she had somehow angered him even more. She knew she was right when he stated flatly, "I didn't come here to talk about Doc Fitz *or* that damned cat. I came here to talk about *us*."

Rosie attempted a step back that Tag would not allow as he pressed, "No, we have to talk. Times are changing in Deadwood, Rosie. There's talk that the President wants to settle the Indian question once and for all, and that he's going to order General Custer to bring Sitting Bull and his

135

hostiles to their knees. When that happens, this whole territory is going to open up. We're going to have to be ready to stake our claim legally to everything we have here, or chance losing it. I want us to be ready for that move."

Tag halted, his expression softening unexpectedly as he whispered, "I want to make things legal between *us,* too. Rosie, I want—"

"No, Tag! No!" Rosie jerked herself free of his embrace. She snatched up the dish linen she had dropped earlier and crushed it tight against her, continuing, "How many times do I have to tell you the same thing? We're business partners and friends—that's all!"

Beside her in two swift steps, Tag ripped the cloth from her hands and stared at the carefully embroidered initials. "These aren't *your* initials, Rosie, and they aren't mine! Whose are they?" His face flushed an angry red. "You're living in a dreamworld, Rosie. He doesn't want you! He doesn't want any woman to get close to him again!"

Rosie fought to still her quivering lips. "He *will* want me. When he's ready to love again, it'll be me he'll love."

"No!"

"Yes!"

Tag grasped her shoulders and shook her hard. "He'll never love you the way I love you! He'll never want you the way I want you, and he'll never *need* you the way I need you."

Refusing to accept his tormented words, Rosie rasped, "You don't need me, Tag. You don't need anybody. You're one of the most self-sufficient men I've ever known."

"I *was.*"

"You *are!*" Rosie's words snapped with sudden outrage. "Don't try to make me think I've made a cripple out of you! I won't believe it!"

"You won't? Well, you can believe this, then." Tag jerked her closer. She could feel his strong body tremble, could taste his breath on her lips, could feel the heat of his gaze scorch her as he rasped, "I won't let anyone take you from me. You belong to me just as I belong to you, even though you won't let yourself admit it. But you will, Rosie, you will. . . ."

Sliding his hands into her hair, Tag held her fast under his lips as he kissed her brow, her eyelids, her temple. The warm line of his heated kisses trailed across her chin, circled her lips tauntingly to drop to her neck and the deep vee of her wrapper. With a practiced hand, he loosened the tie and Rosie gasped. She didn't want it to be this way again between them, for Tag to settle each argument with the persuasive power of his lips and the heat of his body. She didn't want him to think that he could buy her with his passion. She didn't want to feel herself being absorbed into him as she did now, to ache for the touch of his hands, knowing that she was naked beneath the heavy pink satin of her wrapper. She didn't want . . .

Suddenly thrusting Tag away, Rosie stepped back. The gaping satin of her wrapper revealed an intimate glimpse of lush, white flesh beneath and she jerked it closed.

"I said I have other plans for my future, Tag. I can't seem to make you understand that I mean what I say, but I suppose that's my fault. I thought you could accept the feelings we share as mutual consolation."

"Consolation!" Tag paused, holding her silent with the intensity of his gaze. "I don't believe you feel 'consolation' when I hold you in my arms, and I know damned well I don't."

"Don't try to tell me what I feel."

"It seems I have to! Rosie, you have the love you always wanted right here, in my arms, but you can't see it because of the dream you've lusted after all your life! You'll never be happy with a man who can't love you the way you want him to."

"He *will* love me!"

"He won't!"

"He will, I tell you!" Suddenly unable to bear another moment of the conversation that was tearing her in two, Rosie rasped, "Get out, Tag! I don't want you here anymore!"

Tag went suddenly still. His handsome face drained of color. "You don't mean what you're saying."

Rosie closed her eyes against the heat building beneath her lids. She opened them a moment later, her voice as hard and cold as a blade, "I meant exactly what I said. I made a mistake lettin' things go on as they have for so long between us. I told myself that underneath the paint and satin and behind the smiles, I was still payin' my way, and you knew that as well as I did. I told myself that we served each other's purposes well, but I can see that I was wrong."

"You don't mean what you're saying, Rosie."

"Yes, I do." Rosie's eyes were suddenly brimming. "Please go, Tag. And don't come back here. I don't want you to come back."

"Rosie . . ."

"If you want to dissolve our partnership, I'll understand." She took another fortifying breath. "I can work anyplace in Deadwood. The men like me."

"No!" Tag's compactly built body went rigid. "I won't let you go back to that life again!"

Rosie paused to summon a professional smile. "Tag, honey, you don't really have any choice in the matter."

"I don't, don't I?"

With a sudden step forward, Tag swept Rosie off her feet. In a blur of motion that stole her breath, Rosie felt the bed beneath her back. She attempted a protest that was blocked by the pressure of Tag's mouth against hers as she struggled against a kiss that was more anger than passion. Forcing apart her lips, his tongue seeking hers, Tag ripped apart the closure of her wrapper to find the soft flesh beneath. His hand sought the warm, moist crevice between her thighs, caressing her boldly as he tore his mouth from hers to suckle her breasts.

Realizing the futility of struggle, Rosie went suddenly still beneath him. She closed her eyes, only to feel Tag go still as well. He rasped, "Rosie, look at me. Tell me you want me."

Rosie slowly opened her eyes. Her gaze was frigid. Infuriated, Tag rolled himself fully upon her, pinning her wrists to the bed with one hand as he unbuttoned his trousers with the other. His voice a harsh growl, he whispered, "I'll prove

138

to you how you feel if I have to! I'll show you how it's supposed to be between us . . . and I'll *make* you say the words!"

His words killing the last flicker of emotion within her, Rosie closed her eyes again. As she had so many times before, she summoned the warmth of a familiar hearth to mind. She watched the colors of the flickering flames. She saw the white kitten playing there, and standing beside the small feline she saw the man who had brought her, unsoiled and pure, through so many nights such as this when her body was being used so basely. She slipped into her phantom lover's arms and hid there, knowing it was there she would remain until she could—

"Rosie!"

Her eyes snapping open, Rosie saw Tag's stricken gaze. Numb inside, she heard him say, "You're thinking about *him* now, aren't you?" He shook her roughly. "Tell me!"

Rosie responded levelly, without emotion.

"I've lain under men before, and I will again, if I have to. But I won't pretend with you. I won't let you believe that this is anythin' more than—"

Suddenly free of his weight, Rosie watched as Tag drew himself to his feet and refastened his trousers. His dark eyes on her face, he spoke in a voice as devoid of emotion as hers had been moments earlier.

"All right, Rosie. You win. You always win, but this time when you win you lose, whether you realize it now or not. You don't have to worry about leaving the Nugget. I told you before that our partnership wasn't dependent upon my use of your bed, and I meant it. And you don't have to worry about my knocking at your door in the middle of the night, either. You see, there're plenty of warm, female bodies out there a lot more willing than yours. A gold piece will buy me just about any one of them." He gave a hard laugh. "And the truth be known, a crook of my finger will probably do just as well. You see, most *women* like *me,* Rosie. It's too bad that you're no longer included in that group, but I guess it's for the best."

Tag walked to the door. His hat in his hand, he turned

back to look at her. "Your bed is your own, Rosie. I hope your phantom keeps you warm."

The door clicked closed behind Tag. Realizing she had made no effort to close the wrapper that Tag had stripped open moments earlier, Rosie drew herself to her feet. She raised her chin and fastened the belt tightly around her waist. She picked up the dishcloth Tag had discarded so angrily and walked unsteadily toward the chest in the far corner of the room. Kneeling before it, she lifted the lid and looked down at the neatly monogrammed linens within. She added the cloth to the coffer in silence. She would be ready when *he* came for her. She would love him as he had never been loved before, and she would make him forget all the terrible years behind him, just as he would make her forget hers.

Rosie sighed, unaware of the tear that trailed down her cheek. As for Tag—she hoped he would be happy without her, because she knew now there was no other way.

Tag pulled Rosie's door closed behind him and stood stock-still as the full significance of the last few minutes registered fully in his mind. Incredulous, he wondered how he had made himself believe it would never come to pass. He wondered if it was purely vanity that had made him think he could make Rosie overcome her feelings for that man, and he wondered how he could have been so wrong.

Straightening his shoulders, Tag placed his hat on his head and prepared to step out into sight. He remembered what he had told Rosie a few minutes earlier.

There're a lot of warm, female bodies out there more willing than yours. A gold piece will buy me just about any one of them.

Tag gave a short, bitter laugh. The trouble was that he didn't *want* anyone but Rosie.

Forcing himself from Rosie's door, Tag walked toward the street. He paused as he reached the crowded walkway, lost in painful thought. A husky voice at his elbow turned him with a start toward the flashy saloon girl who had appeared unexpectedly at his side.

"What's the matter, Tag, honey? You look like you've got the weight of the world on your shoulders."

Ella O'Connor searched his face with a knowing gaze. Hesitating only a moment, she slipped her arm under his and smiled.

"This must be my lucky day. It's kinda early, but why don't you step down the street to the Grubstake with me for a while. That's my territory, Tag, honey, and unless those little goose bumps that are runnin' down my back right now are doin' me wrong, you're in the market for a change." She drew his arm tight against the side of her bulging bosom. "What do you say?"

Tag looked at Ella's brightly painted face. Ella had none of Rosie's vibrant natural beauty, but her darkly kohled eyes were as honest as they came. She didn't pretend to be anything that she wasn't, and her goals were firmly fixed in reality, not a dreamworld that would never materialize. She was exactly what he needed right now.

"Come on, give it a try," Ella coaxed him softly. "I'll even let you cry on my shoulder, if you like. Hell, anythin' that'll get you that close will do."

"I'm not in the mood to cry, Ella."

Ella's eyes took on a hopeful gleam. "What *are* you in the mood for, Tag, honey?"

Slipping his hand over hers where it still rested on his arm, Tag smiled. "Well, maybe we'll just take that walk to the Grubstake and see."

Leaning against him with a hoot of unabashed excitement, Ella purred, "Lead on, Tag. I've been waitin' for this day for a long time."

Tag turned into the Grubstake a few minutes later. Forcing a smile for the sake of the beaming saloon girl on his arm, he suddenly despised himself for his deceit in leading her to expect more from him than she would get. He was approaching the bar when he realized that his attempt to distract his mind would not change the agonizing truth. Rosie was going on without him.

Doc looked up and shuddered, the lines on his whiskered face turning down revealingly as Miriam Higgins appeared unexpectedly in his doorway. His office hours, always irregular, had been especially long that afternoon and he had been looking forward to a trip to the Nugget. His heart had begun warming at the thought of the pleasures awaiting him there *until* . . .

"I can see you're glad to see me, Jerome."

Miriam's nasal tone sent another shudder down Doc's spine. "That so? Looks to me like your eyesight might be gettin' poor. Maybe you should have a doctor check it."

"Humph. . . ." Choosing to ignore his response, Miriam walked boldly into the office. She looked pointedly at the vacant chair beside his desk, finally prompting, "Well, am I invited to sit down?"

"By all means!" Doc suppressed a groan. "What's on your mind, Miriam?"

"Obviously not what's on yours! You're practically salivating. How long has it been since your last drink?"

"*Too* long, not that it's any of your business! I was gettin' ready to fix that, so if you don't mind gettin' to the point. . . ."

"I suggest you hold on to your patience, Jerome! You ought to thank me for keeping you from your vices, even if it's only for a few minutes."

"Well, if it's thanks you're lookin' for, you're wastin' your time. What's on your mind?"

Miriam drew herself up primly. "You've heard the news about General Custer. . . ."

"What news is that? All I've heard are some ugly rumors."

"*Ugly* rumors?"

"Ugly, indeed."

Miriam's sharp nose twitched. "And what news might you be considering ugly?"

"The tale that Josiah Cribbs brought into town this mornin' about General Custer takin' the Seventh Calvary on an Injun hunt that's supposed to wipe out Sioux resistance once and for all."

Miriam dropped the bundle she carried onto his desk. Doc squinted at his neatly bound laundry, then looked up at the woman's tight expression. "Well, are you goin' to sit or not?"

"I'm not certain I want to exchange thoughts with a man whose mind has been altered by alcohol to the point where he can't even *think* clearly!"

"My mind's a helluva lot clearer than yours, it seems to me!"

"I'll not tolerate profanity in our conversation, Doctor Fitz!"

"Profanity!" Suddenly unwilling to allow the hardheaded woman to tower over him a moment longer, Doc drew himself stiffly to his feet. Annoyed that he still need look up to meet her hard-eyed gaze, he puffed out his sagging chest and growled, "Seems to me the person who's bein' profane here is you—gloatin', just like the rest of the damned fools in this town, over the prospect of the bloodshed to come!"

"You're a fool, Jerome—a fool who can't see past an unfortunate necessity to the glorious future that will be won."

"You're so sure of that, are you, Miriam?"

Miriam blinked under the craggy-faced doctor's scrutiny. "I don't know what you mean."

"I mean you're so sure that this 'unfortunate necessity' to which you're referrin', really *is* a necessity. And you're so sure that marchin' on a bunch of Indians who are fightin' for their holy land will bring a 'glorious' future."

"Of course, it will! Once the Sioux have been subdued, all the other tribes will see they have no chance against the U.S. Army! This country will be opened up legally for all time, and a great influx of enterprising settlers will bring this land to its full potential!"

"What makes you think it isn't at its full potential now, the way the Almighty made it?"

"Because it isn't!" Miriam's thin face flushed. "You know that as well as I, and you can stop pretending to be holier than thou with me, Jerome! You know this land is rich, not only in gold, but with endless resources. You

143

know what's said of the prairie that surrounds these gold-laden hills . . . that the grasslands are the richest that the eye of man has ever seen . . . that there's more gold from the grass roots up than there is from the grass roots down! Think of the great herds this land can support! Why, cattle raised here could eventually feed the whole nation! Families, immigrants, and native-born alike, who've found it difficult to earn a decent living in other areas of the country could come here and lead rich, meaningful lives! We could have a whole new generation of Americans here, people who will—"

"I think you're forgettin' somethin' with all that lofty talk, Miriam." Doc pinned her with his steely eyed gaze. "You're forgettin' that this land's already occupied."

"By whom? A few ignorant savages who'll never truly appreciate its full worth?"

Doc paused in response, accustomed to the blind prejudice of the words the stiff-faced woman spoke, but never more infuriated by it than he was at that moment. "No, by people who revere the sanctity of the hills and the gods who inhabit them."

"Gods!" Miriam rolled her small black eyes with disgust. "Don't tell me you *believe* gods live in the peaks of the hills, gods who speak in rolls of thunder and send forth bolts of lightning when angry! You're a Christian, Jerome! You're blaspheming!"

"No, it's you who's blasphemin', and you're too ignorant to realize it!"

"Ignorant!" Miriam raised her sharp, haughty chin. "You will apologize for that insult, Jerome, or I will leave your office this instant!"

"I'm not about to apologize, Miriam." Maintaining firm control on his rising temper, Doc continued slowly, "The truth is the truth, and the truth here is that you're not seein' more than a few feet beyond that nose you've got stickin' up in the air. You're not seein' the slaughter that General Custer's advance on the Sioux will bring."

"Slaughter? General Custer is invincible, and everyone knows it!"

144

"I'm talkin' about the slaughter of the Indians!"

Doc's response obviously taking her aback, Miriam was momentarily quiet. "Any deaths that will be incurred within the Indian nation will be an unfortunate necessity. War is war."

"And slaughter is slaughter."

Doc's eyes narrowed with concern as he assessed Miriam's thin face. The woman was beginning to breathe unevenly and her color had deteriorated to a pasty white. The physician in him overwhelming his anger, he took her arm.

"Are you all right, Miriam?"

Miriam jerked her arm free. "No, I'm not all right! I dislike being called a bloodthirsty warmonger, and I demand an apology!"

His back effectively raised at her response, Doc felt all concern drain away. He took an abrupt step backward. "I can see you dislike facin' the truth."

"The truth? How fine and generous of you to take up the cause of the *innocent* Indian. What is your solution to our problems here then, *Doctor* Fitz? Would you have us lay down our arms and allow the savages to swarm all over us? Or would you suggest that we invite their chiefs into Deadwood as our guests?" Her lips noticeably whitened and trembling, Miriam continued a trace more softly, "And if you feel as strongly as you claim about our invasion of this Indian domain, what are *you* doing here in Deadwood—on *holy Indian ground* where you're not wanted?"

Realizing Miriam had asked a question for which he had no logical response, Doc shook his head slowly. "Unlike you and the others who think violence as the only answer to the Indian question, I never claimed to have a solution to the problems here, Miriam."

"What about the violence the Indians are perpetrating every day on peaceful wagon trains?"

"Which are trespassing on their land?" He shrugged. "I don't know."

"What of those who come here in hopes of a better future for themselves and their families?"

145

"I suppose the Indians are looking to their future in the hills, too."

"You're a damned, unpatriotic jackass!"

Doc could not resist a smile. "Miriam, such language!"

But Miriam did not smile in return. "You didn't answer my question, *Doctor.* If you feel so strongly about all this, what are you doing in the Black Hills with the rest of us *interlopers?*"

Finding himself without a clear-cut response, Doc shrugged again. "I suppose I'm here because I'm gettin' old. For me this will probably be the last frontier, and I suppose it makes me feel more alive to be a part of it. I'd just as soon be here as anyplace else."

Miriam drew herself rigidly erect. Unconsciously noting the effort she expended in doing so, Doc found his concern thrust from his mind by the sharpness of her next comment.

"It's very easy to sit back and criticize those of us who vigorously seek a solution to our dilemma here and applaud General Custer's efforts to guarantee our rights. Tell me, Doctor, where will *you* stand if all this comes to out-and-out warfare?"

Slowly going as rigid as the pale widow standing before him, Doc replied with careful restraint, "Madam, I served nobly in the U. S. Army durin' the war between the states. I saw and was revolted by the slaughter, and I told myself then that there wasn't any cause worthy of the shedding of such a great magnitude of blood. *But . . ."* Doc paused, his gaze riveting. ". . . *But* I served my country nobly and well until the war ended. Some might say that I'm not the man I was then . . . and maybe they'd be right . . . but I'll tell you now that there hasn't been a moment before or since that day when my devotion to my country has faltered."

"So . . . ?"

"So, with those things said, I'm *still* tellin' you that I'm not goin' to applaud a march that'll end up in wholesale bloodshed, and that's that!"

"How easy it is for you, Doctor!" Miriam's small, dark eyes filled unexpectedly. "You haven't lost someone you loved here in this land! You don't go to sleep at night wondering whether his grave will one day be profaned by savages! You don't carry the doubt in your mind whether you'll be able to be laid to your final rest . . . final rest . . ."

Swaying, Miriam raised a hand to a forehead that was suddenly covered with perspiration, and Doc grasped her arm supportively. Realizing that she was trembling, he urged her to sit, growling gruffly as she resisted. "Don't be pigheaded, Miriam! Sit down before you fall down!" Waiting only until she complied, he took her wrist and checked her pulse. Her heart was racing but strong, but her flesh was cold. He was not fooled for a moment into thinking that she had simply overreacted to their argument.

"You didn't come here today to deliver my laundry, did you, Miriam? You didn't come here to discuss General Custer either. How long have you been feelin' this way?"

"W . . . what way? I don't know what you mean."

"You know damned well what I mean! This weakness, these sweats. . . ."

"I haven't been sleeping well, lately, an . . . and I think I'm developing a cold—maybe a fever."

"Your temperature's as normal as mine."

Miriam flicked him a caustic glance. "Is that supposed to reassure me?"

"I didn't say your *liver* was as normal as mine, damn it! Just answer the question!"

"What question?"

"Miriam . . ."

"About a month."

"You've been feeling sick for a month and haven't done anythin' about it?"

"I considered going to see Doctor McCormick . . ."

"Doctor McCormick! That old quack?"

". . . but I came here instead."

His gaze still assessing, Doc noted that the widow's color had begun returning. The vacant look in her eye was fading, and he suspected she would soon be her old bellicose self. It was now or never.

147

"Unbutton your blouse."

"I beg your pardon!"

"I said unbutton your blouse." Doc gave a snort of disgust at the widow's shocked expression. "Don't worry, I won't attack you. There's a whole bevy of belles at the Nugget that serve my needs very well, thank you. Did you or didn't you come here for my professional help?"

Miriam's spine was regaining a revealing rigidity, forcing Doc to press, "Well?"

"Yes."

"Then unbutton your blouse."

Miriam's long, thin fingers moved to the buttons on her blouse and Doc walked quickly toward the examination table where his stethoscope lay. He had known better than to ask the widow to lie down so he might examine her more easily. He snorted again. Her frozen inhibitions would never allow a prone position.

Returning to the chair beside his desk where the widow still sat obediently, Doc was surprised to see that she had made fast work of her chore, that her blouse hung open to reveal a spotless white camisole that covered surprisingly full breasts. He was momentarily taken aback. Strange . . . Years in his profession had left him quite adept in assessing the attributes of the female form, even while it was fully clothed, yet he had never realized that this woman was so well endowed.

Doc shook his unkempt head, eliciting a frown from the silent widow. He supposed he had been distracted from the obvious by the acid of the woman's personality and the constant challenge in her eyes. But somehow, that challenge was absent as he approached her, pulled his chair in front of her, and sat abruptly. He checked her eyes—now clear, her ears—as shiny and clean as a babe's. He instructed briefly, "Open your mouth," knowing he never thought to see the day he'd say those words to her.

He placed the stethoscope against her chest. The steady thump of the widow's heart echoed in his ears—perhaps a bit faster than it should—but Doc had seen that reaction to his ministrations before. The widow was nervous, but her heart was as sound as a dollar.

He inched closer, his knees brushing the widow's as he reached around to the back of her neck where he searched for lumps that would indicate a problem. He slid his fingers under the tight bun confined there, startled at the softness of a few graying locks that loosened at his touch. A long strand curled against the side of her throat, lending an unexpected vulnerability to the widow's formerly prim appearance as he slid his fingers professionally down the side of her neck and pressed the hollows at its base. He reached inside her blouse, maintaining a professional façade as he pressed her armpits in a like manner. A fragrance wafted up to his nostrils, a bodily scent that was warm and pleasant, and he was momentarily startled by his reaction as his hand brushed her breast.

Suddenly aware of the danger there, Doc forced his mind clear of extraneous thought. Concluding his examination a short time later, he drew back, surprisingly relieved, to find the widow's sharp, black eyes on his face.

He responded succinctly to her unvoiced question. "You're as healthy as a horse."

"Am I?"

"Did you doubt it?"

The widow's long nose twitched, but somehow the tartness was absent from her tone as she replied, "I wouldn't have come here today if I didn't have some doubts, would I?"

Something about her response made Doc look closer at the widow. He was surprised to feel a little flicker in the area of his heart as he caught a fleeting glimpse of sadness. His voice also devoid of its former curtness, he inquired simply, "You're not sleepin' well, Miriam?"

The widow shrugged and avoided his eye. "No."

"Somethin' on your mind—I mean, other than General Custer's attack on the Sioux?"

Miriam looked up sharply, the bite in her gaze fading when she saw no sarcasm was intended. "No, not really."

"Come on, you might as well tell me. There's nobody else to tell."

The widow shrugged again, her gaze flickering off to a spot on the far wall. "I . . . I've been dreaming disturbing dreams about Jonas. . . ."

Doc paused in response. "Every night?"

"Yes."

"What else?"

"I've been sleeping so poorly that I've lost my appetite."

"That so. . . ." Doc pondered the widow's unexpected plight. His old heart began a slow pounding as professionalism forced him to pursue a tact he was strangely reluctant to voice. "You're all alone here, Miriam. It's a difficult life for a woman. You have friends or family back home, don't you?"

Miriam looked back at him. *"This* is my home."

"You'd lead a much easier life if you went home."

"I told you, *Deadwood* is my home now." Miriam stood abruptly, her hands moving to the blouse that still hung agape. She fastened the buttons with shaking fingers. "I'm going to stay here, in Deadwood, and when I die, I'm going to be buried on the hill beside Jonas."

Doc stood as well. His brow knit into an unconscious frown when he found himself disturbingly close to the shaken widow. He looked up soberly into her eyes, his voice emerging just short of a whisper. "You're too young to think about dyin', Miriam. You have a lot of good years ahead of you. You should be thinkin' about livin'."

Miriam raised her chin in a way that sent her gaze down her nose, but Doc felt none of his customary annoyance as she replied, "I am. That's why I came here today, to see if you could help me."

"All I can do for you is to give you a prescription for a tonic to build you back up and restore your appetite. And maybe another prescription for a sleepin' powder when you're havin' a bad night."

The widow's eyes were suspiciously bright. "Well, give them to me, then."

"But I think the advice I just gave you would be more effective in helpin' what ails you."

Miriam took a step backward and reached for her reticule. "Just give me the prescriptions, please." She looked back at him, and Doc found his old heart pounding a little harder. "How much do I owe you?" And before he could respond, "I brought your clean laundry. Let's just consider it an even exchange."

"But —"

"The prescriptions, please."

Acutely aware that the widow was barely able to maintain her composure, Doc scribbled the appropriate marks and handed her the sheet, strangely reluctant to have her leave.

"Miriam, I think —"

But the widow was already walking toward the door. She paused there to say unexpectedly, "Thank you, Jerome."

Doc was watching from the doorway a few moments later as the widow's tall, erect figure moved down the crowded street with a familiar, purposeful step. He found himself following the sway of her slim hips and remembering the surprisingly silky texture of her hair. The scent of her body returned to his mind and he remembered the way his hand had brushed —

Doc awakened from his bemusement with a sudden snap.

He must be going crazy!

A shaken man, Doc grabbed his hat and burst out onto the street. His eye fixed on the doorway of the Nugget, he started forward at a pace just short of a run.

Rosie adjusted the neckline of her red satin dress, aware that the depth of its curve was bringing the first smile of the day to the lips of a few appreciative fellows at the bar. Bart Mellon and Timothy Ryan's glances were just short of leers as she looked back at them from her customary table and batted her lashes flirtatiously. They raised their glasses to her and she blew them a kiss, then looked away.

The din of the crowded saloon grew louder as Rosie surveyed the scene with a smile so stiff that it hurt. Damn it all, where was Tag? The sun was preparing to set and she hadn't seen him since he had left her cabin that morning. Sheila was handling the poker table well enough, but it wasn't like him to be late. She hoped nothing was wrong.

Rosie paused on that thought. As far as things stood between Tag and herself, the situation was *right* for the first time in years. She knew that now. She had been more cruel than she had realized. Tag loved her. He really loved her. She was uncertain why, but she supposed the reason made little difference. Tag was handsome and kind, and more of a man than any other fellow she had known. He'd find the right woman for him without any problem. That was the way it should be, because she had found the right man for her many years ago.

Rosie's smile slipped into a frown as she glanced up at the clock on the wall for the fourth time that hour. She didn't love Tag the way he loved her, but she was worried.

As if in response to her thoughts, Tag appeared in the doorway and Rosie's heart began a rapid pounding. Her anxious gaze elicited a polite nod as Tag made his way directly to the poker table and slid into the chair Sheila gratefully vacated at his approach.

Rosie's spirits plummeted to her toes. Well, what had she expected? She had sent Tag away. He was a gentleman and he would behave like one by keeping a polite distance from her and observing his promise to maintain their relationship on a purely business level. It was what she had wanted. The trouble was that she had not realized how much getting what she wanted would hurt.

Rosie forced her smile brighter as her spirits plummeted lower. Her fingers tightened around the glass in front of her. Suddenly realizing she had yet to take a sip, she raised it resolutely to her lips and drained it dry. The fiery liquid burned all the way to her stomach and she gasped. A short laugh escaped her throat. Damn, she was getting soft! It was time she stood on her own two feet again in a way she suddenly realized she hadn't for a long time.

Rosie stood up and surveyed the bar. She had been neglecting her duties while she had spent the time worrying. She had not been circulating, rubbing shoulders with the customers to keep things running smoothly, and it was time to correct that oversight.

A spot cleared for her at the bar as she approached and Rosie's smile broadened. The men liked her — genuinely liked her — and she liked most of them. She was especially fond of the two young prospectors, Bart Mellon and Tim Ryan, and she laughed as they extended their arms toward her in welcome as she neared. Adding a deliberate sway to her step, she walked boldly toward them to the hoots and whistles of appreciative onlookers. Bart slipped his arm around her waist when she stepped to his side and spoke in a mock whisper.

"Rosie, darlin', you're the girl of my dreams, do you know that?"

"That so?" Rosie fluttered her thick eyelashes. "Now don't go tellin' me what we were doin' in those dreams. You might make me blush!"

Bart's blue eyes sparkled into hers. "There you go, spoilin' all my fun!" He drew her closer, then shot a respectful glance toward Tag's table. "If only you wasn't already taken. . . ."

Refusing to allow her smile to falter, Rosie pinched Bart's smooth cheek and whispered with a pursing of moist, rouged lips, "Whether I am or not doesn't mean that I can't have a drink with a handsome fella like you."

The young prospector slapped the bar with his hand. "A drink for the lady, Barney! And keep 'em comin'."

Rosie raised a speculative brow. "You wouldn't be tryin' to get me drunk so you could take advantage of me, would you?"

Bart went suddenly sober. "I might if I thought it would work. Would it?"

"Not a chance in the world, Bart, honey."

"I figured as much." His despondency temporary, Bart smiled again. "Guess I'll have to be satisfied with lookin' into them big, beautiful blue eyes. . . ." Turning back to the bar, he called out, "What's holdin' up them drinks, Barney?"

Rosie's smile widened. Business as usual. She darted an

153

unconscious glance at Tag, her smile momentarily dimming. Almost as usual. . . .

Interrupting her sobering thoughts, Doc Fitz appeared in the saloon doorway with an expression that was almost frantic. Rosie watched his dash to the bar, seeing true panic in his eyes as he shouted for a drink. She nodded unconsciously to Bart's steady stream of flattery, managing to better each witticism with one of her own as Doc downed his first drink in a gulp, then gulped a second and a third. Her brow knit with concern. Something was wrong.

Excusing herself with a low comment that left her admirers laughing, Rosie elbowed her way to Doc's side. Appearing lost in thought—thought that obviously paralyzed him with fear—the graying physician stared into his glass completely unaware of her presence beside him. Something *was* wrong.

"You're not doin' much for a lady's ego today, Doc."

Doc's head jerked up at the sound of her voice, but his smile was weak as he responded, "Rosie, honey. I didn't see you standin' there."

"I know, and *you* know that isn't normal, especially for you, you old lecher." Rosie poked him in his bony ribs. "What's goin' on, Doc? You got a secret you want to share with old Rosie?"

Her question did not have the reaction Rosie anticipated as Doc's grizzled countenance suddenly paled. "A . . . a secret? Hell, no, I don't have any secrets!" He blinked. "None at all."

Her concern growing, Rosie slid her arm around Doc's shoulders. "Are you all right, Doc?"

Swallowing thickly, Doc looked at his empty glass then back up into her face. He blinked, then raised a hand to her cheek. He patted it gently, responding in a confidential tone, "I'm all right now, Rosie, now that I have a couple of drinks under my belt, but I had a damned frightenin' experience." He shook his head. "I must be gettin' senile."

"If it's one thing you aren't, it's senile, Doc. I can attest to that."

A shade of his former panic returned briefly to Doc's

eyes. "You wouldn't think so if you'd have seen me a little while ago, standin' by the door of my office watchin' the way Mir—" Doc halted abruptly and shuddered. "But that's all over with now that your beautiful face is lookin' down at me and your voice is whisperin' in my ear, Rosie, honey. You're the best medicine this old doc could have prescribed for himself."

"Am I, now?" Rosie read sincerity in Doc's eyes and true warmth stirred to life inside her. She liked this old man. He made her feel good inside, temporarily filling the gaping hole that Tag had left behind. Bowing to impulse, she pressed a hard, short kiss against his mouth. Surprising her, he flushed.

"Now what was that for?"

Rosie squinted in mock anger. "Don't tell me you're complainin'!"

"Hell, no!"

"Well, didn't anybody ever tell you not to look a gift horse in the mouth?"

"You're not a horse, Rosie."

"That's a point. . . ." Rosie laughed. "Well, maybe it's because I like you, Doc."

"I didn't think you gave me that kiss because you hated me."

"And maybe it's because I think you're really my friend." She paused. "A girl needs a friend sometimes."

Doc's expression became slowly assessing. "That so?"

Doc's gaze became more speculative and Rosie realized that the situation between them was gradually being reversed, with Doc beginning to wonder about *her* unexpected behavior. Realizing she was not ready for questions, no matter how well intended, Rosie broke the silence of the moment by bumping him with the curve of her hip and giving him a broad wink.

"You keep a careful hand on that glass tonight, Doc, because I have to be leavin' you now. I got some work to do. There's a few fellas over there that need my help in their celebration."

Aware that Doc's gaze remained fixed on her as she sauntered away, Rosie suddenly realized that without conscious intent, she had taken his mind off his problem, whatever it was, by substituting her problem in its stead.

Glancing toward the poker table in the rear of the room, Rosie felt her heart sink. Tag dealt the cards there without a hint of a smile on his handsome face. She knew how he felt, because, strangely enough, she felt the same way. She was already missing him. She hadn't realized that in giving Tag up as a lover, she would be giving him up as a friend as well. She hadn't wanted it to be that way, but she supposed she couldn't really expect anything else.

Carefully affixing her professional smile, Rosie turned back to the bar. Avoiding Bart's warm reception as she stepped up to the rail, she did not see Nellie enter the saloon, excitement on her brightly painted face as she walked to the nearest table and whispered in Sheila's ear. Neither did she see the titter of excitement that spread through the Nugget as word was passed from one saloon girl to another.

Tired of the steady banter she need maintain in order to keep Bart's mind and hands occupied, Rosie excused herself with a quip that left the men laughing a short time later. She sat at a corner table where she could watch the progress of the night's activities undisturbed. Noting that Bart was looking for her a moment later, Rosie signaled Terri to take her place at Bart's side. She was surprised to see the small redhead nudge another girl toward the young prospector, then turn to approach her.

Rosie frowned as the girl neared, uncertain of the reason for her unnaturally sharp tone as she asked, "What's the matter, Terri?"

"I . . . I'd like to talk to you for a minute, Rosie."

The girl's brown eyes held hers as Rosie studied her unexpectedly sober expression. Terri was one of her quieter girls, a hard worker who kept to herself. She had never considered the slightly built redhead pretty, but at close range she saw a pale beauty that had previously escaped her. She also saw a determination in the girl's expression that she had not witnessed there before.

"Sit down. What's on your mind?"

156

Terri sat abruptly. She took a deep breath that should have been fair warning before asking bluntly, "Is it true that Tag and you are finished?"

Rosie was momentarily unable to answer. A thousand shrieking responses rose to her mind as she replied with a surface calm she did not feel, "What business is it of yours?"

"It's not my business now, but I'd like it to be." Her expression suddenly apologetic, Terri continued in a rush, "It's goin' around the saloon right now that Tag spent most of the day in the Grubstake with Ella O'Connor." Terri's lips twitched. "Everybody knows he wouldn't be with another woman if things were all right between the two of you. I'm sorry, Rosie . . ." Terri paused, obviously discomfited, "I'm not tryin' to make you uncomfortable, but the truth is, I've had a deep feelin' for Tag ever since I came here. If he's free now, I'd like to know because I'd be real good to him."

Rosie could feel herself go rigid. Ella O'Connor. . . . Her response dripped with ice. "I'm not interested in your plans for Tag."

"Don't be mad at me, please, Rosie." The girl's eyes pleaded her understanding, "But you know that Ella O'Connor. She's a hussy. She isn't good enough for Tag. She'd only make him miserable."

"But *you* could make him happy. . . ."

Terri nodded, a revealing brightness appearing in her eyes. "I'd sure try."

"Try then. . . ." Rosie raised her chin. "Tag's a free man." She gave a short laugh. "But it looks like you're goin' to have to get in line."

A limp strand of hair escaped from the fiery mass piled atop Terri's head as she stood up. It lay limply against her thin white neck, making her appear strangely pathetic in Rosie's eyes as she whispered, "Thanks, Rosie."

"Don't thank me."

The girl walked back to the bar and Rosie swallowed against the steadily growing lump in her throat.

Rosie was suddenly disgusted with herself. She was a dog

157

in the manger, that's what she was! She didn't want Tag, but she didn't want anyone else to have him.

Rosie took a steadying breath. Well, Tag deserved more than that. He deserved the best. She hoped he would get it.

The effort almost beyond her, Rosie drew herself to her feet. Forcing herself to a natural pace, she walked toward the rear door of the saloon. In her cabin a few minutes later, she leaned down and picked up the white kitten that came scampering up to meet her. She rubbed his small face against her cheek, whispering hoarsely, "There's only one man for me, Silky. There's *always* been only one man. But I love Tag, too, in so many ways, and I wish him well, really I do. It's just that it hurts so much to lose him. . . ."

Staring at the doorway through which Rosie had just disappeared, Tag resisted the urge to slap down his cards and go after her. Instead, his emotions under tenuous control, he signaled Sheila toward him and stood up abruptly to give her his chair. Without a word of explanation, he walked to the bar.

Raising a glass of bourbon to his lips a moment later, he downed it in one gulp, then set it back on the bar with a snap. Rosie didn't belong to him anymore. He gave a caustic laugh. She had never really belonged to him. He knew the break between them was as hard on her as it was on him. He had read that much in her eyes, but there was little consolation in knowing that although Rosie needed him, she didn't *want* him. He wished . . . he wished . . .

"Tag. . . ."

Turning at a touch on his arm, Tag looked down into Terri Walsh's pale face. "What is it, Terri?"

"Are you all right?"

Tag's eyes narrowed. So that was what all the whispering was about. The girls would be scrambling to make their mark on the boss now that they thought Rosie was out of favor. Tag looked at the small saloon girl a moment longer. No, he was being unfair. Terri was a sweet girl, almost shy. It had been difficult for her to approach him. He attempted a smile.

"I'm all right, Terri."

"Can I do anything for you?"

"No."

"You'll let me know if I can?"

"I'll let you know."

Terri paused, started to say something else, then changed her mind and walked away.

The irony of the situation a bitter pill indeed, Tag signaled for another drink.

Thirteen

Drake growled a necessary admonishment as his horse moved restlessly under his attentions. His own impatience soaring, he looked around the small clearing outside the cabin where he tended the recalcitrant animal. The sun shone through the umbrella of trees on the perimeter, weaving a lacy pattern of shade against the ground. It beckoned him, and he wondered how he had come to be standing in the bright sun, perspiring needlessly, when he could just as easily have ministered to the beast in the shade.

Drake mumbled an appropriate oath under his breath. He wasn't thinking clearly, that was why. He hadn't been able to think clearly since that day almost a month ago when he had first ridden over the hill and found Carolina.

Three weeks. . . . Drake frowned at the thought. He'd accomplished little work during that time with most of his attentions centered on his two charges. Drake paused, realizing he wasn't being completely fair. Carolina had been assuming more and more responsibility in the cabin during the past week. He knew that had it not been for his horse's unexpected injury the previous week, he might have attempted the journey to Deadwood sooner.

Drake glanced toward the spot just outside the cabin door where he had begun accumulating provisions. Traveling alone in the dead of winter with rations that need last him until the trails again cleared, had not necessitated as much preparation as the two-day trek in clear spring weather which they would begin the following day.

The impatient animal moved again, eliciting another sharp rebuke. Waiting until his horse was again still, Drake ran his hand down the animal's foreleg, his concentration intense as he searched for sensitivity in the area that had been badly swollen a week earlier. The fool animal had stumbled on a trail he had traveled countless times before, almost throwing him. He had known immediately the beast had done himself damage and he had known what that would mean.

In some ways he supposed the delay had been for the best. Carolina had needed more time to be physically up to the difficult journey. Her head wound had healed well but her strength faded quickly. Worrying Drake deeply, however, were the severe headaches that had begun to plague her and the nightmares that allowed her little sleep. His concern was that her head wound had not healed as well inside as it had outside. Carolina needed a doctor.

But if the mother's condition was an anxiety, the babe's most certainly was not. A smile touched with unconscious pride tugged at Drake's lips at the thought of Suzannah. The infant was thriving.

Drake surveyed the silence around him, intensely aware that the true danger in the journey they were about to undertake did not lie in Carolina's uncertain physical condition. They were safe here. His presence in this portion of the hills, far from the frantic activity of Deadwood and other mining camps, had gone unnoted by the Indians. Once they rode onto the well-used trails, their situation would be entirely different.

Drake stood up, released his horse's tether, and drew him along into the shade. Restless and strangely reluctant to return to the cabin, he frowned in the direction of the stream. Snatching a cloth and soap from his shaving basin in passing, he paused minutes later at a spot where the stream widened into a shallow, natural pool. He stared at the sunlight glinting on the rippling water, becoming acutely aware of the perspiration that soaked his shirt. He stripped it off, breathing deeply as the bite of the spring air touched his damp skin. Submitting to impulse he sat abruptly on the bank and pulled off his boots and socks. Standing, he un-buttoned his pants and stripped them off as well. He tossed them onto the ground as he stepped into the water.

Drake paused, his breath catching in his throat at the first shock of icy water against his naked skin, then walked in deeper. At its deepest point the water reached to his thighs. Hesitating only a moment, he lowered himself into a seated position on the sandy bottom and began soaping himself. His mind drifted.

He remembered Carolina's emergence into the yard an hour earlier. Believing herself unobserved, she had raised her face to the sun. Standing there, her slender frame almost lost in the oversize dress that was becoming more worn by the day, her long brown hair streaming unbound past her shoulders, her small face sober and her eyes clear of guile, she had appeared almost a child.

But she was not a child.

A warning voice sounded again in Drake's mind. Yes, those guileless eyes. . . . He had learned the danger in Caro-lina's eyes, where little was hidden, and from which he seemed able to hide little in return. He had also discovered the threat in her quick mind that perceived much that went unsaid, and he had learned to steel himself against the ap-peal of her vulnerability, the trust in him that never waned, and the inexplicable innocence about her that both con-fused and perplexed him. He had told himself during periods when he had felt the hard core of him weakening, that he was not seeing the total woman in Carolina—that her forgotten past, her fear of the future, and her depen-dence upon him, masked her true self. He had reminded himself that she was a woman, a trap into which he had fallen before, and a trap he did not intend to fall into again.

Halting his energetic efforts with the onset of numbness, Drake stood up abruptly. He ran his fingers through his dripping hair as he walked back toward the bank of the stream. A brisk breeze prickled against his wet skin but he ignored the chill. He had faced worse circumstances in his desperate past.

Snatching up the cloth he had dropped over a low bush,

Drake stepped up onto the bank and rubbed the excess water from his hair. He then dried his chest and arms. His life had depended upon his strength and endurance then, even as it did now, but with one difference that could not be more marked if it had been branded into his soul. He was no longer responsible solely for his own life, and the weight of that realization was heavy indeed.

A slow agitation growing inside him, Drake dropped his toweling onto the nearby bush and leaned over to pick up his pants. He slid one long leg into them and then the other. Driven by an unconscious sense of urgency, he turned back to the cabin when fully dressed, his step just short of a run.

Finding Carolina standing outside the cabin upon his approach, Drake stopped short at an expression in her light eyes that kept him farther at a distance than a spoken word. He realized with a jolt that she had slipped back into the haunting shadows of her past.

He waited uncertainly. . . .

Carolina raised her hand to her temple as distant echoes sounded in her mind. There was no field of flowers this time. There were angry words . . . shouts. She didn't want to remember them. She didn't want to relive pain and fury. She didn't want to know that the father of her child . . .

The world suddenly spun around her. Carolina closed her eyes as a nausea, quick and overwhelming, rose in her throat, and she fought the desire to retch. The pain in her head that had been the bane of her existence returned and she was suddenly ill, more ill than she had ever been. . . .

Strong arms closed supportively around her, stilling her rocking world and Carolina gasped with relief.

"What's wrong, Carolina?"

"Drake . . ." Carolina's voice erupted in an unrecognizable rasp, her next words leaving her lips before she realized they had been spoken. "I'm afraid . . ."

Drake's handsome face went still. "Are you sick?"

"No . . ." Realizing that the nausea had fled as quickly as it had come, Carolina mumbled, "No, my head. . . ."

163

"Another headache. . . ."

Carolina closed her eyes against the abrupt onslaught of pain, hardly realizing that Drake had picked her up and carried her inside the cabin. She resisted as he attempted to lay her down.

"No."

"Lie down now and close your eyes. The headache will fade."

"But—"

"Please . . ."

That word, so difficult for him to say. Carolina could not refuse it.

Lying down, she closed her eyes.

She had been sleeping too long. . . .

Still squatting beside the fire, Drake turned back toward Carolina, his jaw tight with concern. He glanced toward the window, at the bright light of afternoon shining there. Carolina was so still. It worried him. It seemed he worried when she slept and worried when she didn't. He knew that sleep was the only medicine available when she suffered another of her headaches, but that was somehow little consolation when he saw her lying there, so still.

Drake drew himself to his feet. He walked to the side of her bed, resisting the urge to place his palm against her forehead. Carolina had begun resenting that gesture and he supposed he couldn't blame her. He need remember that Carolina was a grown woman, not a child under his care, and he couldn't treat her like one.

Standing over her, Drake allowed his gaze to linger on Carolina's smooth, motionless face. No, she wasn't a child. He remembered telling himself at one time that she had little true beauty. He wondered how he could have been so blind. Her hair, recently washed free of the grime of her ordeal, was shot with golden highlights that shone with life. Her eyes, although as pale and clear as glacial ice were paradoxically capable of incredible warmth. Thick stubby lashes shielded the shadowed mystery in those eyes with unconscious appeal that was free of flirtatiousness, and he had come to realize that the features he had considered plain only remained plain until she smiled.

Carolina whimpered in her sleep and Drake crouched beside her. He unconsciously took a lock of the long brown hair that fanned across her pillow into his hand. It was warm and filled with life. It glowed, just like Carolina.

He knew the reason for her most recent headache. He had recognized that look in her eyes. She had had another flash of memory that had been too frightening to accept. Somehow he knew that the terror of the Indian raid was not all that haunted her.

Carolina moved, then awoke with a start. Her eyes were wild in the moment before she saw him crouched beside her and Drake reached instinctively for her hand.

"How do you feel?"

Carolina was momentarily breathless. He saw the effort she expended at control. Her hand was cold as ice and he gripped it tighter.

"What scared you?"

"Nothing. . . ." Carolina shook her head. "Nothing."

"Tell me, Carolina."

"I don't want to talk about it."

"Tell me. . . ."

Snatching her hand from his, Carolina drew herself to a seated position. She swung her feet over the side of the cot as he stood up. Irritation twitched at his lips as she drew herself to her feet as well. He noted her step was unsteady as she walked to the table and looked down at her sleeping infant.

Suddenly impatient with her silence, Drake said flatly, "You remembered something."

"No."

"Yes."

"Yes, I did!" Carolina raised a shaking hand to her brow. ". . . but I don't want to remember those things! Angry voices . . . furious shouts . . . fear. . . ."

"Whose voice did you hear?"

"I don't know!" Carolina's face whitened and Drake

165

gripped her shoulder supportively. It was thin, incredibly fragile, just as she was.

"Sit down."

"Don't give me orders, Drake! I won't sit down! I'm not afraid. I'm *not!* And I don't hear those voices. I *won't* hear them." Carolina covered her ears with her hands and he felt a moment of panic as he saw hysteria flare in her eyes.

"Carolina . . ."

The babe awoke unexpectedly with a sharp cry and Carolina dropped her hands abruptly. She blinked as Suzannah squirmed and cried again. Her hands unsteady, she relieved the babe of her wet linens and rewrapped her. Her daughter in her arms, she looked up at Drake minutes later.

"I'm sorry, Drake." Turning, Carolina sat on her cot and adjusted the babe against her. He thought he saw her blink back tears before she looked up again to speak in a whisper, "You were right. I did remember something . . . anger, and then something terrible that happened, but I couldn't remember what it was."

Drake offered tentatively, "The attack on the wagon train. . . ."

"No. Something else . . ." Carolina paused in an effort to retain her newly won control. She attempted a smile. "B . . . but I'm not afraid anymore. We'll be in Deadwood in two days. . . ." She waited for his confirmation.

"That's right."

"I'll find out what happened then. I'll find out everything."

Drake did not respond.

"You'll be rid of us then, Drake." Carolina's smile faltered. "You'll be able to get back to work."

Silence.

"Drake . . ."

Suddenly realizing he was drowning in the welling depth of Carolina's eyes, in the aching need to comfort her with the words she longed to hear, Drake reached deep within him for the strength to resist. Picking up the discarded wet linens, he turned toward the door. He felt Carolina's eyes on his back as he pulled it closed behind him, and he acknowledged with a curse the gravity of the mistake he had made. . . . that first day, when he had mounted his horse and ridden over the hill.

Night had fallen with its usual swiftness. Within the cabin all was silent, but Drake was restless. He did not have to see Carolina's face to know she was asleep. In the time they had shared the cabin, he had come to recognize the different sounds of her breathing during the night—the deep, slow rhythm of restful sleep; the steady cadence of wakefulness; the short, quick breathing that preceded the onslaught of frightening dreams; and the rapid, breathless gulping that had so often awakened him to Carolina's full-blown nightmares.

Inhibiting Drake's sleep was the realization that this was the last night he would listen for those sounds in the silence of his cabin. That thought was heavy on his mind as he strained his eyes into the darkness toward Carolina's bed, as he reviewed the fear he had seen in Carolina's eyes earlier in the day and his own reaction to it. He thought of the restlessness inside him and of the uncertainties to come, and he wondered . . . He wondered what the next few days would bring.

Carolina moved restlessly. She had been drifting in the gray world between sleep and wakefulness when an uncertain sound had awakened her. She listened, realizing as Drake turned and drew the blanket over him that his wakefulness had stirred hers as well. Awake, her mind returned to the mysteries locked in her mind that were never far from conscious thought.

The gold band on her hand glittered unexpectedly in the light of the fire, drawing her attention, and Carolina frowned. It seemed to beckon her, to warn her. . . .

The shadowed memory invaded her mind again. She saw the meadow filled with flowers. She saw a strong male form in dark relief against the brilliance of the sun. The shadows masked his features but she heard the deep sound of his voice and felt the touch of his hands. He moved and the shadows lightened. His face grew clearer and her heart began a rapid pounding. She could almost see . . .

Suddenly trembling wildly, Carolina covered her eyes. She didn't want to see! She didn't want to feel the uncertainty that was slipping over her, to feel fear returning. She didn't want to remember that he . . . that he . . .

Forcing the memory away, Carolina thought of the three weeks she had spent in this wilderness and the peace Drake had afforded her. She thought of the unknown that awaited her beyond the cabin door, of the world she could not remember, and she wondered . . . She wondered what the next few days would bring.

Fourteen

Miriam looked around her small cabin, her gaze critical as she unconsciously smoothed her tightly bound hair and adjusted her apron. The furnishings were sparse. A few things had survived Jonas's and her trip West, such as the bone china teapot with matching cups and saucers that were prominently displayed on the rather crude side table in the corner, the china bowl and pitcher on the nightstand beside her bed, and the large, black stove with its spacious oven that she had refused to leave behind. Otherwise, the cabin was rather primitive, no better or worse than the others in a town where gold was king. There was one exception, however. *Her* cabin was spotlessly clean.

Miriam's thin lips moved into a smile. Jonas had always prided himself on having the cleanest home of all his friends — he had told her that often — and in the time since he had gone on to his reward ahead of her, she had made certain that it remained that way. It was her memorial to Jonas — to his smile, to his pride in her, and to their love for each other.

Dr. Fitz's grizzled countenance chose that moment to pop before her mind's eye and Miriam's smile faded. She sniffed with annoyance. That old fool could live in a pig sty without a word of complaint, she was sure. His office, with the single room behind it that was his living quarters was proof of that. She'd never seen a more disorganized, cluttered, unclean —

Miriam sighed. It had been almost two weeks since she had visited Jerome in his office. She disliked admitting it, but the tonic he had prescribed, not to mention the sleeping draught, seemed to have done the trick. She now slept dreamlessly and well. There had been an immediate improvement in her appetite, and her energy level had risen along with it. She was almost her old self.

Miriam looked at the table and the dried apples she had prepared earlier. She told herself that her sudden inclination to bake had nothing to do with the fact that Jerome had once told her that he was a slave to apple pie and could not resist it. Miriam shrugged. Well, even if it did, she certainly owed Jerome a debt of gratitude. She hadn't been at all pleasant that day in his office, and she regretted some of the things she had said . . . especially since Jerome seemed to be holding a *grudge*.

There could be no other explanation for the way Jerome had been avoiding her, even taking to dropping off his laundry at her back door with a note. Granted, she had not been at home when he had called the first time, but she could swear that he hadn't even knocked the second time. And the truth be known, she missed their conversations. Their divergent points of view were a true challenge to her active mind, even if she often found his liberal attitude infuriating. She had felt at a loss without that challenge, almost as if she were stagnating within these four, pristine, *lonely* walls.

Oh, it wasn't as if she didn't have friends! Mary McCullough, the dear saint of a woman that she was, stopped by at least once a day to talk, even though her conversation usually centered around her husband's latest trip into the hills and the strike she knew was forthcoming. And there was Josie Whalen . . . Of course Josie had little time for conversation with nine young ones hanging on her skirt. A familiar sadness touched Miriam's mind. She envied Josie the joy of her children. She wondered why some women had child after child while others were unsuccessful in conceiving a single one.

Miriam frowned. She supposed she could ask Jerome that question. The only problem was that knowing Jerome as she did, she was wary of his response.

Shrugging again, Miriam scooped out a handful of her precious flour and added a bit of lard. She had always been told that her pastry was as light as a feather, and the truth be known, she missed cooking for a man. The thought touched Miriam's mind that she missed other things as well. . . . Miriam felt herself flush. Well, she was a normal, healthy woman, wasn't she? She had loved Jonas dearly and had enjoyed their intimacies. She missed being held in his strong arms. She missed the comfort of his warm body flush against hers, and she missed knowing, as the sound of his heavy, steady breathing echoed in their room at night, that she meant more to him than any other woman in the world.

The memory of Jerome's knees rubbing accidentally against hers that day in the office returned unexpectedly, and Miriam recalled the discomfort she had experienced — the tightening in the pit of her stomach, and the way her heart had begun pounding. Miriam sniffed again. She also remembered that Jerome had jumped away from her as if he had been bitten by a snake. Things had not been the same between them since.

The disquiet that thought evoked more than she was prepared to face, Miriam cleared her mind as her hands worked the delicate pastry. Drawing the cooked pie out of the oven a short time later, she was unable to avoid her uneasy thoughts any longer. Whatever the problem between Jerome and her, she intended to clarify it and put it to rest. He was due to pick up his laundry today. He couldn't possibly have a clean shirt left — not that he had allowed that problem to bother him in the past. But he would come. Miriam smiled. She would just leave the door open so the aroma of her pie would filter out into the yard and let nature take its course.

Extremely pleased with herself, Miriam walked to the door and opened it wide. Pausing there, she surveyed the street, her expression freezing as she caught sight of Jerome's untidy figure walking purposefully up the street. She recognized the determination in his gait and she groaned aloud, calling herself all kinds of a fool. No one had to tell her where he was heading or whom he was going to see. An apple pie, no matter how warm and golden brown, no matter the thought with which it had been prepared, could not compete with the music, the laughter, the inane frivolity and cheap liquor at the Nugget. Miriam gave a harsh laugh. What did Jerome need with apple pie when a *tart* like Rosie Blake was available?

Miriam's clever pun afforded her little amusement as Doc slipped through the doors of the Nugget and out of sight. Her spirits plummeted. Turning back into her cabin, she slammed the door behind her, furious at the tear that slipped down her pale cheek. She was a fool, a pathetic, lonely old fool, that's what she was! An apple pie could not compete with smiling red lips wreathed in a come-hither smile. She had always known that. So why did it hurt so badly?

Doc Fitz was thirsty. It annoyed him to realize he'd been more thirsty than usual of late. It annoyed him even more to know that he'd been getting less pleasure than usual out of quenching that thirst. Somewhere in the back of his mind a voice nagged, but Doc carefully avoided acknowledging it. Damn it all, he was forty-nine years old! He deserved good food, good drink, and good times. He had earned them! So why had the joy of it all begun slipping?

Doc pushed his way through the door of the Nugget and headed for the bar without a sideward glance. Could his present mood have to do with the two young fellas who had been brought to his office that morning, mortally wounded? They couldn't have been more than twenty-two or -three, either of them, but however old they'd been, they had been fools. Everybody knew that the only safety through Indian country lay in being a part of a well-armed wagon train. Scouts riding out front and guards at the rear—that was the only safe ticket to arriving in Deadwood in one piece. As for stragglers, even when attached to well-armed trains . . . well, they signed their own death warrants, just like that big Swede had a week earlier. These two boys, however . . .

Refusing to continue with that thought, Doc slapped his palm on the bar. "Barney, put a drink down in front of me and make it fast! I've got a deep thirst to quench!"

Aware of the balding bartender's assessing glance, Doc snatched up the glass the moment it hit the bar in front of him and downed it in a gulp. He gasped, belched, and opened his mouth to speak again, only to have the sober-faced bartender steal his thunder.

"I know . . . 'Keep 'em comin', Barney!' "

Unamused by the fellow's imitation of his gravelly tones, Doc glared. He watched as his glass was again filled to brimming, his thoughts drifting despite himself.

Those two boys . . . He shuddered. One had had a bullet through his gullet. He hadn't lived five minutes after reaching his office. The other had had a bullet in the chest. That poor fella had lived for three, long, pain-filled hours. He had turned his back on his office and headed here the minute the undertaker had taken them away. He remembered too clearly for comfort the agony in the one fella's blue eyes as he had gasped, "Indians . . . Billy and me didn't see 'em until it was too late."

Yes, too late. . . .

Futility rose inside Doc, sending his blood surging up to his face in a hot flush. Killing . . . killing . . . When was the land going to be wiped free of bloodshed? When was it all going to be over and done?

Downing the second glass of red-eye in a gulp, Doc paused a moment to catch his breath, then tapped the bar. Barney refilled his glass without a word, allowing him to reflect on his own silent question. When was the bloodshed going to be over and done? He remembered asking himself the same question during the war, when he had watched countless young men die in the same way those two had a short time earlier. He hadn't had the answer then and he didn't have it now. He stared down into the amber liquid in his glass. And he wasn't too far gone yet to realize that he wouldn't find the answer there.

Lifting his hat from his head, Doc ran an unsteady hand through his uncombed hair. The world seemed to go from one bloody war to another, and here he was in the middle of it all again! He shook his head as the warming effects of the liquor began to blur the images of the two young men in his mind, allowing his thoughts to drift. But it seemed that even if he wasn't involved in out-and-out bloodshed, he was smack in the middle of a war of another kind.

Miriam Higgins's thin, unsmiling face came to mind, and

173

Doc unconsciously shivered again. The woman haunted him! It had been two long weeks since Miriam's visit to his office, and he still hadn't fully recovered from the shock of his reaction to her that day. He looked at the amber liquid swaying gently in the glass in front of him, wondering — not for the first time — if it had begun eating at his brain. His grizzled countenance dropped into familiar downward lines. Well, he wasn't a doctor for nothing, and if there was one thing that he had learned over the years was that there was a time when a man had to take his medicine and like it. Following that line of thought, he had prescribed his own treatment shortly after Miriam had left that day, which was to stay away from the sour-faced old widow until he had his head on straight again. He had followed that treatment, but the truth was that he hadn't been able to like himself while doing it.

Doc raised his glass and surprised himself by taking a sip and returning the glass, still half filled, to the bar. He hadn't liked himself too much . . . that was putting it mildly. He had felt like a yellow dog sneaking up to the widow's house and dropping his laundry outside when she wasn't looking! He had felt even worse when he had picked up his neatly bound clean laundry the same way, following that procedure for two weeks until he now felt like a complete ass. He doubted he would be able to stand his own medicine — or himself — another day if he continued his cowardly actions.

So he had stopped to ask himself — what was he afraid of, anyway? Miriam Higgins could freeze a man with a glance and reduce him to a squirming worm with a few, well-chosen, acidic sentences. If allowed to speak as much as a paragraph, she could totally emasculate even the strongest of men. He knew all that, but the knowledge had never frightened him before. The trouble was that she hadn't done any of those things to him that day in his office. She had done much worse. She had allowed her mask to slip. In doing so, she had touched his heart. . . .

He had admitted it! So there! He had glimpsed what lay beneath that dour façade the widow sported for all to see. He had seen past the campaigner, the woman-with-a-cause exterior that was so much a part of her. He had seen past the caustic, vitriolic, unyielding woman to a lonely woman who was suffering – and in a moment of sheer insanity, he had actually longed to comfort her!

But worst of all was the *way* he had longed to comfort her! Damn!

Doc downed the last of his drink and tapped the polished surface of the bar again. A flicker of movement at the rear of the saloon caught his eye interrupting his thoughts as the door opened and Rosie Blake stood momentarily framed there. The roar of the busy saloon dimmed for a moment, and he knew why. It was because the men who had chanced to be looking in that direction when she appeared had been struck momentarily speechless at the sight of her. He knew that group included him as well.

Doc took a deep breath. There wasn't anything in the world more beautiful than Rosie in that black lace dress that showed just enough of her to tease a man into salivating and left enough to his imagination to make him wish for more – even an old geezer like himself. But the truth was that he valued Rosie's friendship and loved her dearly. He knew she felt the same. What was more, he worried about her. His gaze blurring, he squinted in her direction. Suddenly recognizing the look in her eye, he silently groaned. Rosie worried about him as well, although he sometimes wished she didn't, and damned if this wasn't one of those times!

Doc forced a smile as Rosie walked directly toward him. He couldn't help a flush of pride knowing that this beautiful young woman had chosen him, above all the other young and good-looking men in the saloon, to greet first, but he knew Rosie had her reasons. Some of the reasons he knew, but others . . .

Rosie drew closer. As always, the sight of her beauty up close knocked all other thoughts from Doc's mind.

Rosie slid into the spot next to Doc at the bar. She looked into his bloodshot eyes, her heart warming as she smiled.

"I can see you got a jump on me this afternoon, Doc, honey."

"I'd say I have." Doc smiled, his unshaven face wrinkling into familiar lines that gave Rosie pleasure. "But I'm not so

175

far gone that I can't appreciate what I'm seein'. Rosie, honey, you look good enough to eat."

"Doc, the things you say!" Rosie winked boldly.

"Rosie, you'd better watch yourself. You just took ten years off my life with that wink. I start gettin' dangerous about the age of thirty-five."

"Why, Doc, you can't fool me. You aren't much more than thirty-five years old at any time."

Doc laughed. She knew he was truly amused at her flirtatiousness even though he knew it was part of the game. His eyes actually twinkled as he whispered, "That's right, honey, and Jim Clark's old dog doesn't have fleas. . . ."

"Oh, Doc . . ." Rosie leaned against his side as Doc's smile widened. "You're such a clever fella."

"As for you, Rosie, you're—"

But Rosie was no longer listening as her attention was caught by Tag's appearance in the saloon doorway. She suddenly realized that she had been hungry for the sight of Tag, and that her heart still did that little flip-flop in her chest when she saw him. She supposed it always would.

The lump of sadness inside Rosie expanded as Tag removed his hat and catching her eye, nodded in greeting before walking toward his usual table in the rear. He had followed that same procedure for the past two weeks, and she had watched with bittersweet amusement as the bar girls took turns making a play for Tag, only to be turned down politely. She had heard, however, that Tag had not been turning down Ella O'Connor's advances as well. She wondered if it was true. She wondered if he cared for Ella, and she wondered what she could do about it if he did.

"You don't look so good, Rosie. . . ."

Rosie turned back to Doc, her smiling mask carefully in place. "Is that your medical opinion, Doc?"

Doc raised his brow. "When are you goin' to tell me what's goin' on between Tag and you? You know what everybody's been sayin'. . . Is it true? I'm having trouble figurin' it out."

"That depends on what you've been hearin'."

"I've been hearin' that you and Tag are through for good . . . but from the way that fella looks at you sometimes . . ."

176

Rosie's smile stiffened. "Tag and I are good friends, Doc. That hasn't changed. We're business partners, and that hasn't changed."

Doc squinted. "So you're tellin' me what *has* changed is that—"

"—Is that Tag is a free man when it comes to pickin' another lady for his personal life."

"Hummm. . . ."

Rosie felt Doc's assessing gaze down to her toes. The old fella wasn't as drunk as she had first thought, and for a minute she wished he was. She'd get nothing past him in his present condition, and she wasn't sure if she was up to giving him the answers he seemed determined to get. If she wasn't so fond of the old coot . . .

Doc continued speculatively, "Does that mean you're free and on the lookout, too, Rosie?" Not allowing her time to respond, he continued more softly, "Because I've been seein' a lot of fellas tryin' to get close to you in the past couple of weeks, but I haven't seen you give any one of them special attention."

"Maybe that's because I already got myself another fella, Doc. Did you ever think of that?"

"That so?" Doc looked genuinely surprised. He glanced around the room. "I haven't seen anybody in particular hangin' around you of late . . ." He grinned and wiggled his hairy eyebrows. ". . . except me. You wouldn't be meanin' me, would you, darlin'?"

Rosie laughed aloud, then leaned closer. "You old rascal, of course I don't mean you."

Doc's face fell. "Rosie, you're breakin' my heart. . . ."

Rosie leaned closer to Doc and rubbed her cheek affectionately against his. She grimaced as his whiskers abraded her tender skin, but her expression sobered as she spoke. "I've got me a new man. That's the truth, Doc, but you don't know him. You're goin' to like him, though, when you meet him, and that should be soon because he's due to come back here to take me away with him. You're goin' to like him because he's a lot like you. He's good and kind . . . and he cares about me."

Suddenly sober, Doc slid his arm around Rosie's shoulders

and drew her closer. She realized he was attempting to afford them a little more privacy, and she leaned against him, unable to resist quipping, "Doc, honey, you're givin' me goose bumps."

"Am I now?" Doc's smile was gentle, "When all I was tryin' to do was to find out more about this fella of yours. I want you to be happy, Rosie."

Rosie was again as serious as he. "There's only one fella who can do that for me, Doc, and *he's* the one."

Doc looked unconvinced, and Rosie felt his concern. "Who is this mystery man of yours, honey, and how long have you known him? If I don't know him, that means he hasn't been in Deadwood lately."

"Don't worry about me, Doc." Rosie stroked Doc's cheek. "I've known this fella long enough to make it count. He saved my life, you know. . . ."

"He did. . . ."

"Yeah, when I was back home." For a moment the pain returned, but Rosie shook it off. "And he told me that he wanted more than anythin' in the world to make everythin' right for me again, but he couldn't . . . not then."

"Why not, darlin'?"

"Because he was married." When Doc stiffened, Rosie hastened to add, "He didn't cheat on his wife or anythin', Doc. He wouldn't do that—and I loved him more because of it." Rosie swallowed against the thickness in her throat. "He just took me in his arms and held me, and he told me he'd fix it so's nobody would hurt me again. He meant what he said, too. . . ." Rosie felt the heat of tears beneath her eyelids at the memory. "He beat up . . ." Her voice broke, forcing her to pause.

Doc took up in her stead. "But that was a long time ago, darlin'." Rosie could see Doc fought to understand her sketchy tale. "You said it was before you left home. That was . . . how many years was it? And if he has a wife—"

"Years don't make any difference, don't you see, Doc? Besides, he isn't married anymore, and the last time I saw him—"

"When was that last time, Rosie?"

"About four months ago."

"Oh."

Rosie could tell Doc was confused. She saw him glance uncertainly at Tag, and she shrugged.

"Tag knew about my fella from the first. I thought he understood how I felt, but I found out he didn't and . . ." Rosie paused to swallow. "I didn't want to hurt him anymore, Doc, so I called it off between us."

"Rosie, honey . . ." Doc tightened his arm around her shoulder and pulled her closer, "Are you sure you didn't make a mistake? Tag's a gentleman. He'll take good care of you."

"So will my fella."

"You're sure?"

"I'm sure."

"Just as long as you are. . . . But will you promise me somethin', darlin'?" When Rosie nodded, Doc continued, "If anythin' should go wrong, you'll come to me, won't you?" He smiled, so gently that Rosie thought her heart would melt. "If I don't have the medicine you need to fix things, I promise you I'll find it."

"All right."

Realizing the danger in her rapidly deteriorating emotional state, Rosie swallowed thickly, then forced herself to draw back from Doc's casual embrace. With the aid of long practice, she reaffixed her professional façade, but Doc seemed unimpressed with her effort. Determined to wipe the concern from his expression, she leaned toward him and boldly kissed the tip of his impressive nose. She laughed aloud at the bright red smudge she had left there.

"You're not goin' to wipe my kiss off now, are you? I'll take it as a personal insult if you do."

Doc glanced into the bar mirror and laughed, despite himself. Rosie's spirits rose as he responded, "Not on your life, Rosie, honey. Not on your life."

Rosie walked away from the bar to the sound of Bart Mellon's roar of laughter as Doc turned toward him. Turning back, she spoke loudly enough for her voice to be heard clearly over the guffaws at the bar.

"You leave that man alone, you hear? He's a special

179

fella, and he has *my* brand on him."

Doc preened himself to the tune of low hoots and whistles as Rosie turned unconsciously toward Tag to see he had not even raised his head from the game. The relief that swelled inside Rosie was tinged with pain. It appeared that Tag had effectively wiped himself free of her brand at last. With a tug at her heart, she wished him well.

Determination in her gaze, Ella O'Connor pushed open the door of the Grubstake Saloon and stepped out onto the street. She shivered as the chill evening air touched the exposed flesh of her bulging bosom and drew her satin wrap around her.

"Where do you think you're goin', Ella?"

Ella turned back to the jowled face of Gus Ricks. She despised his small, piglike eyes and the way they ate greedily at her. It was that gaze and those fat, moist hands, always pawing her, that had driven her out of the saloon.

"I'm gettin' a little fresh air, that's what I'm doin'. You got any objections?"

"Yeah, I got objections!" Gus's voice turned to a snarl. "I don't pay you to get fresh air. I got a room full of customers to entertain."

"I've been treatin' them customers real good tonight, and you know it, so don't you go complainin' to me! I'll come back in when I'm good and ready!"

Gus took an aggressive step toward her and Ella forced herself not to cringe. Gus liked to throw his weight around, and there was plenty of that — about three hundred pounds of it packed onto his average frame. He liked a lot of other things, too, things that he didn't want to pay for and things that she couldn't stomach — especially with him. She had paid her dues when she had first started at the Grubstake, but she wasn't about to cater to him anymore. She had seen what happened when Gus lost his temper, but she knew if she backed down now, she'd never get out from under his thumb — that same thumb that had seemed to be screwing down harder and harder on her of late.

180

And she knew why.

"Gettin' real independent lately, ain't you?" Ella controlled a grimace of distaste as Gus motioned toward the saloon down the street. His sagging chins swayed in a way that revolted her as he sneered, "It couldn't be because you've taken up with a fancy man, could it?"

"If you're callin' Tag Willis a 'fancy man,' well, I'd say you're right. He sure enough is . . . damned fancy, but I don't see you complainin' when he comes in here and spends all his free time settin' up drinks at the bar." Ella punctuated her statement with a sharp nod. "And this here woman's the one who got him to come to the Grubstake in the first place."

"I don't need Tag Willis in my place!" Gus's ruddy complexion darkened apoplectically. "And if you're not careful, I'm goin' to show you that I don't need you, either."

"Oh, you got me workin' here because you're full of charity, is that it, Gus?" Ella laughed sharply. "You know damned well that half the boys inside come here because of me — because nobody shows them a good time like me!"

Gus advanced another step, but Ella stood her ground as he rasped, "You're pushin' me too far, Ella. You're goin' to find yourself out on the street if you ain't careful."

"And you're goin' to find yourself without one of your best girls, too, if you don't keep your greasy hands off me while I'm workin'!" The true cause of her fury surfacing for the first time, Ella continued shrilly, "You don't throw no special weight with me just 'cause you're the boss! I get *paid* for givin' a fella a good time and I — "

"But you're givin' it for free to Willis, ain't you?" Uncaring that their argument was beginning to attract the attention of passersby on the street despite the din coming from the crowded saloon, Gus grabbed her arm roughly. "Ain't you! I'm the boss here. What's that fella got that I ain't?"

Tearing her arm from his grasp, Ella responded in a hiss, "You're foolin', ain't you? Hell, you must be blind!"

Gus's beefy arm snaked out with a pounding slap that snapped Ella's head to the side, and she stumbled a few steps backward. Grasping a nearby wooden support, she steadied herself, hardly able to see out of her right eye for the pain throbbing there as she rasped, "All right, you filthy pig! Have it your way! I'm out on the street all right, because the only way you'd get me back inside that pen of yours would be to drag me." And as Gus took another aggressive step toward her, she rasped, "And I'm tellin' you now, you'll hit me again at the price of your life. I got me a man who'll protect me. . . ."

Gus's advance halted abruptly. The fleshy bulge hanging over his straining belt jiggled ludicrously as he shook his head. "Tag Willis ain't your man. He's just usin' you. . . ."

Ella forced a grin that caused her physical pain as she silently cursed the overweight lecher still challenging her. "Yeah, and he's usin' me real well. He ain't about to let me go, so you take yourself right back inside and tell all them lonesome fellas that you just lost your best saloon girl, and if they want to find her, they can come to the Nugget, 'cause that's where I'll be!"

Turning, her step more unsteady than she chose to reveal, Ella started down the street. The hairs on the back of her long, slender neck prickling, she waited for the sound of Gus's heavy step behind her, but it didn't come. Not daring to look back, she made steady progress along the crowded walk.

Then it came to her. Damned fool that she was, she had burned her bridges behind her, all the while knowing that everything Gus had said was true! Tag had been hanging around her for the past two weeks, but she knew it wasn't for the reason she had led everyone to believe. His heart was aching, and he needed somebody who wasn't a part of the Nugget to keep his mind off his pain.

The truth be known, she considered it a privilege to do that for Tag. He had been real generous to her, and he was a true gentleman, something she hadn't seen much of in her life. It was her own personal humiliation — one that she dared tell no one for the embarrassment it caused her — that Tag and she were nothing more than *friends*.

Friends. . . . Ella's stomach squeezed tight and she felt an accompanying tightness in her groin. And all the while, every night when Tag had sat in the Grubstake beside her and looked at her with those eyes as black as coal, when he had spoken to her in that voice as smooth as velvet, she had wanted to show him how good she could be for him. She had known from the start she could be better for him than that uppity slut who had turned him out. But she had also known she needed to bide her time.

Well, she had gone and done it, now. She couldn't bide her time any longer. She had no choice but to go to the Nugget. The Nugget and the Grubstake were the best saloons in town, and she had determined long ago that she would never take a step down when a step up was possible.

Ella paused abruptly, aware that the Nugget was only a few yards away. She stared at the gaudily painted false front of the building, realizing that the fact that it had any paint at all was unusual. That had been Tag's work, setting it a step above the others, just as he was a step above all the other men in town. Ella swallowed convulsively as tension knotted in her throat. Maybe . . . just maybe, he would take her a step up as well.

Pressing a hand against her throbbing cheek, realizing she could do little about the swelling there, Ella raised her chin. She adjusted the neckline of her dress, aware that her greatest attributes were liberally exposed to be appraised and appreciated. She then licked her fingers and ran them against the upward sweep of her bright yellow hair. She lowered her shawl and tied it tightly around her hips so the full curve of her backside was clearly outlined. She wanted the fellas inside to look up when she entered, and she wanted them to keep looking.

Satisfied that they would do just that, Ella did as she had always done when her situation became dire. She took a deep breath, raised her chin, and stepped through the doorway of the nearest saloon.

"I'll be damned, will you look at that!"

Willie Simpson's low comment made little impression on Tag. He had developed a new method of survival during the past two weeks, which he employed stringently during the hours he spent in the Nugget. That method had saved his life, and had saved the lives of several of the men who had thought

183

his departure from Rosie's bed had made a place for them in his stead.

Tag gripped the cards in his hand tighter. The past two weeks had been a living hell from which he was uncertain he would ever escape. Watching Rosie in the saloon every night, knowing that he need get his fill of her with covert glances when the full warmth of her body and heart had formerly been his to savor, had been torment beyond belief. But her body and heart were his no longer. Her heart belonged to a phantom the young, abused Rosie had created in her mind. He knew if she had her way, her body would belong to her dream man as well.

He had not been deceiving Rosie, however, when he had told her that her phantom lover would never be hers. He believed what he had said so intensely that he had not been able to set Rosie adrift in a town where she would be forced to sell the only commodity available to her to make her way. He told himself that Rosie would come to her senses when the fellow returned. She would finally see the man for what he was, and when she did, he would be there to pick up the pieces.

The problem was that he knew it would not be as simple as that. Rosie had lived her fantasy for too many years. It had become a part of her and he feared — he worried to the point of desperation — that with that part of her gone forever, there would not be enough of his Rosie left to go on.

Tag briefly closed his eyes, then purposefully reshuffled the cards in his hand. He had remained cordial to Rosie during their estrangement, but it had not been easy. Bart Mellon didn't know how close he had come to having his roving eyes blackened when he looked at Rosie the way he did. His partner, Tim Ryan, didn't realize that he had been flirting with death on more than one occasion, and that scruffy, lecherous old man, Doc Fitz . . . Tag's lip twitched. The only thing that had saved Doc when he had had his arm wrapped around Rosie so tightly earlier had been his certainty that Rosie *liked* the old man . . . really liked him for some reason he had never been able to comprehend. He only hoped the old fool knew that there were limits to Rosie's affections for him. If he didn't, Tag was prepared to make *sure* he understood . . .

even though he was certain Rosie would never forgive him.

So, he had employed his method. He had come into the saloon each night and kept his head down. He seldom looked up at Rosie, most especially when she was busy entertaining the men at the bar. He had made one mistake in looking up earlier. The sight of her leaning against Doc's side and smiling into his wrinkled old face had tied his stomach into knots that would be with him all night long.

When that method failed, which had been more often than not during the past two weeks, he went to see Ella. Without a speck of conceit, Tag realized he could have any woman he wanted in the Nugget with just a snap of his fingers. One by one, the girls had made certain they made that fact clear, but none of them had struck a chord within him. Ella O'Connor was different. She was the right medicine, making him conscious of the fact that she wanted him without asking anything in return. She was easy to talk to and good company, if you didn't mind a woman who flaunted the obvious. He genuinely liked her and she—

"Do you believe it, she's comin' this way! Didn't anybody tell her that she's in the wrong saloon?"

Breaking his own cardinal rule, Tag looked up. Startled at the physical manifestation of the woman he had been thinking of only a moment earlier, he remained motionless as Ella approached, appraising the attributes that made her the most popular girl in the Grubstake. She was a big woman, all right, at least eight inches over five feet tall, and she had the womanly proportions to match. He flicked an unappreciative glance over her bright orange dress. The color was wrong for her. It clashed with the brassy shade of her hair. The neckline was too low, and that fringed shawl she had tied around her hips . . . well, he supposed it served its purpose. There wasn't a fellow in the saloon who wasn't following the sway of that backside as she came closer. Dressed as she was, Ella appeared to be a cheap piece of merchandise. He supposed some would say her appearance suited her, but he knew better. Ella's heart was big and open. She liked him and he liked her, and whatever she was doing here tonight he was certain he would—

Tag stood abruptly as Ella neared. He took a step forward and took her arm, the sudden iciness inside him spreading to his tone as he questioned sharply, "What happened to your face?"

Surprising him, Ella flushed. She raised a hand to her cheek, shrugged, and forced a laugh. "I ran into a bedpost?"

The ice thickened. "I asked you what happened."

"What difference does it make what happened?" Ella's voice rose shrilly. Recognizing the signs, Tag motioned Sheila toward him. Ignoring the inquisitive glances of the players at the table as Sheila assumed his seat, he took Ella's arm and ushered her toward an empty spot in the rear of the room. He seated her and sat beside her, his stomach churning. Ella's eye was almost closed and a great blue bruise was already beginning to spread on her cheek. It hurt him to look at her.

He repeated, "Your face . . ."

Ella's eyes filled unexpectedly. "If I ran into a bedpost, or if the bedpost ran into me, it don't really make much difference, does it?"

Surprising himself with the vehemence of his reply, Tag stated flatly, "It does to me."

Ella covered his hand with hers. "I guess I shouldn't have expected anythin' different from you, and I thank you for carin', but I didn't come here to make trouble, Tag. I don't *want* trouble."

"Who did this to you?"

Ella stiffened. "I won't tell you."

Frustration sent a hot flush of color to Tag's face. "Tell me, Ella, and I'll make sure it doesn't happen again."

Ella's lips twitched revealingly, and he realized for the first time that she was not as cool about the whole affair as she would have him believe. That realization frustrated him further as she struggled to speak.

"Tag, please . . ." She gave a short laugh. "I don't usually say please to a man, but I will to you. I want you to forget about my face. It don't mean nothin' . . . but if you really want to help me, there's something you can do."

Tag rolled his hand around hers, a switch of positions that left his hand on top as he gripped hers tightly. "Name it."

186

"You can give me a job."

Tag's momentary hesitation brought the brightness of tears back to Ella's eyes. She shrugged. "Sorry I asked."

She attempted to stand, but he wouldn't let her.

"Wait a minute, Ella."

"No."

"Ella, the job's yours, anytime you want it, but I want to know why you're leaving the Grubstake."

Tag watched the play of emotions across Ella's heavily painted face. He saw the indecision there.

"If I tell you, will you promise me that there won't be no trouble?"

"No trouble."

Ella gritted her teeth revealingly. "That greasy pig, Gus." She gave another hard laugh. "He thinks he's irresistible. Well, he ain't, and I don't work no place where I ain't got freedom of choice." Ella's expression changed to one of sudden earnestness. "I'm a hard worker, Tag. You won't be sorry you hired me."

"I know. Come on." Feeling a furious urgency building inside him, Tag drew Ella to her feet. He escorted her to the bar. Strangely, for the first time, the ache did not soar to life inside him as Rosie turned her beautiful face up to his.

"Rosie, you know Ella, don't you?" And at Rosie's nod, "She's working for us now. Get her settled. I'm going out for a while."

"Tag, you promised!"

Ella's strong hand clutched his arm, but he gently dislodged it. "I know. Don't worry. I don't break promises."

Turning on his heel, Tag strode toward the door. His fury building, he did not see the glances the two women exchanged. Neither did he see the look in their eyes that said they would never be friends.

Gus Ricks was fuming. Bumping roughly into a short brunette saloon girl as he turned back into the Grubstake, he nearly knocked her from her feet, but no apology was forthcoming. Instead, he snapped a biting remark that raised eyebrows as he turned toward the bar.

Damned whores! They were all alike, playing free and easy when they came looking for a job, and then getting high and mighty when they thought they had a little backing.

Gus slipped behind the bar and grabbed the nearest bottle. He sloshed the liquor into a glass and downed it in a gulp, his eyes returning to the doorway. Ella would be back. He had only to be patient and she'd come crawling back, begging for her job. He'd have her just where he wanted her then.

Suddenly realizing that he was salivating, Gus rubbed the back of his hand against his mouth, then poured himself another drink. He had known this was coming the minute Ella had walked through the doorway with Tag Willis in tow two weeks earlier. Looking at her, you'd have thought that she had the king of England on her arm, she was that proud. He hadn't had to look at the other girls to see their reactions. All he had had to do was to listen to the buzzing that ensued.

It had made him sick, the fawning they did over Willis. It had made him just as sick to see Willis's pretense, with his impeccable manners and courtesy toward women who weren't worth a damn any day of the week. But he had let it go on. He had told himself that Willis's money was as good as anybody else's, but there were some things that he hadn't been willing to tolerate.

The look on Ella's face when he had grabbed her plump backside earlier in the evening had been the last straw. She hadn't always been so standoffish — no, not Ella. He remembered when all he had to do was crook his finger and she came running. That had been in the beginning, just after she had arrived on a wagon train with a few other girls, her pocketbook and stomach empty. He had made good use of her then. It was his privilege. After all, girls like her were a dime a dozen and she was lucky to be working with a roof over her head and food in her stomach. She had *him* to thank for that.

Admittedly, he had been watching Ella more closely since she had started seeing Willis. He had wanted to make sure she remembered her place — that she knew who the boss was. He hadn't liked that haughty look he had seen growing in her eye, and he knew now he had been right all along.

His eyes still on the entrance of the saloon, Gus waited. It had been all he could do not to grab that haughty bitch by her hair and drag her back inside, but he had known instinctively that would be the wrong way to handle things. Ella had been right in one thing that she had said. She had too many regulars in the Grubstake . . . too many fellas that came there especially to see her. He couldn't afford the possibility of offending them. But he'd get her. . . . She'd be back, and then he'd—

Pausing, his glass halfway to his lips, Gus gulped audibly as Tag Willis suddenly appeared in the saloon doorway. It wasn't the size of the man that had stopped his thoughts dead, or surprise at Willis's appearance there when his own saloon was normally at full steam. It was the look on Willis's face . . . a rage that turned his dark eyes to stone. It took only a moment to realize that *he* was the cause of the man's fury, and in that second, Gus's heart almost stopped.

Gus took a step back, searching frantically for the gun he kept under the bar. He saw it then, at the far end. He made a quick rush toward it, only to be caught a few inches short of his mark as Tag reached across the bar and grasped him by his damp shirtfront.

"Don't try it, Ricks!"

"Let go of me!" Gus attempted to dislodge Willis's grip, but his hands were shaking too hard to be effective. He shouted to his bartender. "Leon! Throw Willis out of here!"

It didn't take longer than a moment to see that Leon had no more desire to tangle with the furious gambler than he had himself. Realizing he had no choice, Gus brassed it out.

"What do you want, Willis?"

"From you?" Willis's gaze was scathing. "Nothing! But I've got something to say to you, and I'm only going to say it once. Ella won't be coming back here. Stay away from her. If you ever touch her again . . ." Willis paused, his voice dropping to a lethal whisper, ". . . you're a dead man." He waited a moment and hissed, "Are you listening, Ricks?"

Gus could not stop shaking. He knew Willis's reputation—never a harsh word when a softly spoken word would do—backed up with a backbone of solid steel. He could feel the

189

bite of that steel as he scraped, "I . . . I don't want her back. . . ."

"I know what you want, Ricks . . . but you won't be getting it from Ella anymore." Willis twisted his shirt tighter, choking him, raising his massive bulk to his toes. "Do you hear me, Ricks?"

Gus struggled to swallow. He nodded.

"I can't hear you."

"I said yes. . . ."

"I still can't hear you. . . ."

"I said yes! Yes, I heard you!"

Willis's gaze turned to a black, burning heat as he prompted, "I heard you . . . *Mister Willis* . . ."

Gus could feel himself pale. "I . . . I heard you, Mister Willis."

Falling back against the sideboard as Willis released him unexpectedly, Gus heard the shattering of glass, but he was conscious only of Willis's whisper as he leaned closer and spoke again. "Don't forget what I said. If you do, you won't live to regret it."

Gus was still staring at Willis's back as it disappeared through the doorway. Snapping abruptly out of his fear-induced paralysis, he looked around him. He saw the faces turning away from him. He heard the snickers and the whispered jokes. He felt the contempt and a deep, burning humiliation that he could fight in only one way.

Forcing a smile, he raised his voice above the muted din around him. "I guess it's time for a drink. Step up to the bar, boys! This round's on the house!"

Gus watched the surge toward the bar, knowing the scene his customers had witnessed would dim in their memory with the aid of the liquor they swilled. He growled a sharp command to his bartender.

"Keep 'em happy and keep the drinks comin', but remember. Only *one* round's on the house."

Sliding his massive bulk out from behind the bar, Gus started toward the rear of the saloon. He wiped a heavy arm across his brow and upper lip, aware that his shirt was soaked with perspiration. The sudden realization that the dampness

190

marking his trousers had no relation at all to perspiration was a further humiliation he could not shed.

A deep, consuming rage slowly filling the void where fear had reigned only moments earlier, Gus slipped through the rear door and slammed it closed behind him. His fleshy chest heaving, he gasped a low oath.

"I'll get Tag Willis for this—him and that blond whore. No matter how long it takes, I'll get him . . ."

Rosie stood at the far end of the bar, a few feet from the spot where Tag had dropped Ella O'Connor in her lap a short time earlier. Ella hadn't stayed with her any longer than it had taken for her to explain the system at the Nugget. Her instructions had been a waste of time in any case. Ella didn't need explanations. She was an old hand at the game—wise beyond her years, and hard as nails.

Rosie followed Ella's progress across the saloon, watching as she stopped beside a tall stranger who stood observing the poker game. She saw Ella lean against the fellow and smile with a few whispered words. The fellow nodded and continued to watch the game, and Ella remained there as well. Rosie's lips tightened. Ella was faking it. She was resting . . . biding her time . . . looking busy without getting herself involved. She had tried that tack herself when she had first started in the business, but she had soon learned that she couldn't get away with it for long.

Rosie's startlingly blue eyes narrowed. She knew what *her* reason had been for faking it those many years ago. Shyness . . . concealed fear . . . uncertainty. . . . But Ella didn't suffer from any of those maladies. No, that woman had something else in mind.

Suddenly realizing that she was shaking, Rosie picked up her glass and emptied it in a gulp, her lips separating in a gasping breath as the liquid burned all the way down. She had needed that. She glanced toward the door, remembering the look on Tag's face before he had left. He had been furious because someone had struck Ella. The bold hussy had probably deserved it, but she hadn't missed the opportunity to play that bruised face for all she could get. And she had gone to the right man for sympathy.

A hard, gnawing ache started inside Rosie. Tag had always protected *her*. He had always kept *her* safe, and she realized only now how much she had taken for granted these last few years. In her heart she knew Tag still protected her, that he always would, but it somehow hurt to know that he had included another woman under that special sphere of protection — especially a woman like Ella O'Connor.

Rosie paused in that thought. Some would say that Ella and she were of the same breed, but Rosie knew differently. She had heard about Ella, and she knew Ella was using Tag for all she could get. Rosie never had. She had always tried to give as much as she had received with Tag. When that had been no longer possible, she had put an end to things between them.

Regretting that move for the first time, Rosie felt her throat fill with suppressed tears. She had turned Tag free, only to throw him into the arms of a grasping hussy who didn't know the meaning of fidelity . . . who would use Tag and then break his heart — if she didn't get him killed first. . . .

As if in answer to her disturbed thoughts, Tag walked back through the doorway and Rosie's heart gave a sharp leap. Her spirits plummeting a moment later, she watched as he approached Ella and took her arm. She saw the concern in his expression, and she fought true tears as Tag touched Ella's bruised cheek gently.

Taking a deep breath, Rosie walked directly toward Tag. She saw his eyes narrow with scrutiny as she approached. Her heart ached at the lack of love in his gaze as she halted at his side and placed her hand lightly on his arm.

"Are you all right, Tag?"

Tag's dark eyes held hers in silence for a long moment before he nodded. "I'm all right now, Rosie." He forced a smile. "Ella has a fondness for poker. I was just telling her that we've been looking for another dealer."

Rosie knew what was coming and her heart stopped. She made herself respond, "What about Sheila? She — "

"Sheila doesn't want to deal full time. Ella does . . . don't you, Ella."

Tag turned toward the buxom blonde. Rosie felt her animosity rise as Ella pretended surprise, then nodded a silent assent. Tag turned back to Rosie.

"Ella won't be working with the rest of the girls at the bar, so you won't have to keep an eye on her after all."

Returning to the bar minutes later, aware that Ella remained at Tag's side, Rosie struggled to retain her smile. So Tag was taking his protection of Ella a step farther. It hadn't taken him long to put the years they had shared behind him.

Rosie reached the bar as Oscar struck up a gay tune at the piano, and submitting to impulse, she touched Bart Mellon's arm.

"Dance with me, Bart? I'm in a mood for some fun tonight."

"Then you've come to the right man, honey!"

Laughing aloud as Bart gave her a mad whirl, Rosie retired to the inner core of herself, seeing the face of the man who would take her away from the Nugget, from Tag, and from the need to smile when her heart was breaking.

Rosie's laughter sounded momentarily over the energetic tune being hammered out on the much abused piano in the corner of the room, jerking Tag's attention from Ella's smiling face. The sight of Rosie dancing in Bart Mellon's arms was a knife that cut deeply, and his heart bled. Unable to look away, he recalled the look in Rosie's eyes a few minutes earlier. He knew what she had been thinking—that he hadn't taken long to replace her in his bed. She had then wondered how long it would be before he would replace her completely. The answer to that question he knew Rosie would never ask was simple.

Never.

Rosie laughed again as Bart took the opportunity to draw her closer, and Tag wondered if the wound inside him would bleed him dry.

"Tag, about dealing . . ."

Tag's head snapped back toward Ella at the sound of her

voice. He could not manage a smile as he replied, "You told me a few nights ago that you had always wanted to be a dealer. I figured this was your chance. I hope you don't mind my putting you on the spot."

Ella hesitated uncharacteristically, her eyes meeting his with an honesty that Tag knew instinctively was not feigned. "Yeah, but you'd be takin' a chance with me dealin'. I'm not experienced. I might lose you a lot of money." She swallowed. "But I *can* make you a lot of money if I work at my regular job."

"Do you *want* to work at your regular job? If you do, it's all right with me."

Ella blinked. He saw the effort she expended to retain her control as tears filled her eyes. She whispered hoarsely, "Only with you."

"Ella . . ." Tag's voice was gentle. "You'll never know how much I appreciate that, but I'm a one-woman man . . . and you know who that woman is. . . ."

"Yeah, I know."

"Do you still want the job dealing?"

"Yes."

"It's done, then." Turning the conversation onto safer ground, Tag looked more closely at Ella's rapidly darkening bruise. "Maybe you should have a doctor look at your eye. Doc Fitz is at the bar."

Ella's response was direct. "That old coot? No thanks!"

Tag laughed aloud and squeezed Ella's arm. "I always knew you were smart. Well, let's get going on your training. I'll take over the poker table and you can watch. Sheila's heart's not in the game. In a few days you'll be dealing rings around her."

Assuming his seat a few minutes later, Tag dealt the cards, his own words ringing in his ears. *Sheila's heart's not in the game.* . . . The truth was that his wasn't in the game either, not anymore. He knew where his heart lay—under the heel of a beautiful woman who cared about him too much to let him love her.

Standing behind Tag, looking down on his smooth, neatly

194

trimmed hair as his head turned this way and that in quick assessment of the table, Ella barely resisted the urge to touch him. In the space of two short weeks, this man had done more for her than anyone else had done in her entire life, and he had done it all without asking anything in return. She had made her offer and had been turned down in the most gentle of ways.

I'm a one-woman man, Ella . . . and you know who that woman is. . . .

Yeah, she knew, and she was glad. Because she knew how things would stand when that one-woman man was hers. And he would be.

Ella took a step closer to the table with a silent vow. He would be.

Fifteen

The everlasting hills . . . that phrase rebounded in Carolina's mind as the laboring donkey underneath her struggled up yet another rise. The animal stumbled, righting itself with its next step as Drake's head snapped around toward her from his position riding directly ahead. She saw his concern. It was a concern for her and her child that had not lapsed since that first day three weeks earlier, when for all intents and purposes she, as well as her child, had been born.

In an attempt to escape that thought, Carolina turned her attention to the babe who slept so soundly in the swinglike contraption Drake had made for her. A blanket carefully wrapped around her as she rocked gently to and fro with the rhythm of the animal's plodding gait, she appeared as content as if she were in her mother's arms.

Wishing that she were able to feel that same sense of security, Carolina surveyed the landscape through which they traveled. An eerie discomfort again prickled up her spine. Majestic pines stood tall and proud all around them, towering far above their heads. In the profound silence broken only by the sounds of their steady progress, they had traveled up and down over rough divides where the sun seldom shone and the hush was almost oppressive. Afforded a clear view at the top of the last rise, she had seen that the growth of pine was endless, covering low-lying ranges of hills that extended in great rolling waves to a horizon where other ranges lay like cloud banks against the sky. The panorama had been vast in scope, somehow unearthly or primeval, appearing untouched by the hand of man, but Carolina knew the greatest threat lurking in this wilderness was human in kind.

Realization of that danger had grown stronger in her mind as the hours had lengthened and the journey had progressed from early morning when it had been barely light, to late afternoon. They had stopped only long enough to answer nature's call, to eat, and to allow Carolina to feed her daughter, and with each passing hour her physical discomfort became more acute.

The donkey took another jolting step, and Carolina suppressed a groan. She was uncertain, but she suspected that she had never ridden astride before. She was painfully sure, however, that her legs were not responding well to being stretched around the sides of the barrel-bellied animal underneath her for hours on end, and that her back and arms were now stiffly frozen into the posture of maintaining a firm grip on the saddle.

The donkey stumbled again and the groan Carolina had suppressed for so long escaped her lips. Drake turned immediately toward her and Carolina felt her face flush under his assessing gaze.

"What's the matter?"

"Nothing. . . ."

Carolina avoided his eye. She did not see the flicker that moved across his face the moment before he drew up his horse and dismounted. At her side, he hesitated only a moment before grasping her by the waist and lifting her to the ground.

To Carolina's humiliation, her aching legs refused to support her and she grasped Drake for support. Her flush darkened as Drake muttered under his breath and abruptly scooped her from her feet to carry her toward a leafy bower beside the trail. He sat her on a log, his voice gruff as he commanded, "Stay here."

"But Suzannah . . ."

"I'll get her."

Her sleeping daughter in her arms a few minutes later, Carolina watched as Drake secured their mounts and turned back toward her.

"This is as good a place as any to stay for the night."

Carolina looked around her. The foliage was thick and the cover of trees dense, but she was suddenly acutely aware of their vulnerability. A tremor shook her as she realized they would be unshielded from watching eyes during the night . . . from any possible attack that might occur . . . from the painted face that haunted her in the darkness.

"Carolina . . ."

Crouching beside Carolina, Drake took Suzannah from her arms and lay the child gently on the ground. He then grasped Carolina's trembling shoulders.

"Don't do that, Carolina. Don't drift away."

"I wasn't." Carolina swallowed in an attempt to regain control, drawing heavily from Drake's strength. "It was just that face that keeps haunting me. . . ."

"Forget that face."

Drake's lips twitched as he brushed a straying wisp back from her cheek. She recognized the gesture as an unconscious sign of Drake's concern. As it always did, it fortified her where words failed, dimming the image of the demons of the dark awaiting her.

Carolina looked up at the sky visible through the heavy cover of trees overhead. The light of day was rapidly fading. Her heart began pounding.

"I . . . I think we should build a fire before it gets too dark."

"No fire."

"Why?" She paused. "Indians? But we haven't seen any sign of them . . . have we?"

"No."

Something about the haste of Drake's response sent a chill crawling up Carolina's spine. She glanced toward Suzannah, still sleeping soundly, then looked back at him, her gaze searching.

"Are the Indians going to find us, Drake? Are they going to finish what they started three weeks ago? When we close our eyes tonight will they come up—"

"Carolina, listen to me. There's no reason to be afraid. I said I'd take you to Deadwood, and I will. Nobody's goin' to hurt you or Suzannah. We're as safe here as we were in the cabin."

When she was unable to force words of response past her frozen throat, Drake shook her gently. "Do you trust me?"

Carolina managed a stiff nod.

"Then you know I won't let anythin' happen to you — either of you." When she still did not respond, Drake urged softly, "Talk to me, Carolina."

With a supreme effort, Carolina rasped, "Yes."

"Yes what?"

"Yes . . . I believe you."

Drake searched her expression a moment longer. "Good." Releasing her, he drew himself to his feet. "Stay there and rest. I'll set up camp."

Carolina attempted to stand. "I'll help."

"No."

"I want to help."

"What you want to do, and what you're able to do, are two different things. You're as stiff as a board."

"I'll be all right."

"That's right, you will be. I'll take care of that, but in the meantime you'll do what I say and sit there."

The muscles in her calves taking that moment to tighten spasmodically, Carolina did not respond. Taking her silence for assent, Drake turned toward his horse. Suddenly realizing that she was helpless to do anything else, Carolina watched him stride smoothly away.

Silently cursing himself a short time later, Drake mounded the dried leaves scattered on the ground and spread the heavy fur robe on top of them. The comfort that meager padding would afford during the night was negligible, but he was determined to do whatever he could to spare Carolina additional pain.

It was his fault. . . . Drake assessed Carolina covertly, noting the rigidity with which she turned her head, and her unconscious grimace as she leaned over to change her daughter's wet linens. He should've realized that Carolina was still weak . . . that the ordeal she had suffered would have left any woman poorly equipped to handle an extended journey such as theirs, even an accomplished rider — which Carolina was not. Her obvious inexperience with the fundamentals of riding astride had caused her more than common discomfort, which he knew she concealed for his sake. She was paying the price of her inexperience and he knew she had not yet seen the worst of it.

That thought heavy on his mind, Drake returned to the donkey contentedly chewing at some nearby foliage and removed the blankets secured on his back. The problem was that he had spent little time thinking about Carolina's discomfort after they had ridden over the first rise and he had seen Indian signs everywhere he had looked. He now believed that his decision to avoid the usual trail might have saved their lives. Several times during the afternoon they had passed spots where groups of five or six unshod horses had paused to wait. It hadn't taken more than a quick examination of the tracks while Carolina was otherwise involved during their infrequent stops to see that the Indian ponies had departed hastily from those points of cover. Drake suspected he knew what had prompted their haste, and he wondered how many other travelers had failed to reach their destinations because of them.

Drake looked back at Carolina. He recalled their departure from the cabin in the early morning hours. He remembered that there had been little rejoicing in that departure, either from Carolina or himself. He knew the reason for Carolina's feelings was apprehension at facing a world she could not remember. As for himself, he was at a loss. He was anxious to be relieved of responsibility for Carolina and the baby's care — *wasn't he?*

Drake's gaze lingered on Carolina, the fall of her hair against her smooth cheek, her small features, her petite stature. His stomach tightened. Carolina and her child were a hindrance, an impediment in the path of the goal toward which he had looked for seven long years. That goal had become a part of him, a reason for existence when there had been no other motivation to go on. He could not — he *would* not — allow anyone or anything to stand in his way of realizing it.

But still . . .

Unable to bear Carolina's obviously pained movements another moment, Drake strode toward the sleeping robe where she sat and dropped the blankets there. Kneeling beside her, he took the clean linens from her hands and proceeded to change Suzannah. He scooped the babe up into his arms a moment later.

"I'll take care of her if you need a few minutes of privacy."

Carolina flushed at his outspokenness, even as she attempted to stand. She had difficulty accomplishing that simple task, and he stood abruptly, holding the babe in one arm as he eased her to her feet. Carolina attempted to conceal her pain as she walked away but the effort was useless, and the long, difficult ride ahead of them loomed more darkly in Drake's mind.

Carolina stepped out of sight into the foliage, and the small, down-covered head lying against Drake's chest bobbed up. Bright blue eyes attempted to scrutinize him, but the babe's neck, seeming no thicker than a bird's, was not up to the task and he cupped it with his palm, supporting the effort.

A smile tugged at his mouth as Suzannah's gaze fixed on his face. The babe's fine lips moved as if attempting to speak, and the total innocence of the small bit of humanity so vulnerable in his arms, brought an unexpected lump to his throat. He knew she probably saw no more than a shadowed outline, but he was somehow certain that she recognized that outline, just as she did his voice and his touch. She was such a bright little thing and he knew that she . . .

Bringing his thoughts to an abrupt halt, Drake was suddenly disgusted with the depth of his personal fantasy. The child was *three weeks old*. . . . He was endowing her with abilities she could not possibly possess and with attachments impossible for her to make. He was playing a fool's game, just as he had done in his past. He'd be damned if he would continue.

Waiting only until Carolina was once again seated on the sleeping robe, Drake returned the child to her. He paused, despite himself, as Suzannah began rooting against her breast

201

and Carolina's hands moved to the buttons on her dress. Catching himself, Drake forced himself to look away.

The sound of the babe's suckling done a short time later, Drake glanced back at Carolina. He had felt her gaze follow him as he had worked around the camp. He knew that she had assessed the single fur robe and the two blankets piled upon it that he intended them to share. There had been no need to gauge her reaction. She trusted him.

Drake sat back on his heels and reached for the sack of food nearby. Why shouldn't Carolina trust him? He had spent three weeks with her, caring for her and for her child, nursing her through sickness and through dark, fear-filled nights when he had often feared he might lose her to the demons in her mind. The only trouble with that thinking was that he wasn't being honest with her. He was telling her what she wanted to hear, that they would be in Deadwood by this time tomorrow night, when he knew that there was a distinct possibility that they might never reach their destination at all.

Withdrawing his knife from the sheath at his waist, Drake sliced the beef jerky in long, narrow strips. They would have meager fare tonight, but he knew Carolina would not complain. He almost wished she would, so he might be distracted from the harsh realities they faced in this insecure spot, and the uncertainties in his own mind that caused him even more discomfort.

Drake glanced unconsciously at Carolina. She was holding Suzannah, rocking her as the babe's eyes fluttered slowly closed, and in that moment he was certain that he had never seen a more beautiful sight than this woman and child.

Angry with his straying thoughts, Drake spoke abruptly. "It'll soon be dark. We'll bed down early so we can be up at first light."

No response—but then Drake hadn't really expected one. He watched as Carolina slowly lowered the sleeping babe to the robe beside her, then looked up at him. Countless unspoken questions were reflected in her eyes, but he knew she would not ask them—not now while she was straining so hard to present a brave façade. He also knew that as daylight waned, her façade would begin to crumble.

Sitting beside her a moment later, Drake handed Carolina a piece of jerky which she obediently raised to her lips. He saw the determination with which she bit into the stiff meat and jerked off a bite-size piece. She chewed without speaking, accepting the canteen when he passed it to her and drinking deeply. His heart reacted strangely when he fitted his mouth over the spot from where she had drunk a moment earlier. So distracted was he that he was unprepared when Carolina finally spoke.

"You saw signs of Indians today, didn't you, Drake."

Drake paused in response to the question that was not really a question at all, causing Carolina to press quietly, "Please, Drake, tell me the truth. I know you don't want to frighten me, but I want to know."

"What do you want me to tell you?" Drake knew he could deceive her no longer. "Do you want me to tell you I saw signs of Indians — because I did — most of the way. Do you want me to tell you they could come upon us at any time — because they could. Do you want me to tell you that we wouldn't stand a chance if a band of five or six of them attacked us — because we probably wouldn't."

Carolina began trembling and Drake cursed aloud, then continued, "You said you wanted to know the truth, but another part of that truth is that we've managed to avoid the Indians all day. From what I can tell, they're ahead of us, possibly by a day or so. They aren't expectin' anybody to be travelin' this trail through the mountains. If I'm right, they'll be watchin' the regular wagon train route to Deadwood." Drake paused, his eyes searching Carolina's frightened expression. "And the rest of that truth is that we're probably in the clear for today, because those Indians, if they're still around here, are probably doin' just what we're doin' right now, beddin' down for the night."

Carolina stared at him, appearing unable to respond, and Drake was suddenly disgusted with his inept handling of the situation. He continued softly, "If you're wantin' the *complete* truth, I'll have to say somethin' else, too. We've got the upper hand in this whole thing, with us knowin' the Indians are around and them not knowin' we're behind them. We've got just one more day and we'll be in Deadwood, and I don't think those Indians have a chance of gettin' us before then."

Carolina still did not respond and Drake shook her gently. "Did you hear what I said?"

Drake held his breath, awaiting her response.

"I heard you."

Drake dropped his hands from Carolina's arms. "All right. Suzannah's already asleep and we should be doin' the same, but first we have to do somethin' about your stiffness or you won't even be able to mount up tomorrow."

"I . . . I'm all right." Carolina attempted a smile. "I'll be fine."

"The truth, remember?"

"The truth?" Carolina hesitated, then attempted a smile as she continued more softly, "I hurt like the devil."

Carolina's wobbly smile touching him more than he was prepared to admit, Drake ordered curtly, "Lie down on your stomach. I'll take care of it."

Danger . . . the approaching night . . . the threat she had seen behind every bush during those brief moments while Drake had disclosed their true situation . . . floated away on waves of intense, almost debilitating pleasure. Lying on the blanket as Drake had directed, Carolina moved under the strong, kneading pressure of his hands as he slid his fingers up into her hair to massage her scalp for long, sensuous moments. She was silent as he returned his soothing attentions to her neck, her upper arms, her shoulder blades. She bit back an ecstatic groan as he sought out the fine tracing of her spine through the material of her dress and trailed his magic down the aching column to eliminate each point of pressure there. He curved his hands around her rib cage with gentle, healing strokes. She felt his fingers sink into the curve of her waist, then slide onto her hips to massage them gently. He cupped her buttocks in his hands, squeezing them, kneading them, affording her a relief from an ache that had seemed to penetrate to the bone. But he was not satisfied to stop there. He attacked her thighs with firm, mending strokes, rubbing the muscles with a circular motion until she thought she might burst with the pleasure of it. The cramping in her calves yielded to his touch, then the soreness in her ankles and feet. Carolina groaned aloud as Drake worked the delicate arches, then each individual toe with relentless thoroughness.

When she thought she could stand no more, Drake slid his hands upward, sweeping the tender flesh that he had tended so well minutes earlier. With a swift intake of breath, Carolina realized he was starting all over again. . . .

His brow perspired despite the chill in the air, Drake slid his hands back up into the silky warmth of Carolina's hair. With a firm, even touch that belied the rioting emotions inside him, he massaged her scalp, wondering at the fine torture he had set himself as he prepared to repeat his ministrations of a few minutes earlier. His breathing became labored as he traced Carolina's hairline with his fingertips, the curve of her ear, the slender column of her throat with a steady, healing pressure. He told himself that his attentions were merely a continuation of the care which had begun when Carolina had first entered his life those few weeks ago. He told himself as his hands followed a course to the base of her neck, then her back and upper arms that he felt nothing but the pleasure of relieving Carolina's pain.

Sweeping aside a few straying strands of hair, Drake traced again the straight line of Carolina's spine, exerting gentle pressure as he sensed the greatest points of pain. Carolina reacted sharply to his touch, and he whispered a soft reassurance as he stroked that pain, cajoled it, coaxed its retreat, his heart beginning a slow pounding as Carolina arched her back gently in response.

Carolina's eyes were closed, her lips parted, her breathing was accelerated. His touch was affording her a relief close to pleasure, and Drake recognized those same emotions were rising inside himself. A familiar warning sounded in his mind as his fingers curved around her rib cage, grazing her rounded breasts, and Drake caught his breath. His hesitation momentary, he continued his healing pursuits to rediscover the minute curve of her waist. His fingers moved warmly against the fragile bones there and he wondered again at the supreme delicacy of this small woman as he curved his palms around her narrow hips.

Sliding his hands to Carolina's buttocks, Drake soothed the tight muscles there with gentle pressure. Suddenly aware that his hands were trembling, Drake looked up again at Carolina. His heart beat faster. There was no resistance to his touch. She trusted him.

Trust. . . .

Drake slid his hands down her thighs, carefully avoiding the warm delta between. He patiently worked the strained muscles, eliminated the tension in her slender calves and ankles, caressed the high arch of her foot, denying an inexplicable desire to touch it with his lips. Then her small, even toes. . . .

Damn!

Drake drew himself abruptly to his feet as Carolina turned over and sat up with a new ease of movement. Not realizing that his eyes were as cold as ice, he saw her gaze become puzzled as he stated flatly, "Get yourself ready for sleep. I'll be back in a few minutes."

Inexplicably furious, Drake stomped off into the fringe of trees.

The sounds of night were all around her . . . frighteningly close. Stretching out her hand, Carolina touched the wooden box Drake had brought with them from the cabin. In it Suzannah lay secure and warm. She heard the sound of her babe's steady breathing, but even that comforting sound afforded her little relief. With the fur robe beneath her and the blanket covering her, she was protected against the chill of the night, but her comfort stopped there.

Refusing to turn, to reassure herself with the sight of Drake's presence where he lay no more than a foot away, Carolina knew that the distance Drake had abruptly put between them could more accurately be measured in miles. Swallowing against the fear that grew greater with every flickering shadow, with every rustling branch, Carolina felt the strain of that distance tremble inside her.

In the absence of light, the forest had become an intimidating force for which she was ill prepared. Sounds magnified by her apprehension roared loudly in her ears. Damp, musky smells took on almost human scents. Anxiety played cruel tricks of ever expanding proportion on her mind as Carolina tasted the bitter essence of a fear—a taste she could not expel. She dared not close her eyes. She knew what awaited her in sleep.

Carolina swallowed the tears that rose in her throat. Drake . . . so strong . . . so close . . . *so angry*. . . . She was uncertain what she had done to arouse that anger. She wanted to turn to him, to feel the concern in his touch. She wanted him to relieve her mind of fear just as he had relieved her body of pain with the magic of that touch. He seemed to know her body and her mind better than she knew them herself, and she silently wished—

But it was senseless to wish. Drake had withdrawn from her and returned to the hard, cold Drake. The change was so great, so complete that she had begun wondering as the shadows closed around them if the Drake she had believed him to be had been merely a figment of her need.

That question more than she could bear to face, Carolina forced herself to close her eyes. She strove for a sleep that would ward off the fiends of the dark, but it would not come. She fought to escape the echo of gunshots and pounding hoofbeats that grew gradually louder within her mind, the cries of pain, and the moans of the dying. The sounds became more shrill, more vivid, and suddenly before her closed eyelids was the terrifying, painted grimace she had come to know so well. Cringing under the relentless scrutiny of the image's dark, soulless eyes as it hovered over her, Carolina saw the war ax poised and glinting. She heard the swish of air as the blade descended. She felt the searing pain, tasted the blood . . . !

"Carolina. . . ."

Frozen with fear, Carolina did not respond to Drake's whisper. Nor did she react when his arm slipped around her waist from behind, as he drew her back against him and curved his body around hers, cupping her with its warmth. She felt the hard, male length of him pressed against her back as Drake draped his blanket over her to enclose her in a silent cocoon of safety, but she remained motionless.

"Go to sleep."

Drake's voice was warm, caring, almost loving. . . .

Life returned slowly to Carolina's frozen limbs and mind. Not trusting her voice, knowing she could not convey with words the emotions that filled her heart, Carolina covered Drake's hand with hers where his palm lay flat and warm under her breasts. And she prayed, as she had never prayed before, that Drake would never leave her.

Dawn flickered through the cover of trees as Carolina awakened. Realizing abruptly that she was alone, she reached out to grasp the wooden box where Suzannah lay. The warmth of her child was reassuring as she touched her.

Squinting into the semilight, Carolina looked around the glade for a sign of Drake. She realized that the animals were already saddled, loaded, and ready to go just as Drake stepped into sight. His hat shielded his eyes from her gaze as he looked at her. A night's growth of beard shadowed his chin, but that shadow somehow added to the reassurance of his presence as a slow warmth spread through her.

Drake spoke without preamble.

"It's time to go. I've already changed Suzannah. You can nurse her when she wakes up. We'll eat on the trail."

Carolina nodded and threw back the blanket. She slipped on her shoes and rose quickly, her sore muscles protesting as she shrugged into the jacket that lay nearby and walked into the foliage. Emerging a moment later, she walked toward the donkey standing placidly nearby, noting for the first time that the animal's back was heavily loaded.

Drake spoke in response to her confusion.

"You'll be ridin' with me today."

Not waiting for her response, Drake lifted her up onto his horse. Taking a moment to carefully affix Suzannah's hand-made swing to the saddle, Drake swung himself up behind her.

Carolina swallowed against the intense contentment that shot through her as Drake drew her back against his chest and spurred his horse into motion. Drake's body supporting her . . . his chin brushing her hair . . . his arms circling her. . . . Carolina breathed deeply of the reassuring scent of him, realizing she was as close to happiness at this moment in Drake's arms as she could remember ever being.

Drake glanced at the sky overhead, noting the position of the brilliant sun that had flickered through the cover of trees throughout the day. It was approaching midafternoon. Drake adjusted Carolina's weight against his chest. She was sleeping and he was grateful for that. She had lain silently awake much of the previous night. He had sensed her fear and had tried desperately to ignore it. He had told himself that Carolina need face down her fears sooner or later. That thought had been echoing in his mind when he had seen her jump with fright and begin trembling. A part of him had agreed with that insistent voice in his mind even as his arm had reached out of its own volition to draw her close.

Drake closed his eyes briefly, remembering the sensation of drawing Carolina into his arms. He had heard himself whisper a soft reassurance as he had drawn her back against him, and he remembered telling himself that this was little enough to do for this slight young woman who had suffered so much. But he had known even then that his rationale was based on self-deception. He had consoled Carolina because he wanted to console her. He held her close because he wanted to hold her close, and when she had accepted him and clutched his arm closer, his feelings had fluctuated between intense pleasure and a strange kind of pain.

He had not made a conscious decision to have Carolina and her babe ride with him that day, but it had taken only a moment, long enough for Carolina's slight weight to settle against him after he had slipped into the saddle behind her, for him to realize that he had wanted it that way for myriad reasons he did not care to examine. Now, hours later, he knew no other manner of travel had been truly feasible. Carolina was already exhausted, and the most dangerous part of the journey lay ahead of them.

Carolina turned, adjusting her head against his shoulder in sleep. Drake felt a flush of heat as her lips brushed his throat. Her eyelids fluttered and he wondered what it would be like to feel those thick, stubby lashes under his lips. Her sweet breath fanned his face and Drake unconsciously separated his lips to taste it. It tasted warm and pure, the way he had known it would, and he wondered—

A soft snorting, then a restless whimper cut into Drake's dangerous thoughts. He glanced toward the sack swing swaying gently against the saddle. He felt Carolina stir the moment before she spoke.

"I think Suzannah's hungry."

Grateful for the opportune interruption of his straying thoughts, Drake responded gruffly, "So am I. We'll stop for a few minutes. We're going to have to come out into the open soon in order to follow the wagon train trail and we'll need our wits about us."

Carolina stiffened, but she did not respond as he reined his horse and dismounted.

The light of day was rapidly failing. A knot of apprehension thickened in Carolina's throat as they rounded another curve in the trail. Looking up at Drake, Carolina did not dare ask the question foremost in her mind. They had returned to the saddle after a quick stop hours earlier, but the journey had not gone well after that. Uncertain whether she had conveyed her anxiety to her small daughter, she had struggled with the babe's unusual fretfulness for the greater part of the time since.

Forced to hold the babe most of the way in order to stop her wailing, Carolina had had no need to ask Drake how dangerous the child's crying could be. In her anxiety, she was certain that there was not an Indian within fifty miles who had not been alerted to their position by Suzannah's persistent wails.

210

They had stopped time and again in an attempt to alleviate Suzannah's discomfort and Carolina realized the danger in that situation as well. More frequent stops, valuable time lost, and night would soon be upon them.

A shudder ran down Carolina's spine as she anticipated the approaching darkness. Drake's arms tightened around her spontaneously.

She could feel Drake shift his position behind her and she knew he was attempting to see her face, but she kept it steadfastly forward.

"You're wastin' your time tryin' to hide from me, Carolina." Drake's voice softened. "Don't worry, we'll get to Deadwood tonight."

"How can we possibly make it?" Suddenly realizing she had revealed her anxiety with those few words, Carolina continued with a supreme attempt at control, "It'll be dark soon and there's no sign of civilization in sight."

"I never said you could classify Deadwood as civilization. Deadwood's a minin' camp, just like any other. It's a gatherin' spot for every adventurer, prospector, gambler — whatever dregs society has left over. It's not civilized because it isn't a part of the United States and there's no law. It's nothin' much more than an open sore on the landscape any way you look at it."

"But it's safe from Indian attack." Carolina regretted her words as soon as she spoke them.

"Yes, it's safe." Drake turned to scan the lengthening shadows. "We'll be there in a few hours."

"A few hours. . . ." Carolina looked down at a fretting Suzannah. Her arms were numb and her back was breaking.

Drake spoke again as if in answer to her thoughts. "But first we have to do something about Suzannah."

Drawing his horse to a halt, Drake dismounted and took Suzannah from Carolina's arms. Carolina waited for him to help her down as well but he did not. Instead, he walked off the trail, drawing the horse and donkey behind him. Securing the reins on a tree, he disappeared into a thicket with Suzannah in his arms. Puzzled, Carolina was about to attempt dismounting by herself when she heard Drake's soft baritone. . . .

"Oh, Suzannah, don't you cry for me, for I come from Alabama with a banjo on my knee. . . ."

Drake's soft serenade continued and Carolina was uncertain whether to laugh or cry. Hard, cold Drake . . . the recluse . . . the man who never smiled. . . . She swallowed against the emotion that filled her throat. No one had ever been kinder to her than Drake. She knew that instinctively. She also knew that no one had ever shown her as much love, and that she had never cared for anyone the way she cared for Drake. She—

A sound in the brush and Drake emerged with her sleeping daughter in his arms, his expression as close to a smile as Carolina had ever seen it. Suzannah safely in her sack moments later, Drake mounted and spurred his horse into motion.

Drake's arms were around her again, and Carolina relaxed. All was suddenly well with her world. They would be all right. She was sure of it. As sure as she was that it was meant to be the three of them . . . together.

The road ahead of them was clearly lit by a great silver moon as the small party plodded steadily onward. Drake scanned the shadows around them, a gradual excitement pervading his senses. He knew how close they were. . . .

Carolina's head bobbed against his chest and Drake carefully tucked her more firmly into the circle of his arms. Carolina had taken all she could stand. It had not been easy for her to face her fears, to ignore watchful eyes she imagined behind every rock and tree. He had silently shared her anxiety as he had passed the long hours of the day scouring the horizon for a sign of movement. They had been lucky, incredibly so, but he supposed it was time that Carolina had a bit of luck.

Urging his mount up the final rise, Drake felt a new anticipation building inside him. Secure in their safety at last when he reached the crest of the hill, he paused to look down on the wood and canvas town below them. Lit by hundreds of kerosene lamps, the ugly declivities wrought by the hand of man shrouded in shadows, Deadwood assumed the guise of a

212

fairyland from above, a twinkling oasis of sounds and safety — a harbor of dreams — but Drake knew nothing could be farther from the truth. He had visited Deadwood only once, but he knew that there were more dreams lost than realized in that merciless camp. He knew the streets teemed with life of an impermanent kind, that the only certainty there lay in the certainty of change, that most of the men now laughing and joking in the dozens of saloons and dens of vice would have left town, one way or another, within a few months' time, and that their would be no shortage of others to take there place. Residents of Deadwood were there for the short term, not unlike himself. The land had little value to those men, aside from the quick riches it would yield, and they cared little for those who would follow after them.

But under the cover of night, few of these things were apparent to the naked eye. For a few short hours each day, Deadwood could be viewed as a place of beauty. Carolina had had too little beauty in her life of late. He didn't want her to miss this.

"Wake up, Carolina," Drake whispered gently. "We made it to Deadwood. Wake up, darlin'."

Unconscious of the endearment that had slipped past his lips, Drake watched as Carolina stirred and raised her head. He waited for the gasp of realization that was not long in coming as she looked down on the camp below them. He felt the sudden pounding of her heart and he heard the thickness in her voice as she rasped, "It's beautiful. . . ."

"Only from up here." Suddenly uncomfortable with the myriad feelings assaulting him, Drake forced a more casual tone. "We're going down now. The trail is steep. Hold on tight to Suzannah's swing. Are you ready?"

Carolina's heart began beating a rapid tattoo against the arm he had wrapped around her waist as he started the slow descent into town. He was guiding his mount cautiously when he suddenly realized that it was all over. He had delivered Carolina to Deadwood as he had promised. His responsibility for her ended there. After some rest, he could go back to his cabin and resume his work without interruption, and by the end of the summer he, like so many other men here, would leave the Black Hills and everything in it behind him.

Carolina turned to look up into his face. Her expression was a mixture of excitement and trepidation that touched his heart with a supreme sadness. Like Carolina, he had been waiting for this moment for three, long, wearying weeks.

. . . So why did he feel so damned bad?

Sixteen

Doc cursed aloud, moving just quickly enough to dodge the barrel that bounced and rolled down the street past him. Hoots and whistles sounded from the passing throng in approval of his fancy footwork as the barrel came to rest with a bang, rocking the support of a nearby awninged storefront. Doc held his breath, realizing a moment later as the wooden awning shuddered into stillness that it was stronger than it looked — good news for the evening revelers standing beneath it too numbed by red-eye to have the inclination to move.

Looking back into the street, Doc spotted the real villain in the affair. A lopsided freight wagon, with its separated wheel lying splintered in a nearby rut, dominated the center of the thoroughfare, its contents, including several more barrels similar to the one that had nearly claimed him, sprawled across the muddy road. He grimaced with disgust, realizing that traffic would be held up for hours until the wagon was fixed and the freight reloaded. Of course, that meant soaring tempers and in all likelihood, a few more customers for his doctoring skills — just when he had thought he was through for the day.

Congestion, the chronic affliction of Deadwood's streets, always appeared to be worse at night, and he supposed for good reason. Night brought all the rats out of their holes — human rats, that was, who had spent the daylight hours with a pick and shovel in their hands or with their backs bent over a gold pan. Doc looked around him, assessing the best way to pass through the jammed walkways where men of all

215

shapes and sizes watched the melee of cracking whips, shouted curses, protesting oxen, and agitated travelers unable to move past the uncommon impediment. Most onlookers appeared highly amused by the frantic antics of the bull whacker and the stalled wagons behind him, but few seemed inclined to lend a helping hand. Doc shrugged. He supposed he shouldn't have expected anything different.

Deciding on the best course of action, Doc pressed boldly into the crowded walkway, elbows clearing the way past two swaying prospectors engaged in a deep conversation. Judging from their slurring tones, neither would remember a word that was said the next day, but he supposed it made little difference. There wasn't much of any consequence to talk about in this town that appeared to have been forgotten by both God and country.

Doc paused to consider that thought. He must've had a worse day than usual if he was thinking about the Almighty's influence on this town in general, and in his life in particular. He shook his head. Either that or he was getting old.

"Hi there, Doc, you old reprobate!"

Doc turned at the sound of his name, his grimace spreading into a smile at first sight of Heddy LaRue's paint-bedaubed face. Heddy was a right good hand with the brush. He knew that was so because he had seen her without that makeup when she had been taken ill some weeks back, and he had decided then that paint covered a multitude of sins in many ways. With her small eyes heavily darkened with kohl and her sallow complexion brightened with two bright spots of red strategically placed, not to mention those ruby red lips with the dress to match, she looked considerably better than she had that day. As a matter of fact, she looked downright inviting! Doc puffed up his chest and tipped his hat.

"Hello there, Heddy! You're lookin' mighty fetchin' tonight."

"Well, you come over to the Melodeon and visit me tonight, and I'll show you just how fetchin' I can be." Heddy took a step closer and rubbed herself against him. "I got a real fondness for professional men, you know—especially gray-haired professional men with *experienced* hands."

216

Doc laughed. "Oh, yeah, my hands are experienced, all right."

Heddy bumped against him suggestively. "Doc, you're makin' my heart go pitty-pat. Don't you disappoint me, hear? I'll be waitin' for you."

Turning away with a batting of her eyes, Heddy continued down the street. Grinning, Doc did the same. He had always liked Heddy. Not many women were able to take him by surprise in more intimate exchanges, but he remembered the last time he had visited Heddy's room nonprofessionally. She had been real happy to see him, and she had done more than surprise him when she had gotten down on all fours and . . .

Well, that was another story . . . one he wasn't ready to go over now. He had other fish to fry.

Stepping through the doorway of O'Neil's General Store, Doc advanced toward the counter, taking the time to scan the numerous display tables he passed en route. They were spread with all manner of merchandise from ribbons to pickaxes, all in a disarray that was almost dizzying, but he knew what he wanted.

"Hello there, Doc." Bob O'Neil's deep voice did not suit his skinny frame. Nor did it suit his pale complexion and rapidly thinning blond hair, as he continued with his usual comradely fashion, "I've missed you here of late. Where've you been doin' your shoppin'—at George Brown's broken-down shack?"

"What kind of a question is that? You know I only patronize my friends, Bobby boy."

Bob rolled his eyes and laughed aloud. "All right, what're you after?"

"Well, it's this way. I'm after somethin' special for a friend's birthday."

Bob wiggled his pale brows. "Is that a *girl*friend or just an old pal?"

Doc sniffed. "I don't have any *old pals* in this town. It's for a *lady*."

"Well we ain't got many of them in Deadwood, either. Where'd you find her?"

Doc felt a moment's true annoyance. "I'd say you'd better

217

quit while you're ahead, if I were you, *Bobby boy,* or I might tell you that I find that comment downright insultin' to my friend and ask you to mind your own business."

Bob blinked, appearing to realize that he had struck a nerve, and Doc realized that he probably wondered why. If the fellow wasn't such a fool, he might tell him, but deciding it wasn't worth the effort, he asked abruptly, "What have you got in the way of ladies' combs?"

"Combs to comb the hair, or fancy combs like the girls at the Nugget use?"

Doc's expression was just short of scathing. "I wouldn't give a lady a plain comb for a present, now would I?"

"I don't know. Some of the ladies —"

"A fancy comb, Bobby boy! That's what I'm lookin' for."

"All right, all right!" Bob took a few steps away to return a moment later with a metal tray. "Take your pick."

Doc had never seen the like! The combs that the snickering proprietor offered appeared more like varied species of exotic insects than they did hair ornaments, with their brightly colored stones glinting in the light and wispy feathers dangling. Doc scratched his head.

"Damned if I know which one to choose."

Bob O'Neil's sharp nose twitched with suppressed amusement. "I could probably help you with your choice, beings I've got experience in this kind of thing with all the *ladies* comin' in here to shop. But since it ain't none of my business . . ."

"I didn't say it was none of your business. I said, I might be *tempted* to tell you it's none of your business."

"In that case, what color's the lady's hair?"

Doc grinned. "Black as midnight, shinier than a full moon, and soft as silk. . . ."

"Hmmmm . . . buying the combs for Rosie, are you?" Doc's gaze narrowed into slits which caused Bob to continue with a rush, "I'd say the tortoiseshell combs . . . these here ones, for afternoon. Rosie's got good taste. She'll like them. And then these here ones decorated with them shiny stones for when she wears that black lace dress." He shook his head. "I ain't never seen anythin' like Rosie in that black lace dress."

Doc's grin reappeared in a wink. "Yeah, me neither. . . . I'll take them both."

Doc walked out through the doorway a few minutes later. He slipped the small package carefully wrapped in white paper into his pocket and paused to look again at the littered street. As he had expected, there had been no change in the status of affairs, except for the growing crowd of spectators that had filtered out from nearby saloons. Realizing the chaotic scene was not about to improve, Doc employed the same tactic as before, using his elbows liberally to clear his way.

About to cross the street, Doc stopped dead in his tracks at the sight of the big fellow approaching on a huge black bay. The stranger reined his horse to a halt just beyond the damaged wagon, allowing Doc an opportunity to study him more closely. Silently acknowledging that the fellow was one of the biggest men he had seen in a long time, Doc realized it was not as much his height which was so impressive, since that was difficult to judge, mounted as the fellow was, as the sheer breadth of him. Those shoulders and that powerful chest bespoke labor of an uncommon kind, as did the biceps that strained against his coat and the long, heavily muscled legs that gripped his horse's sides. He had never seen the fellow before. He was certain of that because he knew he would not have forgotten the look of silent menace about his unsmiling features and rock-hard jaw. He doubted much escaped those eyes almost obscured by the brim of the worn, black hat he wore pulled down on his forehead. The fellow had the appearance of a man who was hard through and through—in striking contrast to the young woman perched on the saddle in front of him.

Doc paused to consider the woman. She was small, of an incredibly petite stature. She was no true beauty, but there was something about her—the way she held her head, those great pale eyes and small features. She reminded him of a dainty porcelain doll his Emma had kept on the bed at home. Emma had said the doll must be handled carefully because it was so fragile it could easily break. Looking at the young woman, he had the same feeling about her, that she—

Startled from his thoughts as an unexpected fight between

219

two prospectors broke out within the crowd, Doc stepped to the side as one of the men was propelled violently backward into the street. The fellow staggered, striking the big bay's hindquarters with a smack, forcing the animal to sidestep into one of the stranded oxen. The surprised beast responded with a bellow and a toss of his head that sent the horse rearing wildly.

The young woman's terrified scream sounded over the street noise as the big man fought to draw his mount under control. Doc moved spontaneously toward them, holding his breath as the frightened animal reared again. An unexpected wail sounded over the commotion around them as the big man reined his excited mount to a standstill, and Doc pressed purposely forward. He knew an infant's cry when he heard one.

Reaching the animal's side as the big man placed the sack that had been hanging on the side of the saddle into the woman's arms, Doc realized a baby was cradled inside it at the same moment he viewed the barely restrained fury on the big man's face. The fellow dismounted and swung the woman and child down onto the street beside him.

Doc heard the man's brusque inquiry. "Are you all right, Carolina?" At the woman's nod, he instructed tightly, "Wait here."

With a few long strides, the fellow stepped into the fight continuing a few yards away. He emerged a few minutes later leaving both men lying on the ground, staring up at a night sky that Doc doubted either of them was in a condition to see.

Out of the corner of his eye, Doc saw the young woman sway. He gripped her arm spontaneously, his physician's eye appraising her sudden pallor and the fine mist of perspiration that had appeared on her forehead and upper lip. In a moment, the big man was back beside them, but Doc was too intent on the woman's condition to pay much attention to the deadening look the fellow gave him as he brushed his hand from the woman's arm.

Doc stated flatly, "I'm a doctor. This woman isn't well. I suggest you pick her up before she falls. My office is over there."

The baby in his arms, Doc walked quickly through the crowd as it parted with silent respect. He paid curious onlookers little mind as he reviewed the situation in his mind. The babe was obviously less than a month old and the woman was unnaturally pale. She had not recuperated fully from a possibly difficult birth and the fright, the noise and confusion, plus her own exhaustion, had been more than she could stand.

Doc stepped into his office and turned toward the big fellow, seeing his concern as he held the woman without a sign of effort.

"Put her down on the couch."

"No, I'm all right. I can stand."

Ignoring the young woman's protest, the big man lay her on the couch. He reassured her with a few softly spoken words, then turned, with a look of pure steel.

"Give me the baby."

Doc relinquished the child and stepped to the woman's side without comment. He noted unconsciously that the fretting babe quieted the moment she was in the big man's arms, but the child was not his immediate concern. Doc looked down into the young woman's pale face. Smiling, he took her hand.

"My name's Doctor Fitz. What's yours?"

Uncertain why, Carolina hesitated in response to the doctor's simple question. She felt strange, almost as if the quick progress of events since they had entered Deadwood had happened to someone else . . . someone she didn't know. She glanced at Drake to find his gaze intent upon her. He did not smile, but she was somehow strengthened.

"My name is Carolina Brand."

The doctor's smile settled comfortably into the deeply etched grooves on his face. She found herself at ease with that smile as he stated simply, "A pleasure to meet you, Carolina. Deadwood didn't greet you too well tonight. I wish I could say that kind of disorder doesn't happen often here, but that would be a barefaced lie. I don't think you'll have anythin' to worry about from now on, though. Your husband made sure that the fellows around here will give you a wide berth from now on."

Carolina glanced again at Drake. His expression had not changed although she could feel a flush rising to her own cheeks.

"Drake isn't my husband, Doctor." And when the doctor appeared confused, "The wagon train I was traveling on was attacked by Indians. I was wounded. Drake found me and took care of me."

"Wagon train?" The doctor paused. "When was that?"

Carolina's heart began a slow pounding. "About three weeks ago."

"Was that the Harper train?"

Carolina's heartbeat turned to sudden thunder in her ears. She strove to catch her breath. "I . . . I don't know."

"You don't know?" The doctor glanced at Drake, then back at her when there appeared to be no clarification forthcoming from either direction. His obvious concern did little to soothe her rapidly increasing anxiety as he pressed, "I don't know what you mean, dear."

"I . . . I can't remember. . . ." Shutting out the light of harsh reality for a brief moment, Carolina opened her eyes again to rasp, "I had a head wound . . . I can't remember anything but my name." Her voice had an hysterical ring, even to her own ears. "I thought someone here would be able to tell me . . . maybe recognize me. . . ."

"Relax, dear. Don't upset yourself." The doctor patted her hand. "Will you let me examine you? I think it would be best." And when she responded with a stiff nod, "How old is the baby?"

"Three weeks old. . . ."

"Then you had the baby about the time of the attack. . . ."

Gunshots, the thunder of pounding hooves, screams of the wounded and dying resounded vividly in Carolina's mind. She fought to overcome them.

"Yes. Drake helped me."

The doctor looked at Drake again. She thought she saw new respect in that gaze before he turned back to her and touched the scar on her forehead.

222

"This is the wound . . . yes . . . it looks to be healin' nicely. How have you been feelin'?"

"Very good."

"She's been feelin' weak."

"No, I haven't!" Carolina was suddenly angry at Drake's contradiction. "I've been feeling better and better."

"*Better* doesn't mean too much, considerin' . . ."

"Considerin' what?" Doc Fitz turned toward Drake, relieving Carolina of the responsibility of response. She was inwardly grateful as he continued, "Maybe *you'd* better tell me what happened, Mister . . . ?"

"McNeil."

The doctor shook the hand Drake extended as Drake began a recitation of the events Carolina knew so well. The deep, familiar tone of Drake's voice rumbled on, but the words escaped her. She felt so strange. . . . She had been feeling fine, even excited as they had made the tortuous descent into Deadwood. She remembered the lights of the camp had twinkled like a thousand fireflies as they had drawn closer, but the sounds that had risen to greet them had been distinctly human. Music, laughter, good-natured shouting. . . .

Then, gradually, the tenor of things had begun changing. Up close the fairy-tale quality of the view became tarnished. The fireflies became kerosene and coal oil lamps that released a familiar, unpleasant odor into the air while casting flickering rays of light into the intimidating darkness beyond. The structures so picturesque from afar became lopsided tents with stained canvas, scattered hither and yon like mushrooms on the forest floor. The permanent structures which she had unconsciously viewed as havens from the threat they had escaped so miraculously on the trail, were no more than log cabins with occasional gaudy false fronts from which raucous music, the stench of beer, and the sounds of garish laughter resounded.

Carolina attempted to sort out her thoughts. But she had been fine in spite of all that. She had merely gripped her babe's swing more tightly and leaned back into the safety of Drake's arms.

Then she had heard the thudding of fists, grunts of pain,

and excited shouts. A chill raced down Carolina's spine in vivid recall. Yes, she remembered. . . . Two men had been fighting and Drake's horse had reared. She had screamed, fearing that Suzannah would swing from her grasp, but Drake's hand had closed over hers, holding the babe secure, even as he had brought the animal under control. Drake had dismounted and swung Suzannah and her to the ground and then she had seen him . . . one of the fellows who was fighting. His nose and mouth were bleeding profusely. Blood ran down his neck, staining his chest like a mortal wound. . . .

A familiar queasiness returned and Carolina raised a trembling hand to her head. She had seen others similarly stained with blood . . . but they had been lying on the ground, never to rise again. . . .

Drake had waded into the fray and her heart had all but stopped. She remembered clutching Suzannah as he swung his fists and closing her eyes, only to open them a moment later to see two men lying on the ground. She had not been able to catch her breath for the split second before she realized that neither of them was Drake.

Stirred from her uncertain reverie by a touch on her arm, Carolina looked up at Dr. Fitz.

"You've had a rough time of it from what this fella tells me."

Carolina blinked. She didn't want anyone to pity her. She just wanted someone to help her remember.

"I'm all right." Carolina attempted to sit up, only to have the doctor restrain her gently.

"Drake says he wants me to check you over, and I'm thinkin' neither one of us is big enough to back him down. What do you say?"

Carolina looked at Drake, noting the tight lines of tension around his mouth. The shadows of concern in his eyes forced her concession.

"All right."

Doc turned to Drake. "If you'll go outside for a few minutes . . ."

"No!"

The single word, spoken in unison by Drake and herself,

brought a brief smile to Carolina's lips. She was still smiling on the inside when Doc Fitz looked up from a cursory examination a short time later.

"You seem to be just fine to me, other than bein' a bit too thin and maybe a bit too pale. But I'd venture to say that rest and some good, nourishin' food is the best medicine for what ails you."

"What about my memory? I want to be able to remember, Doctor Fitz."

The gray-haired doctor shook his head. "No, I don't think you do."

Carolina saw Drake stiffen behind the doctor's back even as a flash of anger sent the blood rushing to her cheeks.

"I *do* want to remember! I *have* to remember. . . ."

"And you will, when you're ready."

"But . . ."

"Answer me this, Carolina. What happens when you try to remember?"

A familiar trembling started inside Carolina. "Nothing . . . nothing happens. I try and try, but all I see and hear over and over again is the attack, the gunshots, the screaming. . . ."

"Then . . . ?"

"Then? Nothing. Everything goes dark. I want someone to fill the darkness in for me, Doctor Fitz. I want to know who I am other than a name. I want to know where I came from. I want to know if Suzannah has family somewhere."

"What about your husband?"

Carolina stiffened. "He's dead. They were all dead. Everybody. . . ." Carolina took a shuddering breath, then pressed determinedly, "But you said the 'Harper' party. . . ."

The doctor looked hesitant. "That's what everybody calls it for want of a better name. A wagon train arrived here a couple of weeks ago. The fella in charge said they came across the remains of a train when they strayed off the regular trail." The doctor's brows furrowed into a wiry line. "He said everybody had been dead a while, that there were only men—no women—and that most of the wagons had been burned or looted. But they found some papers with the name Harper on

225

them. That Harper fella was from Illinois."

"Illinois . . ." Carolina searched her mind to no avail. Her throat filled with tears, but she swallowed them, determined. "Wasn't there anybody waiting for that train, or expecting it? Do you think if I asked . . . ?"

"Carolina, dear"—the doctor's expression grew almost pained—"if you're expectin' to discover your past in Deadwood, you've come to the wrong place, because the truth is that Deadwood has no past. Another truth is that there's not one of us here who's really sure whether it has a future, either. In some ways, Deadwood is like you, Carolina. It sprang up in the wilderness—nobody seems to know how, but worse than that, nobody seems to care. The population keeps changin'. Here today and gone tomorrow, just like that fella who found those Harper papers. I don't think I could direct you to even one of the fellas that arrived on that train with him, but even if I could, it wouldn't do much good. All anybody cares about in this camp is how much gold dust he has in his pouch, or the location of the next strike. Everythin' else is unimportant."

"But . . ."

"Don't worry . . ." Dr. Fitz's hand tightened around hers. "It's not uncommon to have a memory loss when you've had a blow on the head. It's usually short term. Yours is worse for good reason, I believe. I'm thinkin' your mind knows that your body isn't up to the strain of rememberin', and it's not goin' to let you remember until it's good and ready. Don't worry, the time will come."

"What am I supposed to do until then, Doctor?"

"I can't tell you that, dear."

"But . . ." Carolina looked at Drake. His expression was stiff. She read in his gaze that he didn't believe a word the doctor had said. She looked back at Doc Fitz as he spoke again.

"I'm goin' to write you out a prescription for a tonic to build you up again."

"I don't need medicine. I'm all right. Besides, I don't have any money."

"Carolina, dear. . . ."

Carolina was adamant, despite the throbbing that had begun in her head. She wanted to get away from this office. She wanted to go someplace where it was quiet and still, where she and Suzannah would be safe from the confusion in which her mind was circling. She wanted to feel Drake's arms around her. She wanted . . . she wanted . . .

Carolina closed her eyes. She wanted to go back to the cabin with Drake.

"Give the prescription to me, Doc." Drake interrupted for the first time as Carolina began fading rapidly before his eyes. He was grateful that this old fellow had checked Carolina's physical condition, but the truth was that he didn't believe a word of the mumbo jumbo the fellow had said about her memory, and he hadn't needed a doctor to tell him that Carolina needed rest and more time to recuperate.

Not waiting for Doc Fitz to respond, Drake continued, "If you'll tell me where I can get a room—"

"There aren't any rooms available in Deadwood."

Suzannah took that moment to declare her impatience and Drake rocked her lightly with a gentleness that belied his growing agitation.

"What do you mean there aren't any rooms?"

"You're not goin' to find a place of your own to sleep in tonight unless you're totin' a tent on the back of that donkey you had trailin' from your lead."

Acutely aware that Carolina watched him intently, Drake pressed less politely than before. "There're wagon trains comin' into Deadwood every day. Where's everybody stayin' if there aren't any rooms?"

"In their wagons, or in those tents I was tellin' you about. Some sleep right out there on the ground in a bedroll until they can put up some kind of shelter for themselves."

Drake's eyes narrowed into slits. "What about the hotel?"

"We have one hotel, if you can call it that, and there isn't room for another flea in it."

"You're tellin' me that this woman and child have to sleep out in the open tonight in a town full of drunks. . . ."

Drake could feel his ire rising. He was startled when the

227

doctor shook his head. "No, I didn't say that."

"Then what did you say?"

"I said you weren't goin' to find a room of your own, but I'm thinkin' I just might be able to find a place for this young lady and the babe until she gets settled. As for you . . ."

"I'm not worryin' about me." Drake's tone was brusque. "I'll get by."

"I don't want to go anywhere without you, Drake."

Drake frowned at Carolina's unexpected interjection. He had somehow expected it, and the realization only made things more difficult. "You don't have any choice, Carolina."

"I do." Carolina sat up determinedly. Drake could tell her head was still swimming as she raised her chin unsteadily. "I won't go."

Drake gritted his teeth as he replied more slowly than before, "As I said, you don't have any choice."

Carolina's lips parted in an objection that was never voiced and her face flushed. Ignoring her discomfort, telling himself that she need become accustomed to the idea of separation sooner or later, Drake addressed the doctor who observed them both curiously. "Where's this place your talkin' about takin' Carolina to?"

"The cabin of a *friend*."

Not certain he liked the way the old doc stumbled over that last word, Drake followed him out the door a few minutes later, extremely conscious of Carolina's rigid posture as she walked ahead of him.

"What a little beauty!"

Miriam's voice broke the silence of her small cabin. Her heart fluttered in her breast as she looked down into the sweet perfection of the baby in the arms of the huge fellow who had been introduced to her as Drake McNeil. She glanced again at the baby's mother who sat stiffly on a nearby chair. She was such a pale, delicate young woman.

An unexpected knock at the door a few minutes earlier had raised her from a chair by the fire where she had been reading before going to bed. Not dressed for company, she had been uncomfortable when she had opened the door and seen Jerome standing there along with a handsome couple and a baby.

Jerome . . . Miriam gave an annoyed sniff. Of late he had become a ghost who appeared and disappeared mysteriously when it was time to drop off or pick up his laundry. It was almost comical. She often heard his step outside in the yard, but she couldn't count the times she had raced to the door without reaching it in time to see him.

Oh, she had it in for the old fool, all right, but there hadn't been a moment's doubt in her mind what her response would be when Jerome had ushered the unexpected threesome into her small cabin, introduced them, and related their difficult circumstances.

"Carolina and the baby are welcome to stay here as long as necessary." Miriam glanced at the bed in one corner of the small cabin and the small settee in the other. "I'm only sorry that I can't offer Mister McNeil accommodations, too." Aching to touch the child, Miriam looked up at the tall man. "May I hold Suzannah?"

Drake did not answer her and Miriam suddenly realized that he was hesitant. Flustered, Miriam turned toward the young woman who responded with an attempt at a smile.

"If you like, but Suzannah's getting hungry. She may get restless."

True to the woman's word, the babe squirmed as soon as Miriam took her into her arms, but Miriam's elation was undimmed. She looked down into the babe's exquisitely formed features. The sweet scent unique to an infant reached her nostrils and an incomparable warmth flushed through her veins. She looked up again at the big man as she rocked the babe gently. "You might ask at the livery stable to see if they have any room for you. Will Reed sometimes lets paying customers sleep there."

"That's all right, ma'am." Drake McNeil was polite, but his eyes were so cold that Miriam almost shivered as he continued, "I won't be here long. I'll be goin' back to my claim as soon as I've had a chance to rest up a bit."

Carolina stiffened visibly, and Miriam was caught as much

229

by the shock his statement seemed to cause the young woman as she was by Drake McNeil's unaffected mien. It was obvious to Miriam's keen eye that Jerome was aware of Carolina's increasing anxiety as well. He proved it by his next statement.

"Don't you go worryin' about Drake, Carolina. He's welcome to sleep on the couch in my office if he doesn't mind hangin' off it from the knees down. *And,*" he added with a chuckle, "if he doesn't mind the late hours I keep."

Miriam could not suppress a low, "Humph!" that turned all heads in her direction as she fixed her small eyes on the old geezer's gay expression. She added tartly, "I'd say this *young* fellow could teach you a thing or two about keeping late hours if he so chose, Jerome."

Miriam paused, her gaze narrowing. She did not intend to allow the old fool to believe she would let him off easily for the distance he had maintained between them the last few weeks, and for leaving notes with his laundry when a few words of conversation would have been more appropriate. But she would die before she would admit that she had missed him terribly. Instead, she raised her thin brows with a pointed look. "I should think he could teach you a few things in other areas as well."

But Doc was not biting.

"Maybe so . . . maybe so." Jerome looked too relieved to satisfy Miriam as he turned to McNeil. "Well, I think Carolina is in good hands now. If you want to come back to the office with me, you can settle yourself and your animals for the night."

The big fellow nodded and Miriam could sense the young woman's growing apprehension. Her old heart bleeding for the poor, lost dear, Miriam realized that she had not become so benumbed to matters of the heart by her own personal tragedy in losing Jonas that she could not sense the reason for the young woman's agitation. And so, she found herself offering, "You will come back for breakfast tomorrow, won't you, Mister McNeil?" Her smile turned to acid as she added, "Of course, that invitation also includes you, Jerome."

"Why thank you, Miriam!" Doc's false enthusiasm did not fool her as he continued, "But the truth be known, I'm not

230

sure that I'll be risin' with the chickens tomorrow."

Miriam bit back a response as she gazed with silent disdain into Doc's bleary eyes. Uncertain why, she turned back to the big man and pressed as sweetly as she could manage, "May I expect you, Mister McNeil?"

The fellow's nod and his short, "Thank you, ma'am," brought Carolina to her feet and Miriam felt an almost maternal relief. Jerome had briefly recounted the young woman's story, and her heart had immediately gone out to her for the suffering and loss she had endured. But she had learned long ago that unusual circumstances bred unusual circumstances . . . and it was obvious that Carolina had developed a strong attachment to the fellow who had saved her life. The dear girl was too young and too sweet to be so alone. Somehow, she couldn't bear the thought of those haunted eyes growing more shadowed, and the thought of what losing someone else she held dear might do to the girl.

The babe took that moment to whimper loudly, a sound that caused both Carolina and Drake to step spontaneously toward her. Their display of mutual concern only confirmed her thoughts as Miriam consoled the child gently.

"I'll be expecting you, then, Mister McNeil. It'll be so pleasant to cook for a man again." Unable to resist a last stabbing gibe as the two men turned to the door, Miriam added, "Of course, we 'chickens' will be happy to have you peck at our table if you're so disposed, Jerome — *but we won't count on you.*" Satisfied that she had momentarily stopped the old coot in his tracks, Miriam smiled broadly into the infant's uncomfortable wail and cooed, "All right, young lady, your mama will take you now, as much as I hate to give you up."

The door closed behind the men without further ado, and Miriam placed the babe in her mother's waiting arms. A sudden swell of emotion caused her voice to crack as she whispered earnestly, "My dear, I'm so glad to have you both here."

Having abandoned a silent Drake McNeil to settle into temporary quarters in his office, Doc walked briskly along the jammed street. He reviewed the events of the past few

231

hours in his mind. Drake McNeil and Carolina Brand were an unlikely couple. He sensed that the young man was uncomfortable with the situation between them and the dependence Carolina seemed to have developed on him.

Doc unconsciously nodded. The big man was right in being cautious. Transference . . . that's what it was. Carolina had suffered a traumatic experience. She had no recollection of her recently departed husband. The shock of seeing him devoid of life under such horrendous circumstances, combined with her own dire physical state, had probably been too much for her mind to accept. As far as Carolina's memory was concerned, her husband might never have existed. Enter Drake — a handsome fellow, obviously concerned for her welfare and attached to the infant, the only other person in the unfamiliar world into which she had awakened, and the stage was set for another tragedy in the making. He had seen it in Carolina's eyes when Drake had declared his intention to leave within a few days.

Troubling Doc was the fact that he had seen something else as well in Drake McNeil's eyes. He had seen an unnatural coldness, a grim determination that approached the fanatical. That fellow would not be easily swayed from any course he had set for himself, not even for a lovely young woman and child who needed him. He feared that Carolina would be the one to suffer as a result.

Doc sighed and rubbed his chin. Well, one good thing had come out of the strange affairs of this night. He had finally found a way to end the estrangement between Miriam and himself — a problem that had caused him considerable discomfort. He had felt like such a worm . . . but that was all over and done now . . . almost.

He remembered his disquiet as he had knocked on the door of Miriam's cabin earlier. His heart had pounded like a drum. He had felt as nervous as a boy, and the steely look in Miriam's eye had not provided much relief — not until she had spotted the bundle that Drake McNeil carried in his arms.

Strangely, he had actually believed for a few minutes that Miriam was going to thank him for the imposition he had fostered upon her. Instead, to his intense relief, she had given him a few parting gibes that had restored his faith in her. Doc grinned. The woman had a truly wicked tongue. She raised acrimony to a true art form. He was uncertain, but he believed he actually admired her in some strange way for her sheer inventiveness in that regard. Doc's grin faded. He *was* certain of another thing, however. He didn't admire her for anything else.

Yet, contrary as it seemed since Miriam was truly a homely sort, she had almost looked beautiful when she had first looked down at the infant. Her small eyes had glowed and the smile that had graced her lips had nearly melted his heart. She had been on her good behavior after that, except for those few gibes, and he had been almost ashamed of the way he had counted on the presence of others to protect him from a more virulent assault.

There was a deeper reason, however, one Doc would not readily acknowledge, for not trusting himself to go to Miriam's cabin alone at night. His reaction to Miriam's appearance in that soft blue flannel robe, with her graying hair released from its bun to hang in a single braid down her unyieldingly erect spine, had been proof that he had been wise in taking such precaution.

Experiencing a familiar tug in his groin when he allowed his thoughts to dwell on Miriam, Doc cursed aloud and hastened his pace along the crowded walk. Damn! Senility began in the strangest of ways. . . .

Shaking off his somber thoughts as the doorway of the Nugget came within view, Doc patted his pocket and the small package he had placed there earlier. Dear Rosie was twenty-one years old today! He knew she would not remember having mentioned her birthday in casual conversation with him months earlier, but he had not forgotten the date. In the time since, he had recalled it often to mind in sober self-ridicule when the sight of Rosie became too sweet for him to bear.

Dear Rosie. She needed some cheering up, all right. Tag Willis had eyes for no one but her, but Ella O'Connor, the rapacious tart that she was, was doing her best to change all that. Her campaign was so blatant that he, who had a place in his heart for even the most outrageous of people, *could not stand her.*

Doc stood momentarily in the doorway of the saloon, searching the rowdy crowd with his gaze. The usuals were at the bar . . . Willie Simpson, Josiah Cribbs, Timothy Ryan, and, of course, Bart Mellon. Doc's lips twisted in a wry smile. That Bart didn't take no for an answer, that was sure. Rosie had sicced every girl in her employ on him at one time or another, and he still followed her around like a puppy dog.

Spotting Rosie where she stood with a few patrons at the end of the bar, Doc unconsciously sighed. Ah, yes, sweet Rosie. . . . The sight of her never failed to wipe thoughts of all others from his mind, but as the dear girl turned and he glimpsed her face, Doc frowned.

Rosie had a smile on her lips, but there was a deep sadness in her eyes. He saw it there, although he knew few others would. Sweet Rosie was sick to the heart without Tag and that was the truth of it, no matter how she denied it. He knew no amount of attentions from an old fool like him would fill that void, but he also knew that he could add a little sparkle to that smile if he tried.

Stepping into the crowded saloon, Doc walked briskly across the floor. Bart Mellon had gravitated to Rosie's side and had slid his arm around her waist. Doc paused only a moment before tapping the young fellow on the shoulder. When Bart turned, Doc cleared his throat loudly enough to claim the attention of Rosie and all others in the vicinity.

"Excuse me, Bart, but Rosie's fella has just arrived and you'll have to unhand her now."

Bart glanced quizzically around them, then looked back at him. "Yeah, where is he?"

"Standing right here in front of your nose, you damned, young fool!"

Slapping Bart's arm from Rosie's waist, Doc drew Rosie away from the bar with a proprietary glance calculated to induce the laughter that sounded along the bar. A backward look as Rosie walked beside him toward a corner table revealed that Bart wasn't amused, but Doc couldn't care less. The grin on Rosie's face made it all worthwhile.

Pulling out Rosie's chair as gallantly as he could manage, Doc waited until she was comfortably seated before assuming the seat beside her. He signaled to Barney at the bar and he knew it would only be a minute before the fellow put two drinks in front of them. He sighed with contentment. It was great being a friend of the boss.

"What are you grinnin' at, Doc, honey?" Rosie pinched his cheek. "You look like the cat that ate the canary."

"Do I?" Doc picked up Rosie's hand and raised it to his lips. "You're good for me, you know that, young lady? You make me feel good just lookin' at you in that purple dress."

Rosie fluttered her eyelashes at him and whispered coquettishly, "Don't you go tellin' me purple is your favorite color, Doc, 'cause if you do, I'll go right out and buy myself a whole wardrobe of purple clothes."

"It's not the color, Rosie, and you know it. And if you weren't just twenty-one years old *today* . . ." Doc withdrew the package from his pocket with a flourish and placed it on the table in front of her. "Happy birthday!"

"You remembered!" Her eyes filling unexpectedly, Rosie stared at him for a few minutes, then said hoarsely, "You know, there're some times when I regret bein' twenty-one years old. Why'd you have to get born so many years before me, Doc?"

"Poor timin', Rosie . . . poor timin'." Doc's momentary sadness disappeared as he directed, "Open your present!"

Surprised to see that Rosie's fingers were trembling, Doc watched as she slowly undid the folds of the paper. Her expression said it all as the combs came into view.

"They're beautiful, Doc!" Fingering the tortoiseshell combs first, Rosie then picked up the evening combs. She swept up a few straying wisps at the back of her neck and pressed them into the luxurious mass piled atop her head. "How do they look?"

"How else could they look? Beautiful!"

Leaning toward him, Rosie threw her arms around Doc's neck and kissed him soundly on the mouth. "You're too good to me, Doc. You're the only one who remembered my birthday."

"Am I now?" Doc glanced automatically at the table where Tag somberly dealt cards.

Rosie's gaze followed his briefly. "Tag's too busy with Ella to think about much else . . . and I'm glad, I really am. But you know . . ." Rosie's voice dropped a notch softer, "I would've been a whole lot happier about it if Tag had tied up with somebody other than Ella. She isn't good enough for him, and I don't mean because of her occupation."

"You don't have to explain yourself to me, Rosie. Ella's a little too hard for me to swallow, too, but you're wrong, you know. Tag hasn't forgotten you. He's just fillin' in the time until —"

"Don't say that anymore, Doc, please." Rosie's eyes again brimmed. "I'd rather see Tag set on somebody else, even if that somebody was Ella, than have him pinin' after me, 'cause there's no use in it. But I don't want to talk about that anymore, either." Rosie forced a smile. "Tell me what you've been up to today to bring you here so late. You had me worried. I thought you'd slipped off to visit Heddy LaRue or somethin'."

Doc's eyes popped open wide. "How'd you know about Heddy? Can't a man have any secrets in this town?"

Rosie smiled. "Why, Doc, you're blushin'! Could it be because Heddy gave you one of those special treatments she saves only for *special* customers?" Rosie winked and poked him with her elbow. "How was it, Doc?"

"That's for me to know and for you to find out!" Rosie's grin widened and Doc muttered, "Damn!"

"Heddy likes to brag, Doc, and you're one of the best catches in town as far as the girls are concerned. They keep talkin' about 'experienced hands'. . . ."

Doc could feel himself flush more darkly, even as suspicion took seed in his mind. "Rosie Blake . . . did you have one of your spies out on the street a few hours ago . . . is that it?"

Rosie winked again. "That's for me to know and for you to find out."

"Hummm." Thwarted by Rosie's quick mind, Doc sought to switch the subject to more comfortable grounds. "Well, I guess there isn't any use in my tellin' you that it was a good deed that kept me out of here . . . because you probably heard all about the ruckus on the street already."

"The ruckus?" Rosie raised her handsomely shaped brows. "Doc, there's a ruckus on Main Street just about once every hour. You can depend on it as much as you can depend on the sun risin' tomorrow mornin'. What was so different about this one to get you so excited?"

"If you'd have seen the fella that put a stop to it, you wouldn't ask." Doc shook his head. "I'll say one thing. He isn't the kind you'll forget once you've seen him. He waded right into a fight between Bobby Monroe and Phil Baxter, and damned if he didn't clean up the street with both of them without even raisin' a sweat!"

Rosie's silence coaxed Doc to continue. "It wouldn't be a mystery how he managed it if you'd have seen the size of him. I figure he stands at least four inches over the mark of six feet — all brawn and muscle, too. A good-lookin' fella, but a real intimidatin' sort with those hard eyes and that square jaw. I know *I* wouldn't go up against him in a fight."

Rosie went suddenly as still as a statue. Her gaze was fixed on his face, and when he took her hand he found that it was cold. She was trembling.

"What's the matter, Rosie?"

Rosie swallowed, her beautiful face suddenly pale. "What color hair did this fella have, Doc? Black?"

Doc nodded.

"Were his eyes green?"

Doc scrutinized Rosie's tense expression. "Honey, what's the matter?"

"His eyes, Doc . . . were they green?"

Rosie's agitation mounted and Doc's concern grew. "I don't remember. They were light . . ." He paused. "Yes, I believe they were green. . . ."

"Doc, he —"

Rosie's words came to an abrupt halt in midsentence. Her lips parting, she stared at the doorway with such rapt attention that Doc could do no more than follow her gaze. Startled to see Drake McNeil standing there, Doc watched as the fellow's light eyes swept the room with a cursory glance that did not reach into the corner where they sat before he started for the bar.

Rosie was on her feet in a moment and Doc grasped her arm. Confused, he asked again, "What's the matter, Rosie?"

Her eyes great glowing saucers as she turned back to him, Rosie whispered, "It's *him,* Doc. He's come for me at last!"

Doc was too startled to react as Rosie shook off his grip and started toward the bar. Uncertain what to think, he looked at Tag to see him watching Rosie as well. His heart seeming to stop, Doc recognized the torment in Tag's gaze . . . and then he knew. Rosie's secret lover had arrived at last.

Her heart pounding like a drum, Rosie approached Drake with a measured step. She appraised his broad back with her gaze, knowing the power Doc had described was not confined solely to his overwhelming stature. Lean and mean . . . she remembered some had used those words to describe Drake back home, but she knew better. She knew that Drake had never been mean . . . only strong and determined. In truth he was kind . . . the kindest man she had ever known . . . and she worshiped him.

Standing behind Drake, Rosie sought the courage to speak. She had been waiting for him for so long. Unconscious of the curious glances she received, she took a steadying breath, wondering somewhere in the back of her mind if she looked her best . . . if Drake would think she had changed . . . if he would still find her beautiful. He had always said she was beautiful.

"Drake. . . ."

At the sound of her voice, Drake turned toward her. Pinning her with the cool green of his gaze, he did not immediately respond, and Rosie remembered. She had been a young girl, her face battered and bruised from the beating her stepfather had just given her for resisting his attentions. She had picked herself up from the forest floor her clothes askew as her stepfather fled through the foliage at the sound of approaching footsteps. And then she had felt those green eyes upon her.

She had cowered, frightened, until Drake had extended his hand toward her. She had felt his outrage, but she had not responded when he asked the man's name. He had seen that she was too terrified to speak, and he had miraculously understood. He had put his arms around her and for the first time, she had not cringed at a man's touch. She remembered that she had felt at home in Drake's arms as she had never felt at home before. She had known at that instant that he was the man for her, that he always would be.

A softening appeared around Drake's eyes that was not quite a smile. "How are you, Rosie?"

"I'm fine, Drake, especially now that you're here." Rosie's grin was tremulous. "I've been waitin' for you to come back to Deadwood. What took you so long?"

Appearing suddenly aware of the curious glances they were receiving, Drake picked up his drink and took her arm. He caught Barney's eye.

"Bring the lady a drink." He ushered her ahead of him and seated her politely. He took a cautious sip of his drink and replied to her question. "Things are goin' slower than I expected at my claim. I'm thinkin' that I'll need a few more months there before I've got enough dust accumulated to be able to leave."

Drake paused. "You're just as beautiful as ever, Rosie." He looked down at her left hand. "I see no man's laid claim to you yet. What's wrong with the fellas around here?"

Rosie's smile came from the bottom of her heart. "There's nothin' wrong with them, Drake." She laughed. "I practically have to beat them off with a stick."

Drake looked deeper into her eyes, then turned to look at the table where Tag openly watched them. "I thought you had a special fella. The last time I was here it looked to me like Willis wanted to stake a claim."

"No, Tag's a friend. There's nobody special. . . ."

"How come?"

"Come on now, Drake. You know I'm waitin' for you."

Rosie smiled as Drake's cool eyes warmed. She knew that warmth was just for her . . . that it was with him always . . . that he had carried it inside him for seven long years . . .

"You've always been my special girl, Rosie."

Drake's gaze changed, and she knew he was remembering. She read the same distress there she had seen that day in the woods. He had looked out for her after that, watching, never knowing that the man who abused her lived in her own home. She remembered the day he found out. . . .

"I'll always be your special girl, Drake." Her heart in those words, Rosie paused when she did not get the response she had hoped for. Instinct told her Drake was not ready to declare himself yet. She didn't want to rush him. She wanted it to be just right between them when he did. She tried for a lighter note. "What brought you back to Deadwood—not that I'm complainin,' because I missed you like the devil."

Drake's expression tightened unexpectedly. She saw a curtain drop over his gaze and she felt a moment's fear at the distance that slipped unexpectedly between them.

"What's wrong, Drake?"

"Nothin's wrong." Drake's expression slowly relaxed and Rosie breathed more easily. "I had somethin' to take care of. I'll be goin' back to my claim in a day or so, but I didn't want the night to pass without seein' you and makin' sure you're all right." He paused. "Seein' you is like takin' a breath of good, clean, Texas air, Rosie. It makes a man feel real good inside."

Loving him so much at that moment that it hurt, Rosie questioned tentatively, "Have you found a place to stay tonight? Everybody tells me there ain't a bed to be had in town." She offered hesitantly, her heart pounding more rapidly than before, "If you're stuck, you can always stay at my place."

Not batting an eye at her offer, Drake shook his head. "That's all right. I've got a place to stay."

"Lucky man. . . ." Rosie cursed her misfortune. "How'd you find it?"

"It found me. Doc Fitz is lettin' me sleep in his office."

Rosie's mouth fell agape. She turned and looked at Doc where he now stood at the bar. She laughed. "That Doc, he always was too quick for me. I'm goin' to have to tell him that I don't like him stealin' my thunder."

"Speakin' of sleepin'. . ."

Drake lifted his hat and ran his hand through his hair. Rosie recognized the gesture. It meant that he was either exhausted or upset, and she wished with all the fervor in her bursting heart that it was her hand instead of his that raked his hair as he continued, "I've been on the trail for two days. There were signs of Indians, so I didn't get much sleep. I figure it's time to make up for it." Rosie sensed the smile that did not make it to Drake's lips as he looked at the drink Barney slipped in front of her. "I won't be waitin' for you to finish that drink because I'll be sayin' good night now." Holding her gaze a moment longer, Drake whispered, "You're a special person, Rosie . . . real special."

Tossing down his drink, Drake drew himself wearily to his feet. Standing beside him, Rosie slipped her arms around his waist and hugged him close. Drake's arms closed around her and she felt his cheek rest against her hair the moment before he stepped back and turned toward the door.

Watching until Drake disappeared from sight, Rosie turned abruptly toward the rear of the saloon. Emotionally spent, she walked unsteadily across the floor, unaware of curious glances from the bar. Outside, she leaned against the back door and breathed deeply of the night air. Drake had returned, as she had known he would. He loved her. She had seen it in his eyes. The trouble was that he didn't realize how much, yet. How long had he said he would be in town? A few days? A few days wasn't enough, but it would have to do. He'd go back to his claim afterward, but she knew he'd come back for her before he left the hills. She'd wait. She had already waited seven long years. If she had to, she'd wait a lifetime.

Rosie started slowly toward her cabin. Drake would come back to see her tomorrow, and if he didn't, she would go to him.

Rosie unconsciously smiled. So Doc, the old dear, had confirmed her faith in him by sensing the good in Drake without even knowing who he was. He had been kind to Drake. She would have to thank Doc . . . someday. . . .

Drake pushed open the door of Doc's office and stepped

241

inside. He fumbled for the lamp, giving a sigh of relief as its meager glow illuminated the darkness. He was weary to the bone. He glanced around him, his gaze skimming the much abused desk, the crude wooden table that obviously served for both examinations and surgery, the cabinet on which were stacked worn medical journals, the ragged rug that covered the dusty floor in front of the fireplace, finally coming to rest on the dilapidated couch squeezed into the corner of the room. The old geezer was right. His legs would hang off it from the knees down, but he knew it would make little difference once he put his head down.

Wasting no time, Drake stripped off his coat. He sat down heavily on the nearest chair, pulled off one boot, and then the other. Standing again, he removed his shirt and pants. Down to his brief underclothes, he walked directly to the couch, lay down, and pulled the blanket over him.

Sleep did not come. Instead, the events of the day flashed across his brain in a blurred parade, with Carolina's face emerging brightly before his mind's eye. It was not a happy face. It bore the expression of betrayal he had seen there when he had announced his intention to return to his claim within a few days.

Suddenly angry with the myriad emotions assaulting him, Drake jerked the blanket up over his shoulders and closed his eyes. Damn it all, what had she expected? He hadn't misled her. He had delivered her to Deadwood just as he had promised. His obligation to Suzannah and her was done.

Miriam Higgins. . . . Drake's mouth twitched with a strange discomfort. The woman had practically glowed when she saw Suzannah. He had been reluctant to relinquish the child to her eager arms, and he wondered why.

Carolina's face returned to his mind's eye. Her expression was sober and touched with anguish. Somehow that anguish resounded inside him as well. It stabbed at his heart more sharply than a knife, but he forced it aside, determined to think no more.

Another image far more beautiful than Carolina's plain, pale countenance intruded into the void. He was uncertain what had driven him to see Rosie when his only thought after leaving Carolina had been to find a place to lay his head, but he was glad that he did. He supposed he had wanted to reassure himself that the innocents of the world who had suffered cruelly at the hands of wicked and traumatic circumstances *could* survive. He had felt Rosie's womanly body tremble when she hugged him, and he had known that she was remembering that first day in the forest as he was. Rosie was a woman now—intoxicatingly beautiful—but to him she would always be that child whom life had flayed so cruelly.

Dear Rosie. . . . She and he were bound by personal tragedies that had left indelible scars. It hurt him to know that Rosie's suffering had not been limited to the hands of an abusive stepfather, that even after she had escaped him, she had been forced to walk a hard road to survive. Some would condemn her for the choice she had made, but he knew he never would. He, too, had played the game of survival. He, too, had functioned by casting aside thoughts of a present beyond bearing by focusing on a point in the future where he would put all indignities to rest once and for all. Rosie had risen above her circumstances. She no longer paid her way in the only currency available to her. She had been forced onto a difficult way of life at a time when she should have been safe in the bosom of her family, but there had been no safety for her. And when she had needed him most, he had been unable to help her.

He remembered arriving in Deadwood a few months earlier and being startled to find Rosie comfortably ensconced as part owner of one of the best gaming establishments in town. He remembered her smile when she had reminded him that she had kept her promise to meet him there. He had almost forgotten that promise, written in a letter in Rosie's childish scrawl almost a year earlier. He had been surprised that she had not. He was pleased to see that they were both at the brink of meeting their goals. Rosie's goal was to be financially independent enough to have a hearth of her own with a white kitten sleeping beside it. His goal, however, was a commitment signed in blood. . . .

Carolina appeared suddenly before Drake's mind's eye, unbidden, in silent appeal. His stomach clenched into a tight knot. She was alone, without a home, without a past, and without funds. He recalled the faces of the men he had passed on Main Street upon entering town. He would not have Carolina depend upon the likes of them for the support of her child. He would not have her forced to follow Rosie's path in order to survive.

That thought so offensive that he was temporarily nauseated, Drake steadied himself with deep, cleansing breaths. He would take care of it tomorrow. He would provide for Carolina and the babe, and when that was done, he would leave with a clear conscience and a free heart.

A voice in his mind rose in stinging challenge. A free heart? He had no heart. It had been stripped away seven long years ago.

A titan-haired image from his past suddenly rearing its head, set Drake's heart to a vicious pounding. Rage, hatred, a killing fury, inundated his mind—emotions with which he was familiar—emotions he had learned to handle with a promise he had made himself those seven years ago—emotions he controlled by allowing himself no emotion at all.

Love? He had been capable of love once, but not anymore. Decency was another matter. He would do the *decent* thing tomorrow.

That thought clearing his mind of its former turmoil, Drake closed his eyes. Within moments, he was asleep.

"All right, man, you love the woman! So what are you goin' to do about it?"

Tag turned with a start at the unexpected voice that emerged from the shadows of the alleyway where he had gone to escape the picture of Rosie in the big Texan's arms. He had abandoned his poker table to Sheila the moment Rosie had stepped out of sight through the back door of the saloon. He had thought himself alone, but he was not.

Recognizing the gravelly voice and keenly resenting the question, Tag stared at Doc as he stepped into the light.

"What business is it of yours, Fitz?"

"If you're too dumb to know, then I guess I'll have to tell

244

you. Anybody with half an eye can see Rosie's special to me. I want to see her happy."

Tag felt a familiar anger rising. "Well anybody with half an eye can see I'm not the man she wants. Weren't you watching? There's only one man for Rosie, and that man isn't me."

"That's a pity, because she isn't goin' to get him."

The antagonism between the two men flaring, Tag's response was just short of a snarl. "What're you talking about?"

"Keep a civil tongue in your head, Willis, or I'll knock it off!" The old man made a visible attempt to draw his anger under control before he continued more softly than before. "What's wrong with you, anyway? I know you don't like me, but if you'd take the time to use the good sense God gave you, you'd see that we both want the same thing. We both want Rosie to be happy, only it looks like I'm the only one who can see that *you're* the fellow to do that for her."

"Me?" Tag was genuinely surprised. "I thought *you* were bucking for that position."

"Me? I'm not that much of a fool, Willis! I'm more than twenty-five years older than that little girl, and there are times when I feel every damned year of it. Rosie needs better than what I can offer her at my age. And the truth be known . . ." Doc paused and added with a catch in his voice, "She's like a daughter to me."

Tag gave a mocking laugh. "Are you trying to tell me that you'd look at your own daughter the way you look at Rosie? I don't believe you."

"Well, I'm not dead, you know, and Rosie's a damned powerful woman. It's just that she isn't the woman for me . . . much as I have days when I regret it."

Tag was incredulous. "Well, I guess you aren't the old lecher I thought you to be."

Doc looked up sharply. "Yes, I am . . . a lecher to the core . . . but not with Rosie or any woman as innocent as she is."

Tag was not surprised by Doc's use of the word "innocent" in reference to Rosie. Somehow it gave him more respect for the fellow knowing he saw past the obvious to Rosie's pure heart.

"Well?"

Tag frowned. "Well, what?"

"Well what are you goin' to do about it, you young fool! You're goin' to have to wake Rosie up! She's in for some big heartache, and I've got the feelin' that she can't stand too much more."

Tag drew himself tensely erect. "I'll ask you again. What are you talking about?"

Doc took a step closer, his voice dropping to a troubled whisper. "I don't know what kind of a game that big fella is playin' with Rosie, but she's way off track if she thinks he came back to Deadwood for her. I admit it looked that way for a few minutes inside, but it isn't so. The truth is that he came back to Deadwood with a woman."

"A woman!" Tag took a spontaneous step backward, the breath knocked from him as if from a blow. If Rosie knew . . .

". . . And a child—an infant."

Tag's stomach knotted painfully. "I . . . is the baby his?"

"No, I don't think so."

"You don't *think* so?"

"How would you expect me to know for sure?" Doc's stance became belligerent. "I wasn't there when it was conceived, and I only know what they tell me!"

"Who is this woman? Where is she? Why is she with McNeil?"

Doc's jaw tightened at the barrage of questions, but Tag was too disturbed to notice. He remembered the expression on Rosie's face when McNeil appeared in the doorway, and he remembered thinking that he'd do anything to have Rosie look at him that way just *one* time.

"The woman's name is Carolina Brand. She's the only survivor from that burned-out wagon train that was found a while back. Right now she's stayin' with Miriam Higgins. As for why she was with McNeil, he's the one who found her. He brought her here so's she can find her family and go back home."

Furious at being misled, Tag snapped heatedly, "Damn you, Fitz! If McNeil was only delivering the woman here—"

"There's more to it than that. I've seen the way McNeil looks at the woman . . . and the way the woman looks at him." Doc shook his head. "There's more to it than that, I tell you."

"That's not enough to put Rosie off. She's waited for McNeil for a long time."

"I know."

"You know?" Tag felt jealousy rear its ugly head. He remembered how difficult it had been to make Rosie tell him about the shame she carried behind that brave façade. He had told himself that he was special to her because she had never told another man the whole truth. He demanded tightly, "How much do you know?"

"Calm down, Willis. Whatever you're thinkin', Rosie only told me that this fella she was waitin' for had saved her life, that she had waited for him for a long time, and he was comin' back for her."

Tag nodded. The jealousy inside him deepened, turning in another direction as he rasped, "I suppose he *did* save her life in a way, although it didn't happen the way Rosie makes it sound. Only Rosie knows what she really means when she says that, but if McNeil hadn't happened upon her those years ago when he did, if he hadn't reacted in the way he did . . ."

Tag's voice drew to a gradual halt. He shuddered, jealousy fading into despair as he continued without a hint of his former animosity, "If we're putting all our cards on the table here, Doc, then I'll tell you this. You're right. I love Rosie. I've wanted to take things between us a step farther for a long time, but Rosie wouldn't hear of it. She told me from the beginning that she was waiting for McNeil, that he was coming back for her someday, but I only had to see him once to know what was inside that man. I thought it was just a matter of time before she'd relegate that part of her life to the past, where it belongs, and that we'd go on together from there. I wanted that more than anything in the world. But I was wrong. I underestimated the depth of pain Rosie hides behind that beautiful mask. She needs to put it aside forever, but there's only one man who can do that for her."

"That'll never happen with McNeil. The man is cold as ice inside."

"Not to Rosie."

Tag saw the old doc's gaze flicker. "If I don't miss my guess, Carolina Brand doesn't think McNeil is ice inside, either, but that's not the real problem here, Tag. The problem is that he *is*. I've seen that look he has in his eye before. He's a man with a mission . . . revenge, maybe . . . but whatever it is, he isn't goin' to let a woman . . . *any woman* . . . get in his way. He told Carolina that he's goin' back to his claim in a day or so, and he didn't bat an eye when it looked like her heart was fit to break. I'm thinkin' it wouldn't be any different with Rosie."

"She wouldn't be able to take that, Doc. If he turns his back on her . . ." Tag's voice cracked revealingly. "I . . . I don't know what she'll do."

Tag saw his own concern mirrored in the old man's eyes as Doc paused, then asked abruptly, "The point is, what are you goin' to do?"

A familiar hopelessness assaulted Tag. "What *can* I do? Rosie cut me loose. She doesn't want any part of me anymore."

"You're wrong." Doc's unexpected words ignited a spark of hope inside Tag as he continued, "Rosie won't admit it, but she's hurtin' because you took up with Ella so soon. She figures your feelin's for her weren't so deep if you stepped out of her bed and into Ella's without battin' an eye."

Tag was momentarily stunned. "Ella? I guess I should've figured what people would think, but I thought it was plain enough how I still feel about Rosie. Ella's a friend, Doc, somebody to talk to. She needed some help, and I gave it to her. She's grateful . . ." Tag hesitated before continuing, "But I haven't accepted her gratitude in the way she's been offering it to me . . . partially, I suppose, because I don't do things that way, and partially because Rosie's the only woman for me, and as long as she's within sight, I'm not about to take up with another."

"Well, I suggest you do somethin' about it, then, before it's too late."

"I've been telling myself the same thing, but when McNeil

walked through that doorway, I figured it *was* too late."

"It isn't." Doc turned away abruptly, tossing casually over his shoulder, "I'll let you know what I come up with."

Doc was gone as quickly as he had appeared, leaving Tag behind in the darkness. Staring into the shadows into which the old man had disappeared, Tag relived the nightmare of seeing McNeil walk through the door of the Nugget. His greatest fear had come true, but another nightmare now stood waiting in the wings, ready to materialize just as vividly.

A cold knot of fear tightened in Tag's stomach. He didn't want that to happen . . . not to his beautiful Rosie. He had to prevent it, but how . . . ?

Squinting in the bright light, Doc strode back into the Nugget. He was squinting for another reason as well—a pounding in his head that seemed to magnify the sounds of the bawdy music and drunken laughter into a painful din.

Stopping for a cursory glance around the crowded room, Doc continued on toward the bar. Rosie hadn't returned, and he wondered what that meant. Had she gone to seek McNeil out? No, Rosie wouldn't do that. He shook his head, regretting it a moment later as it throbbed all the harder. He muttered a curse. He *never* got headaches anymore. Headaches had been a daily occurrence for him during the war, but not since.

Doc recognized the significance of that thought. It didn't pay to care. Caring brought pain, but he had a surefire cure for the kind of pain that ailed him.

"Barney!" And when the balding bartender looked up, "Pour me a drink, and leave the bottle."

His glass filled a moment later, Doc raised it to his lips, almost choking as Barney snatched the bottle from his hand and returned it to the ledge behind the bar.

"I said leave it!"

"It's against orders."

"Whose orders?"

"Rosie's."

Doc glanced around him. He was getting madder by the minute. "Rosie isn't here."

"She is as far as *I'm* concerned. All you have to do is ask for a refill, Doc, and I'll pour."

"That's a waste of valuable time!"

Barney nodded pointedly. "Yeah, I know."

"Damn!"

Raising his glass back to his lips, Doc drained it and slapped it back down on the bar. "Fill it up!"

Watching as the amber liquid rose slowly to the rim, Doc jumped at the sound of Ella's throaty voice at his elbow.

"You'd think you were a three-year-old the way you're treated here. It beats me why you tolerate it, Doc."

Doc turned slowly toward Ella's sympathetic expression. He was not deceived. "What do you want, Ella?"

"What makes you think I want somethin'?"

"I'm not too old and not too drunk to see the obvious. Come on, out with it. What do you want?"

Ella's sympathetic expression faded. "You don't like me, do you, Doc?"

"How'd you guess?"

"Why?"

"Because you're out to get what you can get here, at anybody's expense." Doc's eyes narrowed. "And both those 'anybodies' happen to be friends of mine."

Ella raised her chin. "I don't know what you're talkin' about."

"Don't you? Well let me explain so there won't be any misunderstandin'. You're out to hook Tag, and I've seen the way you look at Rosie. If you have to cut her down in the process, it won't bother you one little bit."

"You're not bein' fair to me, Doc."

"Fair? What's fair?"

"Fair's admittin' that every other girl in this place made a play for Tag after Rosie threw him out, and nobody's come down on them."

"Rosie doesn't know what she wants."

Ella's eyes hardened. "I do."

"That so?"

"That's so, and I'm not ashamed to tell you that I go after what I want. And while I'm at it, I'll also tell you that it won't do no good followin' Tag outside to put a bee in his bonnet about Rosie, because it won't work. He's just about fed up with the way she's been treatin' him, and I'm tellin' you now, that when he's ready to turn to somebody for a sympathetic ear and a warm body, I'll be there to supply both."

"That time will never come."

"Think not? Well, I guess we're goin' to have to see which one of us is right."

Looking up as Tag reentered the room and waved her back to the table, Ella straightened up and smiled broadly. "I'll be leavin' you now, Doc. And don't waste your time worryin' about Tag. I'm goin' to make him real happy. And you don't have to bother tellin' him what we was just talkin' about, either, 'cause I ain't been shy about lettin' him know how I feel. He's goin' to take me up on my offer sooner or later. You know he will."

Watching as Ella walked back toward the poker tables in the rear of the room, Doc felt a strong urge to wretch. Hard as nails was that Ella. She'd bear some watchin'. . . .

Realizing that his head was pounding even harder than before, Doc tossed down the last of his drink. Gasping, knowing better, he slapped the bar for another.

Walking toward Tag, a smile on her face, Ella silently assessed his expression. Tag was upset. That dark-haired slut had done it on purpose, too, throwing herself at that big fella when she knew that Tag was pining away for so much as a smile from her. Inwardly fuming, Ella maintained her smile with sheer strength of will. She'd get that bitch for that, one way or another. And she'd take good care of Tag, too, just like she had told Doc at the bar. She wasn't afraid of that old drunk and his threats. She wasn't afraid of anything except having to go back to work for a pig the likes of Gus Ricks. Tag was her way out. She was going to take it, and *nobody* was going to get in her way.

Pausing at Tag's side, Ella leaned against him warmly for a

moment before resuming her seat at the table. He acknowl-edged her with an absentminded smile, but even that meager effort sent little shivers down her spine.

Ella sat down and picked up the cards. Her mind repeated a single word.

Nobody.

Seventeen

Carolina moved restlessly, unable to sleep. She looked again toward the window of the widow's cabin and the darkness beyond. The night was endless. Nightmares had returned vividly, awakening her time and again to a familiar terror. The pounding of horses hooves, gunshots, cries of the dying, and the blood. . . . Carolina breathed deeply in an attempt at control. The blood. . . .

Shuddering, she had drawn on the image of Drake in defense against her haunting dreams. She had ached for the comfort of Drake's arms, the solace of his voice, and the concern in his touch. The events of the day had paraded endlessly across her anxiety-clouded mind. She remembered Drake's awakening her when Deadwood first came into sight, and she remembered her exhilaration. She recalled the protective curve of his arms around her as they had ridden slowly down the main street. She remembered knowing instinctively that she had never felt so content and so safe, despite the unrestrained revelry around her.

A familiar despair rose in Carolina's throat. What had gone wrong? She looked at the makeshift cradle that Drake had carefully transported from the cabin in the hills. She knew the reason he had gone to such trouble to bring it with them, although she was certain he would deny it if asked. He had wanted Suzannah to feel secure and unthreatened in the familiarity of the only haven she had ever known. As her child slept peacefully, the wooden box resting atop the small work table Miriam has drawn up beside her bed, Carolina knew she did.

But Suzannah was an infant, unconcerned and unaware of the shift in the pattern of her life that would soon change its course so drastically. She did not know that the man who had delivered her into the world and watched her take her first breath, who had cared for her when her own mother had been too ill to attend her, who had changed her and rocked her to sleep in his strong arms and who had sung her into peaceful oblivion in his uncertain baritone, was preparing to walk out of their lives forever.

Carolina paused, her thoughts weighing heavily on her heart. Suzannah did not know, but she did. She knew that Drake's strength, his concern, the compassion he fought so hard to conceal would soon be denied to her. But it was more than that. The feeling she had experienced that first day when she had awakened to the pain of childbirth in a world she did not know and had found Drake crouched by her side, had not waned. Even disguised as he had been by a heavy beard and dark hair spilling onto his shoulders, she had recognized him. He was the man she had known would come . . . the man she had awaited all her life.

Carolina looked down at the plain gold band on her finger. She could not remember the man who had put it there, but she knew . . . she was somehow certain . . . that he would never have been able to be to her what Drake had become in three short weeks of her life.

Carolina paused again, considering that thought. With no basis for comparison, how could she be so sure? The answer was suddenly clear. She had seen the strengths of Drake, but she had also seen the weaknesses. She had glimpsed scars inside him where large, gaping wounds had once torn him apart. She knew they had crippled him in ways that could not be viewed with the naked eye. She had felt those scars healing in the weeks they had spent together. A softer man had begun to emerge—the man she had sensed was inside him if she would only seek him out. She *had* sought him out without conscious thought, and with the healing of Drake's scars had come a healing of her own.

Drake needed her and she needed him in order for them both to be complete. Yes, it was so clear to her now. . . .

A few days. . . . Drake had said he would stay in Deadwood for a few days before returning to the cabin. She had seen his eyes when he had said the words. They had been as cold as ice. For some reason, the scars had become raw once more.

The sun rose over the mountain, dispelling the darkness outside the window and bringing forth the new day in brilliant celebration of life, and Carolina's heart began a slow pounding. The fears she had suffered through the night faded as suddenly as the darkness, and a celebration began inside her as well. She was abruptly certain she had worried for naught. Drake wouldn't leave her. Because of his scars, because of the past that still haunted him, Drake struggled against those things that he knew as instinctively as she, but he could never desert her. He had a few days to realize it. It would be enough.

In her bed a short distance away, Miriam stirred. Throwing back her blanket, Carolina slipped her legs over the side of the settee. She was anxious for the day to begin.

Drake awakened to the new day with a start. Momentarily disoriented, he glanced around the unfamiliar room, realizing he was in Doc Fitz's office. The order of things slipping into place, he recalled that he had finally managed to fall asleep the previous night, only to hear Doc Fitz stagger through the doorway a few minutes later, bumping and crashing, appearing not to miss a single piece of furniture on his way toward his small room in the rear. The smell of liquor about the old man had been so strong that he had wondered if the fellow had indeed bathed in the devil's brew, and he had begun to understand the widow's sharp glances and even sharper gibes. But that was Doc's business, not his.

Throwing back his blanket, Drake swung his legs over the side of the couch, peculiarly at a loss. He wondered if

Carolina had spent a restful night . . . if the babe had allowed it. He was uncomfortable with the suddenly driving desire to see her, to touch her.

Annoyed at the direction of his thoughts, Drake stood up and reached for his clothes. He was fully dressed moments later, but it took only a glimpse in the mirror to see that he was a disreputable sight with a heavily shadowed chin and roughly cut hair. He knew his appearance had been far worse three weeks earlier when he had first come upon Carolina. He had no doubt that he had appeared more animal than man then, yet there had been spontaneous trust in her eyes when they had met his. He wondered what he would see in her eyes now. . . .

Turning with a snap, Drake snatched up his hat and started toward the door. It made little difference what he would see. In a few days' time, Carolina Brand would be nothing more than a memory.

Miriam had put forth her greatest effort for breakfast. Fresh eggs from the chickens she tended so carefully behind her small cabin, generous portions of her jealously guarded smoked ham, biscuits that melted in the mouth, and the good, strong coffee that Jonas had always said started his day with a sharp shove.

Miriam looked up from her plate and cast a covert glance between the two who sat opposite each other across the table. She raised her hand to the bun at the nape of her neck, fingering it for loose strands in the way she did when anxious. Her mind registered that all was well with her severe coiffure, even as it registered that the situation between the two young people appeared dismal.

Despite her effort, breakfast had been an uncomfortable meal. Carolina had picked at her plate and had flushed with embarrassment when she had finally put her fork down with the contents barely touched. Drake had eaten well, but she doubted that he had tasted a bite. The conversation had been halting and awkward. Had it not been for

The Publishers of Zebra Books
Make This Special Offer
to Zebra Romance Readers...

Suzannah's opportune interruptions, she supposed there would have been little conversation at all.

Miriam withheld a smile as she recalled the first time Suzannah's wail interrupted the uncomfortable silence. Carolina and Drake had jumped up simultaneously in a manner that was almost comical. At a word from Drake, Carolina had resumed her seat to allow him to attend to the babe. She had been surprised at that, but she realized that she shouldn't have been, since the big man with the cold eyes had obviously had full responsibility for the baby until Carolina had recuperated from her ordeal.

A greater surprise had come when the big fellow had turned back to the table with the babe changed and dry in his arms. In the brief moments until he had put the babe into Carolina's arms, his eyes had been cold no longer.

In a morning of surprises, however, the greatest one had come much earlier, when she had first opened the door to Drake McNeil's knock and seen him standing on her doorstep. Shaved, bathed, and well groomed, wearing what appeared to be a shirt recently purchased under his light jacket, he had almost taken her breath away.

So handsome. . . .

As dumbstruck as Miriam had been with Drake's impressive appearance, she had known intuitively that the look on Carolina's face as he had entered, the relief and the joy the quiet young woman had attempted to conceal, had little to do with the way he looked. She had sensed another thing as well. The big man was inhibited by her presence and was waiting for the right moment to speak to Carolina in private. She wondered what he had to say.

As if in response to her thoughts, Drake cleared his throat, drawing her attention as he spoke.

"I have some things I have to take care of this morning. Thank you for breakfast, Mrs. Higgins. It was very good."

Carolina rose silently to her feet. Miriam could almost feel the young woman's heart leap when Drake addressed her.

"I have some last-minute arrangements I'd like to make if

you can come with me, Carolina."

"Of course. I'll get Suzannah."

Miriam winced. Carolina's reply was too quick, too anxious. She interjected softly, "Don't disturb the child. I'll be happy to take care of her until you return."

Carolina paused and Drake responded in her stead.

"We won't be long."

Certain she could hear Carolina's heart falling to her shoes at the sudden coldness in his voice, Miriam turned toward Suzannah. Her blood began a slow boil. The fellow was either possessed of a cruel streak, completely insensitive, or blind—she was uncertain which. But she knew one thing for sure: Drake McNeil held Carolina Brand's heart in his big, callused hands. She only hoped he would not crush it.

Carolina shivered at the nip in the morning air and pulled her coat closer around her. She glanced up at Drake as he walked silently beside her. He was so tall, so handsome. . . . She had paid so little attention to his appearance in the past that it had come almost as a shock when he had entered Miriam's cabin that morning and she had realized how truly handsome he was. She, on the other hand . . .

Carolina raised her chin, aware that her average appearance had suffered as a result of her recent ordeal. She was even thinner than she had been, and more pale. A short glimpse in Miriam's mirror that morning had confirmed that dark shadows under her light eyes made them appear even larger, almost overwhelming in her small face. Her baggy dress did little to add to her feminine appeal, and as she had worked her hair into a single braid in an attempt at control of her thick, unmanageable locks, she had deplored the look of herself. But she had cast those thoughts aside as she attempted to do again. This new Drake . . . this handsome Drake . . . was the same man whose heart had touched hers through long days and nights in the wilderness. They had been bonded by the unusual intimacies they had shared. She had grown close to Drake. She sensed it was the same with him. She *knew* it was. Appearances meant little.

But still . . .

The rough, muddy ground underneath their feet turned to an uneven boardwalk and Carolina looked around her, startled at the dense mass of male humanity surging along the narrow street. The sounds of construction that had appeared to resume at the first light of day grew louder, and the traffic in and out of the saloons and commercial establishments was already heavy. Her step faltered and Drake looked sharply toward her.

In answer to the inquiry in Drake's eyes, she responded, "Miriam said it's Sunday . . ." She was momentarily embarrassed at the admission that she had needed to be informed of the day of the week as she continued, "I didn't expect . . . I mean, it's the day of rest. . . ."

"There're no churches in Deadwood and no day of rest, either." Drake squinted down at her. "The only thing that sets Sunday apart from any other day of the week here is that it's usually busier because miners from the surrounding camps come in to get their mail or supplies and to have a little fun."

The bellow of an angry bull whacker interrupted Drake as the fellow attempted to turn his team on the street. A stream of profanities more colorful and emphatic than Carolina had ever heard rent the din, and she flushed. Drake's eyes narrowed further, seeming to find her lacking. His apparent disapproval darkened her flush as they made their way through the confusion of unloading freight wagons at every door and the ever-increasing crowd on the walk.

Shouted oaths, the crack of the lash, loud complaints from tired cattle, and the resonant braying of mules echoed behind them as they continued down the street, but the uncomfortable silence between Drake and her remained. She had almost despaired at it when a disheveled fellow staggered out of a nearby saloon and lurched toward them. Drake's arm snapped protectively around her waist, removing her from the man s path. It was the first time Drake had touched her that day, and Carolina's heart took on a glow that gave her the courage to ask, "Where are we going, Drake?"

Drake's only response was to survey the street more closely. Appearing to spot the establishment he sought, he pushed through the doorway minutes later, ushering her along beside him. Just inside the entrance, he drew her aside and frowned down into her face.

"I'm going back to the cabin in a day or so, Carolina, but there are some things that need to be done first."

Carolina's heart turned to lead. "Things?"

Drake glanced around the crowded store, obviously frustrated at the lack of privacy. When his gaze returned to her face it was determined.

"I want to be sure you and Suzannah are provided for before I leave. You need things . . . clothes. . . ."

Carolina took a step back. She didn't want Drake's charity. Neither did she want his pity. She raised her chin. "I don't need anything."

"This is no time to be stubborn! If you don't want to think of yourself, think of Suzannah. How do you expect to survive until you go back home?"

. . . until you go back home . . .

"Carolina . . ."

. . . until you go back home . . .

"Carolina, are you listening?"

"Yes."

"You'll need some necessities. . . ."

"No."

"What do you mean, 'no'?"

Carolina avoided his eye as she fought to overcome the lump in her throat. "I mean you've done enough for Suzannah and me already. You're not responsible for us, and you don't have to spend your money on—"

"Look at me!" Drake grasped her arms, interrupting her

260

protest with visible anger. "I didn't spend every day and night for three weeks nursing you back to health just to throw you to the wolves here in Deadwood."

"I'll be all right. I can take care of myself and Suzannah."

"Doing what?" Drake's eyes were beginning to spark fire. "Tell me! Doing what?"

A slow panic grew inside Carolina as she searched her mind. What *could* she do? She had no money, no shelter, no means of support. She had no one but Drake. . . .

"Answer me."

"I don't know!"

Strangely weak once the admission had passed her lips, Carolina relied heavily on the support of Drake's hands as he continued harshly, "Well, I know. You're going to do as I say . . . now. You're going to buy whatever necessities you need and then we're going to arrange for a place for you and Suzannah to stay until you're physically fit enough to leave Deadwood."

"Leave Deadwood? Where would I go?"

"To Sioux City. From there it's only a short journey to Illinois. Your wagon train came out of Illinois. You can contact the agency that sponsored your train. Someone is bound to know you."

Carolina did not speak. The meaning behind Drake's words was clear. He wanted her to go back home . . . wherever that was . . . anywhere, as long as it was away from him.

"Carolina . . ."

Carolina blinked. She owed Drake so much. The least she could do would be to allow him to leave her with his mind at rest.

"Yes."

"Yes?"

"Yes, you're right. Suzannah and I must pick up our lives. You're very kind to want to help us. Thank you."

The fire in Drake's eyes grew to a threatening blaze. "I've told you before, I don't want your thanks!"

261

Dropping his hands abruptly to his sides, Drake held her gaze in silence for a moment before he ordered, "Let's get on with it."

Standing at the counter a moment later, ignoring the obvious curiosity of the thin, balding storekeeper, Drake said flatly, "The lady needs some clothes."

Watching as Carolina looked through a short rack of ready-made dresses, Drake could not remember ever being more angry. Infuriating him even more was his realization that he was angry at himself. But he was out of his depth, and he knew it.

You're very kind. Thank you.

Drake's anger flared anew. He didn't want gratitude from Carolina. He wanted to be free of the concern that had surged anew when he had noted her pallor and the shadows under her eyes that had told him all he had needed to know about the kind of night she had spent in Miriam's cabin. He wanted to be free of the desire to protect her, to console her, to keep her never far from his sight. He wanted to be free of the need to touch her, to keep her in the circle of his arms. He wanted to be free to follow the course he had set for himself seven years ago . . . to accomplish the goal that was the only possible balm for a wound that still festered inside him after all those years. He wanted to be free. . . .

He *would* be free.

Drake's eyes narrowed as Carolina fumbled with a small white tag attached to the dress in her hand. He heard her gasp as she turned it over.

"The price isn't your concern, Carolina."

Carolina was obviously distressed. "But . . . perhaps if I bought some material and sewed the clothes myself . . ."

"You don't have time."

Carolina did not respond. Suddenly impatient, Drake took the dress from Carolina's hand. He scrutinized it with a critical eye. It was blue, a simple style with little decoration. He didn't like it very much. He continued looking

262

through the rack and after a few moments, withdrew a pink cotton decorated with a fine white lace.

"Do you think this one will fit?"

"It's too expensive."

"Will it fit?"

Carolina's lips tightened. "I don't know."

"The young lady can try the dress on in the back room if she likes." The gaze Drake turned on the storekeeper who had interrupted their exchange hastened the man to add, "She'll have complete privacy there."

Drake watched as Carolina disappeared into the back room a few moments later, both dresses and the necessary undergarments and accessories in her hands. He was prowling like a hungry bear when she finally emerged and paused uncertainly in the doorway.

"Will this do?"

Would it do?

It took only a moment for Drake to see that Carolina was sincere in her question, that she had no realization of the picture she made in the pale pink cotton that lay smoothly against her slight proportions. Standing as she was, her light eyes uncertain, her cheeks borrowing a pale color from her dress, the lace that graced the high collar and cuffs accenting her fragile femininity, she was so lovely that it hurt. He took a spontaneous step toward her as a slurred, grating voice sounded behind him.

"Ma'am, you're the prettiest thing these old eyes of mine have seen since I came to this godforsaken hole! Damned if I ain't goin' to give you a kiss!"

Drake stepped into the path of the drunken miner with a menacing growl. "Get out of here, fella, while you're still able."

Too far gone to recognize his danger, the unsteady fellow persisted, "Just one kiss, buddy. Hell, it'll be like a visit to heaven."

Drake's voice dripped with threat. "One more step, and I can promise you you'll pay heaven more than a visit."

Appearing to recognize the sincerity of Drake's words,

the fellow staggered back through the doorway onto the street.

Drake turned back to Carolina, his voice gruff. "The dress is fine."

Carolina disappeared into the back room. Emerging clothed in her old dress, she stated flatly, "I think we should go now."

Drake took both dresses from Carolina's hands and a firm hold on his patience. Emerging onto the street a few minutes later, he glanced around in silent scrutiny. The old sot with amorous intent was probably propped up against the nearest bar by now, Carolina and her pink dress forgotten. The only trouble was, *he* hadn't forgotten.

A warning bell sounded in Drake's mind as he looked down at Carolina's averted face. She had grown so quiet. He was uncertain what she was thinking, and he didn't like it. He liked even less the barrier her unnatural silence was erecting between them, but he'd be damned if he'd let it affect what he had set out to do.

His expression firmed as she looked up. "Doc Fitz can probably direct us to the best transportation out of Deadwood for you and Suzannah."

Carolina's step faltered, and Drake gripped her arm. "Are you all right?"

"I'm fine."

Carolina's response was too quick. She was *not* all right. Her color had paled and she was trembling. Damn! Drake slipped his arm around her shoulders. "On second thought, we can do that another time. I think you've been away from Suzannah long enough."

Carolina's relief was immediately apparent. Guiding her back along the crowded walk, Drake drew Carolina closer against his side, intensely aware that he was as relieved as she to have put off the final details of separation. And he cursed himself because of it.

Smiling, Rosie stepped out into the brilliant morning

264

sunlight. She nodded a flirting greeting to familiar customers lingering nearby and started on down the street, her step brisk. She had found it difficult to fall asleep the previous night for the glorious dreams that had filled her mind after Drake's arrival, but sleep had finally come. She had awakened surprisingly refreshed and anxious to begin the day. Dressing quickly, Rosie had chosen to wear a vibrant azure dress that was styled more modestly than the rest of her gowns, knowing the color deepened the blue of her eyes to a flattering degree and enhanced the natural highlights of her hair. She had applied the barest minimum of makeup that could be expected of a woman in her trade, and surveying herself critically in her mirror, she had been pleased with what she saw. Her heart beating a rapid tattoo, she was certain Drake would be, too.

Rosie's smile brightened. She had laid her plans well. She did not intend to wait for Drake to come to her. She would use every minute . . . every hour, to make him see as clearly as she that they—

The crowd in front of her shifted, and Rosie stopped short with a gasp. The world swayed around her. No, it couldn't be . . . ! That couldn't be Drake walking toward her, looking more handsome than he had a right to be, with one arm loaded with packages that she knew instinctively were not purchases for him, and the other wrapped securely around the shoulders of a woman.

The light of happiness within her darkened to fury as Drake walked directly toward her. And Rosie wondered why, in all her imaginings, it had never occurred to her that Drake might want another woman. . . .

Carolina walked silently in the protective curve of Drake's arm, but there was no joy inside her. More than anything, she wanted to get away from Drake now, to divorce herself from his concern, from his kindness . . . and from his pity. She had seen the pity in his eyes when he had forced her to face her true situation for the first time.

265

Alone, homeless, without funds or means of support for her child and herself, without knowing anything more about herself than her name, she was totally dependent upon his charity. She had wondered briefly why she had never viewed her situation in that way before. It had not taken her long to realize that she had not because she had deceived herself into seeing more in Drake's kindness than he was prepared to give.

The pain of that acknowledgment still fresh, Carolina paused as the crowded walk thinned momentarily, allowing her a view of an extremely beautiful woman who stood stock-still in their path. Shock, jealousy, and then rage flashed in the woman's expressive eyes in a fleeting moment of revelation before the woman smiled.

Drake's arm fell from her shoulders as they drew within a few feet of the woman. She was startled by the affection in his voice as he said, "Good morning, Rosie. I'd like you to meet a friend of mine, Carolina Brand."

And Carolina wondered why, in all of her imaginings, it had never occurred to her that Drake might want another woman.

"Come right on in, Jerome. . . ."

Miriam stepped back from the doorway of her cabin to allow him entrance, and Doc knew in that instant that he had made a mistake. Trying not to shudder as he raised a foot to step over the threshold, he suddenly saw himself as the proverbial fly accepting the invitation of a smiling spider. It was not a comfortable feeling.

He balked.

"I . . . I had some things to talk over with McNeil and Carolina, but I can see they aren't here. I don't want to disturb you. Maybe I'd better come back later."

"Don't be ridiculous. They should be back any moment. You can wait for them here." Grasping his arm, Miriam jerked him inside with surprising strength, then pushed the door closed behind him. He could almost see her eyes glow

266

as she said, "You didn't think I was going to let you slip away again, did you?"

Doc swallowed with a gulp, momentarily without response as the proximity of Miriam's tall, erect form caused his heart to flip-flop in his chest.

"All right, out with it, Jerome! What's gotten into you!"

"What's gotten into me?" Recovering, Doc took a deep breath, determined to take his humiliating secret to his grave. "What's gotten into you is more like it! I was beginnin' to feel like a leper the way you've been avoidin' me."

Miriam's small eyes widened to twice their size, and Doc inwardly congratulated himself for turning the tables on his sharp-witted opponent. Unwilling to allow her time to recuperate, he continued in a rush, ". . . Never answerin' the door when I came to drop off my laundry, skitterin' out of my way on the street whenever you could. . . . Damn, Miriam, a man would start to think you've got somethin' to hide!"

"Jerome Fitz . . ." Miriam took an aggressive step forward, her eyes narrowing. "You *never* knocked on my door and you know it!"

"I did!"

"You didn't!"

"I did!"

Miriam's voice took on a warning tone. "Jerome . . ." She stared at him, asking suddenly, "What *is* that? Is that a pimple I see growing on your nose because of that great lie you've just told?"

Doc raised his hand to his sizable proboscis, then snapped it back to his side as Miriam shouted, "Aha! Caught you, didn't I?"

"You didn't catch me doin' anythin'!" Doc shook himself, hesitant to continue his verbal jousting with the clever widow. "If there's anythin' that's plain to see, it's that we've somehow been perpetuatin' a misunderstandin' between us these last few weeks. I sure am glad that I came all the way here this mornin' just to set it all straight once and for all."

"You didn't!"

"I did!"

"You didn't!"

"I did! Oh, damn it, Miriam, let it rest, will you?" Despising the plea that had entered his voice, Doc continued, "I think there're more pressin' problems to discuss today than a few bent feelin's between us. The plight of that poor young woman you were kind enough to take in last night, for instance."

Miriam glanced toward the babe who slept in a small wooden box on a nearby table. All sign of agitation faded as she responded in a voice totally unlike her formerly shrill tone, "And the plight of that darling infant, too."

There it was again, the softness in that thin face, the glow that imparted a beauty to Miriam's homely features that tugged at his heart . . . and another less conscientious part of his anatomy. Doc resisted the urge to shake himself again. He *was* going crazy!

"Yes, that *darling* infant, too." Doc continued, grateful for the distraction, "Confidentially, can you tell me what in hell's goin' on between that young woman and McNeil?"

"Nothing, more's the pity."

"Miriam!" Doc was truly shocked. "I can't believe you said that, a respectable widow like you! Carolina Brand lost her husband no less than a month ago!"

"A month . . . a year, what's the difference? Carolina's husband is dead and she can't even remember him. She's too young to spend her life alone, especially in this hard land, and this dear child needs a father. If she's found someone she can love, someone who loves her and the child—"

Doc gasped. "So that's the drift of things. . . ."

"No, it isn't."

Perplexed, Doc all but shouted, "Then what in hell are you talkin' about, Miriam?"

"Don't you yell at me, Jerome Fitz!" Her back going ramrod stiff, Miriam looked down her nose at him, stimulating a familiar annoyance as she continued, "My dear Jonas never yelled at me, and I won't allow any other man

268

to yell at me, either!"

"Oh, no? Well, how in hell are you goin' to stop me?"

"You will cease those profanities immediately, *Doctor* Fitz, or you will leave my house!"

"Oh, you won't throw *me* out."

"Oh, no? Why not, may I ask?"

"Because you want to get to the bottom of this mess with McNeil just as much as I do."

"Mess?" Quick to catch his slip, the widow pinned him with her gaze. "Do you know something that I don't know, Jerome?"

Damn!

A knock at the door interrupted opportunely, turning Miriam to it with an incredibly sweet, "Come in!"

The door opened to reveal the young couple they had been discussing. One look at Carolina's pallor and Doc moved to her side. He dislodged McNeil's clutching grip and ushered her to the nearest chair. The vein in her temple was pulsing rapidly, but the rhythm was strong and even. He patted her hand.

"It looks to me as if you've overdone things this morning, dear. Have you taken your tonic?"

"We haven't had the prescription filled yet." Responding in her stead, McNeil continued stiff-faced, "I'll get it done right now."

"Yes, I suggest you do."

Watching as the big fellow dropped his packages on the nearest chair, Doc waited until the door had closed behind him before looking directly into Carolina's eyes and continuing, "And while he's gone, you and I will have a nice talk. Would you like that, dear?"

The young woman did not reply.

A smile frozen on her lips, Rosie walked toward the gaily painted false front of the Nugget Saloon. She had not questioned her direction after her meeting with Drake and the unexpected Carolina Brand. Their conversation had been

269

brief and she was returning to the only home she knew—to the only security in her life. She paused at the saloon door, realizing that this security was a poor substitute for the love that had filled the greater part of her life with hope.

Pausing there momentarily, she acknowledged shouts of welcome from the bar, but she saw nothing but the wan face of the woman Drake held so protectively in the curve of his arm.

I'd like you to meet a friend of mine, Carolina Brand. . . .

Suddenly certain she would retch, Rosie covered her mouth with her hand and turned at a run. Fleeing down the alleyway, she felt her breath catch in her throat as her cabin came into view. Through the doorway in a moment, she stumbled toward the washbasin, remaining there until the painful spasms ceased. She had not realized that she was not alone until she felt a touch on her arm and heard Tag's voice behind her.

"What's the matter? Are you sick?"

Unable to speak, Rosie staggered to the bed and sat weakly. Her eyes closed, she raised her face to the wet cloth Tag sponged across her brow and lips moments later. She did not question the concern in his voice as he repeated, "What's wrong, Rosie?"

Her voice emerged in a harsh rasp. "Drake has himself a woman. . . . She's a pale, weak-looking thing, hardly a woman at all! She's not good enough for Drake . . . not woman enough for him. She could never make him happy!"

"Are you sure you know the full story, Rosie? Maybe you're wrong . . . jumping to conclusions."

"I saw them together." A thread of hatred entered Rosie's tone. "I saw the way she looked at Drake."

"I think the way Drake looked at her is probably more important."

A sob escaped Rosie's throat. "He looked at her as if the sun rose and set in her eyes."

"I don't believe it."

"He did!" Rosie sobbed again. "He did!"

Tag paused in response. He sat beside her on the bed and slid his arm around her and Rosie leaned full against him for support. Dear Tag . . . dependable Tag . . . he loved her. She only wished she could love him in return.

Rosie attempted to withdraw from Tag's comfort only to hear his whisper, "No, Rosie. Stay still and listen to me for a moment. I think you're torturing yourself unnecessarily. I think you've got this thing all wrong."

"No."

"Yes, listen to me. Drake came into town with the woman last night. He found her wandering in the hills. She's the only survivor of that wagon train that was discovered burned out a few weeks ago. He's been taking care of her and her child."

"There's a child . . . ?"

"It's not his, Rosie."

"How do you know?"

"I know."

"She was with Drake all this time . . . in his cabin . . . alone . . . ?" Rosie's heart fell into shreds.

"She was sick. She's not well yet. Drake is trying to make arrangements for her welfare, that's all."

Rosie stared up at Tag. She read an earnestness there and she knew he wanted her to believe him. She wondered at the selflessness of a man who would defend another man to the woman he loved, just so she might be happy. She wished she had as generous a heart. But she did not.

"How do you know all this, Tag?"

"I made it my business to know."

"And you didn't tell me?"

"I didn't think you'd want to hear it from me and I figured you'd find out sooner or later."

Rosie's throat choked once more. "I saw her face, Tag, and I saw his."

"You're wrong, Rosie."

"I'm not."

"I wish you weren't, but you are."

Breaking down into sobs, Rosie clung to Tag. She felt his arms go around her. She felt his cheek against her hair. She felt his hand stroke her back and she whispered, "You still love me, don't you? I thought you had found someone else."

"Never."

"Oh, Tag, why doesn't Drake love me the way *you* love me?"

Tag was momentarily silent. She felt his hand on her chin as he raised her face to his. She heard his whisper as he attempted a smile. "Why don't you love me the way I love you? I wish I knew the answer to both those questions."

Panic touched Rosie's senses. "What am I going to do?"

"Stop worrying, that's what you're going to do. Everything will be all right. You'll see."

But Tag's words were no more than empty sounds. She had seen Carolina Brand's face, and she had seen the way Drake looked at her. Realizing she could stand little more, Rosie sought refuge from her fears by summoning the picture in her mind that had brought her through the darkest days of her life—the fireplace, the tall man standing beside it, holding her in his arms—but it was no good. The man had become a shadow whose touch she could not feel and the fire in the hearth was dying. If it went out, she did not think she would survive.

Shuddering anew, Rosie was uncertain of the moment when Tag lifted her onto his lap, when he tucked her head against his neck and began rocking her as he would a child. In the safety of his arms, she allowed her tears full rein.

Standing outside Rosie's cabin, Ella peered cautiously through the window, her breath catching in her throat. Rosie in Tag's arms. . . .

She drew back, the sight more painful than she could bear. She had seen Rosie in the doorway of the saloon, and she had seen Tag follow her when she had fled. Something had gone wrong for the little bitch, and she was not above

272

using Tag for consolation, then tossing him aside when her need for him was gone.

Tag was a fool! He couldn't see past Rosie's bright blue eyes and soft white skin. He didn't realize that *she* could do more for him than the little witch had ever done. She'd never take him for granted, either . . . hell, no. She was too smart for that.

Refusing to look back, Ella turned into the alleyway and made her way toward the street. She'd get her chance, and when she did, she'd use it. Then Tag would be hers for good.

Yes, her time would come. . . .

Exhausted, her tears spent, Rosie closed her eyes as Tag tucked a pillow under her head and drew the coverlet up over her. She felt his mouth brush hers and heard his rasping endearment the moment before he drew himself to his feet and walked toward the door.

Releasing a sigh as the door closed behind him, she saw Drake's image again before her mind's eye. It was no good. Tag's words of consolation meant little. She had seen the tenderness in Drake's eyes when he looked at that woman. He had been protective, concerned. He had touched the woman easily, as if at ease with the intimacy.

A burning jealousy surged anew, striking a pain so severe within her that Rosie temporarily lost her breath. Her eyes wide, her breathing restored moments later, Rosie made a vow.

She'd get her chance, and when she did, she'd use it. Then Drake would be hers for good.

Yes, her time would come. . . .

Eighteen

The sounds of revelry had increased as daylight waned, but they held little attraction to Drake as he walked along the crowded street. Stepping down off the brief boardwalk, he continued to the end of the street and the stable located there, uncertain of the reason for his visit even as he turned in through the doorway.

"Somethin' I can do for you?"

There was no need to turn to recognize the origin of the voice. The odor of Deadwood's livery stable proprietor was more powerful than the nearby stalls.

"No, nothin'. I just came to check on my bay. He was favorin' his right foreleg on the way here."

"There ain't nothin' wrong with that animal." The old fellow rubbed his beard with a grimy hand. "He's just ornery. That pack animal you got ain't much better. Damned if he didn't kick me. Near to broke my leg."

Drake scrutinized the old man's expression. "Is that right?"

"Yeah, that's right, and after I fed and watered him so nice, too. But don't worry, I ain't goin' to charge you extra. It served me right, I guess, forgettin' that there ain't no gratitude forthcomin' from animals."

The old man limped away, but Drake hardened himself against his obvious pain. The old boy had it right. If a man didn't learn by experience, he deserved everything he got.

Taking only a minute to satisfy himself as to the status of his animals, Drake walked back out onto the street. He paused, noting that Deadwood had started to come alive with lights that softened the tawdriness so apparent during the day. He allowed his thoughts of a few minutes earlier to wash over him.

Gratitude was a short-lived emotion. Even if it wasn't, he neither needed it nor wanted it from anyone, most especially a woman. He had been trapped by gratitude once before when he had been foolish enough to believe it could earn him love. He had trusted deeply because of it, only to learn the hard way that gratitude soon turned to resentment and resentment to treachery . . . that was the way of things. He would never be taken in again.

That thought still fresh in his mind, Drake found his gaze returning to the opposite end of town as it had so many times that day. The traffic on the street impeded his view of Miriam Higgins's cabin, but it was of little consequence. It drew him strongly without visual persuasion.

Lifting his hat from his head, Drake ran his hand through his hair, then settled it squarely back on his forehead. It had been a long day which had not started particularly well. Carolina's bout of weakness after they had finished shopping that morning had unsettled him. He remembered her pallor and her trembling as he had curved a protective arm around her. He had cut short their ill-timed meeting with Rosie in order to rush Carolina back to the cabin. He owed Rosie an explanation for that. He would explain the reason and more tonight. Carolina would need all the friends she could get when he was gone, and he knew no one could find a truer friend than Rosie.

His gaze focusing on the garish false front of the Nugget Saloon, Drake gave an unconscious nod and started purposely forward, unwilling to admit that he was running out of excuses to keep him away from Miriam Higgins's cabin. He reviewed the activities of the day.

After Doc Fitz's sharp admonition, he had gone directly to the pharmacist's shop to fill the prescription Doc had ordered. He had returned immediately and watched as Carolina had taken the first dose. Strangely enough, he had been annoyed with the lack of privacy afforded Carolina and him in the widow's cabin. There were many things that he wanted to say to Carolina that were impossible in the presence of others . . . but he was somehow uncertain exactly what they were. He supposed that was the reason he had left in disgust shortly afterward, only to return later in the afternoon to find the same situation prevailed with Miriam Higgins fluttering around Carolina and him, privy to every word they spoke.

As for Suzannah, it appeared that Miriam took every opportunity—each peep of sound the babe made—to pick her up or stand hovering over her. So involved had she become in pampering the infant that she had even spoken of borrowing a "proper" cradle, when Drake knew Suzannah was perfectly content sleeping as she was. It annoyed him—more than annoyed him—and he had felt a surge of pure satisfaction when Carolina had spoken up, telling Miriam that would not be necessary.

Miriam had, however, been able to provide for the child in a way he had not. Upon his return to the cabin later that afternoon, he had found Carolina sorting through a mound of infant's clothing. He had been startled by Miriam's ability to produce the apparel when he had been unable to uncover clothing for the babe anywhere in town, at any price. Uncertain of his reaction to Miriam's success where he had failed so miserably, he knew only that Suzannah had looked truly beautiful in the pale pink embroidered sacque in which she was dressed, the first article of proper clothing she had ever worn.

A sadness had slipped over Drake on seeing the babe so clothed, as he felt her slipping gradually farther and farther away from him. He had mentally chastised himself for that reaction. He had wanted to be relieved of responsibility for Carolina and her child, to be able to turn his back on them without the need to spare them another thought, *hadn't he?*

To that end, Drake had spent the entire afternoon in trips back and forth to Miriam's cabin, attempting to settle Carolina's future as best he could. He had visited the nearest bank and opened an account for Carolina and her child with an amount that had greatly lightened the weight of his precious pouch of gold dust. He had told himself that his peace of mind would be worth the weeks of work that would be necessary to replace it. He had then visited Doc Fitz at his office. Between an extremely painful case of poison ivy which had left the stricken prospector almost unable to button his drawers, and a knife wound that had come about as the result of a lover's spat, he had managed to discuss the safest modes of transportation back to civilization. He had left Doc's office with a clear decision as to the particular conveyance Carolina should use when she was strong enough to travel. He would see about arranging for Carolina's passage tomorrow.

Those details accomplished, he had then gone about the purchase of supplies for his return to the cabin. They were presently piled and ready for pickup in Bob O'Neil's General Store. He had somehow expected a sense of great relief would accompany that realization, but it had not. To the contrary, the sinking sensation that had begun inside him the first night in Deadwood, after he had pulled Miriam's cabin door closed and left Carolina behind him, had grown greater with each task he had performed until it was now a deadening ache. Damn, but he needed a drink!

The Nugget grew closer, and Drake released a silent sigh as the aroma of baking bread wafted from the bakery nearby. He was reminded of the afternoon meal he had eaten alone, and the evening meal he had also eaten in his own company. He had spent the entire time remembering that Carolina had barely touched her plate that morning. He knew her appetite was suffering as a result of her uncertain circumstances and he had a driving desire to console her, to hold her close and tell her that all would be well.

The doorway of the Nugget loomed in front of him, but Drake found himself continuing past despite his thoughts a few minutes previously. He looked at Miriam Higgins's cabin as he approached, and his stubborn chin hardened.

He was determined. He would get a few minutes in private with Carolina at any price.

The cabin was silent except for the steady sound of Suzannah's even breathing. Carolina smiled at the contented expression on her daughter's smooth, flushed face, then adjusted her new chemise and buttoned up the front of her bodice. The fabric of her dress was crisp underneath her fingertips, a reminder of the shopping expedition with Drake that morning that had ended so abruptly.

Despite her discomfort, Carolina had changed into her new clothing at her first opportunity, determined that the ragged dress she had worn for the greater part of the time she had spent in the hills with Drake would get another well-needed laundering. Carefully folding away the pink dress that Drake had selected, she had slipped on the simple blue cotton. A glance in the mirror had revealed that the dress was little more than adequate. She had taken the time to rebraid her hair and wind it into a simple crown atop her head but the effort had made little improvement on her appearance. She had despaired at the memory of the beautiful young woman named Rosie Blake whom Drake had introduced as a "friend." Drake had introduced her as a "friend" also. The memory cut deeply, when in her heart she knew her feelings for him far transcended that simple term.

Carolina looked up at the knock at the door, her arms tightening around the babe in her arms. She called out softly with a bid to enter, grateful that Suzannah was too content from her recent feeding to awaken. The door opened to reveal Drake's familiar figure, and Carolina's agitation soared. Drake had stopped by several times that day, appearing more angry with each visit. Uncertain what to expect next, she had searched her mind for the cause of his annoyance, to no avail. She had caught herself staring at the closed door after his most recent departure, then had self-consciously glanced back to see Miriam regarding her with a knowing gaze as she had offered, "Mister McNeil is a difficult man, but it's obvious that he's deeply concerned about Suzannah's and your welfare."

A spontaneous defense of Drake had risen to Carolina's lips then, but she had bitten it back. Miriam was a good woman. She simply did not understand the kindness of which Drake was capable, or his gentleness. She knew few would. As for the bond between Drake and her, there was little use in attempting to explain something Drake obviously strove to deny. Most of all, Carolina knew that Miriam would never understand that with Drake's leaving she would lose a part of herself, and the thought of that loss, when she had already lost so much, was almost more than she could bear.

Placing the child in her cradle, Carolina did not see Drake scan the room or his obvious relief to find her alone. Suzannah settled, Carolina turned back to Drake to find his expression intense.

"How are you feeling, Carolina?"

Carolina could not manage a smile. "I'm fine. Suzannah's fine. You don't have to worry about us."

"I told you before, I don't *have to* do anythin'."

Drake walked toward her and threw his hat on a nearby chair. The sheer size and breadth of him was achingly familiar. She remembered being held against that broad chest and hearing his heart thud against her ear. She recalled the scent of him, the warmth of him buried beneath layers of rigid control. She remembered long nights when she could not sleep, when the sound of Drake's voice speaking softly in the darkness had drawn her back from the edge of the terrifying void in her mind from which the demons of her dreams emerged. She remembered the comfort in his touch then, and those light eyes assessing her as they did now. For fleeting moments as she had looked into their clear depths, she had felt she could see directly to his heart. She had known that his heart was battered and bruised as she somehow felt hers was as well, and she knew instinctively that in each other's arms the healing that had begun could be

279

raised to a far more glorious emotion than either of them had ever known. She knew . . . but Drake did not. Worst of all, she now feared that having lived for so long without emotion in his life, he no longer cared.

"I've been wantin' to talk to you alone, but there hasn't been much chance with Mrs. Higgins constantly underfoot and Doc Fitz hangin' around."

The resentment in Drake's tone surprised Carolina. She responded instinctively. "Miriam's been very kind, and Doctor Fitz is concerned."

Drake's expression tightened further as he came to stand beside her. Carolina was confused at his reaction. *He* had brought her to Miriam's cabin and *he* had left her behind in the hands of strangers when she had clearly said she wanted to stay with him. *He* had turned her down. *He* was leaving her. . . .

"I'm plannin' on goin' back to my claim tomorrow."

"Tomorrow. . . ." Carolina's heart fell. She bit back the words that sprang to her tongue.

"There's no point in my stayin'." The sensuous curve of Drake's lips twitched. "You'll be well enough to travel in a little while. I've already looked into makin' the arrangements for Suzannah and you when you are."

"You did." Carolina raised her chin. "What if I don't want to leave Deadwood?"

"You don't really have a choice, do you?" Drake was suddenly angry. His strong fingers bit into her flesh as he gripped her shoulders. "You want to find out who you are. You want to find your family, don't you?"

"I'm not sure that I do. . . ."

The words she had suppressed slipped past Carolina's lips. They drew Drake's handsome features into a frown as he responded sharply, "What do you mean?"

"I . . . I mean . . ." Carolina closed her eyes briefly, shaking her head. "I don't know what I mean. Oh, Drake." Her restraint slipping away, Carolina took a step closer to him, her pale eyes pleading for his understanding, "I'm not sure I want to remember! Memory only brings pain."

280

Drake's jaw hardened. His hands dropped back to his sides. "You can run away from memories only so long, Carolina. Then you have to turn around and face them. If you're unhappy with what you see, then it's up to you to go on from there."

Drake's emotional retreat was obvious and Carolina was suddenly ashamed. She could not, she *would* not, bind Drake to her with her need. Taking a deep breath, Carolina attempted a smile.

"I suppose you're right. I'll leave by the end of the week."

"You'll wait until you're strong enough to leave."

"I'm strong enough now."

"No, you aren't!"

Carolina did not immediately respond. When she spoke at last, her words were a hushed whisper. "I can't seem to please you, whatever I say or do. What do you want from me, Drake?"

Drake took an instinctive step backward and Carolina realized belatedly that she had only worsened an already tense situation as he muttered gruffly, "Do what you want. You will anyway."

A sound at the door interrupted their exchange, turning them toward it as it opened unexpectedly. Miriam paused in the doorway, obviously at a loss as she looked uncertainly between them. Carolina's heart squeezed tight as Drake returned Miriam's stare for a moment before snatching up his hat from the nearby chair.

Miriam's protest echoed in the tense silence. "Don't let me rush you, Mister McNeil. I only stopped back to drop off a few packages. I'll be going out again."

Carolina knew instinctively that it was too late. Drake had retreated behind his impenetrable façade. He would not emerge again.

Confirming her thoughts, Drake replied bluntly, "I'm going. Good night."

The door closed behind Drake as Miriam's gaze eloquently expressed her regrets. As silent as the widow, Carolina turned away.

Drake strode away from Miriam's cabin, Carolina's whispered question echoing in his mind.

What do you want from me, Drake?

He had been incensed to hear voiced aloud the question that had drummed unconsciously at his mind. He had taken refuge in anger as he had done so often in his dealings with Carolina. He was only now beginning to recognize the cowardice in that refuge.

The familiar sounds of evening in Deadwood grew louder as Drake slipped into the crowd at the end of the street and allowed himself to be moved along with the tide of merrymakers surging along the walk. Bawdy songs mingled with harsh shrieks of laughter as he passed a nearby saloon, but Drake was numb to their attraction.

What do you want from me, Drake?

He had seen despair in Carolina's silver eyes as she had asked that question. He had silently shared that despair as he had perused her subtle loveliness, clearer to him than it had ever been when he saw her in the plain blue dress he had disdained earlier in the day.

A burst of song from the saloon ahead of him interrupted Drake's thoughts. Grateful for the intrusion, Drake stopped in his tracks, turning a sharp glance at the men who piled up behind him with loud protests. Hesitating only a moment longer, he turned into the entrance of the Nugget and perused the crowded room. His gaze touching on the person he sought, he started forward unconsciously.

He paused at the bar moments later.

"Rosie . . ."

Rosie's head snapped toward him at the sound of his voice. He saw a flash of an unrecognizable emotion in her eyes the moment before a smile of incredible beauty burst across her lips.

"I was wonderin' when you were comin' back to see me, Drake."

"Well, you didn't have to wonder long."

Rosie made him feel good . . . a welcome relief from the torment of every moment he spent with Carolina. He was inordinately grateful when Rosie turned her back on her companions and took his arm to lead him to a nearby table.

Seated a moment later, Rosie leaned closer, her heady scent teasing his nostrils as she spoke over the din of boisterous prospectors nearby, "Where've you been? I missed you today."

"I've been busy makin' some arrangements. I'll be leavin' Deadwood soon."

"When?"

"I was thinkin' of leavin' tomorrow, but I may have to put it off for a day." His aborted conversation with Carolina returning to mind, he continued, "I have to settle a few things first."

"Tomorrow. . . ."

Rosie's disappointment was apparent.

"I have to get back to my claim, but I have a favor to ask of you before I do. It's about Carolina."

There it was again, that flash in Rosie's eyes that was gone so quickly that he was uncertain if he had imagined it.

"About Carolina?"

"Carolina's goin' to be needin' a friend."

Rosie was momentarily silent. When she spoke her voice was husky. "Sounds like this is real important to you."

Drake was surprised to hear himself respond, "It is."

Rosie's glorious eyes glazed over momentarily before she responded, "Well, then it's important to me, too. You can depend on it. I'll be visitin' her real soon."

"Thanks, Rosie."

Intensely relieved, Drake could not refuse when Rosie responded with the return of her smile, "Now that that's taken care of, I'm not goin' to let you get away from me so easy. You just sit still for a minute." Rosie signaled the bartender. "Two drinks, Barney."

Curving her hand around his, Rosie smiled up into his eyes. "We got a lot of catchin' up to do, and I'm intendin' to

283

enjoy every minute of it."

The lonesome, abused young girl Rosie had once been was clearer to him in that moment than ever before. Drake was unable to refuse her.

"Looks like Rosie's got herself a new fella. . . ."

Tag's head snapped up at the sound of Ella's voice. The brassy blonde was smiling as she stood beside him near the rear wall of the room, but he was not as he responded sharply, "That's Rosie's business, Ella, and nobody else's."

Ella drew back visibly from his sharp rebuke. "I didn't mean nothin'."

"Didn't you?"

"Well, maybe I did." Ella raised her chin, challenging him unexpectedly. "I suppose I wanted to make you see that Rosie's usin' you now, just like she always did. Everybody knows she has eyes for that big fella, whoever he is. She hasn't been herself since he came to town."

"Did it ever occur to you that if everybody could see Rosie has eyes for McNeil, that I could see it, too?" Tag's gaze hardened. "Let's get one thing straight, Ella. I don't need you or anyone else to tell me how to handle my private affairs."

"I wasn't tryin' to tell you how—"

"You were trying to lead me. I don't like being led, and I don't like people who try."

To his surprise, Ella's eyes filled. She swallowed with obvious difficulty as she placed a hand on his arm. Tag felt the depth of her sincerity as she whispered, "I'm sorry, Tag. It's just that it hurts me to see you watchin' her and feelin' so bad. I keep thinkin' that I could make you feel better if you'd just give me a try. I'm good at makin' men feel good, and I'd never be better than I would be with you, I promise you that."

"Ella . . ."

"No, you don't have to say nothin'. I mean, I know you

284

ain't interested yet. I was just tryin' to explain why I said what I said. The only thing is that I didn't give you credit where it was due, that's all. I didn't think you could see past your feelin's for Rosie." Ella swallowed again. "You ain't mad at me, are you, Tag?"

Tag hesitated in response. "No, I'm not mad at you, but I want to make something very clear to you, Ella. I consider you my friend, but while Rosie's in the picture, you'll never be more to me than that."

"But she's —"

"You don't know Rosie. You only think you do." Tag's anger swelled again. "*I* know Rosie, and I won't tolerate a word spoken against her, is that understood?"

"I understand."

"Now I suggest you get back to your table. Sheila has other duties to attend to."

Tag attempted to turn away from the thoroughly chastised blonde, but her hand tightened on his arm, halting him as she looked ardently into his face and whispered, "Don't be mad."

Tag scrutinized Ella's apologetic expression, gradually understanding. Ella was as frustrated as he, although he knew the depth of feelings behind her appeal did not approach the dimensions of his love for Rosie. But his own anguish did not give him the right to make others suffer.

His eyes softening, Tag responded, "You don't have to worry, Ella. Nothing has changed here. You still have your job and we're still friends. If nothing else, you've shown me you aren't afraid to stand up to me when you think it's necessary. I respect you for that."

Ella managed a smile. "Well, fancy that . . . a man respectin' *me*."

Tag's smile fell away. "I've always respected you. I don't make judgments on women when it comes to what they have to do to survive."

Ella's smile became shaky. "When you say that, you almost make me believe it's true."

"It's true."

"Thanks, Tag."

"Don't thank me. Just get back to work. Sheila's been sending me dagger looks for the past five minutes."

Ella turned abruptly away from him. Suspecting that she did so to conceal an embarrassing swell of emotion, he watched until she assumed Sheila's seat at the table. He was relieved when her full smile flashed once more.

Ella dismissed from his mind, Tag turned back toward the table where Rosie looked up at Drake McNeil with open adoration. He remembered holding her in his arms earlier that day, consoling her for her unrequited love of McNeil, and wishing he could do so much more. In a way, he had almost been relieved when McNeil had appeared in the doorway, knowing how much it meant to Rosie to see him there.

Tag sighed. He knew, however, that McNeil's appearance was only prolonging the agony by giving Rosie cause to believe her dreams would eventually be realized. They wouldn't. He was absolutely certain of that, just as he knew there would be difficult times ahead for Rosie once she was deprived of her dream, perhaps more difficult than any she had ever experienced. But he would be there for her, whenever or however she needed him. He had no choice. He loved her.

The deep, mesmerizing tone of Drake's voice held Rosie spellbound. The noise of the saloon around her faded, leaving only the sound of his voice as she sat beside him, enraptured. It had been like this before, in that time so long ago when she had been totally alone. Only Drake had cared enough to seek her out, to talk to her so she might regain a feeling of worth. Now, when she had again been so low, he had instinctively sought her out again.

Her hand tightening around his, Rosie smiled. She loved listening to him. She loved hearing about his claim and the cabin he had raised in the hills. She loved knowing that he would remain in the hills until the end of the summer, when he expected he would have enough gold dust put by so he would be able to leave. She had listened intently, but he had not yet divulged his plans from that point on. Despite herself, a niggle of insecurity had begun to torment her mind.

"You're a good listener, Rosie. You make a man feel you could listen to him all night."

"I suppose that's because I could—if that man was you."

Drake was momentarily silent. "You're a treasure, Rosie Blake, and a little too patient for your own good. I think I'm goin' to have to save you from yourself by sayin' good night."

"Not yet!" Rosie held his hand tightly, her gaze ardent. "I never feel better than when I'm around you, Drake. Stay a little longer."

"I don't think so. I don't know whether it's the whiskey or your beautiful face, but I think it's time for me to bed down before I'm too drunk to make it to Doc's office."

Rosie attempted to hide her disappointment. "You *will* come back to see me before you leave . . ."

"I couldn't leave without sayin' goodbye to you, Rosie."

Drake stood up and Rosie stood up as well. She took his arm and walked with him toward the door. Her smile tremulous, she managed, "You're the best thing that ever happened to me, Drake McNeil."

Drake held her gaze for a long moment. "You won't forget about Carolina. . . ."

Rosie's smile froze. Regaining control in an instant, she replied, "I won't forget. You can trust me on that."

In a moment Drake had slipped through the doorway, leaving Rosie with the sound of his voice echoing in her ears. With growing anger, she repeated, "No, I won't forget about Carolina. You can trust me on that."

Resolute, Rosie turned back to the crowded room.

A few steps down the street and Drake paused at the familiar figure of Doc Fitz approaching. The old fellow frowned as he glanced from him, to the doorway of the

Nugget, and back.

Halting beside him, Doc squinted up at Drake. "Leavin' early, are you? I'm thinkin' Rosie wasn't too happy about that."

Surprised at his comment, Drake responded, "Whether she is or she isn't, isn't anybody's concern."

"I suppose not." Doc's bloodshot eyes narrowed further. "I just left Carolina. She and the baby seem to be doin' fine. She tells me you're thinkin' of leavin' Deadwood tomorrow."

"Maybe. . . ."

"I suppose that would be best. That young lady has become too dependent on you." Doc paused. "I'm thinkin' that's a strange effect you have on women, McNeil. I'm also thinkin' you'll be doin' Carolina more harm than good if you hang around too long. She—"

"I'm not interested in what you're thinkin', Doc!" A flush of heat balled Drake's fists. "If I were you, I'd concentrate on dispensin' medicine and keep your advice to yourself." Doc's face tightened as Drake continued, "I'm goin' back to the office now to get some sleep. If you got any objections to my stayin' at your place, say it now."

Anger his initial reaction to Drake's straight talk, the old doc straightened up, his jaw rigid. He replied slowly, "Understand me, McNeil, my first concern is for my patient. She's a fine young woman with a big problem that doesn't look like it's goin' to get any better until she knows the way her life will be goin' from here. I'll be takin' good care of her after you leave, so you won't have to worry about her . . . if you were so inclined. As a matter of fact, I'll say it's my considered *medical* opinion, that given time, the young lady will recuperate so well that she'll be able to put this whole thing in its proper perspective, marry again, and move on." Doc paused. "That much said, I'll reiterate that as far as I'm concerned, the sooner you're out of her life, the better. As for your sleepin' facilities, I offered you my place to stay, and you haven't done anythin' to cause me to withdraw my offer. Since you're leavin' soon, I'm thinkin' things will work out fine anyway."

Drake glared as the old man questioned, "Do we understand each other?"

Drake's gaze turned to ice. "I'd say so."

"Then I'll be sayin' good night."

Doc disappeared through the entrance of the Nugget and Drake started down the street. His expression tightened. It was obvious that news traveled fast in Deadwood, but he knew for a fact that no one but Rosie and him understood the history behind their association. For that matter, it was nobody's damned business, either.

Reaching Doc's office, Drake pushed the door open and slammed it shut behind him, seething. As far as Carolina was concerned, *he* was the only one who was going to make the decision as to when he would leave, and he wasn't going to do that until he was certain she'd be all right. He had moved in lockstep for seven long years, living his life at the command of others. He would not do it again.

Not bothering to turn up the lamp, Drake stripped off his clothes and lay down on the nearby couch, his mind repeating, *no, never again.* . . .

Nineteen

Rosie brushed a raven-colored curl from her shoulder as she made her way down the early morning street. For the visit she was about to make, she had dressed for effect and she was pleased with the result. She looked particularly good in purple—Doc had told her so. And once her shawl had been removed, she knew that the cut of this particular dress, just low enough in the bodice to tease and just tight enough elsewhere to turn heads, would convey the image she sought.

Stepping down off the boardwalk at the end of the street, Rosie looked at the cabin a short distance away. She controlled the urge to sneer. Colorless, and tidy . . . just like its owner the haughty widow Higgins. The first line of laundry of the day already flapped in the morning breeze and Rosie gave a low snort of satisfaction. The widow was right on schedule, a schedule she had known she could count on to allow her time to talk to Carolina Brand in private.

Anguish resurging, Rosie recalled the note in Drake's voice when he had spoken of the pasty-faced Carolina Brand the previous evening. Such a quiet, proper young *lady.* . . . No one had to tell Rosie that the differences between the two of them were more marked than she dared admit. Carolina Brand and she had one important point in common, however. They both wanted Drake.

So, Carolina Brand couldn't remember her past. . . . Contempt filled Rosie's mind. She didn't believe a word of the story the frail Carolina had concocted. Her lapse of memory was a trick to tie Drake to her when all else had failed. As for the woman's physical weakness, she had known others to bear a child and be up on their feet to resume their work within days. Carolina Brand was nothing more than a sly pretender who having lost her husband, had marked Drake for the man's replacement.

But Rosie had already determined that Carolina Brand would not succeed.

Rosie approached the door of the widow's cabin, her heart pounding. Affixing a smile on her face despite her agitation, she knocked boldly. The widow's shocked expression at finding her on her doorstep was almost comical as Rosie greeted her sweetly.

"Good mornin', Widow Higgins. I've come to visit Carolina Brand."

The woman's mouth was still hanging agape as a voice sounded from behind her. "Someone wants to see me, Miriam?"

"It's me, Carolina." Rosie moved into sight, forcing her smile brighter. "Drake asked me to stop by to see if you were needin' anythin'."

Regaining her composure, the widow drew herself up to her full, fleshless height. "Carolina doesn't need anything, especially from you, *Miss* Blake."

"Miriam!" Obviously shocked at the widow's discourtesy, Carolina took an anxious step forward. "Drake introduced me to Rosie yesterday. She's his friend."

"Friend. . . . Humph!" Miriam did not bother to hide her contempt. "Miss Blake has many male friends . . . many *close* male friends, although few of them would acknowledge their friendship outside the Nugget."

"That's right, Mrs. Higgins. I do have a lot of friends—most of them male—and Drake's the best of the lot. I think Carolina understands."

Miriam's thin lips twitched. "Perhaps she doesn't understand well enough."

"Miriam, please. . . ." Carolina was obviously uncomfortable. Noting Miriam's rigid posture at the door and the obvious fact that she had no intention of allowing Rosie en-

291

trance, Carolina addressed Rosie with an attempt at a smile. "If you'll be patient for a few minutes, I'll wrap Suzannah up and walk with you for a while. I need the exercise, and Suzannah would probably benefit from some fresh air."

"You'll do no such thing!" Miriam's thin face flushed as she turned back to Rosie, relenting with obvious displeasure. "Come in, then. I suppose it's the lesser of two evils after all." Ignoring Carolina's shocked gasp at her outspokenness, the widow continued pointedly, "I have some work to do outside. I'm sure you won't be long. . . ."

The door closed behind the old witch as Rosie stated flatly, "The widow doesn't like me, but I don't care because I don't like her much either. She looks down on me because I'm part owner of a saloon. She considers it a palace of vice." Rosie shrugged. "I suppose it is, but I don't pay much attention to the things men do for amusement as long as they behave themselves around me. Does that shock you?"

Silent for a moment, Carolina replied with surprising candor, "I suppose it does, in a way. But I don't think Drake asked you to come by for my approval."

Realizing they were on shaky ground, Rosie walked toward the small wooden crate on a nearby table from which a low whimpering sounded. She looked at the infant inside, a flash of elation flushing her cheeks at finding the child blond and fair-skinned. This baby wasn't Drake's! Drake was a real man. Any child he fathered would *look* like him.

Rosie turned back to the small woman who stood silently behind her. "It looks like your baby is doin' well. She seems healthy." Not waiting for an invitation, Rosie sat casually on a nearby chair. "I suppose you'll be happy to go home after all that's happened."

Avoiding her eye as she assumed a seat nearby, Carolina nodded. "Yes, I . . . I hope to go home with Suzannah someday."

"Someday. . . ." Rosie raised her brows. "Then you haven't remembered where you come from yet?"

Carolina looked up and Rosie was momentarily taken

aback by the intensity in her pale gray eyes as Carolina asked, "Who told you about that?"

"Drake, of course. He told me your whole, sad story last night."

"Drake was with you last night?"

"He sure was."

"Yes, of course. You're friends."

Deliberately ignoring Carolina's response, Rosie smiled. "So, tell me, what are your plans?"

"I don't know that I have any real plans, yet."

"Really? That's too bad. Maybe that's why Drake was so anxious to make them for you, especially since he's hopin' to leave Deadwood soon. He feels responsible for you."

Triumph flashed through Rosie's mind as Carolina raised her chin with a touch of pride. "He needn't. He's done enough for me already. I don't expect anything more."

Rosie nodded in silent assent, adding, "But you know Drake. He looks like he's cold as ice, and I suppose he is to some, but he isn't really like that." Rosie allowed her gaze to drift. "Drake and me come from the same little town in Texas, you know. They used to say he was 'lean and mean,' but I knew better." Rosie's jaw tightened. "They said even worse things about him later, after the trial."

"The trial?"

"Yeah." True anger flashed in Rosie's eyes. "I don't blame Drake for what he did. Hank Sills deserved to die, and if anybody had asked me, I'd have told them that Drake did the right thing when he shot him."

Carolina's eyes widened but she did not speak, allowing Rosie the opportunity she sought to continue, "Sills was his partner and he got what he had comin', all right, but the only problem was that Sills didn't have a gun."

Carolina started trembling. "No, Drake wouldn't . . ."

"Drake said Sills drew first, but they never found the gun. As far as I'm concerned, it doesn't matter. Drake knew what he was doin' when he went up to that hotel room and shot him dead. I was in court when Drake told the jury that he would do it all over again, too."

"No—"

"The trouble was that Sills didn't die too easy. The shootin' turned out to be a bloody mess—somethin' the townsfolk couldn't seem to forget. I was there when they carried Sills out of the hotel, and I know I'll never forget it. His chest was soaked with blood and he was starin' up at the sky, moanin' and cryin'. I can remember thinkin' that there couldn't be that much blood in a man's body. The town turned against Drake because he didn't show any remorse . . . everybody but me, that is. But nobody listened to me very much back then."

Noting that Carolina's trembling had increased and her eyes had become peculiarly glazed, Rosie continued with cold deliberation, "Sills had a lot of friends in town and the trial turned hot and heavy. They sent Drake to prison and I left town a little while after that. I couldn't stand the place without him. But Drake never forgot me and I never forgot him, and when he was ready to get out, we agreed to meet here in Deadwood. I'm not sorry I waited for him, either. Seven years isn't too long to wait for a man like Drake."

Her story winding to a halt, Rosie considered Carolina Brand's oddly rigid appearance. The young woman's pallor had deepened until her face looked like wax, confirming Rosie's original assessment that she was so weak and unspirited that her only defense against life was to grow faint. Carolina Brand wasn't a proper match for a man like Drake in any way.

Stepping back into the cabin at that moment, the widow was beside Carolina in a flash. Her voice rang with concern as she asked, "Is something wrong, dear? Maybe you should lie down."

Rosie stood up as the older woman fluttered around the silent Carolina. It was time to leave. She had no stomach for a woman who chose the vapors over facing life square in the face.

Rosie fought to keep the contempt out of her voice. "Yes, maybe you should lie down, Carolina. You don't look too good." Carolina did not respond and Rosie forced herself to add, "I'm goin' now, but if you need anythin' before you leave Deadwood, just let me know."

Outside the cabin moments later, Rosie headed back the way she had come. Satisfaction at having assessed the pale Carolina Brand correctly was rife inside her as she adjusted her shawl over her shoulders and took a deep, cleansing breath. Her smile, when it came, was as brilliant as the morning sun. She would never have to worry about that woman again.

"You don't need any help from the likes of that woman!" Miriam glanced hotly at the door that had just closed behind Rosie Blake. "You just lie down for a while. You'll feel better soon."

Carolina did not respond and Miriam felt the nudge of fear. Her eyes were glassy, and her body was so rigid that Miriam could not draw her to her feet. She urged, "Carolina, dear . . ."

Still no response. Biting her thin lips, Miriam moved to the washbasin and soaked a cloth. Returning, she dabbed at Carolina's pale face. "Was it something that brazen hussy said? If so, my advice would be to ignore it. She's a cheap bit of trash, the kind that gives little and takes much, especially from a place like Deadwood. She isn't worth thinking about. I just don't know what was in Mister McNeil's mind when he sent her here."

Still no response.

"Carolina . . ."

Panic began to assume control of Miriam's mind. What should she do?

The cabin droned into stillness as Carolina drifted in a world of familiar terrors. She saw *him* again. He lay on the ground, motionless, staring up at the sky. She touched him and he was cold. His chest was red with blood and she shook him. He did not respond and she shook him again. A silent sob echoed in her mind. She sat back and looked at her hands. They were wet and sticky, covered with blood. She rubbed her hands against her dress but she could not wipe the stains away.

Carolina cried out and blinked, her gaze suddenly focusing on Miriam's distressed expression as the widow stood beside her. Her shuddering worsened.

"Carolina, dear, please say something. . . ."

Carolina struggled to speak past the thickness in her throat. Her voice erupted in a croak.

"Drake didn't kill him, Miriam. He couldn't have. . . ."

"Please lie down, dear."

"No, I . . . I have to wait for Drake. He'll tell me it's all a lie."

"But—"

"I'm all right. Everything will be all right when Drake comes."

The words Rosie had spoken echoed in Carolina's mind. It wasn't true. She knew it wasn't true. All that blood . . . Drake could not have been the one to shed all that blood. . . .

Drake's chair scraped against the rough plank floor as he pushed himself away from the table in Deadwood's best café. The small portion of greasy eggs and dry smoked ham that he had just consumed lay heavily on his stomach, silent confirmation of the fact that the best did not necessarily ensure quality in a rough mining camp. He walked to the counter and paid his bill without comment, knowing that he had eaten far worse in his day and that the quality of the food was not the true reason he had left the major portion of his meal on his plate.

Walking up the street moments later, Drake knew he could put it off no longer. His horse and pack mule were loaded and ready. Normally, he would already have been on the trail with Deadwood left far behind by this time of day, but these were not normal circumstances. The sleepless night past had been testimony to that realization, one he could not escape no matter how hard he tried.

His tension growing with each step he took, Drake felt his muscles tighten responsively as the widow's cabin came into view. He had handled things poorly with Carolina since they had arrived in Deadwood, but things had not gone as he had planned. He had not anticipated how difficult it would be to relinquish Carolina when they reached Deadwood. He had not known that the flood of relief he had expected when he turned Carolina and her daughter over to the care of others would never come. He had not realized that he would spend each waking moment attempting to elude thoughts of Carolina, and that he would spend the wakeful hours of the night wondering how she fared.

And he had not known that the wondering would turn to wanting. . . .

Drake resisted the urge to shake himself hard. Carolina was an innocent who had been thrust into his care. She had depended on him for her life and he had done his best for her, but all that was over and done. He had other priorities, objectives toward which he had looked and dreamed for long, empty years. Carolina was a young woman who would do no more than pass through his life.

Or was she?

Suddenly realizing his palms were sweating, Drake allowed himself only a moment's respite before he raised his hand and knocked on the cabin door.

"Who is it?"

Drake tensed at the strange note in Miriam's voice. "It's Drake McNeil."

"Come in . . . come in. . . ."

One step inside and Drake saw the reason for the widow's distress. Standing shakily, her knuckles white as she gripped the chair in front of her for support, Carolina stared at him as he entered. Immediately at her side, he noted the shudder that shook her as he took her arm.

"No, don't touch me." Carolina's voice was a harsh whisper. "Just tell me. I have to know. Did you kill him?"

Drake stiffened. "Who? What are you talkin' about?"

"Is it true? Rosie said you killed him. She said there was so much blood . . . so much . . ." Carolina looked down at her palms, then rubbed them against her skirt before looking up at him again to demand, "Please tell me!"

Miriam interrupted with an edge of panic, "It was that woman you sent here who upset her—that saloon woman."

"Rosie?"

"I was at the door and I heard what she said. She said you killed a man—shot him dead. She went on and on about it, telling Carolina about the blood and—"

Carolina interrupted sharply, "Is it true? Did you kill him?"

A moment's dread filled Drake. The look in Carolina's eyes pleaded denial, but he could not say the words she wanted to hear.

"Yes, it's true."

Carolina's breath caught in her throat as shock and horror widened her eyes. Stabbing at Drake's heart was the realization that reflected even more clearly there was the demise of all that had been between them. His pain at the loss was almost physical as Carolina took an instinctive step backward and muttered, "Oh, God . . . no."

A sudden cry of distress from Suzannah seemed to echo her mother's ragged protest. Drake turned toward the babe only to hear Carolina shriek, "Don't touch her! You have blood on your hands!"

Drake froze, chilled by the revulsion in Carolina's voice. He spoke a single word, a whispered plea.

"Carolina . . ."

"Go away." Carolina staggered backward, stretching out the flat of her hand toward him. "Go away!"

Closing the cabin door behind him, Drake struggled to draw his emotions under control. Despising himself for his incredulity at Carolina's rejection, he silently cursed himself as well for the fool he had been in believing she would never turn against him. His first step away from her the most difficult he had ever taken, he was soon walking rapidly down the street.

Rosie's smile froze as Drake walked through the doorway of the Nugget. The sound of his booted feet mimicked the thudding of her heart as he walked across the empty saloon. Fury darkened his face as he halted directly in front of her and demanded, "What did you tell her?"

"Tell who?"

"What did you tell Carolina?"

"I didn't tell her anythin' but the truth!" The trembling that overwhelmed Rosie was transmitted to her voice as she continued, "I told her we came from the same town in Texas and I never believed all the things people said about you, either before or after you went to jail. I told her I left town just after you did because I didn't want to stay there without you."

The pain in Drake's gaze tore at her heart as he rasped, *"Why* did you tell her?"

Elaborate excuses flashed into Rosie's mind as Drake towered above her, but she could not speak the words. Drake deserved the truth . . . only the truth. Her words trembling on her lips, Rosie responded simply, "I . . . I told her because *she* needed to know, because *I* needed to know . . . and because *you* needed to know."

In the silence that met her shaken response, Rosie felt her world shudder around her. She felt Drake's anguish. She ached with it. She longed to soothe it from his eyes, from his body and from his heart. She yearned so desperately to fill the void within him with her love, a true and honest love that would never fail him. She pined for the chance to show him that she—

Drake turned without response and Rosie realized with a start that the cry of her heart was a silent echo that went unheard in the storm of his anger. Still staring at the door through which Drake had disappeared, Rosie whispered into the reverberations of his wake, "She didn't really love you. I had to make you see . . ."

But the only thing that was now abundantly clear was that Drake had left her.

The door of his office burst open with a snap, raising Doc's head toward Drake as the big man strode toward him. Rising to his feet, Doc sensed rather than saw the emotion

299

Drake restrained as he stated flatly, "I'm going back to my claim. I don't know when I'll be back, so I have a favor to ask of you."

Aware that asking favors did not come easily for this man, Doc responded succinctly, "If I can."

Drake's lips tightened as he drew a bank passbook from his pocket. "This is for Carolina, to tide her over until she's well enough to travel. I've already paid for her transportation back to Sioux City when she's ready to go. The receipt's in there, too. I want you to give it to her—*make* her take it if you have to."

"Why don't you give it to her?"

"I'd rather you did it."

Startled to see that Drake's hand was trembling, Doc accepted the passbook. He held it tentatively as he squinted up into the big man's face.

"You're sure that you don't—"

"I'm sure." There was a moment's pause before Drake added, "Thanks."

Another difficult word spoken, Drake turned back to the door, impressing Doc with the personal price the big man had just paid to ensure Carolina Brand's security. Crossing to the window of his office as Drake closed the door behind him, Doc followed his swift progress down the street, knowing that a man like Drake McNeil would never pay so great a price without good cause. He was still watching when Drake emerged from the livery stable on his big bay and turned onto the road out of town without looking back.

As Drake McNeil slipped from sight, Doc wondered what the big man had truly left behind him.

"We need more cold water, Miriam."

Hardly noting the widow's distress as she turned without comment, grabbed a nearby bucket and rushed out of the cabin, Doc turned back to the wild thrashing of his frail, young patient with a sense of true panic. He rubbed his stubbled chin, at a loss. He recalled the moment he had

300

seen Josie Whalen's boy running down the street toward his office earlier in the day. He had turned instinctively for his bag, and within minutes was following the youngster back up the street.

The boy had stopped short outside Miriam's cabin with obvious apprehension. It had taken only a moment for him to discover the reason for the boy's caution when he opened the door. Carolina, crying out of control, was hardly restrainable. She shrank back as Miriam attempted to console her, a wildness in her eyes as she seemed to see past the woman's frantic expression to a horror beyond. His attempts to help her were met with the same reaction and he had been all but helpless as Carolina's torment had led her into a strangely fevered state.

Doc was baffled. That had been hours ago. This was not a simple case of hysteria. It was obvious the woman was suffering delusions, that she was reliving portions of the massacre which had taken the lives of the other members of the wagon train. He had seen such cases during the war where soldiers on both sides had been mentally affected by the horrors they had witnessed. It worried him to know that for many, the horror never ceased. As he glanced toward Carolina's sleeping child, he hoped that would not be the case here.

The baffling part of her malady, however, was the reason for this sudden onslaught of hallucination. She had appeared to be recuperating from her ordeal so well. The story of Drake's conviction for the killing of his partner, no matter how vividly drawn, did not appear to him to be adequate reason. Nor did the fact that McNeil had spent seven years in prison for the crime. He had witnessed the trust in Carolina's eyes when she looked at McNeil. He doubted trust of that magnitude could have been threatened by Rosie's story—at least not before it had been adequately challenged.

Carolina's thrashing continued and Doc glanced toward the door. Her fever, obviously brought upon by her extreme agitation, soared higher by the minute. If he was not effective in reducing it, if he could not decrease the young woman's anxiety in some way, he feared for the result.

Carolina's flailing gained a new violence and Doc leaned forward to pin the frail young woman's arms to the bed as he spoke sharply. "Carolina, listen to me! You're safe now. The horror is over. Your baby is healthy and sleeping a few feet away. You're with friends. There are no Indians. No one is chasing you. Carolina, are you listening?"

"I see him!" Carolina's sudden response was unexpected. Her eyes grew wide, reflecting a remembered horror as her mumbled words became clearer. "His eyes are open—he's staring up at the sky, but he can't see it! His chest is all c . . . covered with blood. I touched him and he's cold. He's dead!" Carolina's sobbing began anew. *"He* did it . . . oh, God . . . *Drake* did it. . . . I asked him . . . he said he did. . . . Oh, God!"

"Drake did what? Answer me, Carolina."

"Drake *killed* him. . . ."

A moment of sudden realization dawned. Doc's head snapped toward the door as it opened. He roared, "Get over here, Miriam! I need your help."

"Don't you yell at me, Jerome!" Two spots of color appeared on the widow's pale cheeks as she approached and placed the bucket beside the bed. "I'm just as worried as you are."

"This is no time to argue, damn it!" Annoyed, Doc continued tightly, "I need you to tell me just what McNeil told Carolina when she questioned him." Ringing out a cloth in the cold water, Doc turned back to his patient and sponged her face. He turned around to snap, "Well?"

"Well, what? You'll have to be more explicit. I'm not a mind reader, you know!"

"When Carolina asked McNeil if he had killed his partner . . ."

"She didn't say it like that, exactly. She asked him if it was true. She kept saying, 'Did you kill him?' Mister McNeil asked her who she was talking about, and I explained."

"You explained . . . ?"

Miriam hesitated. "Yes. Carolina didn't seem to hear his

302

question, so I explained what she meant, and Mister McNeil answered her. He admitted he killed him."

"So, that's it!"

"That's what?"

Ignoring Miriam's confusion, Doc turned back to Carolina. He shook her roughly. "Carolina!" Miriam's spontaneous protest sounded behind him as he shook her again. "Carolina, look at me! Do you see me . . . can you hear me?"

A slight flicker in the wild eyes looking up into his gave him hope, and Doc continued, "It isn't true. It's a mistake. Drake didn't kill anyone."

Miriam interjected, "But he did."

Turning to shoot the widow a deadening glance, Doc looked back at Carolina and continued firmly, "Drake didn't kill anyone on the wagon train. He wasn't there. He came along later and saved you."

Carolina's gaze flickered again, and she rasped, "He said he did. Oh, God, he said he killed him. . . ."

"No . . . no, it was a mistake. Carolina, look at me." Doc pressed, "Do you trust me?" And when there was no response, "You know I wouldn't lie to you. I'd have no reason to lie. Drake didn't kill anyone on that train. It was a mistake."

Suddenly gripping his hands, Carolina looked at him as if straining to see. "He said . . ."

"Drake misunderstood you. He didn't kill anyone on that train."

Carolina's frenzied gaze held his moments longer. The anguish he read there prompted him to add, "He'll tell you himself when he returns, but you have to rest now. Suzannah will be wakin' up soon, and she'll need you."

"But Drake—"

"He'll be back soon. He'll tell you himself then, but you must rest now. Carolina, dear, close your eyes and rest."

"But . . ."

"Close your eyes. That's right. . . ."

Carolina's protests slowly subsided and Doc released a relieved breath as she closed her eyes at last. Dipping a

303

fresh cloth in the bucket beside his feet, he wrung it out and placed it on her forehead.

"Jerome . . . ?"

Hearing the note of anxiety in Miriam's voice, Doc turned and whispered, "She's all right. She's sleepin'."

"But—"

"Her nightmares are over, for a little while, at least. She'll be all right."

"You're sure?"

"As sure as I can be."

The widow stared at him for a moment before her expression crumbled unexpectedly. Surprising him, she sobbed aloud, then turned abruptly away. Surprising himself, Doc stood up and took the widow into his arms.

Humiliated by her weakness, Miriam drew away from Doc's comforting embrace. "I'm all right, Jerome!" She sniffed and raised her chin, suddenly aware of the untidy appearance she must be presenting. Withdrawing a spotless white hanky from her pocket, Miriam wiped her eyes, unconscious of Doc's strange expression and the fact that he had not taken a step back from her as she strove to pull her emotions under control.

Taking a moment longer to fuss with a few strands of hair that had worked loose from her neat bun during the trying ordeal of the past few hours, Miriam looked up, suddenly annoyed.

"What are you looking at?"

Appearing to snap from his stupor, Doc grated, "Damned if I know! I thought I saw a woman who was upset and needed comfortin', and I was attemptin' to do just that. I guess I was wrong."

"You were wrong, all right!" Doc turned away with a growl but Miriam stopped him short with a quick, "Oh, no you don't. You're not going to move a step until you tell me what just happened with Carolina."

Doc's smile was sarcastic as he turned back to face her. "Does that mean you're lookin' for some answers from me?"

"Well, you *are* the doctor here, aren't you? And Carolina *is* your patient."

"Yes, that's right, but I thought you knew everythin'."

"That only means you were wrong again." As Doc attempted to turn back to his sleeping patient, Miriam tried a more civil tone. "Carolina is resting peacefully, Jerome. While we have the time, I want you to explain what happened."

Checking his patient briefly, Doc looked at Miriam, his expression devoid of its former sarcasm. "It was a mistake, plain and simple, just like I told Carolina." At Miriam's obvious confusion, Doc continued, "Let's start at the beginnin'. I think it's safe to say that Drake McNeil's the only security Carolina had after the wagon train massacre. He saved her life and her child's as well. He nursed her back to health and delivered her safe and sound back to civilization. I also think it's safe to say that Carolina didn't have a realistic expectation of what would happen after they reached Deadwood. After they arrived, she became afraid again. She had come to look at Drake as her savior and he was suddenly withdrawin' from her. For all intents and purposes, she was suddenly alone in a foreign world, and although none of us realized it, she was one step away from panic. Then Rosie showed up, representin' a threat of another kind. Somethin' Rosie said when she related the events of Drake's past in gory detail must've touched a responsive chord in Carolina. It seems to me that in her disturbed state Carolina became confused . . . associatin' the man who McNeil was accused of killin' with someone on the wagon train . . . that fellow she kept seein' over and over with his chest covered with blood."

"Rosie said that, too . . . that after Mister McNeil shot the man, his chest was covered with blood."

"That's it, then! In her unstable condition, Carolina looked for help from the only person she knew she could trust—Drake. When he appeared to confirm that he had taken part in the massacre, she slipped over the edge."

"Well . . ." Admiration flickered briefly in Miriam's eyes.

"It does make a strange kind of sense now that you've explained it."

"The only thing I don't understand is why Drake sent Rosie here."

Miriam gave a low snort. *"If* he did. Something tells me that little tart—"

"I won't listen to any talk against Rosie, Miriam." Doc's voice hardened. "She's a friend."

"So, she's *your* friend, too . . ." Miriam's small eyes narrowed. "Well, well, how that woman does get around. . . ."

Obviously uncomfortable under Miriam's speculative gaze, Doc looked back at Carolina. She was twitching in her sleep and Doc touched her cheek. "Seems to me she's feelin' cooler already."

"That's impossible. She was burning up minutes ago."

Doc snapped the widow an annoyed glance. "Who's the doctor here, Miriam?"

Miriam raised her pointed chin. "I'm beginning to wonder."

"Maybe *you* should check the patient then, *Doctor* Higgins."

Miriam stepped up to Carolina's side. She looked down into the young woman's sweet, still face and touched a hand to her cheek. Her thin lips ticked with annoyance. "She does feel cooler."

"Well, since we're agreed that Carolina is doing better, I suppose I can leave."

"No, don't go yet!" Managing to subdue the sudden flush of anxiety that had forced her protest, Miriam took a short breath and straightened her spine. "I . . . I mean, you must be tired and hungry. I'll fix something to eat."

"No, that isn't necessary."

"Carolina might wake up disoriented. She might need you. . . ." Her throat thick, Miriam was suddenly uncertain if her reluctance to see Dr. Jerome Fitz depart her cabin was due to concern for Carolina's uncertain state of health or something else entirely. Annoyed as Doc hesitated, Miriam snapped, "But if it's that much trouble, you don't have to stay."

"Damn it! You're the only woman I know that asks and answers her own questions! I'll stay, all right, for *my patient's* sake, but I'm tellin' you right now that I'm too tired to argue with you anymore tonight."

Somewhat mollified, Miriam glanced at Carolina's strangely peaceful face, then at the babe who slept quietly nearby. She looked back at Jerome's homely, grizzled countenance, countering automatically, "What you're saying goes both ways. It takes two to argue, you know."

Doc grumbled, then shrugged. "I suppose."

"On your best behavior, then?"

"Agreed."

Aware that she was peculiarly shaken by Doc's single word of agreement, conscious of the fact that Doc was staring at her strangely, Miriam walked toward the stove. She was determined. She would do it. She would be pleasant to Jerome . . . if it killed her.

"Drake will be back. I know he will." Elaborately dressed in pink satin for another evening in the Nugget, Rosie faced Tag in the solitude of her small cabin. Her smile was bright and confident, in direct contrast with her expression earlier in the day when Drake had walked abruptly out of her life.

"What's the matter with you, Rosie? Why can't you understand that McNeil's gone for good?" Tag's handsome face was flushed with color. "I saw him ride out of town, and I heard what he said to you before he left. It's over—whatever you thought was between the two of you is over!"

The rafters rang with the sound of Tag's frustration, but Rosie was not intimidated by it. He had appeared unexpectedly at her cabin door minutes earlier and Rosie's feelings at seeing him there had fluctuated wildly between elation and caution. She became increasingly aware that he was equally upset as he took a step closer and gripped her shoulders roughly.

"You made a mistake going to see McNeil's woman. He won't forgive you for telling her something that he should've been able to tell her himself when he was ready."

"She fell apart when I told her, Tag." Rosie's bright eyes were triumphant. "I knew she would. She's not good enough for Drake and he knows that now. He'll be angry for a while, but when he thinks it all over, he'll see that I exposed her for what she is for his own good."

"Rosie, can't *you* see? McNeil doesn't want you."

"He does. You'll see. He'll come back for me before he leaves the hills for good."

"Rosie . . ."

Rosie's brilliant blue-eyed gaze rose to meet Tag's as she whispered, "He has to come back. He loves me, Tag."

"*I* love you, Rosie, not McNeil."

"He loves me. He'll be back. And when he comes back, I'll be waiting."

Rosie did not see the despair that flashed in Tag's troubled gaze, or the sad acceptance that replaced it as he folded her slowly into his arms. She did not know that as she accepted his comforting, Tag's tormented thoughts vacillated between the knowledge that in Rosie's mind, McNeil would always love her . . . and the fearful thought that believing it might not be enough.

The night sounds of Deadwood resounded outside the windows of Miriam's silent cabin, bawdy sounds that contrasted vividly with the serene picture of Suzannah nursing contentedly at Carolina's breast. Seated at the table a short distance away from mother and child, Doc Fitz exchanged glances with the widow, then cleared his throat. He smiled as Carolina raised her head and looked at him.

"How are you feelin', dear?"

The question was redundant for the answer was obvious. Still, Doc waited for Carolina's response.

"I'm fine now, Doctor Fitz. I don't know what came over me this morning."

Doc Fitz stood up, appearing to hesitate momentarily before walking toward her and sitting on the side of the bed. He took her hand and Carolina felt his concern as he spoke softly.

"You really don't know what happened to you?"

Carolina moved Suzannah protectively closer. "I was upset."

"You were more than upset, dear. You were hysterical. You were hallucinatin' and relivin' the massacre of the wagon train."

Carolina's heart began a slow pounding. "I . . . I know. I couldn't seem to stop the pictures that kept flashing across my mind . . . but I'm better now. It won't happen again."

"Do you know what brought on those vivid recollections?"

"I was talking to Rosie Blake. . . ."

"What did Rosie say to upset you?"

Carolina's heart pounded harder. She was beginning to tremble and Doc squeezed her hand, giving her the courage to respond. "She said that Drake had killed a man and that he had gone to prison for seven years because of it."

"Do you believe her?"

"I . . . I don't know."

"It's true."

Carolina raised her chin and clamped her teeth tightly shut in order to still their chattering. With a supreme effort at control, she managed, "It doesn't make any difference. I know Drake."

"What do you know about him?"

Carolina's light eyes misted. "I know that he saved my life and cared for Suzannah and me. I know that I can't remember anything about my life before I met him . . . that I've forgotten so many important things . . . but that I'll never forget what he did for me."

Doc stared into her eyes for long moments, then pressed, "And you're not confused anymore. You understand that he had nothing to do with the massacre."

"Yes, I know." The gruesome picture of sightless eyes staring up at the sky flashed again before Carolina's eyes, but she blinked the image away, echoing, "I know."

Appearing satisfied, Doc smiled, then stood abruptly. He turned back to the widow. "I think your charge will be fully recuperated tomorrow. Just give her that powder as I instructed. She should sleep through the night."

The widow replied, advancing to within a few feet of the bed, but Carolina did not hear her words. Her mind dwelling on the old doctor's questions, she responded more fully in her mind than she had dared to reply aloud.

Yes, she knew Drake had nothing to do with the massacre. She realized now that she had somehow confused the events Rosie had related with the fragmented pictures in her mind. In some way, Rosie had been testing her, and she had failed the test. She had failed Drake as well, but she was determined that she would not fail him again. She was determined that from this moment on, she would not allow her nightmares to overwhelm her. She would be the woman she knew she could be.

Carolina looked down at the bank passbook lying on the bed beside her. She covered it with her palm as Drake's image returned to mind. She had recognized him the first minute she had seen him. He had been familiar to her, and only now did she fully realize that she had recognized him as another part of herself that had lain undiscovered until that moment. He had lived in her heart before she had met him and he would live in her heart forever. No memories, remembered or buried in the past, would change that.

Snapping her from her thoughts with a word of farewell, Doc Fitz walked toward the door. She followed him with her gaze, recalling Drake's stricken expression the moment before he had pulled the cabin door closed behind him. Regrets, too abundant to be contained, inundated Carolina's mind and she clutched her daughter closer. She knew she would never forget it.

Twenty

"Carolina, the baby is crying."

Her arms submerged to the elbow in the washtub, Carolina looked up across the yard as the widow turned back to her chores. A gentle breeze flicked a strand of light brown hair against her cheek and she brushed it away with the back of her arm as Suzannah's hungry wail sounded more loudly. Wiping her arms on a nearby cloth, she started toward the cabin.

In the month since Drake had left Deadwood, spring had turned to summer. The air had turned hotter in keeping with the change of season and the sun shone relentlessly. Carolina glanced at the long lines of laundry stretched across the yard. They would soon be dry and the next batch would be ready to take their place. With a strong prick of conscience Carolina acknowledged that an entire laundry line for which Miriam would otherwise have found more lucrative use, was filled with Suzannah's linens. The widow and she got along well together, but the full extent of her imposition was never clearer than at times like this.

It pleased Carolina, however, that she had finally grown strong enough to assume a full share of the workload. Miriam had vigorously protested her help at first. She sometimes suspected that Suzannah's and her presence would have been tolerated without complaint just so Miriam might have the pleasure of the babe's presence in her cabin, so attached had the widow become to the child, but it was not in her nature to take advantage of the woman's affection.

Momentarily blinded as she stepped into the dimness of the cabin, Carolina paused in the doorway before crossing to the cradle. She smiled as she reached for the fussing infant inside.

"Come now, Suzannah. You can't be that hungry." Carolina glanced unconsciously at the clock on the wall, then shrugged. "Well, maybe you can."

Scooping up the child, Carolina balanced her expertly in one arm as she unbuttoned the front of her dress. She dragged the nearby chair to the doorway, sat and adjusted the babe in her lap. Suzannah was suckling noisily moments later, and Carolina allowed her mind to drift as she looked down at her beautiful daughter.

An entire month since Drake had left them and Deadwood behind him. . . . Carolina glanced up at the calendar on the wall, knowing that each day had been indelibly marked in her mind. She had not realized that the passage of time could be so cruel an anguish with every minute stretching into an hour and every hour into a lifetime. She winced at the thought of the torment Drake had endured for seven long years while his life was not his own. So much had been explained with Rosie's revelation that last day, yet there were so many questions that still went unanswered.

Carolina unconsciously sighed. Questions without answers had become a part of her life which she now accepted. Her own past was still as great a mystery to her as it had been that first day when she had opened her eyes to find herself lying on the forest floor with Drake crouched beside her. Nightmares continued to fill her nights, but she had learned to bear them. She had also learned to discount the flashing glimpses of memory that teased her. Never more than a moment in duration, they still faded as quickly as they appeared, leaving her confused and anxious to the point where she had given up hope of remembering, and was even more reluctant to try. Her only memory of home was of a cabin in the wilderness where she and Suzannah had spent the first month of their new lives, a place where she longed to return so strongly that she ached with the pain of it.

The sadness in Carolina's expression was reflected in her

312

heart. It was not the cabin that drew her, but the memory of that great bear of a man who had looked at her with eyes greener than any she had ever seen. It was the thought of his strong hands tending her gently, of his powerful arms holding her safe from the demons in her mind through long, dark nights. It was the sound of his deep voice in the darkness as he patiently shared his memories when she had none of her own. It was the feeling deep inside her that although there were countless things they had yet to discover about each other, this man and she were one in ways that were inexplicable. It was the belief that if given a chance, she could banish the shadows in Drake McNeil's cool, green eyes forever . . . and it was the knowledge that she wanted to do that more than anything in the world.

"Hello there, Miriam . . . Carolina."

Carolina came back to the present with a start, her smile spontaneous as Doc Fitz turned into the yard. She watched as he tipped his hat to Miriam in passing and came to stand outside the door.

"Well, you're lookin' bright and chipper this morning." Doc leaned closer and chucked the infant's full cheek. "And you, young lady, are getting plump."

"Plump!" Miriam's thin face bore an expression of exasperation as she came to stand beside him. "The child looks healthy, that's all. Plump. . . ." Miriam's small eyes narrowed as she stared at the paltry excess hanging over the doctor's belt. "If we're to speak of plump, I think we should be looking in another direction entirely."

Carolina watched with amusement as Doc instinctively sucked in his stomach, then deliberately puffed it out once more. "I didn't come here to discuss my figure, Miriam."

Miriam eyed the bundle under his arm with a twist of her lips. "So I see. Your laundry. Put it over there, Jerome, but I must warn you that I'm not certain those pitiful garments will survive another boiling."

Doc dropped the laundry as directed, retorting, "Then don't boil them."

"You want them clean, don't you?"

"You ask the damndest questions, Miriam! Of course, I

313

do!"

"Then they have to be boiled."

Doc's nostrils flared with annoyance. "You know, sometimes I think you have a vendetta against my laundry. You don't boil everyone else's clothes."

"There are very few men who bring their laundry to me in the condition that *you* do."

Doc surprised Carolina by flushing a bright red before exploding, "I don't believe that! I'm a professional man. I don't get dirty!"

"Hah!"

"Miriam . . ."

Turning toward Carolina unexpectedly, Miriam demanded, "Tell him! His laundry is ghastly, isn't it?"

The first true smile of the day pricking at her lips, Carolina drew herself to her feet. "I think it's time to change Suzannah. If you'll excuse me."

"Now, see what you did!" Doc's attempted whisper achieved the volume of a shout. "You embarrassed Carolina!"

"I! Your *laundry* is the embarrassment!"

"Miriam . . ."

Inside the cabin, Carolina tuned out the bickering that continued behind her, her mind drifting back to earlier channels. Drake's image returned again before her mind's eye and she forced away the heat of tears. She took a steadying breath. In control once more, she sang softly to the child in her arms.

"Oh, Suzannah, don't you cry for me . . ."

"No you don't, Jerome. You're not escaping until you tell me if you've accomplished any of the chores that the Natal Day Committee assigned you."

Clamping his teeth tightly closed, Doc took a long look at the sky overhead, at the brilliant sun shining down on them, but his silent prayer for patience went unanswered. Damn! Why did he keep coming back for more of the same from this impossible woman?

314

"Well, Jerome?"

"Since when did you become my keeper, Miriam?"

"The good Lord has spared me that odious task. I am, however, assistant to the chairman of the committee. . . ."

"All right!" Doc glanced up again at the cloudless sky, muttering under his breath, "Spare me the rigors of a righteous woman . . ." And then, "Don't worry, Miriam, the centennial celebration will go forward without a hitch. I ordered the fireworks in plenty of time. They should arrive this week."

"You're sure?"

"That's what I said."

"But —"

"Miriam, July Fourth is almost a month away!"

Miriam's thin face moved into a fine network of lines that revealed her anxiety. "This is our country's one hundredth year. It's especially significant that we celebrate here in Deadwood, where we're still unacknowledged as a part of our great land. Our celebration will force everyone here to recognize that our situation cannot go ignored much longer . . . that Washington *must* recognize us as citizens of the United States . . . that we demand —"

"Save the speeches, Miriam. I've heard it all already."

Miriam shook her finger in Doc's face. "Hearing and *listening* are two distinctly different functions, Jerome."

Doc groaned aloud. "Miriam . . . sometimes I wonder why I punish myself by coming he —"

Halting midsentence, Doc focused not on the hand Miriam poked in his face, but on the one she held behind her back. He reached around her and grasped it firmly, his brows drawing into an intense line as he examined her palm.

"What happened to your hand? How did you burn it?"

"It's nothing." Miriam attempted to draw it back. She winced when he grasped it more tightly.

"*I'm* the doctor, remember? I know a bad burn when I see one. How did this happen?"

Doc examined the wound more closely, noting bits of dirt and splinters of wood had adhered to the raw flesh. He pressed, "Well?"

"I was lifting the washtub off the fire. The handle was hot-

315

ter than I realized."

"This burn has to be cleansed or it'll become infected."

"It'll be all right." Miriam again attempted to withdraw her hand. Frustrated when he would not relinquish it, she continued hotly, "It was my own foolish fault. My mind was wandering. I should've known better."

Doc looked at Miriam, unconsciously wondering if the fine misting of tears he saw in her eyes came as a result of her obvious pain or her extreme discomfiture at having erred.

"We all make mistakes, Miriam."

"Speak for yourself, Jerome!"

Doc withheld a smile. "Well, it seems to me that you've just joined the race of us poor folks who have human frailties."

"Does it?" Doc saw the effort it cost for the widow to raise her pointed chin as she continued, "Well, I don't expect to remain in your ranks very long. I most definitely will not repeat such a foolish mistake again!"

A reluctant admiration of the woman's grit tugged at Doc's mind. He cast it aside to direct with a professional air, "Let's go inside. It's fortunate that I just happen to have my bag along with me today."

The widow sniffed. "You bring your bag with you every time you visit. You have since Carolina was ill. Don't go giving yourself any special credit for intuition in bringing it today."

"No, we mustn't give me any special credit, must we. . . ."

Doc's sarcasm drew Miriam's small eyes to his briefly. She sniffed again. "No. We mustn't."

Resisting a low growl, Doc drew Miriam along with him into the house.

Doc looked up from Miriam's hand a few minutes later, noting that Carolina had disappeared into the yard with the babe after he had refused her help in cleansing Miriam's burn. It was just as well. The poor young woman had paled when she had seen the raw, weeping flesh. He was relieved to be able to treat it in private, especially since it appeared that the cleansing was going to be more difficult than he had originally thought.

Doc examined the wound closely. Several rinses with cool

316

water had not washed the raw skin clean. He would have to pick out the foreign substances with tweezers and there was no use wasting time. He searched his bag.

"What are you looking for?"

"Tweezers." Miriam's hand jerked back, but he held it firmly. "Don't be a child, Miriam. This has to be done."

No response.

Doc looked up at Miriam, surprised to find her eyes brimming as she asked, "Will it hurt?"

Will it hurt . . . ? Doc stared into Miriam's suddenly colorless face. It was happening again. . . . He was seeing past the stiff-faced widow to the vulnerable woman beneath that austere exterior. His heart did a little flip-flop in his chest. He didn't like the way it made him feel as he clutched her hand more gently.

"It may hurt . . . a little."

Miriam's thin lips trembled as if she had been touched by a chill as she attempted to respond. Doc had a strong inclination to warm those lips with his own. He swallowed thickly.

Finally finding his voice, Doc responded hoarsely, "I'll be as careful as I can be."

Miriam's gaze held his for long moments before Doc forced himself to relinquish it. Looking down, he realized his own hands were trembling in a most unprofessional way. That thought sobering, he went immediately to work.

A short time later, Miriam's burn was properly cleansed and bandaged. Somehow anxious to escape but finding himself conversely unwilling to relinquish Miriam's hand, Doc forced himself to stand up. Miriam stood as well. Spots of color had returned to her pale cheeks and Doc saw that although her eyes were still unnaturally moist, her lips were steady. He also noticed that the widow's skin was exceptionally smooth for a woman of her age, and that she had about her a clean scent that was more appealing than perfume. It reminded him of home . . . of happy days and long, contented nights . . . of apple pies in the oven and a warm woman in his lap. It —

"How much is your fee, Jerome?"

Doc blinked. "Oh . . . ah . . . no fee is necessary, especially since I treated you against your will."

"Y . . . you were right, of course. I was acting like a child."

Miriam smiled . . . a true smile that softened the lines of her face and lit her eyes with a warm glow.

There it was again, the woman beneath that brittle exterior. She called out to him, and Doc yearned to answer with a longing that tugged at the manly part of him as strongly as it did his heart. The tugging grew more pronounced. . . .

"Miriam . . ."

Miriam whispered, "You've been kinder to me than I deserve, Jerome. I wasn't very pleasant to you earlier, but I'd like to compensate for that now by saying that I appreciate what you've done . . . for Carolina in coming here every day to visit since she was taken ill, and now for me. Thank you. Thank you most sincerely."

Doc swayed toward Miriam, his lips parting as he tasted her breath. He wanted . . . he needed . . .

His eyes suddenly snapping open wide, Doc gulped. He needed a *drink,* that's what he needed!

Dropping Miriam's hand as if her touch had scorched him, Doc stepped backward. He gulped again as he came up against the table with a smack.

"Jerome . . . ?"

Snatching up his bag, Doc rasped, "I have to be going now. I . . . if you have any trouble with that hand, send someone for me. Goodbye."

All but running as he stepped out through the doorway, Doc tipped his hat in passing to a surprised Carolina and continued on down the street.

Standing at the Nugget bar minutes later, Doc downed one drink, then two. Shuddering, he closed his eyes.

Miriam stood in the doorway of the cabin as Doc turned out of sight on the street. Her expression was perplexed. Carolina looked at the widow's hand and saw it was neatly bandaged.

"Is everything all right, Miriam?"

"Oh, I'm fine." Miriam paused. "But I think Jerome isn't

318

feeling well. He had the strangest look on his face when he left. Perhaps I should make him some soup."

"That would be nice."

"Yes, I . . . I'll do it right now."

Miriam turned back into the cabin and Carolina followed her inside, unwilling to voice the opinion that Miriam looked strange, too. Perhaps she was faint.

Carolina paused to consider that thought. No, that was impossible. Not Miriam.

Carolina put her sleeping daughter into the cradle, and turned back out toward the yard. Drake's image reappeared in her mind as she returned to the washtub . . . and she silently wondered what he was doing now.

Drake straightened up from a long morning working over the sluice. He examined the riffles absentmindedly, scooped out a few of the larger particles of gold, and dropped them into the pouch at his waist . . . and he silently wondered what Carolina was doing now.

Forcing his mind from the pale young woman who haunted his thoughts, Drake scratched his bearded chin and looked up at the noon sky. Another clear day that would allow him to work late. . . . He sighed with relief, grateful that the long, empty evening hours would not be extended, and walked toward the bank.

Standing on the sandy edge of the stream, Drake surveyed the forest around him. It was strange. . . . He had seen no sign of Indians as he had traveled back to the cabin from Deadwood. Nor had he seen any in the time since. He remembered the anxieties he had suffered on the way to that bustling mining camp with Carolina and the babe. He recalled that his apprehension had built with every unrecognized sound and with the rustle of every bush. His sense of relief had been acute when Deadwood had come into view and he had realized that they were safe from attack at last.

The opposite could not have been more true upon his return to the cabin. His emotions barely controlled, he had left Deadwood, ignoring precaution and the ever-present danger of attack. He had followed the main trail as far as possible in order to save time, although there had been no true reason for haste, and he had arrived back at his claim without having looked back.

But that had been then, and this was now. . . .

Lifting his hat from his head, Drake raked his fingers through his hair. A light breeze brushed his damp scalp and he allowed the pleasing sensation for a few moments before replacing his hat squarely on his forehead. In the time since he had returned, he *had* looked back, many times. Emerging vividly before his mind's eye each time was Carolina's expression of revulsion as he had replied to her question with the words, "Yes, I did."

Drake closed his eyes, then opened them again to stare at the sun-dappled water of the stream. He had thought he had paid the price of that day so long ago. To his thinking, he had paid a heavier price than should have been demanded, but he had been released from prison determined to consign that matter to the past and concentrate on the future. He had not known at that time that a slight young woman with no past of her own could be so effective in restoring that pain.

Yes, I did.

Those three words had put an end to something precious. Those three words had raked his heart raw. Those three words had made him turn and run when he had never run away from anything before.

The ache inside him almost more than he could bear, Drake sat down on the dusty bank. His elbows on his knees, he held his aching head, allowing memories full range. He recalled finding Carolina that first day. She had opened her wild, frightened eyes and looked up at him, and her fear had disappeared. Something had happened to him in those first moments. Those clear gray eyes had looked inside him, instinctively searching out a part of him that had gone cold and dead. Life had begun returning at that moment. He had felt it stir again when he first held Suzannah in his arms. The flicker had leaped to a flame when he had bathed the stains of birth from Carolina's slight body, when he had wrapped her as gently as he would a child and had watched over her. It had surged to a full-fledged blaze when Carolina had poured out her heart to him, when she had clung to him in the horror of her dreams, when she had turned to him with a youth and innocence that he had tried so desperately to deny.

But he had been neither young nor innocent and he had tried to keep the emotions that threatened him at arm's length. Bitter memories of his own, goals that he had set for himself many years earlier, vows he had uttered in the depths of his despair, had stood between them, and he had welcomed the protection they afforded. Fool that he was, he had not realized what he had striven to escape until it was too late.

Drake's hand moved instinctively to the pouch at his belt. A recent storm had done its work well. The result had been reflected in the fresh accumulations of small nuggets and dust that filled the small sack. He loosened the tie to look down at the sparkling contents inside. It glittered in the sun, taunting him, telling him that what he had lost was far more precious than the sparkling metal. It whispered that with that bullet long ago, he had lost not only his present, but his future as well. It confided that despite his hard work and careful plans, all the fine, gleaming gold dust in the world could not restore Carolina to him.

Drawing himself to his feet, Drake turned toward the cabin. It was time for his noon meal. Although he had little appetite, he welcomed the hour as respite from the silence of the morning's work. He recalled the satisfaction he had formerly found in that work, when he had made himself believe that an ever-growing cache of gold dust and a goal bitterly set, was sufficient incentive to go on.

Inside the cabin, Drake walked toward the sack hanging on the wall and withdrew a slab of bacon. The silence around him merciless, he remembered an earlier time when he had run from the stream at the sound of Carolina's screams to find her *Indian* quietly munching on the tasty smoked meat as his tail flicked away annoying flies.

He remembered the time when . . .

He remembered . . . he remembered . . . he remembered. . . .

The ache inside him precluding the desire for food, Drake

slipped the bacon back into the sack and walked out of the cabin. At the stream minutes later, he picked up the shovel and stepped down into the water.

Rosie's laughter sounded loudly at the bar. Tag raised his head from the cards in his hand, his stomach knotting. Rosie was gay these days . . . just a little too much so. Her smile was broader, her laughter louder . . . and her eyes were sadder. Scrutinizing her more closely, Tag realized that she had lost weight, too. Her lush figure was just a little less lush and her beautiful face a little drawn. It pained him to know that she suffered, and it pained him even more to know that she suffered for naught

A silent flick of his cards and groans sounded around the table, but Tag felt little satisfaction as he raked in his winnings. Slipping out of Bart's eager reach, Rosie walked casually toward the saloon entrance and looked out into the street. The ritual had begun, and Tag knew he could depend upon Rosie to do that same thing more times than he could count before afternoon faded into evening. He was sick to death at seeing her torture herself, and even more sick of his own inadequacy in being unable to prevent it.

Standing abruptly, Tag motioned to Sheila. He turned toward the saloon entrance the moment she slipped into his chair. At Rosie's side, he whispered, "Looking for something, darling?"

Rosie's smile was a trifle forced as she turned slowly and looked up into his eyes. "You might say I am. . . ." She winked and cocked a brow. "And you might say I'm not."

She had made a valiant effort at being flip, but Tag was not deceived. "Well, if it's up to me, I'd say you're not . . . because I'd prefer to think that the reason you're looking out at the street is that you feel like taking a walk."

"A walk?"

Obviously surprised, Rosie did not resist as Tag drew her along with him through the doorway. "And that suits me just fine, because I was thinking of taking a walk myself."

Glancing behind her as Tag drew her out onto the street,

Rosie protested, "But who'll take care of—"

"Barney will take care of the bar and Sheila and Ella will take care of the tables."

"But—"

"Give it up, Rosie." Tag smiled down at her. "Come on. I feel like having some company."

Rosie did not say the obvious . . . that it was dangerous for him to assume that the return of a casually affectionate relationship between them in the past few weeks since McNeil had left meant anything. He knew it didn't, and he was grateful she hadn't said it. He wanted to believe, as he slipped her arm through his, that it *did* mean something.

"Where are we goin', Tag?" Rosie rubbed the smooth white flesh of her shoulder. "The sun's so bright. I'm not used to bein' out during the day like this. My skin just might burn."

"I'll take care of it." Tag slipped his arm around Rosie's shoulders and drew her against his side. "How's that?"

Rosie fluttered her lashes responsively. "You keep this up and you'll have people talkin' about us." Rosie's smile slipped. "Where *are* we goin', Tag? I really should be gettin' back."

"Don't worry. You won't miss seeing anybody who might show up unexpectedly."

Rosie's expression fell. "I wasn't thinkin' about missin' anybody. I just—"

"Yes, you were." Tag pulled her closer as they wove their way through the milling throng. "Don't bother to hide it. I know you better than you know yourself."

"Do you?" Rosie's eyes misted unexpectedly. "Well, maybe you do. And if you do, you know I'm thinkin' that even though you know I love you in a way I don't love anybody else, I don't want you gettin' the idea that anythin's really changed. It isn't any good you waitin' around. You deserve more."

"I've been trying to tell you the same thing, Rosie."

"It's not the same thing with me and Drake."

"No, it isn't, but I know you won't agree with me right now on the reason I say that."

Tag looked around them, annoyed at their lack of privacy

323

as the late-afternoon crowd surged past them on the walk. Frowning, he stepped unexpectedly into a nearby alleyway and pulled Rosie in after him. He drew her deeper into the shadows, blocking her from view of onlookers with his back as he whispered, "Everything's wrong the way it stands between us now, Rosie. We both know that. The only thing that will make it right again is if we take this whole thing back to where we were before McNeil came between us."

"Drake was always between us, Tag."

"Maybe." Tag's heart began a heady pounding. He was intensely conscious of the crowded street behind them as he whispered, "But there was a time when you and I were close enough that I couldn't see him at all."

"I always saw him."

Tag's lips tightened with sudden anger. "You didn't see him while you were in my arms. I would've known."

Rosie's gaze melded to his with a warmth of another kind as she whispered, "No, not then. It was just you and me then, givin' comfort to each other and passin' the time in between."

"Rosie . . ." Tag moved a step closer, so close that his body was almost touching hers. He felt the heat of her moving through him as he whispered, "I want it to be that way again. I want to comfort you, to help you through these lonely days when you're hurting so bad, and I'm hurting by just looking at you. Let me do that for you, Rosie."

Rosie's eyes filled to brimming. "I can't, Tag."

"You can."

"It won't make any difference, you know. What you and I had is nothin' like what's between Drake and me. In the end, it'll be Drake and me. I . . . if I didn't believe that, I couldn't make it . . . you know?"

Tag's heart twisted with Rosie's anguish. He raised a hand to her cheek. "I know."

"Drake'll be back soon."

"You're so sure, darling?"

"I am."

"And you love him."

"I do."

"Yet you love me, too. . . ."

"Tag . . ." Rosie's voice broke. A tear slipped down her cheek and she brushed it away. "I love you enough that I wish it didn't have to be this way."

"You really believe McNeil will come back for you."

"He will."

"I don't think so." At Rosie's spontaneous protest, Tag continued, "No, listen to me. We've both been wasting a lot of time these last weeks when the plain truth is that you need me and I need you. We made things work between us before. We can do it again."

"No. . . ."

"Yes. It was my fault that everything went wrong. I got greedy. I wanted more than you were willing to give, but I've learned my lesson. I've learned it so well that I'm willing to make a bargain with you here and now."

"A bargain?"

"I want to make love to you again, Rosie." Tag's throat tightened almost to the point of pain. His hand trembled as he cupped her cheek with his hand. Her welling eyes were so blue that he ached with the sheer glory of the color as he whispered, "I want you close to me again. I want to know that I'm the only man who can make you feel the way you do when you're in my arms, because I know that I am."

"Tag, Drake is—"

"Drake isn't here. He's out in the hills somewhere and he may never return. He's a phantom, a shadow you see in your future, not the flesh and blood man who's with you right now."

"But when he comes back for me—"

"All right!" Realizing he could not dismiss that thought from Rosie's mind, Tag responded in desperation, "When McNeil comes back for you, *if* he comes back for you . . . then I promise I'll set you free with no protest. We'll become friends again—just friends."

Tears overflowed Rosie's eyes, making silver rivers down her cheeks as she whispered, "You love me that much . . . so much that you'd do that for me?"

"I love you enough to want to see you happy, whatever it costs."

Rosie struggled against her tears, finally managing, "I want to see you happy, too, Tag. An . . . and if havin' me for just a little while longer will do that, then . . . it's all right."

Elation soared within him, but Tag subdued it, forcing himself to continue, "No, don't agree. Not yet. There's another part to this bargain, Rosie." Tag took a breath, then added shakily, "I made you a promise. I want you to make me one in return. I want you to promise me that you'll stay with me until McNeil comes for you."

"I already said—"

"As long as it takes. . . ."

"What are you sayin'?"

"I'm saying, *until* McNeil comes, *if* he comes. . . ."

Rosie's flushed face went suddenly sober. "So you're sayin', if he doesn't—"

"We'll be together for the rest of our lives."

"Tag . . ."

Rosie began crying earnestly, her body racked with sobs. Resisting the desire to draw her into the comfort of his embrace, Tag whispered, "Don't cry, Rosie. Answer me. Is it a bargain? Rosie, look at me."

Raising her chin with his hand, Tag looked down into Rosie's tear-streaked face. Her response trembled on her lips. He waited, the anticipation excruciating until she finally whispered, "Yes, it's a bargain."

Allowing his elation full rein, Tag crushed Rosie close. He gloried in the familiar warmth of her against him and in the scent of her in his nostrils. He had won his Rosie back and he knew in his heart he would never have to let her go. He touched her hair, her eyes, her cheeks with his lips, and as she raised her mouth to his, he felt the pain of her ragged whisper.

"Tag, I've been so alone."

Rosie's words touched a spot deep inside him where only she lived. That spot surged to life with a tenderness only she could elicit. It forced a response that was more earnest than a sacred vow as Tag whispered, "You'll never be alone again, darling. Never again."

Doc was walking a fine line . . . too fine. He emptied his glass and slapped it back down on the bar, then looked around him. The Nugget was in full swing—unusual for so early in the evening. It was for that reason, as strongly as any other, that he was ill at ease with Rosie and Tag's absence.

A quick look at the tables in the rear revealed that Ella continued to watch the entrance, obviously as anxious as he. He had asked her where Tag was upon his arrival and she had been strangely hesitant to respond. Damn, he didn't like not knowing what was going on! If he didn't know what was going on, he might just slip off that fine line he had been walking and make a real mess of things.

Doc pounded the bar for another drink. Barney responded with his usual ease of pace and Doc eyed him impatiently, then barked, "You're sure you don't know where Rosie is . . . or Tag, for that matter?"

"I told you, Doc, I don't know nothin'."

"Yeah, sure. . . ."

Doc looked at the clock on the wall, his discomfort increasing. It hadn't been easy this past month since Drake McNeil had left Deadwood. The big fellow had been in town just long enough to stir up a hornet's nest, and he had then departed, leaving victims of his peculiar kind of sting behind him.

Doc sighed. Carolina was a victim, all right. She had recuperated from her physical injuries and was well enough to travel to Sioux City to begin searching out her background, but she hadn't even mentioned leaving Deadwood. He knew why, too. She was waiting for McNeil to return . . . *if* he would return. He almost wished that big fella wouldn't come back, because he had the feelin' that Carolina would only have more heartache in store if he did.

Rosie was another victim, although he knew she would never think of her strange relationship with McNeil under those terms. It hadn't been easy maintaining his friendship with Rosie with her knowing that he was visiting Carolina every day. Rosie had never actually come right out with it, but he knew she didn't like Carolina. After her visit to the cabin that day, Rosie had gone out of her way to avoid her, but he had seen the contempt in her great blue eyes whenever Caroli-

327

na's name was mentioned. He didn't think Rosie was right in her judgment of Carolina, and had the circumstances been different, he would have told her so. It hadn't taken much insight to see, however, that Rosie couldn't think sensibly where Drake McNeil was involved, and he had known instinctively that to interfere would be to damage their friendship beyond repair. He wasn't about to do that . . . for anybody.

Then there had been the need to visit Carolina frequently during the past month, which had brought him into more constant contact with Miriam. Talk about walking a fine line. . . . Doc shuddered at the thought of the strange fascination he had developed for that prissy old stick. His aging masculine parts had taken on a new life in keeping with that fascination, and he was damned disgusted with their lack of selectivity.

Then there was Tag and Ella, an unfortunate friendship in his estimation. He had continued to voice that opinion to Tag over the past month while he had nudged the stubborn young fellow in the *right* direction. But although the estrangement between Rosie and Tag had tempered a degree after McNeil's departure, progress in that direction had halted abruptly.

Doc picked up his glass and sipped it reflectively. There he was, the man in the middle, and that fine line had gotten real difficult to negotiate. He had the feeling now that it wasn't going to get any easier. He —

His thoughts coming to an abrupt halt, Doc bit back an involuntary exclamation at the sudden appearance of Rosie and Tag in the saloon doorway. The lights of Deadwood had just twinkled to life on the street behind them, but their glow could not compete with the shine in Tag's eyes as he slipped his arm around Rosie and drew her inside beside him.

Doc studied Rosie more closely as they parted and she turned toward the bar. The desperation never far from the surface of late in her glorious blue eyes was muted. She appeared more relaxed . . . more confident . . . more the old Rosie.

"Hello there, Doc!" Rosie's greeting held a spark of true warmth. "You're early tonight, aren't you?"

"Maybe so. Or maybe it's just that you're late. There's a

whole bunch of dissatisfied customers waitin' at the bar for the sight of you to spark their day. Where've you been?"

To his surprise, Rosie blushed. She glanced over her shoulder at Tag as he made his way toward the tables in the rear. "I . . . we, Tag and me, had some things to discuss. Then we went for a little walk."

"A walk? In Deadwood?"

Rosie flushed even deeper. "Well, just a little one. Then we stopped off and . . ." Halting abruptly, Rosie suddenly laughed. "Will you tell me why I'm answerin' all your nosy questions?"

Doc eyed her closely. "Because you know I was worryin' about you, that's why."

Rosie slid her hand onto his sleeve, her expression softening. *"Don't* worry about me. I'm all right. Tag and me made up our differences, that's all. We understand each other real well now."

"Well, that's encouragin'!"

"Everythin's goin' to be fine."

"Good. Real good. Are you tellin' me that you've made some plans?"

Rosie smiled and reached for the drink Barney put in front of her. She sipped it casually. "No. That won't happen until Drake comes back for me."

The wind knocked out of him by Rosie's unexpected response, Doc watched as she glanced up and responded warmly to a greeting from a passing customer. A sickly grin was affixed to his lips when she looked back at him.

"Somethin' wrong, Doc?"

Doc shook his head. "No, nothin'. Nothin' at all."

Doc turned back to the bar, thinking of that fine line he was walking, and knowing that it had suddenly gotten inestimably finer.

Ella slipped out of her seat at the table, annoyed as Sheila took her own sweet time putting her broad fanny down in her place. She made an appropriately sharp remark that snapped Sheila's head toward her angrily as she started toward the bar.

Carefully avoiding the quietly conversing figures of Rosie and Doc, she walked deliberately to the other end of the bar.

"The usual, Barney."

Suddenly at her elbow, Tim Ryan offered suggestively, "Did you give up the table for the night, sweetheart? I could find some spare time for you if you did."

Ella shot him a brittle glance. "No, Tim, honey. I just got up to stretch my legs . . . not spread 'em."

Tim turned away without response and Ella swore under her breath. Pigs . . . all of them were pigs. . . . The biggest pig of them all, Gus Ricks, had stopped her on the street earlier in the day. He had leered at her with his small eyes and she could tell his hands were sweating when he had told her that he was waiting for her to come back begging for her job at the Grubstake. He had laughed and said that she hadn't hooked Tag Willis yet, and she never would. She had told him then what she thought of him and his opinions. She had come directly to the Nugget for Tag's reassurances, only to get a sinking sensation in her stomach when she had arrived and found both Tag and Rosie missing.

It had taken only one glimpse of the two of them when they returned to know where they had been.

Damn . . . damn . . . damn. . . . Ella tossed back a lock of brassy blond hair that had fallen onto her forehead and picked up her glass. She emptied it in a single gulp and slapped it back on the bar.

"I'm thinkin' that ain't too smart, Ella."

Ella's head snapped up toward Barney. "Who asked you?"

Barney's full mustache twitched. "I thought you liked your job here."

"What's it to you if I do or I don't?"

"I saw how you just sent Tim Ryan skitterin' away. I'm thinkin' that unless you want to go back to your old duties, you'd better keep a clear head. Tag don't like his customers gettin' the edge in a game."

"One drink don't bother me."

Barney shrugged. "Unless I miss my guess, you wasn't goin' to stop at just one. I wouldn't like to see you do that, Ella."

330

"You wouldn't. . . ." The unexpected sincerity in Barney's voice took the edge off Ella's agitation. Barney's bald head shone with perspiration in the light and his pudgy face was sober as Ella studied him more closely. "So how come you're bein' nice to me all of a sudden? I thought you figured I was out to get your precious Rosie."

"Well, I think you might be, but I don't think you stand a chance with everybody watchin' you so close. Besides, Tag ain't got eyes for nobody but Rosie. He ain't goin' to change. I figure you need *somebody* on your side."

Ella scrutinized Barney's expression. "On *my* side?"

Barney raised his double chin. "I'm thinkin' you started out on the wrong foot in the Nugget, and as far as I'm concerned, just as long as you don't think you're goin' to stick that foot in where Rosie's belongs, I'll be on your side."

Ella growled with disgust. "Rosie, Rosie, Rosie. . . . What's so great about her?"

"Rosie ain't got a mean bone in her body, and she's got more heart than any two women I know."

"Your Rosie is smarter than you think she is. And she ain't the innocent, neither. She's just like everybody else. She'll do what she has to do to get what she wants. You wait and see."

"I think she already has what she wants."

"No, she don't. There's somethin' about her . . ." Suddenly realizing that she had hit upon the thing that had bothered her about Rosie, Ella paused. Rosie wanted something that she didn't have. . . . What was it? It wasn't Tag. . . . It wasn't a piece of the business. . . . It wasn't money. . . . A light went on in Ella's mind. She wanted a man . . . a special man. . . . That big fella she was mooning over a month back . . . the one who got her eyes so dreamy. . . .

That was it!

Her heart suddenly beating a rapid tattoo in her breast, Ella gave Barney a short salute. "Thanks, Barney, you've been a real help. I'm feelin' better already."

Ella turned away with a spring in her step. She looked back as Barney warned softly, "Watch yourself, Ella. The only way you're goin' to get what you want and keep it is by not tryin' to take it away from Rosie."

331

"I told you before, Barney. I don't want nothin' Rosie wants."

Ella walked back toward the poker table with a smile. Barney had been nice . . . nicer than anybody in the Nugget had been to her, outside of Tag. She appreciated a kind word. She sensed that even his warning had been meant well. She had been truthful to Barney in return, and she had meant what she said to him. She didn't want anything Rosie wanted, because Rosie didn't want Tag. It was that other fella that she had her eye on. With any luck at all that big fella would come back. And when he did, Ella was suddenly determined that she would do her very best to see that Rosie got him.

The silence of the night was not really silent at all. Echoes of revelry filtered through the cabin window from Main Street, joining the familiar sounds of the widow's even breathing in sleep. Carolina shifted her position on the couch, realizing the discomfort that Miriam, who was so much taller than she, must have suffered sleeping there while she had been ill.

The older woman was now back in her own bed again at Carolina's insistence. She slept soundly, but Carolina knew that the widow still suffered for Suzannah's and her presence. The cabin was small, and the needs of another woman and child shrank its dimensions even further. When Suzannah was restless, Miriam was restless. When Suzannah refused to sleep, Miriam was unable to sleep. Carolina was only too aware that the widow was no longer young, that she rose early in the morning and worked late, and that she paid a stiff price for each and every minute of sleep that Suzannah caused her to lose.

Carolina also knew that despite Miriam's kindness and reassurances, there were times when the widow missed her privacy. She had heard the widow cry occasionally in sleep. She had carefully avoided mentioning those episodes to Miriam because she was certain the woman's pride would make such a discussion awkward. She understood, because she felt the same.

Carolina closed her eyes briefly, amending that thought. The true reason for her own refusal to discuss her nightmares and fears, as well as the fragments of memory which flickered through her mind, was not pride. Drake was the only person with whom she had shared that part of herself. Their confidential conversations and the solace he had returned in his deeds and with his touch when the words had refused to come, had united them uniquely. She did not dare risk weakening that bond, even if only in her mind.

And then there was a matter of her own, personal shame. . . . How could she tell the sober, honest widow that she felt no pressing desire to regain the memory of her own husband who had recently been taken from her so savagely? How could she reveal that with the exception of hoping to learn more about her background for Suzannah's sake, she did not feel driven to find any remaining family she might have? How could she explain that except for occasional bouts of anxiety, she was satisfied to allow her former life to remain a mystery as long as her future was secure? How could she confide that she felt that way because she had seen all she could ever want or need when she had looked up into Drake McNeil's eyes the first time, and that she somehow knew she would find greater fulfillment in his arms than she could ever have found with her husband?

Carolina paused in her thoughts, realizing that the time had come to face a difficult reality. Drake had ridden off and left Suzannah and her behind. He had not done it callously, she knew. He had left a sum to tide her over until she could resume her life and had paid for her transportation back to the state that was probably her home. His kindnesses did not change the fact, however, that he *didn't* want her.

Carolina gave a short laugh that erupted unexpectedly as a sob. He didn't want her, but here she was, waiting for him to return. That was the greatest shame of all. . . .

Carolina wiped away her tears with the flat of her hand. She was a grown woman . . . a mother who needed to put an end to the limbo of her child's and her existence. A familiar anguish beset Carolina, but she forced it away. She had no choice in what she must do. She would confirm the arrangements to leave Deadwood tomorrow, before she could change her mind.

Tomorrow. . . .

That decision firmly made, Carolina closed her eyes only to find the image of Drake waiting, and the truest shame of all was suddenly clear. Drake would never know how much she loved him.

The silence of the night was not really silent at all. It was rent by Rosie's heated murmurs, the small rasps of pleasure that echoed in her darkened cabin, sending ripples of passion through Tag's hungry heart. Rosie's sweet flesh was warm and moist beneath him. Her body was giving and eager, and as he looked down into her clear eyes, Tag knew he had dispelled the lingering shadow between them for a little while.

But he wanted more.

Cupping Rosie's magnificent face with his palms, Tag kissed her brows, her fluttering eyelids, the bridge of her nose. He explored the delicate shell of her ear with his tongue, nibbling the lobe, biting her sharply, only to cover her spontaneous protest with his lips. He swallowed her words, consuming them, hearing them echo deep inside him. They were not the words he longed to hear her speak, but he knew that every word Rosie spoke became a part of him. The sharp ones cut deeply, and the soft, loving words, however scarce, were gems indeed. He cherished them and stored them away in his mind, taking them out when he was alone to allow their glittering facets to warm the emptiness. He knew that should Rosie ever leave him, this treasure he had amassed during the years they had been together would have to suffice for a lifetime — for he could never love another the way he loved her.

Tag's throat tightened. He loved Rosie . . . he loved her so much.

Separating her lips with his kiss, Tag drew deeply from her, swallowing the familiar taste of her, knowing he would never get his fill. Her mouth, the slender column of her throat, the full swells of her breasts. . . . Rosie's skin was so beautiful, so smooth, its fragrance sweeter as her passion soared.

334

Slipping his hand down into the dark, moist muff between her thighs, Tag wove his fingers into the silken curls. Rosie's passion-drugged lids fluttered. Her glazed, azure gaze met his, and he whispered softly against her lips, "It's been so long, Rosie. I've missed you so much."

Tag's skillful touch caressed the moist crevice below. He saw Rosie's eyelids flicker responsively as he found the bud of her desire. He stroked it boldly, his breathing accelerating as Rosie's lips separated. He whispered, "Talk to me, Rosie. Tell me what you feel, darling. Tell me what you want so I can make you happy."

"Tag . . ."

Rosie's single word of response was ragged. He prompted softly, "Do you like this, darling?" Tag's caresses swept the tender slit more broadly and Rosie's body jerked responsively. She swallowed and Tag felt her passion mount. He lowered his head to tug at the roseate crest of her breast. Her gasp drove him to a more ardent assault. She was writhing under him as he moved his fervent ministrations to her other breast, then looked up.

"Talk to me, Rosie. Tell me you want me . . ."

The silence was endless until Rosie responded, "I want you, Tag."

"Tell me you need me."

"Tag, please . . ."

"Tell me how you feel. . . ."

His hands working a familiar magic on Rosie's tender flesh, Tag laved her breasts with his tongue. He thrilled at her groan of rapture as she rasped, "You make me feel good, Tag. You make me feel wanted and loved. You make me feel as if . . . as if we're all alone in the world."

"We are, Rosie." Rosie's gaze met his and Tag repeated softly, "We are. There're just the two of us, loving each other, knowing what each other wants and wanting to give."

The pulse in Rosie's throat was throbbing wildly. Tag's heart took up its rhythm as he continued roughly, "Just as I know you want this now. . . ." Tag's caresses grew bolder, "And this. . . ."

Rosie's body began trembling. Her eyes opened with silent

appeal. "I . . . it's going too fast." Rosie swept his body with her fingertips. "I haven't given you—"

Tag managed a smile, interrupting hoarsely, "Don't worry about me. My pleasure is in you alone tonight, darling. There'll be other nights. Just talk to me. Tell me. . . ."

Tag felt Rosie's first warning shudder as she whispered, "I feel so good. . . . The world is bright and colors are soaring around me. You gave them to me, Tag. You're taking me toward the sun and it's hot . . . so hot. It's growing hotter. . . ."

Rosie's soft groan sent a thrill coursing up Tag's spine. He felt the effort she exerted as she continued raggedly, "I love the way you make me feel, Tag. . . . I love to feel your hands on me . . . *in* me. . . . I love your mouth on mine . . . the taste of you. . . . I love feeling your weight on top of me. . . ."

Tag grasped the crest of her breast again with his mouth and Rosie cried out aloud. She quaked again and Tag inwardly despaired, knowing the time was close. . . .

His own body reacted hotly to Rosie's heightening response and Tag fought an ecstatic swell. Abandoning his tantalizing quest, he paused momentarily, lifting himself to hover over Rosie's nakedness with his own. He knew that if he could, he would spend the rest of his life with Rosie this way, just the two of them, loving, wanting, needing. . . .

With one strong thrust, Tag came to rest within Rosie and exaltation soared within his mind. *His* Rosie . . . *his* love . . . *always* his. . . .

Tag was quivering at the edge of culmination as he whispered, "You make me feel all those things you feel, Rosie . . . all of them, and so much more. I love you, darling. I love—"

Ecstasy burst the bounds of restraint, thrusting words from Tag's mind. It shimmered anew with each pulsing spasm, echoing in Rosie's body as she joined his throbbing rhythm with her own. And as he lay replete upon her, breathing her breath, his heartbeat echoing hers, Tag heard Rosie whisper the words he longed to hear.

"I . . . I love you Tag. I do."

Rosie slid her arms around him and he felt a new trembling begin inside her. He felt her desperation as her voice dropped to a barely audible rasp. "I wish . . . I wish it was enough."

Elation dimmed. A familiar sadness returned to tear at the pit of Tag's stomach. It was not any easier, knowing that Rosie shared his sadness, that she wished with all her might she had not felt forced to say those words.

The fine mist of their passion bonding them, Tag wrapped his arms tightly around Rosie in return. Although he dared not declare it, he knew that while Rosie's mind was wrapped up in his loving, no one else could enter. That thought his consolation, he breathed deeply and pressed his lips against hers. That would have to be enough for now. His only hope was that in the end, it would not have to be enough to last a lifetime. . . .

The silence of the night was not really silent at all. In the distance, creatures of the darkness made their forays, howling, screeching, barking at the moon. Drake's cabin echoed with their calls, and with the last pleading cries of prey that would not see the dawn.

Lying abed, Drake followed a singular, plaintiff appeal to its final dying whimper, and he shook with the pain of it. He shared the misery of that dwindling cry. He had suffered a similar agony. He had been tested against a more powerful foe and lost. He had thought never to face that foe again, but he had been wrong. It had returned when least expected, and he had confronted it with scorn. He had feared it, struggled against it, fought it with all his might, and when all else had failed, he had panicked and run from it. But he had not escaped. He had carried the memory of it within his mind, battling it with each waking moment. His blood had been shed in that battle. He was bleeding still. He was dying from the wounds.

But he was unlike that prey that would never see the dawn. The pity of it all was that the sun would rise for him and he would face the new day to continue dying.

The pity of it all. . . . Drake's heart began a new pounding. Pity was not a word he would accept. He wasn't a helpless animal that had been run into the ground never to rise again.

Long years of frustration and pain had hardened and changed him, but the endlessly lonely weeks just passed had forced difficult truths to gradually emerge in his mind. Why hadn't he realized that a prisoner's dreams need not be a liberated man's reality, and that a foe wears many faces — one of which could easily become his own?

Drake closed his eyes, his throat thickening. *He* had been his own greatest enemy. He had turned his back on feelings he feared *because* he feared them. He had seen horror reflected in eyes that had formerly looked to him with faith and trust, and had not said a word in his own defense because he had wanted a way out.

Drake's harsh, self-derisive laughter echoed in the eerie semilight that had begun filtering through the window. There had been no way out . . . and there was no escape.

Carolina's image was brilliantly clear before his mind, and Drake was suddenly anxious as he drew himself to a seated position on his cot. He would start back to Deadwood tomorrow. If she was there . . . if she would listen, he would know there was a chance. He would explain all that he should have explained to her that last day. If the horror in her eyes remained when he was finished, he would turn his back and walk away.

But if she had left Deadwood . . .

The silver light of dawn creased the night sky and Drake drew himself to his feet, knowing that if she had, her decision would already have been made. He would have to accept it.

Drake reached for his clothes, his hands trembling. In two days he would know.

"Have you thought this over clearly, dear?" Miriam's face was lined with concern as she watched Carolina pack her meager belongings with undisguised haste. "Do you realize what you're undertaking? You'll be making a difficult journey with an infant . . . all alone, to an uncertain destination."

Carolina looked up from her recently purchased carpetbag. She hadn't liked spending a portion of her precious funds for it, but she had known that it was a necessary convenience.

"Yes, I do, Miriam." Carolina regretted the woman's anxiety. "I'm sorry. I wish I could make you understand, but I hardly understand myself. All I know is that last night I suddenly realized that I had to do something to take responsibility for my life—that I couldn't spend another day drifting."

"But . . . weren't you happy here, dear?"

"Oh, Miriam . . . my leaving has nothing to do with the way you've treated me. You've been more generous than I had any right to expect. You've cared for Suzannah and me and shared all you have without asking anything in return. And I suppose that's the point. I have nothing to share in return . . . not the way I am right now, without a past or a future. I finally faced that fact last night, and then I decided that if I can't be the person I want to be, there's nothing left but to find out who I *was*."

"I can understand that, dear, but why must you rush so?"

"Because Mister Williamson will be taking his wagons back to Sioux City this afternoon. It's the safest train—the most carefully guarded one. I'll have to wait indefinitely for it to return again, and I don't think I could bear that now that my decision has been made."

"But what will you do? Where will you go?" Tears filled Miriam's eyes. "How will you care for Suzannah?"

"I'll manage. When I get to Sioux City, I'll make inquiries about the Harper train. There are bound to be records somewhere."

"And if there aren't? You'll be all alone in a strange place with no one to turn to."

Placing the last of Suzannah's linens in the bag, Carolina turned to hug the distressed widow. "I won't really be alone, Miriam. I'll have a friend who's thinking about me and wishing me well."

Miriam hugged her tightly in response, then stepped back with a visible effort at control. "If you're sure you want to do this . . ."

"Miriam, dear, I don't really have any choice."

Miriam took a steadying breath. "Then let me help you." A

tear slipped down the older woman's cheek and she brushed it away. "You only have an hour. I'll change Suzannah."

Carolina stared at the widow as the woman turned reluctantly toward the sleeping child. Her sadness was overwhelming.

"It's true, I tell you!" Charlie Sloan turned to glance at Doc over his shoulder. He winced as Doc wielded his knife with an expert hand, but continued determinedly, "I heard Carolina Brand tell Jim Thompson myself that she would be leavin' Deadwood with us this afternoon."

"Stand still, I tell you!" Doc's disposition was poor and getting poorer by the moment. There were things he liked better than removing a splinter that was deeply embedded in this fella's scrawny posterior. Under other circumstances, he might've speculated over the fact that Charlie wasn't the first to come into his office of late with this complaint . . . or the second, or the third, for that matter. He might've asked how he had managed to get such a large sliver of wood so deep into that peculiar portion of his anatomy . . . and if there was any truth to the rumor that his old friend, Heddy LaRue, had found a new game to play. However, the information the randy fellow had imparted had chased that curiosity from his mind.

"You're confused, Charlie! You must be meanin' somebody else. Carolina Brand is the name of the young woman who's been livin' with the widow Higgins."

"Yep, one and the same."

Charlie was still peering at him over his shoulder and Doc fixed him with a hard stare. "You sure you haven't been drinkin'?"

"I been drinkin', but I ain't drunk. If you don't believe me, just come outside and see. We'll be leavin' in about an hour."

Doc slapped a bandage on Charlie's quivering backside, ignoring the fellow's pained reaction as he growled, "Pull up your pants!"

"You don't have to go gettin' mad at me, Doc! I didn't buy that sweet little thing a ticket and point her at the road out of

340

town. It was that big fella about a month ago who done that. The fella with them cold eyes who paid for her ticket. . . ."

Doc demanded flatly, "You owe me two dollars."

"Two dollars!" Charlie gulped. "Two dollars for takin' out a splinter?"

Doc's temper flared. "Damn you, Charlie Sloan! Pay up or I'll put that splinter right back where I got it!"

"All right . . . all right . . . but that's the last time I ever tell you anythin'."

Doc remained staring at the door for a long moment after it closed behind Charlie. Could it be true? Could Carolina really be leaving Deadwood? Suddenly realizing there was only one way to find out, Doc snapped into motion.

"Don't you worry about nothin', ma'am. We'll take right good care of this little lady." Jim Thompson motioned with pride toward the lumbering wagons moving into position a short distance away. We've got six rifles in front and six in the rear for protection, not sayin' what's in between. There isn't an Indian in the territory that doesn't know my wagons, and they're not goin' to mess with them. We'll be puttin' Mrs. Brand in a wagon right up front behind those rifles where she'll be the safest. Don't you worry about her. I'll treat her like she was my own daughter."

Jim Thompson's words were meant as a reassurance but Carolina could see that they had as little effect on Miriam as they did on her. It wasn't as if Mr. Thompson wasn't a comforting sight. A quiet authority was reflected in his weather-roughened face, and kindness and concern flowed from his gaze, but comfort was somehow beyond her.

Carolina attempted a smile but her effort was a dismal failure. She hadn't expected things to move this fast when she had gone to talk to him that morning. She hadn't expected that the train would be leaving that day and that she would be forced into following through with a decision made only the previous night.

Suzannah whimpered softly from Miriam's arms, drawing her attention, and Carolina was suddenly grateful for the op-

341

portune interruption of her momentary weakness. Suzannah's present was unstable and her future was uncertain, but she did have a family somewhere. Finding that family was little enough to give her daughter when she had nothing else.

"Carolina . . ." Speaking for the first time as he stood beside the widow, Doc Fitz stopped to clear his throat, then continued with a suspicious brightness in his eyes, "You're sure you're not bein' hasty. . . . You've suffered a difficult trauma, dear. You haven't completely recovered from it."

Carolina raised her chin. "I've recovered physically."

Doc nodded. "Yes, you have."

"Then that's all that's important."

"Are you sure of that, dear?"

Carolina's throat thickened as she responded softly, "I have to be sure of something, Doctor Fitz, don't I?"

A call from the rear of the train sounded and Carolina felt her heart begin a wild pounding as she realized the time had come. She walked toward the assigned vehicle, finally turning to hug Doc briefly. She hugged Miriam in turn, then accepted Jim Thompson's hand as she climbed up into the rear of the wagon. The driver turned back to nod politely in her direction, but she could barely see his face for the tears that blurred her vision as Miriam handed Suzannah up to her. She placed the babe in the rough cradle which had served her so well, bittersweet memories attached to it flooding her mind. She was putting it all behind her now . . . the only past she knew . . . the only home she could remember . . . her only love. . . .

At a loud call, the lead wagon jerked forward. Through a glaze of tears, Carolina saw the silver stream that moved down Miriam's lined cheek as her wagon slowly followed suit. She saw Doc take a step closer to the widow to slide his arm around her shoulders, and she was suddenly grateful to the crusty old fellow for the comfort he afforded her.

She waved at the two who stood watching until they could watch no more, then dropped her hand to her side, drained of emotion. She was doing what she had to do. Drake didn't want her. He had left her behind. This was the way it had to be.

Miriam was trembling and Doc drew her closer against his side. He knew his own sadness at Carolina's departure was magnified a hundredfold within the lonesome widow. Surprising him, she leaned against him for long minutes before drawing back to turn toward her cabin. He walked beside her, offering softly, "Carolina will be all right, Miriam. She's a brave young woman."

"But she's so young, Jerome. And she's all alone."

"She'll be fine."

The remaining distance to the widow's cabin was covered in silence. At the door, Miriam turned to look down at him from her superior height. She stared at him in silence for long moments and Doc felt the rise of emotions he had thought long dead as she finally whispered, "Thank you, Jerome."

Leaning down, Miriam startled him by pressing a light kiss against his cheek. The cabin door closed behind her moments later, and Doc stood transfixed . . . and he wondered. . . .

"She's gone! I knew she wouldn't last!"

Rosie's smile was gloating as Tag and she stood in a position of partial concealment, watching the Thompson train move out of Deadwood. Her faultless features glowed with triumph but Tag did not share her elation. He made an attempt to turn Rosie back toward town, but he could see she was unwilling to give up the satisfaction of seeing Carolina Brand ride out of her life forever.

"I was right, wasn't I, Tag!" Rosie looked smugly up at him. "That Carolina Brand wasn't worthy of Drake! She was weak and a coward, and now she's proved everythin' I said by runnin' away. Drake will know I'm right when he comes back. I won't have to do any more explainin'. He'll thank me for showin' her up for what she was and everythin' will be all right between us then. Everythin'. . . ."

Not waiting for his response, Rosie turned back to town. Her step was steady and eager, and walking beside her, Tag could feel her exaltation. Looking at her now, he could almost believe that their hours spent in mutual passion the previous night had never really happened.

Tag's jaw firmed stubbornly. But it had. He knew it and Rosie knew it. He also knew that to Rosie the previous night had no reflection on her feelings for McNeil or the euphoria she now experienced in thinking McNeil was now hers alone again. So he told himself as he had so many times before that McNeil was a phantom. He told himself that *he* was Rosie's flesh and blood man and that they had a firm bargain between them. He told himself that he would hold her to it and that he would be satisfied.

Tag took Rosie's hand. She looked up with a smile and he smiled in return. But the smile hurt, and he knew then that in telling himself all those things, he had lied. . . .

The afternoon sun had reached its zenith, but Drake ignored the grumbling of his empty stomach as he surveyed the wilderness of the trail. He wondered at the strange sense of urgency that had beset him as he had started his journey. His discomfort had increased as the morning had progressed until he was now hard put to resist the urge to ignore caution in favor of haste.

Alert to the sounds of the hills around him, Drake knew he could not afford to be that much a fool. He had already made mistakes that might have cost him more than he could bear to lose.

Drake looked up at the leafy umbrella of trees over his head, verdant against the clear blue of the sky. He found himself mumbling, "Two days . . . Just two more days. Wait for me, Carolina. . . ."

The living silence of the land his only reply, Drake pushed on.

Twenty-one

Miriam looked out the window of her cabin at the leaden sky. She didn't like the looks of it. She had seen summer storms close in with frightening fury in the hills, releasing torrential downpours in a matter of moments. She knew what that meant . . . streets that turned into bogs, polluted wells, laundry that would not dry.

Miriam's thin face tightened as she studied the sky more intently. Her freshly hung laundry flapped and billowed in the heightening wind. She took a risk in leaving it there in the hopes of its drying before the storm broke, and she knew that a week earlier she would have been scrambling to get it off the line. But things had changed in her cabin in the five days since Carolina had joined the Thompson train. She had learned a lesson that day and another in the day that had followed. She had begun to see a new attitude emerge in her life, wherein there was room for risk and uncertainty if the reward to be reaped was great enough.

That attitude was reflected in all Miriam had done since. It had begun to affect the way she perceived people and things, and it cast new lights on the priorities she had set in her life. It was with that attitude that she turned back to the stove and stirred the beef simmering there for that evening's supper. A particularly noisy gust of wind rattled the windowpanes, but the widow ignored the warning, somehow choosing to follow her inclination to continue with what she was doing. She would take the risk of beating the rain.

A heavy gust of wind tugged at Drake's hat and he grasped the brim, tucking in his head against it and cursing under his breath. He glanced at the busy Deadwood street as he descended the steep road into town, noting that the pace of the traffic on the street was a bit more frantic than usual as the skies prepared to open up upon it. He cursed again, certain he would get thoroughly soaked before the day was out and knowing he should not have expected anything different the way his luck was running.

Incredibly, the journey to Deadwood had taken *five* days, with every minute a solemn torment. His horse had gone lame the first day out, forcing him to spend a whole afternoon doctoring the animal. He had spent the next day riding his pack mule at a snail's pace, presenting a ridiculous picture, he was sure, with his legs dangling ludicrously close to the ground and his huge bay limping behind him.

That minor mishap had proved to be the least of his problems, however. Almost immediately afterward, he had run into signs of Indian activity all around him. He recalled his momentary panic, knowing that he would not be able to outrun even the feeblest of Indian nags on his long-eared mount. Strangely, it was not fear for his own personal safety that had caused him the greatest difficulty during the tense days that followed. Instead, he had found himself inwardly furious at his own pathetic timing at having finally come to his senses when it might possibly be too late.

He had managed to escape direct conflict with the roving Indian bands, discovering that the delay had been beneficial in one respect alone. His horse had been sufficiently rested to allow him to enter Deadwood with a modicum of dignity.

Drake revised that last thought. He was keenly aware that there was little dignity in arriving in town unclean, unshaven, and uncertain, and that there was even less dignity in knowing that although he was about to be drenched, the thought of finding shelter had not even entered his mind.

On cue, thunder rolled deafeningly overhead, followed

by a crack of lightning that lit the rapidly darkening sky. His mount shied nervously, but Drake held him with a firm hand as he continued down the street. Lamps flickered to life in the windows around him and the music and merriment so great a part of Deadwood's daily scene continued uninterrupted, but Drake spared it little thought. His heartbeat accelerated as the moment he had anticipated for five long days drew closer.

Miriam's cabin came into sight as the first oversize drop of rain fell. The sky darkened ominously as a few more scattered drops hit the ground, and Drake's heart leaped to a ragged beat as he spotted a slight figure in the yard moving frantically between the billowing lines of laundry. The woman was partially obscured by the flapping folds, but he knew it was Carolina. . . .

Thunder boomed and lightning crackled across the sky as Drake rode into the yard. The rain started in earnest as he dismounted, unable to tear his eyes from the woman's bustling figure. He was within a few feet of her when she turned and saw him for the first time.

Drake stopped abruptly as the woman's beautiful gray eyes widened with incredulity.

The wind whipped them mercilessly with stinging rain, plastering their clothes to their bodies, but neither moved nor spoke. His gaze consuming her, Drake watched as Carolina turned fully toward him. Her words trembled briefly on her lips before emerging in a whisper barely heard over the fury of the storm.

"Drake . . . have you come back for me at last?"

Response was beyond him as Drake closed the final few steps between them, as he crushed Carolina's slenderness against him and strained her close, suddenly knowing he could never have let her go.

Chills ran down Carolina's spine as she adjusted the blanket around her shoulders. She shivered despite the dry clothing she now wore and slid a hand into her damp, unbound hair as she moved closer to the fire. Silent, she watched with a peculiar fascination as Drake stripped down to his bare chest and dried himself with a cloth before accepting the shirt that Miriam handed him. He caught her gaze as he turned back toward the fire and bright golden flecks leaped to life in the cool green of his eyes.

Breathless, Carolina knew she had waited all her life to see that glow there, and she marveled as this beautiful man walked toward her that her dreams could finally have come true when she had come so close to surrendering them.

Sitting on a chair opposite her, Drake grasped her hands and Carolina knew that the tremors that shook him were not caused by a chill. She read in his eyes all that went unsaid as they suffered the lack of privacy that kept them from each other's arms.

The sudden clearing of Miriam's throat turned them toward her as the older woman took an old umbrella from a peg on the wall and reached for her shawl.

"Suzannah's sleeping peacefully, and I know you two won't mind when I tell you that I'm going out for a while to visit Mary McCullough. Her husband went back out into the hills again last week, and she's been alone ever since. I promised her that I'd stop by tonight."

Carolina saw through the older woman's ruse and responded instinctively, "You don't have to do that, Miriam. The weather is terrible. Drake and I . . . we—"

Drake interrupted Carolina's halting statement. "Thank you, Mrs. Higgins."

The widow turned toward the door. "You're welcome, Mister McNeil."

The door closed behind Miriam. Uncertain who made the first move, Carolina was suddenly in Drake's arms. The heat of him was flush against her, his mouth on hers. She closed her eyes, returning his kiss, knowing that although he had comforted her many times, he had never held her like this, that although his touch was familiar, his fervor was stirringly new. Drake trembled as she trembled. His heart thudded against hers. She felt the passionate swell of

348

him and her need surged in response. And she knew as she had always known that they had been created for each other, that no momentary lapse, no strange hysteria, no shadows from the past could come between them to change that basic truth.

As if reading her mind, Drake drew back from her. His regret was reflected clearly in his eyes as he forced a distance between them. His difficulty in maintaining that distance resounded in his voice as he began hesitantly, "Before things go any farther, there are some things about me you should know."

"I know everything about you that I need to know. I don't want to know anything else."

Concern touched Drake's tone. "You don't *need* to know, or you're *afraid* to know. Which is it, darlin'?"

Her heart aching at Drake's uncertainty, Carolina whispered, "Oh, Drake, can't you see? If I allow myself to care about the secrets in your past, then I must care about my own past as well. Neither of us may ever know anything more about me than we do now—yet you love me. Why can't you accept that I can love you the same way in return?" Her voice breaking, Carolina rasped, "I don't care what anyone says about you—"

"Even if it's true?"

"Nothing can change the way I feel. I know all I need to know about you. You found me when I was lost in so many ways. You saved me from my terror and gave me Suzannah's life."

"You're talking about gratitude. It isn't gratitude that I want from you, Carolina."

"Drake. . . ." Pain stirred inside Carolina at Drake's suddenly solemn expression. "Gratitude is only a part of what I feel. Couldn't you tell . . . didn't you know that I recognized you that first day?" And at his look of puzzlement, "I couldn't remember who I was or where I was, but I knew the first moment I saw you that you were a part of me that I had found at last."

Drake was silent. She could see his heart at war with his

mind in the moments that followed. The battle raged in his eyes as his gaze searched her face, caressing her with a touch that was almost palpable. She knew he wanted to believe her. She sensed he tried to accept her words, and she felt his torment the moment before he whispered, "I can't do it, darlin'. I can't accept everythin' you want to give, knowin' that you might eventually find out the things I should've told you today—and hate me for them."

"Drake—"

"If you won't let me tell you for your own sake, Carolina, then let me tell you for mine."

Unable to refuse his appeal, Carolina nodded. She felt Drake's tension build as they sat as they had before, facing each other, holding hands as he started to speak.

"What I've already told you about myself is true . . . that small town in Texas where I was born, and the ranch where I helped my pa run cattle and thought that there'd be no other way I'd ever want to spend my life. But I didn't tell you that things started gettin' hard while I was growin' up. Ranches around us started failin'. Pa died around that time, and I knew the only way I was goin' to save things was by takin' in a partner from back East. I did it against my better judgment, but for a while I thought things might work out. With the additional capital, I was able to buy up some of the surrounding ranches and increase my water rights. One of the ranches I bought belonged to Jake Bradley. Old Jake lost everythin' I paid him in a poker game a little while after that and then he killed himself. I married his daughter."

"Married . . ." A strange breathlessness struck Carolina and she drew back. The image of a church flashed before her eyes. She heard echoes of voices raised in song . . . saw the shadow of a man standing at her side. The man looked down at her—

"What's the matter, Carolina?"

"Nothing." Carolina attempted a smile. "Go on, please."

Drake continued determinedly, "I knew Julia didn't love me when she married me. Maybe there wasn't much about me to love. I was a damned hard case, impatient with myself and with everybody else who wasn't content to work themselves into the ground, but I loved her . . . or thought I did. She was penniless and I figured I could make her love me by making everythin' right for her again. I didn't realize she blamed me for her father's death and hated me for it.

"Things went bad for us, with fightin' and recriminations, until there wasn't much of a marriage left. Then my partner returned from back East and everythin' fell apart. Halpern and I had different ideas about runnin' the ranch and Julia took his side against me. The situation was buildin' up to a blow when I came home a few days early from roundup and Julia wasn't there. It was pretty late, and I figured there was only one place she could be. Halpern was stayin' in town and I went up to his hotel room."

Drake stood up abruptly, his agitation mounting. He took a few steps away. When he turned back, his eyes were cold. "She was with him in his room. I could hear them inside before I knocked, and when Halpern unlocked the door, I pushed it open. She was in his bed, the damned whore that she was, and when she saw me, she started laughin'. It all happened real fast after that. I hit Halpern and knocked him down. He scrambled for his gun and shot at me. He missed. I didn't. He died some time later."

"But if Halpern shot first . . . ?"

"They never found his gun."

"How could that happen?"

Drake's voice dropped to a hiss. "*She* did it. She hid the gun somehow and told the sheriff that Halpern never had one, that I'd shot him in cold blood. Everybody knew that Halpern and I were always fightin' and she said I just used her as an excuse to kill him. There were a couple of empty chambers in my gun, so I couldn't prove that I didn't fire both shots."

"They sent you to prison. . . ."

Drake's expression grew grim. "Seven years. . . . Julia sold off everythin' she could get her hands on and ran the

351

ranch into the ground. The land was auctioned off for back taxes, and when everything was gone, she divorced me."

"Oh, Drake. . . ."

"That was when I made myself a promise." His gaze burning, Drake continued softly, "My pa put his whole life into that land. I told myself that I'd get the money to buy it back somehow, and when I did, I'd build up the ranch and make it bigger and better than it ever was . . . or I'd die tryin'."

Silent for long moments, Drake continued softly, "The Black Hills was the place to go to make fast money, especially when a man didn't have much to lose. Things were goin' along fine, and then I rode over the hill that day and found you. I cursed my luck, told myself that I didn't believe a word you said about not rememberin'. I convinced myself that you had somethin' to hide and made myself believe that I didn't care about you and Suzannah, that all I wanted was to be free of responsibility for you so I could go on with what I had to do. I made myself believe I didn't love you, and when we came to Deadwood and that wasn't workin' anymore, I started to panic. You gave me the way out I was lookin' for that day Rosie came here and you turned on me."

"I didn't turn on you, Drake!" Carolina rose spontaneously to her feet. "I don't really know what happened, but I know I didn't turn against you. Even when I thought you weren't coming back for me . . . when I left on the Thompson wagon train for Sioux City . . ."

"Left . . . ?"

Carolina flushed at Drake's startled expression. "But I couldn't do it. I knew I had made a mistake as soon as Deadwood slipped out of sight, and with every hour that passed I became surer that I couldn't leave if there was the slightest chance you might come back for me. I finally asked Mister Thompson to have somebody bring Suzannah and me back to Deadwood."

Drake did not respond. A slow panic entered Carolina's mind in the moments before he whispered, "So I almost lost you. . . ." The tremor in his voice reverberated in his touch as he gripped her hands, continuing, "I'm not going to let that happen again. I know some might think it's too soon, especially with my past bein' what it is and you not rememberin' yours at all, but I don't see how there's any other way. I love you, darlin'. I want to take care of you and Suzannah and to keep you with me for the rest of our lives."

A flicker of memory returned . . . a sunny meadow filled with flowers, a male shadow hovering over her. . . .

Suddenly furious at its intrusion, Carolina forced it away. She closed the distance between them in a single step as she raised her mouth to Drake's with words coming from her heart.

"How could it be too soon when I know I've never loved anyone more than I love you?"

Enclosed in Drake's arms as his mouth consumed hers, Carolina knew those words were the truest she had ever spoken.

Twenty-two

Carolina fidgeted nervously before Miriam's small mirror. She glanced through the window at the brilliant blue of the sky, unmarred by a single cloud, noting that not a branch stirred on the hillside. The day was clear and the temperature comfortably warm.

It was a perfect day for a wedding.

Inside the cabin, Miriam bustled around the stove. The widow opened the oven door to check on the huge beef roast and potatoes that scented the air with a delicious aroma. Satisfied, she closed it again and checked the pots bubbling on top of the stove, lifting each in turn to sniff, poke, and stir. She glanced toward the sideboard and the pie cooling there, making a mental note. The widow was determined not to allow Drake and Carolina's wedding day to pass without a suitable celebration. As for herself, Carolina knew that the simple vows Drake and she would soon exchange would be the greatest celebration of all.

Carolina turned to consider her reflection once more, silently despairing at what she saw. She would never be more than plain, even in the lovely pink dress Drake had bought her. She wore her hair down, the front locks secured at the back of her head with a pink ribbon, but she was not truly pleased with the result. She would have preferred a crown of braids which was much tidier and which added a few years to her age instead of this simple arrangement, but she knew Drake liked it better this way. For some reason, he thought her hair was beautiful.

Carolina flushed and turned toward the cradle where Suzannah lay sleeping. Within the hour, Drake would be Suzannah's father and *her* husband.

Her heart hammering, Carolina approached the recently washed dishes piled nearby and picked up a cloth. She turned with a start at the sound of Miriam's reprimand.

"Oh, no you don't! I'll do that. I won't have you working in your wedding dress."

"I can't just stand here while you work." Carolina's voice took on the tone of a plea. "I have to do something or the next hour will never pass."

"It'll pass." Miriam walked a few steps closer. Her thin face took on a maternal glow as she appraised Carolina's appearance. "You look beautiful."

"You're prejudiced."

"You look beautiful."

Carolina smiled. "If you insist."

"Drake will be caught breathless at the sight of you. My dear, you are positively glowing."

Miriam's use of Drake's given name pleased Carolina. She knew it reflected acceptance and approval of the subtle changes that had come about in Drake since the day he had walked back into her life and declared his love. A wedding two days later, only long enough to allow the groom to make preparations for their immediate return to his claim, might have been a scandal any other place, but not in Deadwood. The opposite had proved to be true instead, with a genuine excitement being generated by Deadwood's first wedding.

Carolina's smile dimmed. Drake and she had grown even closer since they had declared their love. For that reason, it had been even more difficult to hide from him the dark side of her happiness, the nightmares which had grown more violent, robbing her of sleep, and the brief shards of memory which slashed at her eager anticipation. She knew her anxiety would end when Drake and she were no longer separated, when she would lie in his arms and feel his strength surrounding her. She ached to become a part of Drake and to give to him the only thing she had to bring him. She would give it lovingly, freely, eagerly.

A flash of memory returned unexpectedly . . . a church, a man by her side, his shadowed face. . . .

"Is something wrong, Carolina?"

Carolina returned sharply to the present. "N . . . no."

"You're sure, dear?"

"Yes."

Miriam smiled. "Look outside. A crowd is beginning to gather. Deadwood isn't going to allow Drake and you to get married without witnessing the historic event. It won't be much longer now."

"Yes, only a little longer. . . ."

But the minutes would turn to hours and the hours to a lifetime. And while she waited, Carolina wondered what Drake was doing now. . . .

"That's the third time you've looked at yourself in the mirror. If I didn't know better, I'd think you were fascinated by the sight of yourself!"

Doc's gruff voice rebounded in the confines of his small office as Drake turned toward him with a frown. He was intensely aware of all he owed the short, unpredictable medical man, and for that reason held his tongue. He realized his difficulty with that task was apparent when Doc commented with a short laugh, "From the look of you, I suppose I should be grateful this is your weddin' day or I'd probably be lyin' flat on the floor right now."

Drake made no comment as he adjusted his jacket once more. Damn, it was tight! It restricted movement to the extent that he was uncertain if it would remain in one piece if he forgot himself with a sweeping gesture or two. There were few ready-made clothes that fit across his shoulders properly, however, and he knew that unless he wanted to be married in his shirtsleeves, this would have to do.

Drake glanced at the nearby clock. In less than an hour Carolina would be his wife. Emotion momentarily choked Drake's throat. He had not thought the bitterness could fade and that he could learn to trust again. Carolina had

356

done that for him. She had wiped away all the harshness and anger. He was at peace with the past . . . almost.

Drake glanced again at the clock. Yes, he had time. . . .

Turning abruptly, Drake snatched up his hat and started toward the door, only to be halted by Doc's hand on his arm.

"Where're you off to in such a rush? It's almost time for your weddin'!"

A shadow of the old Drake returned with his curt, "That's my business."

"The hell it is! You're talkin' to your best man, remember?"

Drake paused. Yes, he remembered. "I'll be back in a few minutes."

A few minutes to settle a debt of long standing.

"When are you going to face the truth, Rosie?" Tag grasped her arm, turning her back to face him. His angry question rang in the silence of her cabin as he continued sharply, "Damn it, everybody knows McNeil and Carolina Brand are getting married today. Half the town is planning to be there, invited or not."

"They're goin' to be disappointed." Rosie did not flinch under his verbal assault. "Drake won't marry her, you'll see. He's goin' to come back for me."

"McNeil's been in town for two days. He hasn't come to see you yet, has he?" When Rosie did not respond, Tag demanded, "Has he?"

"He got trapped into sayin' he'd marry that woman! He doesn't want to marry her. He wants to marry me!"

Rosie's voice was rising in pitch and Tag sensed she was losing control. He curled his hands around her shoulders, steadying her as he whispered, *"I'm* the man who wants to marry you, Rosie. Not McNeil." And as her eyes filled revealingly, "McNeil isn't coming back for you. You have to accept it."

The long silent moment that followed was shattered by an unexpected knock. Breaking free of his grip, Rosie walked to the doorway. The glory of her smile as she drew the door open set Tag's heart to an anxious pounding. He stared with disbelief as it swung open wide.

It couldn't be . . .

Drake stepped into the cabin and Rosie's heart took wing. She had known he would come! He wasn't smiling, but that meant little. Drake seldom smiled. She would teach him how to smile again once they were married. . . .

"Hello, Rosie."

"Hello, Drake."

Strangely, Rosie was at a loss for words. She had dreamed of this day for so long. Now that it was upon her, she was again the shy young girl she had once been, adoring this handsome man, her savior whose kindness had lit a path in her dark world. She trembled with the power of her feelings.

"I'd like to talk to you for a few minutes, Rosie." He glanced at Tag who did not make a move to accommodate him. "In private. . . ."

"Of course. Tag, will you please — "

"Whatever you have to say to Rosie, you can say in front of me."

Drake's stare turned cold. "I think Rosie's the one who should make that decision."

"That's where you're wrong, McNeil."

"I don't need you to talk for me, Tag!"

Rosie reached defensively for Drake's hand. The warmth of it sent ripples of pleasure through her, but he surprised her by drawing back, relenting, "No, maybe your friend's right. This'll only take a few minutes."

A shiver of premonition shook her as Drake began hesitantly, "I suppose you know I'm gettin' married today."

Rosie restrained a gasp. No, it wasn't true!

Drake continued softly, "But I had to talk to you before I do. You were a good friend to me when everyone else turned their back on me, Rosie. I let myself forget that for a while, but it's time to set things right." Drake paused, obviously searching for the right words. "I did a lot of thinkin' about what happened the day you went to see Carolina. I don't know your reasons for tellin' her what you did, but I finally came to realize that you only told her the truth. I suppose I can't blame you for that." He paused again. "This is an important day for me. Reverend Smith will be goin' to the widow's house to marry Carolina and me in less than an hour. I'd like you to be there, if you can."

Rosie's smile was frozen on her lips. It wasn't true. Drake was joking. He wasn't going to marry that skinny little stick of a woman . . . that pale, scrawny thing who had turned on him once before. Didn't he know that she wasn't worthy of him? Didn't he know —

"Will you come?"

No! I won't come!

"Rosie?"

"Rosie will be glad to come, McNeil." Answering in her stead, Tag took Rosie's hand, but she was numb to the comfort of his touch. "We'll both be there. We wouldn't miss it for the world . . . would we, Rosie?"

Rosie shook her head. "No." The sound of her own voice restoring her control, Rosie added, "We'll be there."

Drake's gaze searched her face, effectively reducing them to the only two people in the world as he said with an almost debilitating gentleness, "We go back a long way, Rosie. We both have a lot of bad times behind us, but there's somethin' I just learned that I wanted to share with you. I only just realized that we can't change the past. We can only change the way we look at it. I've finally done that . . . and I'm hopin' you can do the same."

Rosie could not manage a reply.

Drake walked toward the door. She fought the desire to hold him back, to tell him he was making a mistake, that she was the only woman for him . . . but she did not. Instead, she watched as he tipped his hat and pulled the door closed behind him.

Drake was gone, but his image was still clear in her mind's eye as Tag questioned softly, "Did you listen to what he said, Rosie?"

359

A knife of pain stabbed at Rosie's heart. "Drake's makin' a mistake. . . ."

Tag was suddenly livid. "He's marrying the woman he loves!"

"No." Her conviction stronger than it had ever been, Rosie raised her chin. "Drake doesn't realize it, but he loves *me*. He proved that just now. When it's over, he'll come back to me. It won't be long, you know . . . not long at all."

Rosie walked toward the dresses hanging in the corner. "I have to get ready, now. Drake wants me to be there. He needs me."

Oblivious of the flush that colored Tag's face, Rosie withdrew one of her precious silks from the rack. She would *always* be there when Drake needed her.

"I now pronounce you man and wife."

A cheer broke from the crowd standing at the perimeter of the yard, but Carolina barely heard the sound, so absorbed was she in Drake's solemn gaze. The vows they had exchanged resounded in her mind.

"Do you, Drake Garrison McNeil, take this woman for your lawfully wedded wife?"

"I do."

The words rebounded joyously within her.

"Do you, Carolina Brand, take this man for your lawfully wedded husband?"

"I do."

The words had been drawn from her heart. She whispered them again as Drake's arms slid around her. He swallowed them with his kiss, drawing the words inside him. She was trembling, shuddering so violently when he finally drew back from her that she could barely stand as well-wishers streamed past with noisy congratulations. She heard Doc's quiet inquiry at her side.

"Are you all right, dear?"

Drake's arm tightened around her, and she knew she need not answer. She was all right. She would always be all right with this man beside her.

Suddenly wishing the festivities were over so she might tell Drake all the things that were in her heart, Carolina looked up to find that same desire reflected clearly in his eyes. She managed a shaky whisper.

"Does the waiting never end?"

Drake did not return her smile as he responded, "Just a few more hours. . . ."

The warmth of the day was fading, slipping into night as Carolina's mount continued on at the modest pace Drake had set most of the day. A chill passed down Carolina's spine at the glorious colors of the sky as the sun made its descent toward the dark outline of the hills to the west. In no more than an hour the most momentous day of her life would come to a close. An almost debilitating joy swept over Carolina. Drake and she had waited only long enough after the ceremony to do justice to Miriam's sumptuous feast before changing clothes and mounting their waiting horses. The beautiful mare she now rode was her wedding gift from Drake. Suzannah slept in a spacious, elaborately padded basket secured to the saddle—a wedding gift from Drake to his new daughter. She had seen the love with which he had tucked the child inside and she had realized in that moment that Suzannah was his child as surely as if his own blood flowed through her veins. She had known it was rightfully so, in many ways.

They had spoken very little during the long hours on the trail. Instead, Drake had spent the time carefully watching the landscape. Realizing their vulnerability on this particular portion of the trail, Carolina had not resented his silence. She had put it to good use as she had studied his broad back for hours on end, marveling at the expanse of his shoulders and the power he exuded from every pore. His strength had drawn her to him from the first. The honesty and integrity she had sensed was so great a part of him had made her feel secure, but it had been the innate gentleness that this big, silent man had striven to conceal, revealed in his actions and in his touch, that had won her.

And she wondered, as she had so many times, at the cruel, inhumane contrivances that fate had used to deliver her to him.

Drake turned toward her unexpectedly, as if sensing her thoughts, and Carolina flushed. The flicker that moved across his expression was almost indiscernible, but it started her heart thudding anew as Drake quickened their pace. He led them off the trail a short time later and her impatience grew as they continued on for a longer distance than she had expected before coming to a natural shelter of rock and trees.

Dismounting, his manner almost brusque, Drake guided their mounts behind the rustic shield which afforded unexpected privacy. He lifted her from the saddle without speaking, his handsome face sober, and stood her on her feet. Placing the babe's basket in her hands, he set immediately about making camp.

Watching Drake from the blanket he had spread on the ground, Carolina nursed her child until her fragile lids fluttered closed. Appearing suddenly at her side, Drake took the child from her and tucked her into the basket.

Carolina was trembling when Drake turned back to face her, as he slipped off his hat, tossed it on the ground and kneeled beside her. He drew her to her knees in front of him. Her body quaked with emotion as he whispered, "Now you belong to me alone, darlin'."

Carolina looked up at him, her pale face flushed and expectant, and Drake's heart began a wild pounding against his ribs. How could he tell this fragile young woman the way she made him feel? How could he explain how many times he had seen her look at him like this in his dreams, her light eyes loving and her lips parted for his kiss? How could he make her understand that he had loved her when he had no longer believed in love, that he had wanted her when he had felt cursed with that desire, that he had suffered more in this last month of separation from her than he suffered during the cruelest years of his life? How could he tell her that she had healed wounds that he had believed too deep to cure and that having her in his arms, knowing she belonged to him alone, was a treasure more precious than gold?

Sliding his hands into her hair, Drake released the ribbon that held the heavy light-brown mass back from Carolina's face. The shimmering strands fell against her shoulders and he wound his hand into the silky softness, inwardly rejoicing as its warmth spread from his fingertips to his heart. He stroked her cheeks with trembling fingers, tracing the line of her brow, the bridge of her nose, the curve of her ear . . . the quivering line of her lips. His voice was a throbbing whisper.

"I remember the first time I saw you lyin' on the hill. Your face was dirty and scratched, your hair matted with blood. You looked to be a child who was about to bear a child, and I was angry with the stupidity that had brought you there when you were so vulnerable. After Suzannah was born, I brought you back to the cabin and washed your face clean and cleansed your body . . . and I knew you weren't a child. I told myself I was angry at the imposition foisted on me by you and the babe. I told myself that you weren't blameless in the tragedy that had delivered you to me and that you were responsible for your own actions. I told myself there was no such thing as innocence, and then when you told me your name . . ."

Drake halted abruptly, searching her gaze. The innocence he had once denied shone back at him from Carolina's eyes, forcing him to continue more softly than before, ". . . I accepted it despite my reservations."

Cupping her cheeks with his palms, Drake drew Carolina closer. He felt her sweet breath against his lips. He breathed it in, tasting it, maintaining the distance between them with growing difficulty as he was driven to continue, "But all the while, Carolina, each time I touched you, each time I tended your wounds, each time I comforted you in my arms, I felt the privilege of it. Somewhere in the back of my mind, even while I fought the thought with every breath, I knew your appearance was a gift that would change my life if I had the courage to accept it. I tried to throw that gift away and to hang onto the bitterness inside me. It was safer that way . . . without risk of lovin' and not being loved in return, or of trustin', only to be betrayed. But I accept that gift now, darlin', and I cherish it. I always will."

Carolina was silent. The small face he had once considered plain grew in beauty as her light eyes filled and a single tear wove a path down her smooth cheek. He brushed it away with his lips, tasting and consuming it. He covered her waiting mouth with his own, slipping his arms around her to enfold her in his hungry embrace. She was lost in his arms, this fragile, slender woman who had turned his life around, but he knew that the power of her had no relation to physical stature. It grew from the truth he read in her eyes, the conviction they shared that every minute of their lives had been leading to this moment, that only together could they ever be truly complete.

Trembling, forcing a separation between them, Drake dropped his hands to the buttons on her dress. He unfastened them, the task familiar, yet not familiar at all as he drew her dress off over her head. The modest undergarments followed as he bared her flesh, his throat so tight at the beauty of her slender nakedness that he could not speak. His own clothes followed, falling in a heap beside them before he went suddenly still. She was so small, so delicate. He reached out tentatively, then withdrew the hand that appeared too awkward to touch her as she need be touched, too rough to show her the tenderness he felt in his heart, too shaken to adequately convey the myriad feelings brimming inside him.

Doubts rose, filling the short distance between them, holding Drake impotent against his riotous emotions. He felt Carolina's uncertainty but he was powerless to assuage it as she searched his face with the liquid silver of her gaze. Her lips twitched revealingly. With a small smile that was almost divine, Carolina wrapped her arms around his neck, closing the distance between them. Freed of his temporary paralysis as their flesh met fully for the first time, Drake swept Carolina up into his arms. Lying on the blanket beside her, Drake proceeded to demonstrate all the love in his heart, with his hands and with his lips, worshiping her with his body as he had never loved before.

His passion at too high a tide to be contained much longer, Drake hovered over Carolina's slenderness, uncertainty again surfacing. His voice was a throbbing rasp as he whispered, "I love you, darlin'. I need you. I want to make you happy. . . ."

Drake's voice trailed away, only to have Carolina take up in his stead, "I need you, and I want to make you happy, too." Her lips trembled revealingly. "Oh, Drake . . . I'm yours, don't you know that? I've always been yours."

Reaching up, Carolina guided him down upon her, her lips parting as he hesitated at the moist delta between her thighs. She gasped as he thrust himself inside her and the spark of passion soared to flame. He heard her rasp of pleasure as he raised her with him on diaphanous wings to a beauty he had never known before. He heard the catch in her voice as she said she loved him, then his own ragged whisper the moment before her soft cry brought them careening from the sustained ecstasy of their love.

Carolina lay still beneath him, her eyes closed, her small face replete. He heard her soft protest as he slipped to the blanket beside her. Cupping her cheek with his palm, he turned her face toward him. He waited until her heavy eyelids fluttered open to whisper, "This is only the beginnin', darlin'. There are so many ways to say I love you."

Then gently, expertly, lovingly, Drake began to show her every one.

Twenty-three

"Watch what you're doin', you damned fool!"

Ignoring the heads that snapped toward him as he stopped still in front of O'Neil's General Store to brush the sawdust from his trousers, Doc darted a look of pure malice at Bob O'Neil. The offending broom still in his hand, the balding storekeeper muttered his regrets, but Doc did not accept them with grace. He growled an appropriate response and walked on, unconsciously aware that he accepted very little with grace of late.

A hot, late-June sun beamed down on Doc's shoulders as he stepped out of the shadows, mumbling under his breath. He didn't like summer in the Black Hills. It was too hot and too dry. It smelled bad, too, with the population of Deadwood steadily growing and sanitary precautions not what they should be. His warnings in that regard had fallen on deaf ears as usual, and he knew it was only a matter of time until his predictions were demonstrated for all to see in the most deadly of ways.

Doc snorted under his breath. He was underestimated and unappreciated in this damned crazy town that was getting crazier every day. He wasn't getting any younger. He wondered why he stayed here when he could be living an easier life somewhere else.

Doc's step slowed to an abrupt halt as two familiar figures emerged from the doorway of the latest tent store down the street. He studied them as they wove their way among the traffic on the congested street. Tag Willis and

Rosie. . . . They had been inseparable since Carolina's wedding to McNeil almost a month earlier, but that didn't fool him. He had looked into Rosie's eyes and seen the shadows there. He knew Willis saw them, too. He wondered how long it would be before the handsome fellow became tired of playing second fiddle to the man Rosie really wanted. And he wondered what Rosie would do when he did.

Rosie and Willis walked directly toward him and Doc paused. Rosie's smile lit her eyes when she saw him, and the first of the reasons he had remained in Deadwood clicked into place. There was nobody quite like Rosie. She demonstrated that anew as she separated herself from Willis upon reaching him and kissed him enthusiastically.

"Doc, you old dog. How come I haven't seen you at the Nugget the past few days? I missed your handsome face."

Doc smacked his lips appreciatively. "It was almost worth stayin' away to get that kiss . . . but not quite. The truth is, I've been busy."

"Too busy to come see your Rosie? Sounds serious."

Willis had remained silent except for his initial greeting, but Doc saw the fresh lines of concern around his eyes as he watched their exchange. Rosie's unhappiness wasn't any easier on him than it was on her. He wondered if love was worth the pain of it all.

He nodded in response to Rosie. "Yeah, real serious. Homer Watson got himself almost buried in a rock slide. It didn't look like he was goin' to make it for a while."

"Poor Homer."

"He's all right now, but nobody's goin' to be hangin' his picture on the wall from now on, that's for sure. He isn't too pretty."

"Poor Homer."

Doc frowned. Nobody ever said, *Poor Doc,* and he sure could use some sympathy right now.

"What's the matter, Doc?" Rosie read his mind. "You don't look too happy."

"Nothin' a half hour of tippin' my glass won't cure." Doc

scrutinized Rosie more closely. "What about you, Rosie? Are you happy?"

Rosie's façade slipped for a fraction of a moment, and Doc knew the truth was the opposite of her bright reply.

"I'm always happy, Doc. It goes with my occupation."

Willis slid an arm around Rosie's waist, and she smiled up at him, but the misery showed through. It was reflected briefly in Tag's face as well as he curled his arm tighter around her and addressed Doc for the first time.

"We have to be going now, Doc. I set up a game for this morning." Tag's smile was forced. "Some fellas can't wait to lose their money."

"You come see me tonight, you hear, Doc? The first drink's on the house."

Rosie pinched his cheek with a wink and he knew he would be there, if only to relieve the sadness Rosie could not quite conceal. He turned to watch as Rosie walked away. The sight of Rosie's firm backside swaying down the street always lifted his spirits. It was having its usual effect when a familiar voice sounded behind him.

"I don't suppose you'll ever change, will you, Jerome?"

Doc closed his eyes, realizing there was no escaping as the familiar voice continued with unexpected softness, "But I suppose a man never gets too old to look at a pretty face. It's only the faces that get too old to get looked at."

Doc's stomach did its usual contortions as he turned around and looked up at Miriam. The circles under her eyes appeared more pronounced than usual and her color poorer. His unshaven cheek ticked with annoyance as he realized that despite it all, his stomach never did a jig when he saw Rosie the way it did when he saw Miriam.

Things had gotten worse in that regard after his enforced monthly stint of visiting Miriam's cabin almost daily while Carolina was staying there. He had found himself looking forward to the sight of the widow's plain, pinched face — even seeing a kind of austere beauty in it. The climax had come the day of the wedding when the celebration was over and Miriam had casually invited him back into her cabin to talk. Hell, the last thing in the world he had felt like doing at that moment was *talking* to her, and he knew it. He knew it well enough to beat a hasty retreat to the familiar haven of his favorite bar, and to stay there until he was numb enough not to think at all.

He had steered clear of Miriam ever since, reverting back to his cowardly practice of dropping off his laundry at her door and running like the devil. His discomfort with his behavior had made him increasingly irritable, more so than usual . . . *a man of little grace.*

He attempted to hide his gracelessness with a smile. "Well, now, Miriam . . . what a surprise seein' you out so early in the mornin'. I thought you did your shoppin' later in the day."

"Obviously, or I wouldn't have run into you today . . . just as I haven't run into you for the past few weeks."

Doc's look of feigned innocence rested uneasily on his sagging features. "I stopped by your cabin to drop off my laundry, you know, but you weren't there."

Miriam's brows rose expressively. "You're getting faster on your feet, Jerome. You were out of the yard before I could reach the door."

"So you *were* home! Well, what do you know. . . ."

"Maybe you should have your hearing checked. I called you several times. Everybody on the street heard me but you."

"You called me?" Doc lied through his teeth. "I didn't hear you."

A trace of the old Miriam returned as her eyes narrowed into a revealing squint. "If I wasn't a lady, I'd tell you just what I think of that prevarication, Jerome, but suffice to say I will ignore it. As assistant to the chairman of the Natal Day Committee, however, it's my duty to ask you if—"

"The fireworks have arrived. I've already arranged to have them set up and fired off on signal. The greatest precautions will be taken and—"

"No little boys blowing off their fingers or tying firecrackers to dogs' tails?"

Doc was genuinely insulted. "I'm a doctor, Miriam! I'm familiar with the dangers involved in this type of affair and I've taken great pains to protect everyone against them."

"Yes, I suppose so." Miriam's thoughts appeared to drift and her small eyes sparkled briefly. "Just think. Our country will be one hundred years old on this Fourth of July. Federal Judge Granville G. Bennett will be present and we'll prove to him that the people of the Black Hills haven't forgotten our nation's birth in the quest for gold. Even if we're not recognized as citizens or accorded the rights of citizens, he'll see that our loyalty to our flag has never wavered. This commemoration will unite everyone in the Black Hills in a common goal. We'll win acceptance in the end, Jerome. I know we will."

Miriam's eyes misted, drawing a similar mist to his own as she continued, "People will be coming in from all nearby camps for the occasion. It's going to be a grand celebration." She hesitated, then continued hopefully, "Do you think Carolina and Drake will come? They shouldn't miss it. It'll be the greatest event these hills have ever seen."

Doc's throat tightened as Miriam inadvertently revealed herself. Despite the lofty goals she espoused and worked toward with such dedication, the widow missed Carolina and the baby. He supposed he had done her a disservice by giving her a family for a short time, only to have it snatched away so abruptly. He despised himself for not being able to allay that loneliness by being the friend she wanted him to be.

"I don't know if they will. It's a long way to travel."

"I suppose you're right." Blinking away her momentary lapse, Miriam raised her chin. Her back was ramrod straight again a moment later as she dismissed her speculation *and him* with a casual glance. "It would be nice to see them again, though. Goodbye, Jerome."

"Goodbye."

Doc watched as the widow made her way down the walk and disappeared into the crowd. His heart sank. She hadn't extended him an invitation to visit or bothered to be truly sarcastic in parting. He hadn't even smelled an apple pie cooking the last time he had sneaked up to drop off his laundry, and he knew she had been expecting him.

Miriam had given up on him.

Doc took a deep breath and released it slowly . . . almost sadly. That was what he had wanted, wasn't it? He had been scared to death of his traitorous old body's reaction every time he got close to the stubborn old crone. He had been haunted by memories that he had thought long dead . . . the comfort of a woman working beside him through anxious days, the consolation of knowing that same woman lay beside him at night, the warmth of her flesh under his hands, the solace of her sympathetic voice in the darkness when life looked too grim, and the knowledge that she cared for him more than any other man in the world. He hadn't thought about those things since the early years after Emma died. . . .

Doc unconsciously sought out Miriam's tall figure on the congested street. He caught a glimpse of her and the fluttering in his stomach started again. Miriam had given up on him, but it was all for the best. He was too old to start over.

Too old to start over . . . !

The widow's pinched, opinionated expression returned before Doc's mind as he suddenly realized the path his thoughts were taking. He gulped and took a spontaneous step backward.

Making an abrupt about-face, Doc started determinedly back down the street in the direction from which he had come . . . muttering under his breath every step of the way.

Bright, sunny days . . . long, loving nights. . . . A smile tugged at the corners of Carolina's mouth. Her new life as Drake's wife in the past month had been a tender idyll surpassing her most sanguine expectations.

Withdrawing her hands from the washtub in front of her, Carolina wiped her perspired brow and tucked a few straying wisps back into her upswept hair. She surveyed the wilderness held back by the few cleared feet of ground on which she stood. She remembered that there had been a time when the wilderness had not appeared serene, when every bush had shielded threat and every sound had raised fear in her mind. But that had been before, when the world was a strange and frightening place, when the void in her mind was a void within her as well, and when she had had little to hold onto except a hope personified by a big man who did not smile.

So much had changed since then. Looking around her, Carolina took comfort in the rustle of the trees, hearing only its peaceful whisper and feeling only the cooling of her brow. The sounds of the night no longer frightened her with Drake's arms around her, and when demons returned in her dreams, they were driven away by a simple word from Drake, a touch, a kiss. . . . Her life was tranquil, filled with a love that was sensitive to her every change of mood, a love that was patient beyond belief, and understanding when she did not always understand herself. The reason for it all was simple. Drake loved her, the woman he had come to know as well as the unknown woman who was a shadow in both their minds. She knew her love matched his in scope. It fell short in only one respect . . . her one, guilty secret.

Shame flushing her with heat, Carolina dropped her hands back into the washtub and scrubbed diligently at Drake's shirt. Slowly raising her hands from the water a moment later, she stared at the plain gold band Drake had slipped onto her finger a month earlier, remembering the moment she had removed the previous band and put it away. *His* face had flashed *clearly* in front of her then . . . a young, smiling face, dissimilar to Drake's in every way with its light complexion, fair hair, and eyes as blue as the sky above her. Her response to the revelation had been a confusing panic. She had reacted by expelling the image from her mind. She had not willingly allowed it access in the weeks since, but it had forced its way back, its warm smile a silent appeal. Strangely, she had been furious at that appeal, unwilling to entertain it, and in her perplexed silence, she had turned to Drake's arms for consolation.

Drake had not refused her.

The shrill call of a bird interrupted Carolina's disturbing thoughts. She looked up into the nearby tree, searching it out. She smiled when she saw it and watched as it raised its beak to utter a more melodious call than the last. Lifting its wings, it then caught a current of air and soared off into the sky. She followed the bird until it disappeared from sight, knowing that Drake's love had freed her heart to soar in the same way.

Carolina's smile slowly fell. Only one fear remained, and Carolina knew she could not escape it. She feared herself—the part of her that was still a mystery—the part of her she fervently wished was gone forever.

Forcing her mind back to the task at hand, Carolina lifted Drake's shirt from the tub and held it high. She imagined the man who wore it . . . a beautiful man, far too beautiful for a woman as plain as she. She remembered the touch of his hands, his softly whispered words of love.

You aren't worthy of that love. . . .

Carolina froze, stunned at the intrusion of the insidious voice in her mind. Her hands suddenly trembling, Carolina released the shirt to fall back into the washtub with a splash.

The day that had formerly been bright with promise became dark with a frightening apprehension as Carolina turned abruptly toward the path to the stream. Running on the uneven ground without regard for caution, she slipped and fell, then picked herself up to run again. She was panting, her chest heaving heavily when Drake came into view. He was standing bare-chested in the stream, perspiration glistening on his broad back and shoulders as he worked. Sensing her presence, he turned. In a moment he had snatched up his gun from the bank and was at her side. His arms enveloped her in safety as he scanned the forest around them.

"What happened?"

"Nothing." Humiliated by her inexplicable panic, Carolina whispered, "I . . . I just needed to see you."

Drake scrutinized her anxiety, then urged more gently than before, "Tell me what happened."

"I don't know." Carolina's response issued from the knot of fear inside her. "I suddenly realized that I might not be what I seem to be, and I was afraid."

"Afraid of what?"

"Afraid . . . afraid you might not want me if you knew . . ."

"Knew what?"

"I don't know . . ."

Dispensing with his gun, Drake tightened his arms around her and Carolina surrendered to their comfort. She felt his lips against her hair as he whispered, "I'm afraid sometimes, too, darlin'."

Carolina looked up in surprise. The planes of Drake's face softened to a tenderness she knew instinctively was reserved for her alone as he continued softly, "Sometimes I tell myself I'm too happy, that this is all a dream and I'll wake up and find myself lookin' out at the sky through bars again, instead of holdin' you in my arms. And other times I remember how close I came to ignorin' those sounds I heard echoin' down from over the hill that first day, and I think what might've happened if I had." Drake's expression became pained. "That's what scares me most . . . rememberin'. I came so close to losin' you that first day. I took you back to the cabin after Suzannah was born, but you had lost so much blood and your fever was climbin'. I didn't think you'd make the night. I remember how angry I was, cursin' my luck for havin' found you, while at the same time feelin' unworthy of the whole miracle I had just been a part of. I was confused by my feelins' and I hid behind my anger until I almost lost you a second time. Sometimes, in the middle of the night, I think what it would be like if I lost you now, and then I'm afraid."

"Drake, I—"

374

"No, darlin'." Drake smiled, a beautiful sight to which Carolina had not yet become immune. Her throat tightened as he continued, "Both of us are sufferin' from the same malady—lovin' each other and bein' afraid it will end." His eyes glittering with a moist brilliance, Drake whispered, "So let me tell you now, so you can put any doubts aside. I love you more than I knew it was possible to love, darlin'. Nothin' could change that, and nothin' ever will, and nothin' will make me happier than provin' that to you every day of my life."

Emotion welled inside Carolina. It was so sharp and sweet that it hurt.

You don't deserve him. . . .

Carolina jumped with a start at the sound of the voice in her mind. Grateful for Suzannah's simultaneous cry which eliminated the need for excuses, she drew back abruptly from Drake's arms. Shaken, she turned toward the trail. She glanced up guiltily as Drake stayed her with a touch. She knew she had not fooled him for a moment when he urged, "Bring the baby back with you. You can stay here while you're feedin' her."

Drake's touch lingered as she turned away from him with a nod. She didn't have to look back to know his gaze followed her every step of the way.

Drake glanced up at the midmorning sky, but his mind was far from the cerulean brilliance above his head. There was no need for him to look back at the stream bank where Carolina sat with Suzannah to know she was there. He felt her presence with every pore of his body. He was relieved that her earlier insecurities appeared to have faded, but his own guilts had not.

No one had to tell him the cause for Carolina's anxieties. It had become increasingly obvious since their marriage that the mystery of her past haunted her. His own guilt lay in the fact that he had deliberately avoided helping her discover her identity. He had made a few inquiries . . . a letter

375

dispatched to the embarkation point of her wagon train, to which he did not expect to receive a reply . . . another letter of inquiry sent to the nearest army post. He had told Carolina that he could do no more, and after their marriage, he had told her that she didn't need anyone but him. The *truth* was simple. He hadn't wanted to help her, because to discover her past would be to share her with it.

It was time to correct his selfishness. But for now . . .

Drake turned abruptly toward the bank. Dropping his shovel as he stepped up onto the sandy surface, he then pulled off his boots and walked toward Carolina. He took Suzannah from her arms and placed her on a grassy patch that cushioned her gently before sitting beside Carolina and drawing her close. Carolina raised her clear eyes to his and he was lost in the wonder of her. He kissed her once . . . twice, his joy profound at her instantaneous response. He raised his hands to her hair and withdrew the pins, watching as the heavy strands tumbled free. He loved her hair. He remembered a time when he had been secretly jealous of the way the heavy mass had caressed her narrow shoulders with each movement, but that time was past. Carolina was now his to touch and cherish, and he adored every inch of her with a humbling passion.

Cushioning her with his arms, Drake pressed Carolina gently to her back. Stretching himself out beside her, he kissed her long and lingeringly. Their lips and tongues tasted and mingled, and the urgency between them grew. He felt Carolina tremble as he raised her skirt to caress the warm nest between her thighs. He saw the flutter of her eyelids. He watched them lower until they were almost closed. He saw her lips part and her breathing become rapid as his attentions became more fervent.

Carolina made no sound as he kneeled before her and stripped away her distracting undergarment. He saw that she was quaking, waiting, trusting him as he separated her thighs. She gasped as he cupped her buttocks with his palms and raised her to him.

The warm delta awaiting him was golden and glowing

376

with warm beads of perspiration. The tangy scent of Carolina's womanliness sent his heart to pounding as he brushed the tight curls with his lips. He felt the shudder that racked her as he kissed them again, pressing his face more deeply within.

Carolina's body jerked with responsive shock as his tongue found the tender slit. She caught her breath as he pressed his lips against it, kissing it, loving her, separating its moistness to find the delicate bud beneath. A groan escaped her lips and she made a soft sound of protest as he drew deeply from it. He looked up to see a shadow of trepidation in her gaze, then the gradual dawning of acceptance as she read in his eyes all the love in his heart. He lowered his head toward her again, his heart rejoicing as she allowed his passions full rein.

Kissing, loving, drawing from her, asking for much in return, Drake felt the rapid rise of Carolina's ardor. Her body was quaking as he supported her gently, seeking her honeyed response, feeling the trembling that began to rock her control. Again a word of protest. Drake raised his head to see apprehension reappear in the glittering silver of her eyes as culmination drew near. His rasping whisper broke the sunlit silence with a soft plea.

"Let your body feel what it wants to feel, darlin'. Let it tell you what it wants to give so I can give back to you in return. Darlin'. . . ."

Refusing to relinquish her gaze, Drake pressed his lips to her body once more. He drew from her with the hunger of long, empty years without end, with the memory of a bitter, joyless quest now abandoned, and with the fervor of a healing love that erased all but the ecstasy of their mutual reward.

Carolina shuddered. She shook again, her eyes dropping slowly closed, only to reopen at his soft command.

"Look at me, Carolina. Give to me, darlin'. . . ."

Quaking spasms, one after another rocked Carolina's slight frame as her gaze touched his. Fastening his mouth against her, Drake accepted her body's homage to his lov-

377

ing, drinking it in, loving it, loving her.

Her passion spent, Carolina was finally still. Poised over her moments later, his heart filled to bursting, Drake whispered, "If I lived a hundred years, I wouldn't be able to give you all my love because it's endless, like the sky." Sliding himself home within her, Drake breathed deeply at her welcoming gasp, continuing with a husky rasp, "So we'll have to take it one day at a time, darlin' . . . each lovin' day."

His passion erupting suddenly in quaking spasms too powerful to withhold, Drake felt Carolina's passion swell as well. Her slender arms clutched him close as his last ecstatic quiver came to an end, and he knew as he lay spent and complete upon her, that seven empty years or seven *hundred,* were worth this moment . . . this woman . . . his Carolina.

The small cabin was fragrant with the smell of freshly baked biscuits and steaming stew as Carolina wiped her perspired brow. The afternoon had turned unexpectedly hot. The dampness within the cabin was a natural buffer against the outside heat, but Carolina was acutely aware that the meal she had prepared with such care ill suited the sultry temperature.

She turned to see Drake watching her intently from the doorway. Despite their loving interlude earlier in the day, she felt a moment's trepidation that was transmitted to her voice as she pressed, "Is something wrong, Drake?"

Approaching without response, Drake came to stand beside her. Looking down at her with a thoughtful, almost troubled expression, he slipped his arms around her. "Nothin's wrong, darlin'. Everythin's right. Suzannah and you have taught me some things that I —"

As if on cue, Suzannah's piercing wail shattered the silence turning Drake and Carolina toward the basket that rocked with the force of her lusty cries. Drake laughed aloud, and Carolina was momentarily in awe of the sound. The man who never smiled. . . .

A slow warmth permeated her senses as he separated himself from her and took the fussing Suzannah into his arms. He smiled broadly as he propped the babe on his shoulder and whispered into her tiny ear, "I'm thinkin' you're goin' to grow up to be an opera singer someday, but anyway you have it, you're goin' to be beautiful, like your ma." At Carolina's automatic protest, Drake challenged solemnly, "Does she or doesn't she look like you?"

Carolina restrained a laugh. "I suppose."

"Is she or is she not beautiful?"

"She is."

"Well?"

Carolina was unable to withhold her smile any longer. "All right. Suzannah's beautiful and I'm beautiful."

Satisfied, Drake looked back at Suzannah's bright face. "Miriam isn't goin' to believe how much she's grown in the month we've been away."

Carolina's smile froze. "Does that mean we're goin' back to Deadwood soon?"

Drake hesitated briefly. "I thought we'd start out tomorrow."

"Why?"

"Because we're runnin' short of a few things."

"Nothing we can't do without."

"The Centennial is goin' to be celebrated in a few days. People will be headin' toward Deadwood from all parts of the hills. The trail will be the safest it's ever been." Slipping Suzannah back into her cradle, Drake curved his arm around her and tilted up her chin. "What's the matter, darlin'? Don't you want to go?"

"I . . . I don't know." Certain only that Drake's plans had started her heart pounding like a drum, Carolina whispered, "It's just that we've been so happy here."

"We'll be happy no matter where we go."

"Yes, I know, but—"

"Trust me, darlin'." Drake drew her closer. "There are some things I have to do . . . some things I've put off that need to be taken care of." Allowing a distance between

379

them, Drake pressed, "You'll be glad to see Miriam and Doc again, won't you?"

"Yes, of course." Carolina attempted to restore her smile. "It's just that I don't want this time to end for us."

"It isn't ending. It's only beginning. I promise you that. I promise you somethin' else, too." His words taking on the solemnity of a vow, Drake added, "I promise you that you'll never be sorry you said the words, 'I do.' "

Drake waited only a moment longer before turning back to Suzannah's fussing wail. The big man cradled her child in his arms as his promise rang in her mind. She knew he had meant every word.

Twenty-four

"What in hell do you think you're doin', Jake?"

Doc challenged the bleary-eyed cook as he stood in the rear of Deadwood's finest restaurant, preparing to dump garbage into the stream. He held the fellow fast with his narrowed gaze. "Don't you know you're pollutin' the drinkin' water?"

"I ain't doin' no such thing. We get our water from a well."

"You get your water from a well, all right, but what about the fellas down farther who use this stream for drinkin' purposes?"

Unblinking, Jake returned Doc's stare. "I got my problems and they got theirs."

Dumping the garbage with a flourish, the fellow made his way back toward the rear door of the restaurant without a backward glance.

Fuming, Doc shouted at his departing back. "The situation around here's gettin' downright unhealthy!"

Angrier still to see that his final admonition had as little impact on the perspired cook as his former warnings, Doc cursed aloud. He glanced around him for the opportunity to continue his argument, but the filthy corridor behind Main Street was deserted. Doc gave a disgusted snort. That stood to reason. Few people, other than fools like him who had taken to patrolling the area in hopes of dissuading offenders from their unsanitary practices, would be able to stand the stench. Troubling him even more than the waste

381

tossed out the back of each establishment where it was left to putrefy in the sun or to be swept away by the stream, was the realization that garbage wasn't the worst of the debris. Improper drainage from outhouses a short distance away was finding its way into the same stream. With the current influx into Deadwood for the holiday, he was aware of the escalating danger there—a danger that was being ignored by everyone but himself.

Taking off his hat, Doc slapped it against his thigh with frustration before running a hand through shaggy hair that was plastered to his scalp with perspiration. It occurred to him that he needed a haircut. Rubbing a hand against his stubbled chin, he recalled that he hadn't shaved for two days, either, and that he hadn't changed his clothes in a longer time than that.

Miriam's disapproving expression returned to his mind, and Doc growled aloud. Damn if the woman didn't have a way of saying "I told you so," even when she wasn't present! But she was right. He had learned the hard way in the past week that few people took advice on sanitary conditions from a man who appeared to break every rule he espoused. She had been right, too, when she had said that if he wanted to be taken seriously, he had to conduct himself in a manner that others would respect.

Stopping short to consider that thought, Doc frowned. The question was, would it be worth the effort?

A few silent moments later, Doc jammed his hat back on his head and headed for the street. The answer was a loud and resounding, "No!" He had washed his hands of causes a long time ago, and if people couldn't accept him or his advice the way he was—if they couldn't see past the surface, however bedraggled it appeared to be—it was their loss.

Stomping out onto the street, Doc raised his stubbled chin and mumbled, "You lose, Miriam!"

"All right, boys. Now!"

With a chorus of heavy grunts, the scores of miners standing side by side in the rapidly darkening north side of Deadwood's main street, strained to raise the heavy pole. Gradually lifting it enough to slip its base into a prepared hole in front of the speakers' stand, they held it steady as others guided the staff's swaying progress toward an upright position with ropes. A shout went up from the surrounding crowd the moment the pole was standing. Working frantically at its base, others pushed crushed rock and dirt into the hole, stomped it down tightly, then stood back as the ropes were shaken free.

Another cheer, louder than the last, rang in the crowded street as the liberty pole stood secure in the dusk of evening, awaiting the stars and stripes to be raised at "dawn's early light."

Perspiring and smiling broadly, Tag stood among the men at its base, leaning on the shovel he had used so deftly only minutes earlier. He was still staring up at it when a seductive voice sounded at his elbow.

"I just love seein' a man with his skin all shiny with sweat from doin' somethin' physical. Hell, there ain't nothin' that's more manly."

Tag turned toward Ella with surprise. The buxom blonde fluttered her lashes, deliberately drawing his smile as he motioned to the fellows around him.

"Well, the street's filled with sweaty, manly fellows right now. I'd say you have your choice."

Ella's full lips drew into a pout. "I said I loved a man who sweats — not a man who *stinks*. I think that counts out just about every other old boy here . . . except you."

Tag tipped his hat, his smile broadening. "I thank you for that, but right now I'm not as tidy as I should be, either."

"You're fine enough for me."

His smile dimming at the familiar ring in Ella's words, Tag picked up his jacket and slipped his arm around her shoulder to urge her along with him as he walked.

"How come you haven't taken yourself a man since you came to the Nugget, Ella? There's a whole pack of fellows just waiting for your nod. There must be at least one good one in the bunch."

Ella leaned against his side and smiled up into his eyes. "I'm just stuck on a gamblin' man, I guess."

Tag did not return her smile. "This gambling man has his woman, and you're too fine a person to waste your time waiting for nothing."

Ella shrugged, but not before Tag saw the flicker of sadness in her eyes as she defended herself brightly. "I ain't wastin' my time. I'm bein' choosy. I got me a good job and I can afford to wait for the right man as long as I want."

"Ella, honey . . ." Tag hesitated. Ella had always touched a soft spot inside him. He supposed that was so because he saw honesty where others saw harshness. Or maybe it was because she allowed herself to be honest only with him. Whatever, Tag knew he truly liked this woman and he empathized with a plight she suffered as well. He offered softly, "Not if the 'right man' you're waiting for is me. I'm a one-man woman, and that's not going to change."

"Supposin' I'm willin' to take my chances?"

"You're wasting your ti—"

Halting midsentence, Tag glimpsed Rosie through the shifting crowd the moment before she turned and walked back into the Nugget. He frowned, his hand dropping from around Ella's shoulder. Their conversation forgotten, he continued briskly, "I'll see you later, Ella. You'd better make sure you get back to that poker table before too long. You're getting to be a real good hand with a deck of cards. Your regulars will be waiting."

But Ella had followed the direction of his glance and Tag knew there was no fooling an old fooler as she said, "Yeah, sure. And Rosie's waitin' for you, too."

No response was necessary as Tag tipped his hat and headed straight for the door of the Nugget. He was through that doorway within a minute. A few moments later his arm was around Rosie's narrow waist. He waited only a second before covering her parted lips with his.

Appreciative yelps sounded from the bar as his kiss lingered. It was Rosie who drew back first, surprisingly flushed as he whispered, "That was just to show you that you didn't see what you thought you saw out there just now."

Rosie's eyes filled unexpectedly. She blinked the brightness away as she leaned against him. "You didn't need to say that, Tag. I don't have any strings on you."

"Oh, yes, you do. I'm your man and you're my woman . . . and it doesn't get any finer than what we have—whether you know it or not."

Rosie did not respond and Tag's heart squeezed with a familiar pain. He smiled as she made an effort to change the subject by chiding him softly, "I hardly know you, all messed up like you are now. Look at you. . . ." Rosie rubbed her palm against his chest where perspiration had soaked through his shirt, then drew off his hat and stroked back his damp hair. "You're almost untidy." She laughed. "Almost. . . ."

Tag whispered suggestively, "I hear some ladies like to see a man sweat. . . ."

"Hummm? Well, the truth is, I like you just about any way you are. I figured you'd be goin' out into the street when those fellas came in askin' for help raisin' that flagpole. It's goin' to be a grand day tomorrow, isn't it?" She paused, her gaze straying from his. "People are comin' into town from all over the hills."

Recognizing that look, Tag cursed under his breath, grating softly, "It won't do *you* any good, even if McNeil does come in for the holiday. He's married now."

"I know." Rosie said the right words, but Tag knew they were just lip service to a hope that would not die. Ushering her along with him toward the back door, Tag waited until they were outside to demand softly, "I want you to tell me something truthfully, Rosie. Have you been happy with me during the past month?"

Rosie's gaze held his without wavering. "I have."

"Do you love me?"

Rosie's gaze flickered. Frustration knotted inside him as

385

she responded with a simple, "Yes."

"But not enough. . . ."

Rosie's eyes grew troubled. "Ella loves you enough."

"I don't want Ella."

"Tag . . ."

"Never mind."

Familiar with frustration, Tag drew Rosie along with him as he started toward her cabin a short distance away. He deliberately changed the subject, attempting a lighter note.

"I'm going to get cleaned up. Maybe I'll use that shower I rigged up for you last week." He winked. "Maybe we'll both use it."

Halting midstep, her expression sober, Rosie curved her hand around Tag's cheek and drew his mouth down to hers. Her voice was husky as she withdrew, and her eyes were filled with a glow akin to love as she whispered, "Maybe we will."

Accepting her generous token, knowing it was the best she had to offer, Tag forced a smile.

Sacrificing her genteel demeanor to an unladylike epithet, Miriam tripped through the doorway of her cabin. Taking a moment to adjust the laundry she held in her arms so that the trailing sheet would not cause her further problem, she continued toward the table, dropping the bundle there as she raced to a pot boiling on the stove. She gave a relieved sigh as she lifted the lid. Just in time. A few minutes longer and she would have burned the small roast. It was totally unlike her to have forgotten it, just as it was unlike her to be so severely off schedule that her chores were extending into evening. But it was all part of a series of unlikelinesses that had grown steadily worse, demonstrating her distraction more clearly than she wished.

Miriam reviewed her circumstances as she had so many times in the past few weeks, in the attempt to ascertain the motivation for her abject unhappiness. Strangely, it had all seemed to start the day of Carolina's wedding, and she was uncertain of the reason. It had been such a beautiful day—so filled with love and promise. Carolina had been such a beautiful bride, and Drake a handsome, if solemn, groom. She had been so pleased with the way her plans for the affair had turned out that she had wanted to share her pleasure with someone . . . someone who had been as close to the happy couple as she. That someone had been Jerome, but it was obvious that Jerome had not wanted to share those moments with her.

Her happiness had eroded quickly after that, with Carolina and Drake leaving almost immediately, and Jerome disappearing from her life as completely as if he had disappeared from the face of the earth.

Only his dirty laundry had remained.

Miriam sniffed with annoyance. The old coot had looked positively seedy when she had run into him on the street, and he had looked even worse at the Natal Day Committee meeting, although he had lived up to the responsibilities entrusted to him. It was a good thing, too, because at the last stroke of midnight, the celebration would begin.

Miriam raised her chin as she reached for the laundry and began folding, reviewing a mental checklist in her mind. The speakers had been designated and were ready. Judge Kuykendall would convene, Reverend Halley would lead the prayer, and Judge Miller would supply the main oration. General Dawson was prepared to read the memorial to Congress he had composed, to pass it around for signature, and to follow through by forwarding it to Washington. The tallest and most symmetrical pole that could be found on the mountain had been planted in front of the speakers' stand, ready for Old Glory. Arrangements for a suitably noisy salute had been made, and every patriotic resident of the Black Hills was prepared to add his own, personal salute—so much so that she feared for the life of any poor fowl that chanced to fly overhead.

Yes, the day toward which she had worked so diligently was poised to explode on schedule—but there was not a spark of excitement inside her.

Oh, Jerome. . . . Miriam wiped away an errant tear. He had disappointed her so. She had been so sure they were alike, that as with herself, Jerome's outward appearance masked a person who was far different inside. She had been certain there was much more to him than his disreputable exterior led others to believe. She had sensed a man of great intelligence and strict moral principles—a man with a strong sense of responsibility to those around him, as well as to his Hippocratic oath. She had also sensed a commonality between them that was innate . . . a closeness that transcended physical aspects.

How could she have been so wrong?

Carefully stacking the last of her laundry, Miriam piled it in the corner and turned to look at the new dress she had made specifically for the Natal Day celebration. It was dark blue, a change from her usual black. She had somehow felt mourning colors were inappropriate on this most special of occasions. She was certain Jonas would not mind.

Glancing at the clock on the wall, Miriam heaved a sigh. It was long past supper hour and the preliminary festivities would soon get under way. The only trouble was that she wasn't hungry, and she had little incentive to celebrate. Somehow, she had not expected it to be this way, with the world outside her cabin merrily preparing for the great event beyond her wildest expectations, while she—

Miriam glanced up at a knock on the door. Hesitating only a moment, she raised her pointed chin. Problems with the ceremony about to commence, no doubt. She should have expected as much. Nothing ever ran smoothly.

Solemn as she drew open the door, Miriam was struck momentarily speechless. Springing into motion a moment later, she threw her arms around the slender young woman on her doorstep with a cry of welcome entirely unlike herself.

"Carolina, my dear!" Finally able to speak, Miriam bit back tears. She looked at the sleeping child Drake carried, her arms aching to hold her, and then smiled up at

388

the big man himself before ushering them inside.

Closing the door behind them, Miriam whispered hoarsely, "My dear friends, welcome back to my home. I've missed you dreadfully."

The darkness of night was lit as if by a thousand lanterns as Deadwood's streets swelled with a milling populace. Miners in every manner of dress and level of sobriety squeezed into the crowded northern portion of Main Street. Gaudily dressed women pushed through a throng where respectable ladies, all too few, stared with awe at the growing spectacle. Ribald laughter mingled with excited giggles as sleepy-eyed children stood side by side with those whose innocence was a faded memory.

Poised and ready for the celebration, the crowd was as one as the countdown began. At the last stroke of midnight, the crowd cheered, artillery boomed, and the first of one hundred anvil salutes began.

Standing at the perimeter of the crowd, Carolina watched the antics with a peculiar distraction. Her distraction had begun when she had entered Deadwood amid the growing revelry. Her anxiety was difficult to explain and even more difficult to hide from Drake as he stood beside her. She felt his arm slip around her and she leaned into his strength, grateful that Suzannah was back at the cabin with Miriam.

Drake's arm tightened supportively. "Are you tired, darlin'? Do you want to go back to the cabin now?"

"I think so." Carolina managed a smile. "Why don't you stay? I can go back alone."

Not considering her suggestion for a minute, Drake drew her along behind him as he turned down the swarming street. Startled when Drake stopped in his tracks, Carolina peeked in front of him to see Rosie and Tag Willis standing directly in his path. She saw his expression soften as he looked at Rosie, and she was struck with a moment's jealousy as he smiled.

389

The change that came over the beautiful saloon girl's features when she looked up at Drake was all too revealing. Love, worship, and a supreme unhappiness flashed briefly across her faultless features in the moment before she managed with false brightness, "So you came back for the celebration. I'm glad because it's goin' to be a wonderful day." She turned to the well-dressed gambler at her side as if in afterthought. ". . . Isn't it, Tag."

The flicker in Tag's eyes disclosed that he saw as much as she, and Carolina suddenly knew that Rosie's distress was echoed in those around her—in Tag, because he loved Rosie and feared losing her—and in herself, because she loved Drake and somehow feared losing him as well.

Anxieties, pain, frustrated love. . . . Carolina fought to subdue her sudden quaking as Drake continued, "We'll be stayin' a few days. Miriam's taken us in."

"You'll come visit me, won't you, Drake?"

The unconscious plea in Rosie's voice tore at Carolina's tenuous control. She hardly heard Drake's softly spoken, "I'll stop by," as he tipped his hat and moved on through the crowd. She looked up with surprise as Drake turned toward her the moment they reached a spot of partial privacy, his expression earnest.

"Rosie's an old friend . . . a good friend."

"I know."

"She got off on the wrong foot with you somehow, but things'll straighten out."

Carolina nodded, wondering how a man as intelligent as Drake could be so blind to Rosie's love for him.

"I know they will."

Appearing relieved, Drake slid his arm around her and within minutes they slipped into Miriam's darkened cabin.

"To the Honored Senate and House of Representatives of the United States, in Congress assembled. . . ."

General Dawson began the memorial to Congress before the assembled multitude. A peculiar silence reigned in the

390

midday street that had echoed with carefully measured anvil salutes through the night, with the sporadic bark of small arms fire in private celebration, and a tearfully and cheerfully received raising of the stars and stripes at dawn's first light. Looking around her, Carolina realized that many of those present had maintained determined vigil throughout the entire celebration, and she had been surprised to see so many of the most weathered of cheeks wet with tears at the reading of the Declaration of Independence. The culmination of the ceremony was clear, however, as General Dawson concluded his determined appeal:

"Your memorialists would, therefore, earnestly request that we be no longer deprived of the fruits of our labor and driven from the country we now occupy, but that the government, for which we have given our lives, at once extend a protecting arm and take us under its care. As in duty bound, your petitioners will ever pray."

The brief silence that followed the conclusion of General Dawson's reading was abruptly broken by enthusiastic whistles, hearty yells of approval, and thunderous applause. Glancing up at Drake, Carolina saw that he was as moved as she. She looked back at the edge of the crowd where the widow held Suzannah securely cradled in her arms to see that tears streamed freely down the woman's lined cheeks.

The tremulous feeling inside Carolina grew as Drake took her arm and drew her along behind him through the dispersing crowd. Uncertain of her feelings, she only knew she was strangely ill at ease in the surging tide of faces surrounding her. She glanced back at the widow who followed close behind them, feeling a need to hold her child but knowing she had no true cause to ask Miriam to relinquish her. Her heart pounded wildly as Drake forged determinedly forward and the traffic on the boardwalk gradually thinned. She was finally able to walk abreast of him and she heaved a relieved sigh, only to come to an abrupt halt at first sight of a man approaching from the opposite direction.

No! No . . . no . . . no!

Carolina's mind screamed in a protest that did not leave her lips. The world whirled around her as the fellow's startlingly familiar blue eyes met hers, as his fair, lightly freckled face blanched of color, as he cried out with disbelief.

"Madeline . . . you're alive!"

Carolina took a step backward, then another. She wasn't Madeline! Not anymore!

She looked up to see shock register in Drake's expression, but her whispered appeal was lost in the din around them. A sea of curious faces pinned her. The blue eyes drew closer. Drake's gaze burned into hers, searing her soul, and as darkness closed suddenly upon her, Carolina cried out — her pain excruciating in the split second of revelation when she realized everything was over and done between them.

The buzz of voices . . . a gentle touch . . . a baby's cry. . . .

The dark mist surrounding Carolina stirred as the cry grew more persistent. It lightened as the sound turned into a wail, eliciting an instinctive response within her. She opened her eyes slowly, snapping them shut again as blue eyes met her gaze.

"I told you to get away from the bed, damn it!" Doc Fitz's voice was gruff as it grew closer. "The sight of you was what made her collapse in the first place. She doesn't need you hangin' over her bed when she's finally comin' around!"

The wail intensified and Carolina opened her eyes. Miriam's cabin . . . she remembered it with warm thoughts of a woman's gentle concern, a haven of safety when she had been floundering in uncertainty, a home second only to a wilderness retreat where her heart dwelled.

"Carolina, Suzannah needs you."

Miriam's voice penetrated the mist of her muddled thoughts and Carolina unbuttoned her bodice spontaneously as Miriam lay the fretful babe beside her. In a moment Suzannah was nursing peacefully.

"Carolina, dear . . . how are you feeling?" Doc Fitz touched her forehead with his callused palm. His face was drawn into deep lines of concern, but she did not reply as she looked past him to see Drake standing a few feet from her bed. He was expressionless, his chiseled features so still that they appeared to be carved from stone. She looked further, her gaze stopping still as it came into contact with moist blue eyes.

She remembered those eyes . . .

Brushing past Dr. Fitz, the fair-haired man took her hand and raised it to his lips.

She remembered those lips . . .

"Madeline. . . ." Tears brimming, he gasped, "I thought I had lost you and the baby forever!"

Carolina's response was sudden and sharp, rising from a knot of pain deep inside her as she rasped, "You said you loved me, but you lied!"

"I didn't!"

"You didn't want Suzannah. You never wanted her or me!"

"I didn't mean what I said that last day, darling." William inched closer. He clasped her hand desperately. "I was a fool. I never realized how much of a fool I was until I had left the wagon train too far behind to turn back. Then I told myself that I'd make up for leaving you in anger by striking it rich and giving you everything you ever wanted."

"You knew what I wanted. You knew from the first day we met." Carolina withheld a sob. "I never wanted to be rich. I wanted a home and the family I had never had. You said you wanted the same thing. You said you loved me that day. . . ." Carolina glanced toward Drake as a tear slid down her cheek. ". . . that day in the meadow. . . ."

"I loved you that day. I love you now."

"No!"

"I do!" William turned unexpectedly to those standing around the bed. His voice quavered as he spoke in soft appeal.

393

"I . . . I'd like to talk to my wife alone if I may." He looked first at Doc and then the widow. "Just a few minutes, please."

Carolina's emotions were under too tenuous control to protest as Doc hesitated briefly, then directed his reply to her. "Just call me if you need me, Carolina."

Her thoughts only of Drake, Carolina glanced at him, then turned away in shame. She knew what she had done to him . . . and what she had made of herself. When she looked back, he was walking out the door. Her heart was breaking when her husband crouched beside her bed, his head level with hers as he appealed to her once more.

"Madeline, please. . . ."

"My name isn't Madeline! It's Carolina."

"All right . . . Carolina. . . ." William caressed her cheek with surprisingly callused fingers but she drew back from his touch. She saw the pain in his eyes as he whispered, "Darling, please try to understand. I love you. I've always loved you. I loved you from the first moment I saw you working in my aunt's kitchen. I didn't care what my mother or my aunt said about the debt I owed my family name . . . that I was stooping below myself. I pretended to listen to them for fear of your being dismissed, but I couldn't stay away from you."

William's trembling hand closed around a heavy brown curl resting against her shoulder. His voice broke as he started to speak again, but he continued determinedly. "I was beside myself with love for you that day in the meadow. You had been avoiding me and when I followed you out there, you wouldn't talk to me. You kept saying you'd lose your position if we were seen. When I finally convinced you to listen to me for a few minutes and we sat down on that log, out of sight of everyone from the house, everything moved so fast. I kissed you and you kissed me back. I don't really know how it happened, except that it was so beautiful between us that I wanted it to go on forever. Your tears cut my heart to ribbons when it was all over, and I'm telling you now, just as I did then, that every touch, every

394

kiss, said what I'm saying now, that I love you."

William's voice broke again. He continued a moment later with obvious difficulty, "I didn't marry you because you were going to have my child. I *wanted* to marry you. I wanted that more than anything in the world. I told you that, and I told my family the same thing. Do you remember how glorious it was between us when we were first married? Do you remember the promises I made when I held you in my arms? I meant every one of them. I still do."

When Carolina did not reply, William's voice dropped to a remorseful whisper. "But the truth is that despite their threats, I never expected my parents to turn their backs on me. I know I didn't handle it well. I didn't realize how dependent I was on the family name and everything it meant. I know now that I was a fool for allowing my parents to manipulate me with their wealth, but it came to the point where I was desperate to prove myself. When the opportunity came to join the wagon train heading into these hills, it seemed like the answer to my prayers. I told myself the stories of Indian attacks were exaggerated, that your fears were childish, and you'd thank me when our future was finally secure."

A shadow of William's appealing smile flashed briefly. "Things were good for the first few weeks on the trail, weren't they, darling? We rode side by side on the wagon during the day, and we lay in each other's arms under the stars at night. You said you loved me."

"I didn't!"

"You did."

The truth slowly emerged in Carolina's mind, and she closed her eyes, her voice a tortured rasp. "I . . . I wanted to believe everything would be all right. I told myself everything would work out because we loved each other, but I was wrong."

"No, *I* was wrong. I was too impatient with our slow progress, and when the wagons started breaking down and the train missed the trail those few times, the delays became intolerable. A feeling started growing inside me that we'd never get there . . . or that when we did, it would be too late. I was determined not to let that happen, and when Curt Martin said he was going to separate from the train and ride on ahead, I told him I'd go with him."

A plea for compassion entered William's eyes as he whispered, "I don't know what came over me to leave you the way I did, but it all looked so simple then. We hadn't seen any signs of Indians and you seemed so well. I thought there would be plenty of time until the baby was born. That's what I told myself, anyway."

William drew her close. He brushed Carolina's lips unexpectedly with his, stirring memories of gentleness she had somehow forgotten. She grew strangely confused as he continued softly, "Your pleas not to leave you were almost more than I could bear, but I told myself it was necessary, that Jimmy Pierce was perfectly capable of driving the wagon in my place, and that his father's wagon was next in line if there was any trouble. I told myself that I was going to make the *first* strike in the train . . . the *richest* strike, and when you continued arguing with me, I was suddenly furious because you refused to see things my way. I said all those terrible things . . . that I wasn't going to let you hold me back and ruin my future just as my parents had said you would . . . that I was leaving, no matter what you said, and that I felt free for the first time since I had slipped the ring on your finger. I said a lot more that I don't really remember, except that I didn't mean a word, even while I was saying it. Darling . . ." A sob escaped William's lips, "I've regretted saying those things with every breath I've taken in the time since."

William clutched her tighter, burying his face in her hair, shaking with the emotion he strove to draw under control. And Carolina remembered. . . .

Yes, William had loved her. He had looked behind her plain face and uncertain background and he had somehow seen something beautiful. He had said the words many times. He had begged her to believe him until, for the few brief moments in the meadow that changed her life, she had convinced herself that she loved him the same way. He had proved he loved her by giving up his family and the promise of a bright future for her. They had married and moved into small quarters which William had despised, and he had promised her they wouldn't be there long. He had wanted so much for her . . . for them . . . and to make him happy, she had pretended to want those things, too. But all too soon those things had taken greater priority in William's mind than his concern for her. He had ridden off and left her with bitter words that had cut her heart to shreds. The pain of his betrayal had vied with soul-shaking humiliation as she had watched him disappear from sight on the horizon.

A sob caught in Carolina's throat, raising William's head from her hair. The anguish on his boyish face could not be denied. She knew everything he had said was true as he smoothed away her tears and then his own.

"I never made it as far as Deadwood . . . not until today. I was too impatient. When I reached Custer, I began working some of the abandoned claims. I had a lucky streak right off and I was certain the others had left a fortune behind while they chased a will-o'-the-wisp in Deadwood. I was going to prove them all wrong. I dreamed of meeting the wagon train with a pouch full of gold when it reached Custer. I imagined the way you'd look when I put the gold in your hands and told you our future was secure. I couldn't wait for the train to arrive."

William's arm tightened around her. His eyes welled anew as he rasped, "I wasn't too worried when the train was late in arriving at Custer. The wagons had broken down often, and I figured it was just more of the same. I was expecting the train any day when the news came that it had been attacked two weeks earlier and there were no survivors.

William swallowed convulsively, his distress deepening. "I wouldn't let myself believe it. I rode day and night to the site of the massacre, but by the time I finally found it, the bodies had been buried without being identified. There was nothing left of our wagon. Everything was gone.

"I rode to the nearest fort, but the army was no help. All they could tell me was that the train had wandered off the trail somehow and that it had been found by another train that had wandered the same way. They said the bodies had been buried immediately without being identified.

"I went back to Custer. It was only after I got there that I realized I had nothing to return to. Strangely enough, a letter from my mother was waiting for me when I arrived. It was directed to general delivery and in it she begged me . . . us . . . to come back. She said she never really believed we would leave. She said she wanted to know her grandchild and she was certain we could all work something out together."

William searched her eyes for understanding as he whispered, "That was the bitterest pill of all — acceptance, when it no longer meant a damn."

William shrugged. "I didn't even answer the letter. I wandered around, but I couldn't make myself leave the hills. I somehow felt that I would remain close to you as long as I stayed." He added hoarsely, "And now I know why."

His eyes glittering, William continued uncertainly, "I shouldn't have left you. You must've hated me when the Indians attacked the train and I wasn't there to protect you. . . . I can't blame you for making yourself forget all the horror you suffered, and I suppose I can't blame you for turning to the man who took care of you. But that's over now. Things are going to be different, I promise you. We'll be a real family and—"

"No." Carolina closed her eyes against the bittersweet swell within her. "I can't, William. I . . . it's too late. I'm not Madeline Markham anymore."

"You are. You're confused, but it'll pass."

"No."

"Yes."

"No!"

William's fair face flushed at her sudden adamancy. Shaken by his obvious distress, Carolina looked away. She allowed Suzannah to slip to the bed beside her and buttoned her dress. She was unprepared for William's trembling touch as he turned her face back toward his, for the plea in his eyes and the tremor of his lips as he whispered a single word.

"Please. . . ."

Carolina was sobbing then, the pain in her heart so severe that she did not think she would survive. The sound reverberated in the silent room, vying with the echo of William's heartfelt plea as his arms tightened around her, as he drew her closer, his tears mingling with her own. She was unaware of the presence of anyone else in the room until she heard Doc's gravelly voice beside the bed.

"Are you all right, Carolina?"

William's arms were still around her, his cheeks as wet as hers as Carolina looked up into the doctor's scrutiny. Unable to reply, she glanced past him to see Drake standing in the doorway. She saw the emptiness in his eyes and felt the hunger in his heart. Pained, ashamed, as empty as he, she looked away.

Twenty-five

A whinny in the distance . . . a low, responsive snort close by . . . a shaft of morning sunlight penetrating the darkness of sleep. . . .

Drake opened his eyes. Snapping them shut a moment later, he groaned aloud, keenly aware that neither the sight nor the smell of the livery stable where he had awakened had forced that spontaneous reaction. His hand came into contact with a bottle as he moved and he clutched it spasmodically. Neither did he have to shake it to know that the bottle was empty.

In a flash it was there again, the image of Carolina and William Markham embracing each other. He remembered their tears, and he remembered with an anguish so severe that it almost stole his breath, that Carolina — no, Madeline — had looked at him and then turned away.

Drake gave a harsh laugh. That was the crux of the problem, wasn't it? During their short month as man and wife, Carolina had proved to him in countless ways that she loved him more than she loved any other man. He had become secure in that love. He had let down the barriers and allowed himself to trust and plan, and to look forward to the future without bitterness. Even now he knew in his heart that Carolina would never choose another man over him.

But Carolina wasn't Carolina anymore.

Drake could not quite believe his stupidity. He had known the true source of the name "Carolina Brand" from the start. Yet, when his suspicions had disappeared, his caution had followed. The rest had been inevitable, and the woman and child, whatever their names, had become a part of him. Drake raised the bottle once more. Empty, just as he was empty. . . .

Controlling the urge to smash the bottle against the nearest wall, Drake looked around him. Despite the chaos inside him, another day had dawned. Looking out at the street through a crack in the stall, he saw the traffic was already thickening. The sounds of construction, never silent for long, had again begun, and as he watched, the first freight train of the day made its way down Main Street. Deadwood had come to life as usual. Nothing . . . and everything . . . had changed.

The familiar sound of Will Reed's cursing as he moved about in the stalls up front brought Drake to a seated position. The old man would soon make his way toward him and he had no desire to be subjected to his scrutiny. Drawing himself to his feet, Drake was almost grateful for the pain in his head that distracted him from his emotional distress. Taking the few steps to his saddlebags, he removed the toilet articles he had carefully wrapped in a cloth and turned toward the rear door and the lethargic stream a few feet beyond. It occurred to him as he stepped through the doorway into the bright morning light that he wasn't alone in his torment — that the woman he loved was suffering as much as he.

That thought sobering, Drake squared his shoulders and walked purposefully forward.

"Can you ever forgive me?"

William looked intently at his wife. His love for her was an aching knot inside him as his question lay unanswered in the silence of the widow's cabin. Dressed in a plain, high-necked, blue dress, she looked more a child than he had remembered, despite the shadows under her eyes that bespoke a sleepless night and their dozing babe in her arms. Her long brown hair was unbound, the front strands drawn back in a style he did not remember her favoring, but she held her slender proportions rigidly erect, in a way that was endearingly familiar. Aside from her direct gray eyes, her features were small and unremarkable. He knew some would say she was plain, but the sight of her touched him in so many ways that he was almost weak with wanting.

But wanting and getting were two different things.

The painful knot inside him tightening, William recalled their parting the previous night. So many things had been left unsettled and unsaid, but he had known that the woman he loved had not yet recuperated from the shock of his unexpected appearance and memories suddenly revived. He had not wanted to press her, but a night filled with dreams of her had raised him from his bedroll at first light. He had shaved and bathed with water from the sluggish stream nearby and had appeared at the widow's door at the first sign of activity within. The older woman had absented herself upon his arrival with a mumbled excuse, and he had nodded his appreciation as she pulled the door closed behind her.

Looking at the living, breathing Carolina as she lowered their child into a basket and turned back to face him, William bit back the words he longed to say. Holding his emotions rigidly in check, he reiterated gently, "Can you forgive me?"

Carolina steadied herself with a hand on the nearby table, silently returning his gaze and he urged her response with a whispered, "Darling . . . ?"

"Forgive?" Carolina was obviously uncertain. "I don't think I can answer that question right now. I don't know if I feel forgiving . . . or if I feel worthy of being forgiven."

Her reply caught him off guard. He returned rigidly, "If you mean because of your 'marriage' to McNeil . . . you weren't yourself. You can't be blamed for your actions. I know that."

"Do you?" Carolina's confusion appeared to deepen.

"How can you be so sure when I'm not even sure myself? The only thing I'm certain of is that I woke up from a living nightmare and Drake was there. I couldn't remember anything, but I recall feeling that I didn't really *need* to remember because I had Drake."

"McNeil played on your need! He took advantage of your gratitude."

"Drake never took advantage of me!"

"He shouldn't have married you!" Anger and jealousy merged in William's ardent protest. "He knew you were frightened and confused. He should've known—"

"I'm the one who should've known, William! *I* was the one who wasn't free! *I* was the one who pushed memories out of my mind because I couldn't bear remembering!"

Carolina's sudden passion snapped William from his jealousy, forcing a pained admission. "And *I* was the one who put you in the position where you were forced to turn to someone else in order to survive. I . . . I'll never forgive myself for that."

Reaching out for her in his distress, William drew Carolina close. Her familiar slenderness felt so right in his embrace. He yearned to draw her closer still, but Carolina remained impassive. His heart sinking, he consoled himself that her reaction was to be expected. She had just left another man's arms. . . .

Forcibly subduing the heat that thought elicited, William whispered, "We have to set the past to rest now, darling. We've found each other and that's the most important thing. Everything will be all right again—just the way it was before."

Stiffening, Carolina drew back from his embrace. "You really don't understand, do you, William? It can *never* be the same for us again, because *I'm* not the same."

William's protest was spontaneous. "I'm not the same either, darling! I'm not the arrogant, immature fool I was before, and if things will be different between us, it'll only be because they'll be better. I'll *make* them better. And I'll make you forget all of this ever happened."

403

Carolina's reply cut cruelly into his heart. "I'll never forget these past months. I'm not even sure I want to forget them."

Managing to keep jealousy at bay, William responded by slipping his arm around Carolina's waist and turning her gently back toward the basket where Suzannah slept. A new quaking began inside him as he whispered, "She's beautiful, isn't she? She's *our* daughter. She's part of us, conceived in love. I made a mistake that almost made me lose you both, but I've learned from it."

Tilting her face up to his, aware that his hand trembled as he did, William whispered with the fervor of long, lost months, "I'll never make that mistake again. You're my wife, Carolina. You were a part of me long before we exchanged our vows. You'll always be a part of me. I want us to live together, to raise our children together, to grow old together. I want to prove I can be the husband and father you wanted me to be. I want everything you've always wanted, but now I want it even more than before. Please give me a chance to prove that I mean what I say. Darling . . . please. . . ."

In the intense silence that followed, William sought to control his emotions. He had been unable to speak the final truth that losing Carolina again would be more than he could bear, but she knew. He read that knowledge in her welling gaze and in her wobbling lips as they parted in a tentative response.

"You . . . you're my husband, William. You're Suzannah's father." The prolonged pause while she searched his fervid gaze was followed by Carolina's barely audible whisper.

"I'll try. . . ."

The holiday was over, but the shock of its aftermath was not. Still stunned in its wake, Rosie turned toward Tag as he entered to slam the cabin door shut behind him. A brilliant morning sun sent shafts of gold through the window as he advanced toward her, his eyes blazing.

"All right, I've checked on it, and it's all true. What I want to know now is what you intend to do about it!"

Tag's voice was filled with unaccustomed anger and Rose knew the pain it masked. She shared that pain, knowing her response would cut him even more deeply as she whispered, "I know what you want me to say, but I can't say it. You want me to say that this whole mixed-up affair with Drake and that woman doesn't make any difference to me . . . but it does. Oh, Tag. . . ." Tag withdrew from her as she touched his sleeve, but Rosie continued determinedly, "Don't you see? Drake isn't married to her. He never was! Carolina or Madeline, whoever she is, isn't the person she made herself out to be. She doesn't deserve Drake, just as I said from the beginnin'. She didn't even tell him her right name. She isn't foolin' me about the rest, either. She knew all along that her husband was alive. She only—"

"You're telling yourself what you want to believe, just as you always have." Tag's expression hardened as he continued stiffly, "But even if you were right, you're forgetting a basic fact. McNeil *loves* Carolina . . . or Madeline . . . whatever her name is. He wants *her,* not you, and whether he's married to her or not isn't going to make a bit of difference in the way he feels about you."

"That's not true!" Rosie drew her pink satin wrapper more tightly closed around her and knotted the tie with shaking hands before looking up again at Tag. "Drake felt sorry for her. He . . . he felt responsible for her and the baby, that's all. When he realizes she doesn't really need him . . . that she *never* really needed him, he'll forget her. Then he'll come back to me. . . ."

"Damn it, Rosie!" Gripping her arms, Tag shook her roughly. "What does it take to make you see what's really happening? McNeil loves that woman! He was shocked senseless when he found out her husband was still alive. He walked right past you on the street last night. He didn't see you or hear you call his name. You didn't even know what happened until the whole town was buzzing about it."

"Drake didn't hear me because he'd been drinkin'."

"Why do you suppose he had been drinking? Because he was happy? Because he was relieved to be rid of the responsibility for Carolina and her child? Because he was anxious to be able to get back to *you?*" Tag shook her again. "Face it, Rosie! McNeil's forgotten you even exist!"

"He hasn't!" Jerking herself free of Tag's angry grip, Rosie took a step backward. "Drake never forgot me and he never will. He was shocked that that woman lied to him, that's all. It . . . it hurt him, but I'll make him forget the hurt. I'll make him feel—"

"What about what *I* feel?" His voice lowering in timbre as it lost all trace of its former anger, Tag took a step closer. His obvious distress was mirrored inside her as he rasped, "Don't you care what I feel, even a little?"

"I do, I do!" Anguish sliced at Rosie. Her voice quavered with the words she forced herself to say. "But you knew from the beginnin' that I was waitin' for Drake. I never lied to you. I kept my bargain to stay with you until Drake came back for me."

"But he *hasn't* come back for you, don't you understand?"

"He will."

"He won't, darling."

"Then I'll go to him."

Tag stiffened. When he spoke again, his voice was gruff. "No, you won't. I won't let you."

"You can't stop me!"

Tag's expression hardened. "Maybe I can't stop you, but I can tell you this. If you go to McNeil now, you can forget about coming back to me when he turns you down." Waiting until the full meaning of his words had registered in Rosie's eyes, he continued even more softly, "I've given you all the love I have inside me to give, Rosie. I've tried to show you in every way possible that I love you more than McNeil could ever hope to love you. I've dreamed dreams for us . . . beautiful dreams . . . but I'm not willing to share those dreams with McNeil any longer. *McNeil doesn't love you* . . . not the way you want him to love you. He's going to make his money in these hills and he's going to move on. When he goes, he's not going to take you. You can follow him if you want, but this time I won't be trailing along behind you. You're going to have to make your decision here and now."

"Tag, please . . ." Tears welling in her eyes, Rosie touched his arm. "Don't make me say the words. I don't want to hurt you."

"You don't want to hurt me?" Tag searched Rosie's anguished expression. "Then tell me what I want to hear. Tell me—"

"I can't! I've already made my choice, you know that! I made that choice over seven years ago, and nothing—*nothing*—will ever change it."

Silent, Tag returned Rosie's impassioned gaze. She felt its touch as it moved slowly over her face, grazing her brimming eyes, her tear-streaked cheeks, as it paused for a long moment on her trembling lips before jerking back up to her eyes once more. The knife of pain sliced more deeply at her heart as he attempted a smile.

"Well, I guess you can't make yourself clearer than that. You're right, Rosie. You were true to our bargain—as true as you could be. I was the one who was fooling himself, not you. You knew from the beginning what you wanted—what you still want—and you're willing to wait for it, for the rest of your life if you must. The only trouble is that I'm not willing to wait that long." Tag took a slow, steadying breath. "I'm sorry, darling, but I think it's time for me to put Deadwood behind me."

"No . . . no, Tag, you don't have to do that. I'll—"

"It'll take me a day or so to straighten out the finances at the Nugget."

"I don't want anything from the Nugget. You can take it all."

Tag's slow smile was sad. "No, I don't think I will." Cupping her chin with his hand, Tag brushed her lips with his.

His voice held a forced lightness as he whispered, "Good luck, darling. I wish you happiness."

The click of the latch as Tag left was simultaneous with the deep sob that escaped Rosie's lips. Suddenly unable to withhold the tumult that followed, Rosie sat down on the bed and covered her eyes with trembling hands. Slowly slipping a hand down her cheek, she ran her fingertips over her lips. They were still warm from Tag's kiss, a kiss she would never taste again.

Raising her head minutes later, Rosie wiped away her tears. She need strike the painful goodbye from her mind. She would do that by remembering that the way was now clear for Drake and her and the life she had always wanted. She would make the best of this second chance that she had been granted, and when she was done, Drake and she would be together forever.

Carolina traveled swiftly along the crowded street. She ignored the curious glances she received and raised her chin higher. She knew what everyone was thinking. A month earlier she had celebrated her marriage to Drake with almost the entire town in attendance. She had made all of those who had celebrated their marriage a part of the cruel farce, and they resented her for it. But she spared little thought for the smiles that had turned to contempt. Her gaze intent on a gently swaying sign at the opposite end of the street, Carolina felt her heart begin a new pounding.

Dr. Fitz had stopped by, concern written in the lines of his haggard face. He had pronounced her fit and had told her without further ado that if she wanted to find Drake, he was probably still in the livery stable where he had spent the night.

Carolina restrained the inclination to run. Anxiety was a thick lump in her throat as she turned into the foul-smelling livery stable and walked cautiously forward. Returning to her mind unexpectedly was Suzannah's response to William when he had held the babe a short time before she left

408

the cabin. The babe had begun cooing the moment she was in William's arms, bringing tears to his eyes, and the ache inside her had deepened.

Maybe William was right. Maybe Suzannah sensed that her father was holding her. Maybe she felt she was home at last when she was in his arms. Maybe William would become more important to the babe than the man whose green eyes had welcomed her into the world . . . whose big, gentle hands had bathed her and cared for her when her own mother couldn't . . . whose deep, off-key voice had ended her fretfulness and had sung her into peaceful oblivion . . . the man who had loved her when she didn't even have a name. Maybe the babe would forget Drake ever existed. Maybe her child could do that.

But Carolina knew she could not.

"Can I help you, ma'am?"

Carolina turned, suddenly uncertain.

"I . . . I'm looking for Drake McNeil. I understand he—"

"I'm over here."

Entering from the rear, Drake walked toward her. His hair was wet and freshly combed. He was clean shaven and his shirt was spotted with water. It was obvious he had just bathed in the stream in the rear of the building, and as she looked at him she realized that despite the shadows under his eyes and his uncharacteristic pallor, this man who had been her husband for so short a time was still the handsomest man she had ever seen.

"I was coming to see you this morning."

"Were you, Drake?" Carolina fought the thickening in her throat. "You left without talking to me yesterday. I wanted—"

Drake interrupted her abruptly. "We can't talk here."

Suddenly realizing that the old man was standing nearby, openly listening to their conversation, Carolina followed Drake as he turned toward the rear entrance. Halting the moment they were out of sight of the door, Drake turned toward her. He had reverted to the old Drake, his emotions carefully hidden behind an impassive façade. Were it not for the careful distance he maintained between them and the fact that he had just as carefully avoided touching her in any way, she might have thought he was completely unaffected by the tumultuous events of the previous day. She whispered hoarsely, "Do you hate me, Drake?"

Drake looked down at her trembling lips. She sensed the quiver that shook him as he responded softly, "No, I don't hate you . . . and I don't blame you for what happened. I should've known better than to think we could go along as if your life before we met had never existed. I should've known it would catch up with us somewhere. I didn't even know your name."

"You did . . . or you thought you did!"

"No." Drake shook his head. His expression slowly softened. "I knew your name wasn't Carolina Brand, but I somehow made myself dismiss the importance of it. I suppose, in the end, it's easier knowing that Carolina Brand never existed. She never did, did she, *Madeline?*"

A shiver passed down Carolina's spine at the alien sound of that name on Drake's lips.

"Don't call me Madeline!"

"What should I call you, then?"

"My name's Carolina . . . Carolina Brand."

"Carolina *Brand*." Drake paused, considering the full significance of her chosen name. "—Not Markham's wife, and not mine."

Carolina took a step closer to Drake, repeating softly, "Do you hate me, Drake?" Hungering for the comfort of his arms, she continued, "I did a terrible thing to you. I made you love me when I didn't have the right. I made you trust me when I wasn't worthy of trust. I planned a future with you when I knew in some dark corner of my mind that a future together could never be. I know now that the reason I didn't want to come back to Deadwood for the centennial was because I somehow knew William would be here."

"So, what are you saying, Carolina?" Drake's jaw grew

rigid. "I saw you and William in each other's arms. You stayed with him last night . . ."

"I didn't!"

Drake's jaw turned to stone. "You didn't come to me, either."

"I couldn't! William's my husband."

"And I'm not."

"William is Suzannah's father."

"And I'm not."

Tears suddenly flowing freely, Carolina forced herself to continue, "You were never my husband *or* Suzannah's father, as much as I truly wanted you to be. Oh, Drake, please try to understand." Moving unconsciously closer until their bodies almost touched, Carolina rasped, "My parents were killed when I was five years old. I had been alone all my life until I met William. Something inside me told me that he wasn't the man I had been waiting for, but he loved me . . . really loved me . . . and that day in the meadow . . . just that one time—" Pausing to regain control, Carolina continued in a rush, "I . . . I made myself believe he was. When I found out I was carrying his child, I was so ashamed. I thought William would be ashamed, too. I thought he would turn his back on me, but he didn't. Instead, he gave up his family . . . a brilliant future . . . everything, to marry me."

Carolina continued softly, "I didn't want to come to the Black Hills. I was afraid for the baby, but William insisted. He said he couldn't leave me behind. I don't really know what happened on the wagon train or how things slowly changed between us, except that when he said all those bitter things to me before he left, I believed him. I hated him, and I hated myself. I was terrified when the Indians attacked, and in that split second while the tomahawk descended toward my head . . ." Carolina's voice dropped to a shamed rasp, "I wished William would die, too."

Carolina struggled to retain her rapidly waning control. Drake's arms slipped around her, steadying her quaking as she continued, "I didn't remember any of this before yesterday—I truly didn't, Drake. I know now that I didn't want to. My heart took over my mind the minute I saw you . . . the minute I heard your voice. I didn't want to give you up."

"You don't have to give me up. We can—"

"Don't you see? It's too late! I'm married to another man. I've borne his child. I was committed to him before I ever met you and I'm still committed to him."

"Committed . . . but do you *love* him?"

"I loved him once. . . ."

"Do you love him now?"

"I'm his wife. . . ."

"Do you love him?"

"I owe him another chance. . . ."

"Do you *love* him?"

"Oh, Drake. . . ." Carolina sobbed. "Yes . . . I do."

Drake's arms dropped to his sides. Carolina gripped them in a plea for understanding.

"The part of me that was Madeline still loves him. How could it be any different? That part of me knows William gave up everything for me, that he hates himself for leaving me that day, and that more than anything else, he wants to make everything up to me. That part of me knows that one mistake doesn't negate the vows I exchanged with William or his right to be a father to Suzannah."

Trembling, Carolina continued softly, "But then there's the part of me that was Carolina McNeil. That part of me will never forget . . . will never stop loving you."

Drake was rigid, his control tenuous. "But Carolina McNeil doesn't exist anymore. She never really did . . . did she?"

Carolina took a shuddering breath. "No."

Drake's jaw twitched revealingly. "Then there isn't much more to say."

"Except I'm sorry. . . ."

Drake did not reply.

"I'm so sorry."

But Drake's eyes were cold. Her apology had not reached

412

him, and Carolina suddenly knew it never would. Drake was frozen inside, just as he had been before. She had done this to him.

Realizing there was only one thing left for her to do, Carolina filled her eyes with the sight of Drake, then turned abruptly. She walked back through the livery stable, ignoring the proprietor's curious gaze as she wiped away her tears and walked out onto the street.

Every muscle in his body tense, Drake stared at Carolina's departing figure until she disappeared from sight. He took a spontaneous step forward, suddenly wondering why he had made no protest as the woman he loved walked out of his life.

The answer was only too simple. He had known the truth the moment he had seen Carolina in Markham's arms. He had read it in Carolina's eyes when she had turned away from him. He had managed to avoid facing it fully the previous night but in coming to him now . . . in being honest and kind, Carolina had made things painfully final.

Drake took a stiff step forward, and then another. Moments later he was saddling his bay. Stopping only to fill his canteen in the stream, he mounted up and rode out onto the street. He paused uncertainly, looking toward the trail back into the hills. The cabin without Carolina? No, he couldn't face that yet.

Turning his horse roughly in the opposite direction, Drake spurred him into motion.

So tense inside that she thought she might snap, Rosie looked toward the upright piano in the corner of the crowded saloon. Nellie and a few customers were singing enthusiastically as Willie plunked out a rowdy tune, adding a new measure of pandemonium to the normal din and testing her forbearance to the furthest degree. Turning back, she forced a smile for the fellow standing beside her

413

at the bar, despite the throbbing in her head.

"So, what happened after that, Doc?"

But her smile did not fool the old practitioner. "Somethin' wrong, Rosie?"

"Nothin' that one of your headache powders wouldn't cure. I haven't been out of this saloon all day. My poor brain is starvin' for a breath of fresh air."

"Then why don't you go out—take yourself a walk. It'll do you good."

"What'll do me good is to find out what's really goin' on in the widow's cabin."

"I don't have anythin' to say." Doc shifted uncomfortably. "You're special to me, Rosie, but Carolina's business is Carolina's business."

Rosie leaned closer to the old man, her gaze intense. "I don't care about that woman. It's Drake I'm thinkin' about."

"Look, honey, everybody knows Carolina's husband materialized from the dead yesterday. And everybody knows Drake isn't with her anymore. That's all I know, except that it isn't as simple as that. I feel kinda sorry for the poor fella."

"Which 'poor' fella?" Rosie was suddenly on the defensive. "If you're meanin' Drake, you're wastin' your sympathy. Drake and I—"

"Drake and I? I thought it was Tag and you."

"It isn't anymore."

Doc gave a low snort. "Off again, on again . . . like a damned spigot."

"No, not this time." Rosie's eyes filled. "Tag's leavin' Deadwood as soon as he can get finances straightened out here."

Doc was suddenly livid. "And you're lettin' him go? You're a damned fool woman, Rosie Blake! You're givin' up a good man for a man who—"

But Rosie was no longer listening. Suddenly still, she stared out the front window at the street for a moment before heading abruptly toward the door. Frantically dodging milling customers and scattered tables, she emerged on the street a moment later and started running down the boardwalk. Intent on the big man who was rapidly riding out of range of her shouted plea, she called, "Drake! Drake, wait! I want to talk to you!"

She continued running, the dust in his mount's wake rising around her, stinging her eyes as Drake's broad outline disappeared from sight. Rosie stumbled to a halt, her breasts heaving as she raised a hand to her throbbing head. Tears unrelated to the coarse dust were hot under her eyelids, but she blinked them away. Straightening her back, she turned back toward the Nugget to meet curious stares with a smile and a jaunty toss of her head.

"That poor fella doesn't know what he missed this afternoon! When he finds out, he's goin' to kick himself around the barn a few times, I'll tell you that."

Sauntering back into the saloon to a chorus of laughter, Rosie returned to the bar. Dying inside, she forced her smile brighter as she chucked Doc's cheek. "He'll be back, Doc, honey. You'll see. . . ."

Twenty-six

More fatigued than he had ever been before, Drake drew his mount to a halt. A relentless sun beat down on his shoulders as he paused to look across the lush centennial prairie. He had heard some say that the land north of Deadwood held the richest grazing they had ever seen. He had also heard it said that the "short-grass country" with its nutritious range, ample water, winter shelter, and sturdy, drought-resistant grasses could be grazed all winter. He had spent a week wandering this virgin soil, and he had discovered that every word he had heard about it was true. This was cattle country.

His broad shoulders hunched as he leaned heavily on his saddle horn, Drake searched the cloudless blue of the horizon. At one time that realization would have excited him, but it now left him strangely cold. He supposed he should not be surprised. He was a different man from what he had been only a few days earlier when the future had been reflected in Carolina's eyes.

Drake raised his hat from his head and wiped his arm across his forehead. The prairie sun was hotter than he would have imagined it to be and his discomfort was growing. Spotting a shady copse a short distance away, he spurred his horse in its direction. He settled himself under its protection a few minutes later and drank long and deep from his canteen. Never far from his mind, the image of Carolina returned vividly clear. He smiled at its bittersweet consolation, ignoring the torments that had made his first few days away from her living anguish. He had become adept at avoiding those torments, so much so that he was certain he'd soon be able to face going back to Deadwood to pick up supplies and say his final farewells.

That thought tightened the knot in his stomach which had become his constant companion, and Drake's smile faltered. In the meantime, Carolina was close to him in sleep.

Wearily, the ache in his heart encompassing the whole of him as well, Drake closed his eyes.

"I'm terribly worried about them." Miriam turned toward Doc, squinting in the bright sunlight as she stopped pinning her laundry to the line. Were she not so relieved to be able to share her concerns for Carolina with another human being whom she could trust to be discreet, she would have told the old coot outright what she thought of his daily visits to the cabin now that Carolina's presence again served as a buffer between them. To be sure, she had not been able to figure out why he felt he needed a buffer. She wasn't that formidable, was she?

Dismissing that thought, Miriam attempted to dismiss the hurt as well as she continued, "It's not that Carolina isn't trying. And William, the dear boy, could not be more attentive and loving." Tears rose to Miriam's eyes. "He reminds me of my Jonas when he and I were young . . . so thoughtful and eager to please."

Doc gave a short-tempered snort. "That so? I didn't think you could remember back that far."

Gasping at Doc's affront, Miriam responded with characteristic spirit, "Oh, you didn't . . . ? Well, if *your* memory hasn't failed you, *Doctor* Fitz, you may recall that I'm several years younger than you are, so I wouldn't make snide remarks about my age, if I were you!"

"Tut, tut. . . ." Doc raised his hairy brows. "I didn't know you were so sensitive."

"There are a lot of things you don't know about me, you old fool! But that's another matter entirely—and if you please, I don't choose to change the subject!" Miriam continued with a slight twitch of the lips, "I'm at a complete loss in this affair. I've tried everything to alleviate Carolina's discomfort. I've even volunteered to turn the cabin over to William and her for a few days, so they might come to terms with things."

Doc's eyes widened. "And you call *me* an old fool! I hope you didn't make that offer in front of Markham!"

"Of course not, especially since Carolina was so adamant about refusing it. Jerome, things aren't going well at all."

"You're exaggeratin'. I've seen the two of them together. They get along well. They're pleasant to each other and enjoy each other's company."

"Just like brother and sister. . . ."

"I wouldn't say that!"

"I would!"

"Well, what do you expect?" Miriam could almost see the hair stand up on the back of Doc's neck as he continued adamantly, "What kind of woman do you think Carolina is? She believed herself married to another man only a week ago! And if I don't miss my guess, that big fella didn't let her out of his sight or out of his arms for more than an hour at a time the whole while they were at that cabin of his."

"Jerome!"

Doc ignored Miriam's flush, continuing, "Then you expect to see her go jumpin' right back into Markham's bed as if the whole thing never happened! It doesn't work that way, Miriam, not with women like Carolina, and I'm surprised that you could think it would."

Miriam drew herself up primly. "I did not relate my concerns to you so you might lecture me, Jerome! I spoke seeking advice."

"I didn't hear you ask for advice!"

"You didn't give me a chance!"

"Well, ask me then!"

Miriam blinked, obviously stunned by his sharpness and Doc silently groaned. He couldn't stand much more of his own contrary feelings. He was only too aware how eagerly he had accepted the opportunity to see the widow on a daily basis again when the excuse had been granted him. He was finding it harder and harder to keep his distance when she appealed to him with obvious distress. He didn't like the way her forthrightness and intelligence continued to spark his admiration, or the way her sharp mind constantly challenged him. Neither did he like the way a simple misting of tears in her birdlike gaze tore him up inside, *or* the fact that she not only seemed totally unaware of his predicament, but couldn't care less. His feelings a damned contradiction that made him more irritable by the moment, Doc barked, "Ask me!"

"All right!" Miriam's thin lips tightened. "What should I do?"

Doc took a necessary step backward. "Is that it? That's what you wanted to ask?"

"Yes."

Doc rolled his eyes. "Do just exactly what you've been doin'. Nothin'! Let them work it out for themselves. They will. That young Markham's got his ways. They're out walkin' now, aren't they?"

"Yes."

"If I don't miss my guess—and I seldom do—he's smilin' that little-boy smile of his right now and workin' his way around Carolina. Don't underestimate him, Miriam. Markham isn't as big and as handsome as McNeil, but he's Carolina's husband and the father of her child. That carries a lot of weight with a woman like Carolina."

"As long as Drake doesn't return."

"What makes you think he will? He's been gone a week."

"He has to come back to Deadwood. He left his pack animal at the livery stable."

Doc's brows shot upward in surprise. "Do you mean to tell me that you went snoopin' at the livery stable?"

Miriam raised her chin proudly. "I did."

Doc's full lips twitched before he asked soberly, "Did you tell Carolina?"

"No. I didn't want to add to her distress."

"Well, at least you were smart enough to keep your mouth shut. . . ."

"Well, I never!"

"I'm tellin' you right now, when that big fella comes back, *if* he comes back, he's goin' to depart again as soon as he loads up his supplies. He won't be visitin' Carolina . . . or anyone else." Doc paused, frowning. "That fella's gone as cold as stone inside. He's got too much history behind him to let him come beggin' after any woman. And as far as Markham is concerned, well, you just take my word for it. He'll break Carolina down. Time is on his side. Right now he's probably charmin' her with pleasant memories. Right now he's probably sayin' . . ."

". . . Do you remember the first time we met, Carolina?"

Carolina looked up at William. They were walking side by side on the narrow path that followed a slow-moving trickle of water that had once been an active stream. A month without rain and summer temperatures that soared daily had reduced its volume, leaving it to drain into unsavory puddles that somehow matched the abused, heavily pockmarked terrain around them. There was little of beauty left in the area of tortured soil where they walked and the sun was too hot to enjoy it even if there were, but Carolina had been unable to refuse William's invitation. She knew they needed time alone together if they hoped to recapture what they had lost. She forced a smile.

"Yes, I remember. Mrs. Fergerson was annoyed with me that day." Carolina gave a short laugh. "She was always annoyed with me. I could never move fast enough, could never clean the kitchen clean enough, could never do anything well enough to please her."

"And you had no hand with biscuits. . . ."

Carolina laughed despite herself as the memory fully returned. "Oh, yes. I was covered with flour from head to toe that day and certain I would be dismissed because of my ineptitude."

"Old Betty knew it, too."

Carolina's smile softened. "But you took care of it. You charmed the old witch, and by the time you were done, you convinced her that cultivating my abilities would be a personal feather in her cap."

William's hand tightened around hers. "I could've strangled the old harridan when I saw her abusing you. I wanted to take you in my arms then and there and snatch you away from her. I wasn't able to stop thinking about you for a moment until I saw you again."

"William . . ."

"You haven't been out of my thoughts for longer than a few moments any day since that time, either. Darling . . ." His voice earnest, his blue eyes bright with growing passion, William gripped her shoulders gently. "Do you remember that day in the meadow?" At her hesitant nod, he continued softly, "I'll never forget it. When I thought I had lost you, I lived it over and again in my mind. It was a day almost like this one. Do you remember how hot the sun was on our skin . . . how right it felt to be in each other's arms? I remember that your hair was like liquid silk splayed out on the ground around us, and that you were so perfect in every way that I felt privileged to touch you . . . to love you. When you wound your arms around me and loved me back, my joy was complete. I cherished that memory and I honestly believed nothing could ever match it. But I cherish a new dream now. In it I hold you in my arms just as I did then, only it's even more beautiful between us because we know what was almost lost. I want it to happen that way, Carolina. I want to make love to you and to know you want it as much as I do."

"I . . . I can't, William."

"Why, darling?"

William's gentle plea touched her heart. She shared his distress as she whispered, "It . . . it's too soon. I'm not ready."

William did not immediately respond. Myriad emotions flashed across his face, flushing his fair complexion with revealing color in the moments before he attempted a smile. But the attempt was costly. It dimmed the eager light she had seen in his eyes only moments previous as he finally spoke.

"I suppose I'll never change in some ways. Impatience was always one of my greatest shortcomings. I wanted you so much that I couldn't wait to have you, and once I had made love to you, I was impatient to have you for myself alone. When my parents turned their backs on me, I was impatient to prove that I didn't need them to survive. I made my greatest mistake when I grew so impatient to get to the gold fields that I rode out and left you. I was a damned fool then, but I'm not going to be a damned fool now."

William drew her close. Carolina felt his trembling as he whispered, "This time it'll be different. I'll wait, darling, as long as it takes for you to be sure, and as long as it takes for you to want me just as much as I want you. I know that time will come."

Not awaiting Carolina's response, William touched his mouth to hers. His lips clung, raising an emotion inside Carolina that was part pleasure and part pain. Her throat was too thick to speak as they walked slowly back in the direction from which they had come. Her head resting against William's shoulder . . . her husband's shoulder, she knew this was the way it was supposed to be.

"If the weather stays this clear, you'll be back in Cheyenne within a week. I'm thinkin' I wouldn't mind travelin' in the same direction myself right about now."

Tossing his carpetbag into the nearby wagon, Tag briefly assessed the chaos of the departing wagon train before turning back to the smiling bartender. "You don't really mean that, Barney. What would Rosie do without you to manage the bar?"

"Yeah, Rosie. . . ."

Barney's full mustache twitched as he glanced back at the Nugget. As the clever fellow had intended, Tag followed his gaze to see Rosie standing tentatively in the doorway of the saloon. A familiar misery began inside Tag as she started toward him.

Keenly aware that departure was imminent as Rosie halted beside him, Tag saw the effort she expended to maintain her smile. The knot inside him twisted tighter as he forced a casual façade.

"Some last-minute questions? You don't have to worry, Rosie. It'll be business as usual at the Nugget with Barney backing you up at the bar."

Rosie's glorious eyes were suspiciously bright. "I'm not worryin' about the Nugget. You fixed everythin' so all I'll have to do is show up every night and smile."

"That's all you ever had to do to bring in customers. The fellows around here would walk a mile for one of your smiles."

"Oh, Tag . . ." Rosie's lips trembled. "You've been too generous. You shouldn't have—"

"Don't tell me what I should or shouldn't have done." Tag glanced around them, growing uncomfortable with the extended goodbye. He knew his weaknesses, and Rosie was his biggest. Another few minutes and he'd be begging her to come with him or telling her what a fool she was for the way she'd been watching the street every day for McNeil's return. Another few minutes and he might even try snatching her up into his arms.

"I'm goin' to miss you, Tag." Rosie took a step closer. "I'll never forget—"

Rosie stopped midsentence, her face whitening as she stared at a point just beyond his shoulder. Turning to follow her gaze, Tag was startled to see Ella standing behind him. Dressed in traveling clothes, she clutched a carpetbag in her hand. She smiled tentatively, then tilted up her chin.

"Toss this bag up into the wagon for me, will you, Tag?" Ella walked closer. "I've been thinkin' that Deadwood ain't all it's cracked up to be. Cheyenne's been lookin' more and more appealin' this past week, so I figured I'd give it another try." She shrugged. "Like they say, there's no time like the present once you make up your mind to do somethin'."

Silent, Tag was suddenly struck with the irony of the scene being played out on the hot, dusty Deadwood street.

423

The woman he loved stood on one side of him, and a woman who loved him on the other—and in between hung all the misery the three of them could make for themselves in this world.

Suddenly disgusted with himself and his own self-indulged distress, Tag made an abrupt decision. Taking the bag from Ella's hand, he tossed it up into the wagon. He turned back to see Rosie had retreated a few steps, her smile frozen. He heard the unnatural ring in her voice as she said, "I guess you'll be leavin' soon, so there's nothin' left for me to say but goodbye and good luck . . . to both of you."

Making no attempt to stop Rosie as she started abruptly back toward the Nugget, Tag watched as she wound her way through the crowded street and disappeared through the doorway with Barney following close behind. He turned at a touch on his arm.

More solemn than he had ever seen her before, Ella whispered, "You ain't mad at me, are you, Tag?"

"Mad?" Tag paused at the question, then slowly shook his head. "No, I'm not mad. You've got a right to go wherever you want to go, but I'd be less than honest if I didn't say right from the start that I'm not promising you anything. You understand that, don't you, Ella?"

"I understand." Ella swallowed, then continued, her gaze earnest. "But I'm promisin' *you* somethin'. I'm promisin' you all the good I got in me, for as long as you want it. And I'm promisin' you that I'll make you as happy as I can."

"Ella . . ."

"And while I'm about it, I might even make you smile." Ella raised her chin, forcing away her sobriety to flash him a flirtatious grin. "How about a little boost up onto the seat so Jake can pull this wagon into line? Then maybe if you sit yourself down right next to me, I'll tell you the joke Tim Ryan told me last night—about the prospector and his cross-eyed mule. It's guaranteed to make you blush—and if that don't work, well . . ." She winked. "I'll just see what else I can do. . . ."

Silently obliging her, Tag waited for Ella to settle herself on the seat. He turned back toward the Nugget, his heart leaping when he thought he saw Rosie's face in the window. Furious with himself when he saw he was mistaken, Tag climbed up into the wagon.

Ella looked up at him as the conveyance jerked into motion amid the noise and confusion of the street. Tag read in her gaze confirmation of all she had offered him so honestly. He was humbled by it.

The wagon train rattled slowly forward. Realizing he would be seeing Deadwood for the last time, Tag looked back as the dust of the town settled in their wake. As he did, Tag slowly . . . deliberately . . . *finally* . . . put the past behind him.

The sound of crickets awakened Drake to the fading light of day. Momentarily disoriented, he looked around him, finally recalling his position in the small, wooded copse where he had reclined earlier that day. Lying still, he sought to clear his cloudy mind. He could not remember the last time he had slept through the afternoon, or voluntarily gone without his noon meal. Contrarily, he found he was still tired and hot, but that he had no desire to eat. He searched his mind further. When *was* the last time he had eaten? This morning . . . yesterday?

Lethargic, with a loss of appetite . . . Lovesick? At his age? Carolina's image returned before his mind's eye and Drake's question was answered. That thought striking him as incredibly ridiculous, Drake burst into laughter. The laughter gained a strange control and he laughed harder, until his eyes watered and his head ached and he could laugh no more. Strangely spent, he leaned back and closed his eyes.

Carolina. . . . He had indulged himself in pleasant memories in recent days, but others had begun slipping through. Most prevalent of all had become the image of Carolina in William Markham's arms, and Carolina's pained expression when she had made her whispered admission.

Yes, I love him.

Those words sharper than a knife, snapped Drake to a seated position. His head swam as he reached for his canteen and drank deeply. Pausing for a breath, he shook the container, realizing it was almost empty. He'd refill it tomorrow. He'd be slept out by then and ready to start back.

With a brief glance at his horse grazing peacefully nearby, Drake lay back down and closed his eyes. Yes, he'd start back tomorrow. He'd pick up his pack mule in Deadwood and head into the hills . . . maybe. Or maybe he'd keep right on going. . . .

His eyes again closing, Drake knew there was no point in running from the ache inside him. It, like the image of Carolina that haunted him, would follow wherever he went. His only respite lay in his growing certainty that he would be able to face things squarely if he knew that the misery he had seen in Carolina's eyes had faded . . . that at least one of them was happy.

In that moment his decision was made. He would go back to Deadwood tomorrow. He'd visit Carolina and ask her if she was happy. He wanted her to be happy.

The light was rapidly fading and a sudden chill shook Drake. Surprised at the sudden drop in temperature, he unrolled the blanket he had used for a pillow and wrapped it around him. As he drifted off to sleep, he heard an echo of Carolina's voice.

Do you hate me, Drake?

He responded simply, truthfully.

"No. I love you."

Drake awakened abruptly from vicious, distorted dreams. A canopy of stars sparkled overhead as a brilliant full moon lit the darkness of the prairie with a silver light, but it was so cold. He shivered, his body aching so badly that he was vaguely uncertain if the wild battering he had received in his nightmares had actually occurred. He drew himself slowly to a seated position and reached for his canteen. One drink and his stomach revolted painfully.

426

The violent spasms past, Drake attempted to settle himself comfortably, but his blanket did little to stave off the chill. He closed his eyes, his head pounding as the discomfort in his stomach worsened. He began shivering violently. Disoriented, he looked around him, wondering if he might not really be on the prairie at all. Maybe hell was not hot, but cold. Maybe it was filled with an eternity of tormenting images . . . a woman he loved but could not have . . . a life with her that would never be . . . a child who had never really belonged to him. Maybe he would pay for his past misdeeds by staying forever in this place, shivering and aching and wanting. Maybe . . .

He was so cold.

"Bring that fella in here, boys. . . . That's it. Put him over there."

Doc watched as the apprehensive miners carried their shaking, barely lucid partner into his office and lay him on a hastily prepared pallet beside other similarly stricken men. Doc noted that they backed up warily, looking at his other fevered, groaning patients with apprehension as they wiped their hands on their pants.

Doc exploded with a bellow. "Damn fools! What are you afraid of? I told you what this is all about! You don't have to be afraid of catchin' what these fellas have—not unless you've been drinkin' the same foul water they have!"

"That so?" Disbelief in his eyes, Harvey White shook his head. "Well, I ain't takin' no chances. I didn't freeze out the winter in this blasted place and sweat out the summer, only to die from some disease before I can get home again."

"Yeah, that's right!"

Growling as the heavily bearded, shorter fellow echoed the same sentiments, Doc took an aggressive step forward. "So you're tellin' me that you're goin' to drop your partner here with me and leave, just like everybody else has been doin'?"

"You're a doctor, ain't you? We don't know nothin' about takin' care of sick people."

427

"I'm a doctor, but I've only got two hands. Look around you! There are nine sick men in this room and many more to come, if I don't miss my guess. They all need attention."

"Well, give it to them, then!"

Inching out the doorway, the shorter fellow slammed the door behind him, leaving Doc fuming. Damn, they were such fools! The town was full of fools!

Rubbing his stubbled chin, Doc restrained the shout of pure frustration. He had warned them! He had told everybody who was anybody in this forsaken wilderness what they were heading for if they weren't more careful. He had looked at that damned stream that ran parallel to Main Street and cursed every pail of garbage that had been dumped into it, and every trickle of effluent that had seeped down from the outhouses on the hill, but it had all been for naught. Nobody had listened.

Doc shook his head. In the past twenty-four hours the afflicted had started dropping like flies and he knew more were to come. The recent celebration had brought a new level of contamination to that particular stream, and it hadn't taken great detective work to trace this sickness back to it. He had worked throughout the night moving from patient to patient, but he knew his limitations. He needed help.

"Here's another one for you, Doc!"

A voice in the doorway was simultaneous with the entrance of four men, struggling with the weight of the big fellow they carried.

"We found this one outside town. I guess he was makin' his way back because he was sick, but he never made it. Where do you want us to put him? Doc . . . ?"

Snapping into motion, Doc walked to the big man's side, then directed sharply, "Put him over there." He motioned to a vacant corner and made a snap decision as he ordered, "And get the Widow Higgins."

"But we gotta go back to our claim. We—"

"Do as I said, damn it!"

Ignoring the grumbling behind him as the fellows walked out the door, Doc grabbed a blanket from his dwindling

428

pile. He crouched down by his newest patient and spread the blanket over him, realizing Drake didn't even know he was there.

William gripped Carolina's arm, turning her roughly toward him. The sound of his anger bounced against the walls of Miriam's cabin as he shouted, "You're not going!"

Trembling from the shock of the brief note from Miriam that she still held in her hand, Carolina shouted back, "Drake's sick. I have to go to him. You can't stop me!"

"Can't I? It's bad enough Miriam went to that pesthouse Doc Fitz set up. I'm not going to let you take the same chance."

Carolina attempted to shake her arm free, her panic growing. "William, Doc thinks it's typhoid!"

"You're not going!"

"I am! You read what Miriam wrote. The sickness comes from contaminated water . . . that stream that runs behind Main Street, or the wells that might have been affected by it."

"Doc Fitz is only guessing."

Her agitation turning into anger when she could not dislodge William's clutching grip, Carolina hissed, "When I was sick, Drake took care of me day and night. He never left my side. Suzannah and I are alive today because of him, and now he needs me. I have to go to him. I owe it to him."

William's grip tightened almost to the point of pain as he demanded harshly, "That isn't the only reason you want to go to him, is it?"

"Let me go, William!"

"Is it!"

Shuddering with fury, Carolina whispered, "You're my husband and the father of my child, William. I'll keep the vows I pledged to you, but I won't abandon Drake when he needs me. I *must* go to him."

"No. Miriam can take care of him."

"He needs *me!*"

"No, *I* need you. *Suzannah* needs you. The past is past and McNeil will have to put it behind him just as we're putting it behind us."

"William . . ."

"No."

Carolina jerked her arm free and turned toward the door, only to have William slip into her path. His fair face set, his voice colder than she had ever heard it, he whispered a final, solemn word.

"No."

The fires of hell were burning him, but they left him strangely cold. Shivering, Drake wandered in a shaded vale where physical torment vied with an even greater tribulation. He saw Doc Fitz's face, and he wondered at the part the old fellow played in this endless ordeal as he attempted to wipe the perspiration from his brow. But he was strangely unable to accomplish that simple task.

Protesting his weakness and realizing the words had not left his lips, Drake forced his eyes open. He was in Doc Fitz's office. How had he gotten there? He recalled awakening from a torturous night of endless bodily purging, feeling more ill than he had ever felt before. The morning had been bright with sunlight, but the brilliant shafts of gold had failed to warm him. He recalled that he had been suddenly desperate to return to Deadwood, to see Carolina and to talk to her. He had needed to ask her something important, but a strange debility had somehow wiped the question from his mind."

"Drake. . . ."

A woman's voice brought Drake back from the darkness into which he was sinking. The sound was familiar and his heart began a rapid pounding as he struggled to respond.

"Drake, can you hear me?"

The shadow above him moved. It came closer as he sought to penetrate the peculiar haze that hung over the room.

"Drake. . . ."

But the curl that brushed his cheek was black, not a light brown in color. The eyes that looked into his were a brilliant blue, not a clear gray. His heart plummeting, Drake tried to speak.

"What is it, Drake? What do you want?"

"Carolina. . . ."

The shadow above him swayed. The voice became choked. "It's Rosie, Drake. I came to take care of you."

"Tell Carolina . . ."

"Carolina isn't here. She's with her husband."

"Tell Carolina . . ."

"She isn't here!"

"Yes, I am, Drake! I'm here!"

There was no mistaking the sound of Carolina's voice. Drake strained harder to see. Carolina's small, almost childlike face appeared through the mist. It was wet with tears.

He tried to speak but no words came. He felt Carolina touch his cheek. He tried again.

"I can't hear you, Drake." Carolina's voice took on a desperate tone. "What did you say?"

But Drake could not respond as the darkness again claimed him.

"Doc! Something's happened to Drake!"

Beside them in a moment, Doc brushed Carolina roughly aside. He looked up seconds later, his lips tight. "He's unconscious, but he's all right."

"No, he's not all right." Her emotions under tenuous control, Carolina ignored Rosie's silent presence beside them. "He's so weak he could hardly speak!"

"Get hold of yourself, Carolina." The sharpness of Doc's tone penetrated her panic, drawing her to attention as he continued, "I'm not going to lie to you. Drake's very sick."

The sound of stumbling steps behind them turned Carolina toward a wrapped body being carried out the doorway. Her head snapped back with growing horror.

His expression severe, Doc responded to her unvoiced

question. "Yes, some of the men in this room will die, but Drake's a strong man. If anyone can survive, he can."

Forcing the return of reason, Carolina nodded. "What can I do to help him?"

"Unfortunately, all we can do is keep him as comfortable as possible. But that won't be as easy as it sounds. This is a nasty illness."

Emotion again thick in her throat as Drake's pallor worsened, Carolina rasped, "Tell me what I need to do."

Moving to Drake's bedside after a few basic instructions, Carolina squeezed out the cloth resting in a nearby bowl and began cooling his brow. She looked up a moment later, suddenly realizing that Rosie still stood a few steps away. Distress drew new heat to Carolina's eyes as she spoke haltingly to the silent saloon girl.

"Drake's so sick. He . . . he was trying to tell me something before, but I couldn't understand him."

"I understood what he said." Rosie spoke at last, her eyes filling. "He said he loved you."

Twenty-seven

The silence of Doc's office was punctuated by the sound of low moans and scuffling feet as exhausted volunteers moved between the pallets of the sick. Weary to the bone, Doc rubbed his cheek, realizing that he hadn't shaved since the first patient had been brought to his office over a week earlier. It occurred to him that he hadn't bathed in that length of time, either, nor had he combed his hair or—

Miriam slipped into his line of vision as she ministered to Pete Smalley, one of the most grievously afflicted. He saw the gentleness with which Miriam bathed the fellow's forehead, and as she turned, he saw compassion reflected on her thin face. He wondered how he had ever thought the woman to be cold and unfeeling.

Miriam turned, briefly catching his eye, but Doc did not look away. Miraculously, she was her tidy self after hours of nursing chores that had stretched into days, and then a week. Not a hair was out of place and he knew that the moment her apron became stained, it would somehow be replaced by another as white as the driven snow. The woman was a wonder . . . a phenomenon. . . .

But she was more than that.

Doc watched Miriam's deft movements with admiration. With a prick of guilt, he realized that his energies could be directed into far more productive channels than observing Miriam Higgins's bedside manner, but he told himself he deserved a pause, however brief, after the grueling pace he had maintained.

Heaving a sigh, Doc allowed himself a moment of optimism. It appeared the worst had passed. No new cases of the disease had been reported in the past twenty-four hours. The contaminated creek had been posted with signs so big a blind man could read them, and nearby wells had been temporarily abandoned. So far, he had twenty-eight cases under his care, all within the confines of his office and private quarters in the rear. He knew Deadwood's "other" doctor was treating a like number. He had lost four patients so far, with several other men's lives hanging by a thread. The next few days while the fate of those patients were decided would be difficult for all concerned.

Still staring at Miriam's erect figure, Doc realized that whatever success he had had in meeting the crisis was greatly due to her. He recalled his frustration until he had asked her for help. Within the hour, the woman had had the situation fully under control, with volunteers reporting for shifts that covered the needs of his patients around the clock.

Of course, there were a few volunteers who did not bother with shifts. His own abilities could not be spared for more than an hour or so at a time and Miriam had worked at his side untiringly. Then there was Carolina . . . and Rosie. It astounded him that the two women, their love for the same man hopeless for different reasons, had been able to work side by side in such accord.

Looking into the corner, Doc saw that Drake, momentarily unattended, was unnaturally still. He moved quickly to the big man's bedside to see his chest still moved in shallow breaths although his continued deterioration was obvious. Drake had been unable to maintain any liquids and his fever still soared after seven dissipating days. He knew that no one, not even a man of Drake's powerful stature and constitution, could hold on much longer if there wasn't a change for the better soon.

A sharp cry shattered the silence of the room. Doc turned to Miriam's look of mute appeal as she took a short, jerking step back from Pete Smalley's bedside. Beside her in a moment, he realized instantly that it was too late. The fellow had breathed his agonizing last.

"Is he dead?"

Doc's response to Miriam's hoarse question was to pull the coverlet up over the fellow's wasted form. Turning abruptly, Miriam walked toward the door, her posture unnaturally rigid and her head high. She reached for the doorknob and Doc followed instinctively. Taking a moment to send for the undertaker when he stepped out onto the street, Doc followed Miriam around the corner into the alleyway beside his office. He called her name.

Miriam halted, but she did not turn around. Her face was still averted when he reached her side.

"Miriam. . . ."

"He . . . he asked me to write to his mother to tell her what happened to him. He said she's old, that he was her only child, and she hadn't wanted him to come out here. He said she'd be alone now until she died, and he couldn't forgive himself for that." Miriam looked abruptly at him. Her face was wet with tears as she whispered, "This is such a cruel land, Jerome. There's so little love and permanence. That young man is dead, and there's no one to mourn him here . . . no one at all. . . ."

"Miriam, dear. . . ."

Doc enclosed Miriam in a comforting embrace. He felt her body rock with sobs and he drew her closer. Strangely, in consoling her, he found he was also consoled in a way he had not experienced since Emma had slipped away. Too tired to fight the effect of mutual solace, Doc rubbed Miriam's back soothingly until her sobs ceased.

Silent as Miriam drew back, Doc saw her face flush as she looked down at him. Her voice was troubled when she finally spoke.

"You're so strong in the face of death, Jerome. I suppose I've disappointed you with my weakness, but I . . . I haven't had as much practice as you."

A surge of warmth rose from the deep, inner core of him as Doc whispered, "My dear Miriam, I hope you never do."

Miriam continued to hold his gaze, stripping away the last of his caustic protection until he added softly, "I've neglected sayin' this earlier simply because I haven't had the time, but I think it's appropriate now for you to know that those men inside would've fared far worse if you hadn't had a hand in their care. You're responsible for much of the progress some of them have made. As for those who've died, you're also responsible for easin' their last hours. I don't suppose a person can be asked to do more than that for another human being."

Miriam's tears were again flowing, and Doc felt his own throat dangerously tight. Swallowing, he added, "You're tired, Miriam. Why don't you go home and rest for a few hours?"

Miriam raised her chin. A familiar glint entered her eyes as she replied with a hint of her old challenge, "What? And have you rescind the only nice things you've ever said to me?" Miriam forced her chin higher. "Come, Jerome, we have work to do."

Miriam's expression was composed, her spine straight, as she walked back down the alleyway beside him moments later. Out of the corner of his eye, Doc saw her lips tremble as they reached the street. He also saw the control she exerted to collect herself as she walked toward the office. Despite his weariness, the urge to do more than soothe this amazingly strong woman was almost overpowering.

Miriam turned the knob and opened the door. Hesitating only a moment, Doc followed her inside.

"Drake, can you hear me?"

Kneeling beside his pallet, Carolina looked down into Drake's gray face. She stroked a damp lock of hair back from his forehead, then ran her fingertips down his gaunt, stubbled cheek. The heat there magnified her fear. She had spent every possible waking hour with Drake since she had been called to his bedside almost a week earlier. She had surrendered her daughter to Josie Whalen's care, knowing the kindly mother of nine would care for Suzannah as if she were her own. She had functioned without sleep and without regular meals in order to remain with him, and she had suffered every time Drake had called her name without realizing she was there. She had barely withheld tears when his body's convulsive spasms had worsened, and hating herself for her weakness, she had forced herself to greater effort. But the effect had been negligible. Drake's condition was worsening, and it terrified her.

In the dark of the night, while she had lain with her head on Drake's pillow, Carolina had become desperate to penetrate the fevered limbo where he lingered. She had talked to him, recalling the first day she had opened her eyes to see him hovering over her in the forest, when she had *recognized* him without ever having seen him before. She had relived with him the long, dark nights after that, when each sound that had echoed into the cabin had seemed to hold a new threat, when he had been her only buffer against the unknown. She had told him how she had treasured the memories he had shared with her then, when she had had no memories of her own. She had laughed aloud when she had recalled his frantic rescue of her from the "Indian" whom he discovered munching lazily on a slab of bacon in the cabin doorway as his tail leisurely flicked away flies. She had touched briefly, with a few, carefully chosen words, on their interlude as man and wife, and she had confessed that she would cherish those moments for the rest of her life. And when neither her laughter nor her tears had failed to rouse him, she had rested her head on his pillow and slept beside him, fearing each moment would be his last.

Carolina glanced up at the clock on the office wall. It confirmed what her aching breasts had already reminded her. Although she loathed to leave Drake with each moment becoming more precious than the last, it was time for Suzannah's feeding.

Drake twitched again in sleep and Carolina glanced to the nearby bed where Rosie worked silently. Drake had been right. Rosie and she had started off on the wrong foot, but their past conflict had been dispelled by their mutual concern for Drake. The path to their truce had been eased by Rosie, who deferred to her in all matters concerning Drake's care. Aware of Rosie's feelings for Drake, Carolina silently admired her for the concession. She feared she could not have done the same.

Carolina drew herself to her feet. As if on signal, Rosie looked up. By unspoken agreement, the beautiful saloon girl would assume her place at Drake's bedside until she returned, and for Rosie's unselfish devotion to Drake's welfare, Carolina was more grateful than she could ever express.

Emerging onto the street, Carolina turned toward the Whalen cabin, her brows knitting into a frown. She wished she could be as sure of her husband's state of mind as she had been of Suzannah's contentment during the past week. William had been furious when she had gone to Drake without his consent. She had seen only glimpses of him since. Each time he had appeared more disturbed than the last, but she had refused to allow his anger to affect her. Whether William *could* not or *would* not understand her reason for going to Drake, made little difference. Drake needed her.

Hurriedly washing her hands and arms in the basin Josie had provided in the yard, Carolina then dried them carefully and slipped on an apron before entering the cabin. Suzannah was restless and waiting and Carolina took her immediately from Josie's motherly arms.

Suzannah was dozing and content when Carolina again surrendered her to Josie a short time later. She was hurrying back down the hill in the direction from which she had come when the sound of William's voice brought her step to an abrupt halt.

"Carolina. . . ."

Carolina glanced toward her husband, then looked away. She was too tired and too dispirited for a confrontation. Her eyes averted, Carolina responded, "I . . . I can't talk now, William. I have to get back."

"But—"

"Please, not now."

Close to tears, Carolina burst into a run. Back on the street, she pushed open Doc's office door and paused breathlessly on the threshold as her gaze darted to the pallet in the corner where Drake lay. Her heart leaping when she saw Drake's eyes were open, Carolina rushed to his bedside, only to have elation crash to despair. His gaze unfocused, Drake mumbled deliriously as she dropped to her knees beside him.

Barely withholding tears, Carolina looked up as Rosie whispered hoarsely, "He's been callin' for you. He keeps sayin' he has somethin' to ask you."

Her heart an aching lump in her chest, Carolina whispered, "Drake, I'm here, darling." Unaware that the endearment had escaped her lips, she repeated, "I'm here. What did you want to ask me?"

Drake's gaze moved waveringly to her face. It settled there for a long, silent moment before Drake startled her by grasping her hand with surprising strength.

". . . have to know. . . ." Drake's voice failed and he tried again. "Tell me. A . . . are you happy?"

Emotion knotted Carolina's throat. Knowing she had never loved him more than she did at that moment, Carolina replied from the bottom of her heart, "When I'm with you, Drake . . . I'm happy when I'm with you."

His gaze clearing briefly, Drake gripped her hand tighter, then closed his eyes.

Still standing on the hillside, William stared down at the street where Carolina had disappeared from sight. The summer sun was unmercifully hot, so much so that he was almost disoriented as he raised his hat and wiped the perspiration from his flushed face.

The agony of long months while he had believed Carolina dead returned vividly clear, and he was almost physically sickened. He had hated himself and had wandered the territory with little regard for his own safety. As fate had allowed it, he had been spared even as much as a close encounter with hostile Indians, while others who had held their lives more precious than he, had not survived. He had wondered then at the cruelty of a fate which had kept him safe while Carolina and his unborn child had not been spared. His question had been answered when he had found Carolina again and had seen his daughter for the first time.

William's heart began a sudden erratic pounding and he cursed aloud as Drake McNeil's unsmiling image flashed before his mind. Jealousy sliced viciously at his waning composure, increasing his physical discomfort. It had been difficult accepting the reality that there was a part of Carolina's love that he could never regain. It had been even more difficult admitting that he had sacrificed that portion of her love forever the day he had ridden away from the wagon train and left her behind. Accepting his own culpability, he had managed to block images of Carolina in McNeil's arms from his mind. He had silently vowed to give Carolina the time she needed for memories of McNeil to fade into the past. He had not anticipated, however, how painful the task would be.

Jealousy swelled over William in nauseating waves. Sitting on a nearby log, he breathed deeply in an attempt to regain control, but his mind continued its vicious torment. Carolina had had no time for him in her haste to return to McNeil's bedside a few minutes earlier. Was she whispering in McNeil's ear right now, telling him she loved him? Was she promising McNeil she'd never leave him again? Which one of them would she choose if McNeil survived?

If McNeil survived. . . .

Hating himself for the hope that was growing stronger within him with each passing moment, William stood up abruptly. His head pounded and his nausea increased, but the thought persisted.

If McNeil survived. . . .

William took a few staggering steps and retched. Sinking to his knees, he retched again and again. Sitting back weakly on his heels, he wiped the perspiration from his brow. Swaying, he looked up at the merciless sun.

If McNeil survived. . . .

Shadows accented the contours of Rosie's flawless features as she drew back rigidly into the corner of Doc's office. The week-long ordeal at Drake's bedside had drained her mentally and physically, but none of the torments she had suffered in watching Drake's horrifying dance with death compared with the torment of the moment she had just witnessed.

Withholding a sob, Rosie recalled Drake's tortured rasp as

he had spoken to Carolina moments earlier.

. . . have to know. . . . Tell me. A . . . are you happy?

There had been only one woman, only one thought in Drake's mind during his brief lucid moment. Carolina.

Not realizing she was trembling, Rosie watched the thin, pale young woman bathe Drake's gaunt face. She had tried so desperately to hate Carolina Brand. She had wanted to believe the woman was not what she claimed to be. She had strained to keep her dream alive, to believe that underneath it all, Drake loved only *her,* but the truth was now too painfully clear for her to deny any longer. Drake had called for Carolina . . . only for Carolina. With each breath a torment, he had inquired for Carolina's happiness, and with his strength waning more each moment, he had taken Carolina's hand.

Rosie forced back a sob. Drake didn't love her the way she loved him. He had never loved her that way. He never would.

A sudden, choking gasp startled Rosie from her thoughts as Drake began shuddering uncontrollably. Rosie took a spontaneous step toward him, only to be thrust aside as Doc brushed past her. Hardly breathing, Rosie watched as Doc worked frantically over his patient before turning at last to Carolina with a few whispered words. Carolina's halting inquiry was answered by a slow shake of Doc's head and Carolina's anguished expression was mirrored within Rosie's heart as well.

No! Drake couldn't be dying!

"Rosie . . ." Suddenly at her side, Doc slipped his arms around her. "I can't let you stay if you lose control."

"But Drake . . ."

"Drake's gettin' the best care he can get with Carolina and you lookin' after him."

Rosie gave a sharp, hiccuping laugh. "Drake doesn't even know I'm here, Doc . . . and he doesn't care! The only person he wants is Carolina."

"Rosie, darlin' . . ." Doc's smile was sad. "I wish things could be different. It isn't easy knowin' that things'll never work out the way we want, no matter how long we waited or how hard we planned. I suppose it would've been kinder if all this had been settled sooner, but —"

"It wouldn't have made any difference, Doc. You can't stop lovin' somebody just because he doesn't love you back."

"I suppose, but—"

A frantic summons from the other side of the room halted Doc midsentence. Within moments he was working his way across the littered floor toward the frantic volunteer who had called him. One glimpse at the still form on the pallet beside the shaken woman and Rosie closed her eyes. She didn't want to watch. It hurt too much to see death all around her now that she could no longer retreat to the dream that had sustained her.

Looking up at an unexpected touch on her arm, Rosie saw Miriam standing beside her. The widow's narrow face was drawn into deep lines of sympathy as she whispered, "You're exhausted, my dear. You've been working too hard. It's time to rest."

"No . . . not yet." Glancing back at Drake's twitching form, Rosie did not question her former enemy's concern as she rasped, "I can't leave. Drake is worse."

"You needn't worry. We'll take care of him while you're gone."

"But . . . but I must *be* here."

Silent for a few moments, Miriam took Rosie's hand. The older woman's eyes misted as she whispered, "I've waited too long to say this already, but apologies are always difficult, especially for a woman who has lived her life quite rigidly, believing *her* way to be the only right way. I was wrong about that, and wrong about you. I've misjudged you, my dear. I saw you as hard, grasping, and uncaring because you had chosen a way of life of which I disapproved. But I've seen you work by the bedside of these stricken men this past week. I've seen the concern you have for their suffering and I've witnessed the true feeling you have for Drake." Miriam paused briefly, then continued more softly than before. "I've also seen what a judgmental fool I've been. I hope you'll forgive my stubborn prejudice, Rosie, although it's truly unforgivable. And I hope you'll be my friend."

Unprepared for the widow's words, Rosie could do no more than nod. At a groan from the nearby pallet, she looked

442

anxiously at Drake, only to hear Miriam whisper, "Drake is as comfortable as possible with Carolina at his bedside. As for his fate, it's in the hands of God, my dear."

At the sound of stumbling footsteps behind her, Rosie turned to the sight of a draped litter being carried toward the door. Gasping, she glanced back at Drake to see her fears mirrored in Carolina's eyes.

Staring, Carolina followed the progress of the covered litter to the door. Her hand closed around Drake's and her fear mounted when she felt no pressure in return. Feeling the bite of panic, she realized he had slipped back into the fitful semiconsciousness where he had lingered most of the week — with one significant difference: he was weaker, dangerously weaker.

Her hand trembling, Carolina reached for the glass beside the bed and raised it to Drake's mouth. He mumbled unintelligibly as she urged, "Drink, Drake. Please, darling. You must drink."

Drake's eyes flickered open, but there was no recognition in his brief, glassy stare. Pressing the glass persistently to his lips, Carolina felt a flood of relief as he finally complied. She drew it back moments later and blotted his mouth as a gruff voice called from the doorway.

"We've got another customer for you, Doc."

Carolina grimaced. The words were revoltingly familiar. She had no desire to turn to see another stricken patient arrive to take the place of the one who had just been carried out. More sickening still was the realization that the twenty-four-hour pause between new cases had not been as significant as Doc had hoped. The outbreak was not yet over.

Shuffling footsteps behind her moved to the opposite corner as the gruff voice continued, "We saw this fella on the hill above the street. He was so weak that he could hardly stand up. He made it most of the way down, but he collapsed outside the door. You should've seen everybody scatter when he hit the ground!"

Carolina frowned as she squeezed the cloth in the basin beside Drake's pallet and bathed his face. Some of the townspeople were still afraid to come close to Doc's office for fear they'd contract the sickness, even though Doc had reassured them they wouldn't. They called the office the pesthouse. *William* had called it the pesthouse, and he had warned her that he'd never forgive her if she brought the sickness back to Suzannah.

"Carolina . . ."

Carolina looked up at the sound of Doc's voice beside her. His strange expression sent an apprehensive chill up her spine the moment before he placed his hand on her shoulder and whispered, "My dear, the new patient —"

A convulsive gasp escaped Carolina's throat as she glanced toward the opposite corner where the new patient was being settled on a pallet.

"William . . . !"

Rosie assumed her place at Drake's side as Carolina made her way across the floor. Her throat tightening, Carolina kneeled beside William and looked down into his flushed face.

"Y . . . you didn't tell me you were ill, William."

"I'm not." Pausing when another cramp doubled him up, William forced himself to continue, "I . . . I'm a little under the weather, that's all. I didn't drink enough water from that stream to get the sickness."

"You drank from that stream?" Carolina felt the rise of panic. "Oh, William. . . ."

"I'll be all right in a day or so. That isn't why I came here. I had to talk to you."

Moving Carolina aside, Doc examined William briefly. His expression darkened. "Whether you want to admit it or not, you're a sick man, Markham. Your temperature's up and you're weak as a kitten. I hate to tell you, but the worst is yet to come. I suggest you lie back and take it easy. We'll do all we can for you."

"I want to talk to Carolina."

"Talking isn't going to do you as much good as resting, but I suppose I can't stop you." Doc looked up at Carolina. "Make sure he behaves himself. Call me if you need me."

444

Hardly conscious of Doc's departure, Carolina stared down at William. The signs of his illness were glaringly obvious — the telltale flush, the chills he couldn't quite hide, the extreme tenderness in his abdomen when Doc had touched him. Carolina briefly closed her eyes. If she hadn't avoided William this past week, she would've seen the sickness coming. She could've helped him before he became so ill that he collapsed. If . . . if . . .

"Carolina . . . please, don't worry."

Her guilt overwhelming, Carolina whispered, "I'm so sorry, William."

"I'm the one who should apologize." William spoke with increasing difficulty. "I . . . I was wrong when I tried to stop you from coming here to help McNeil. You owe him that much, and I suppose in a way, I do, too. I . . . I was jealous and I acted like a fool. It seems that I'm always asking your forgiveness."

"I don't want to talk about forgiveness, William. Let's not talk about anything but getting well now."

Perspiration beaded William's forehead as he raised his head weakly to give the room a cursory sweep. "Where's McNeil? How is he?"

Carolina's heart jumped to a ragged beating as she motioned toward the still figure in the opposite corner. "Drake's over there. He . . . he's not doing well. He was badly dehydrated by the time he was brought in. He can't seem to make it back. . . ." Taking a deep breath, Carolina forced herself to continue, "But Doc and I won't let that happen to you."

"Carolina, there are some things I must say to you *now.*" Clutching her hand, William whispered, "For the longest time while I thought you were dead, I wondered why I had escaped unscathed. I finally realized that I was saved so I could take care of you and Suzannah . . . so I could protect you and love you both for the rest of our lives." William's grip tightened despite the tremor that shook him. He drew her closer, his quaking voice earnest. "Wh . . . when this is all over, I want to take you back East." Overriding her spontaneous protest, William continued, "No, listen, please. I . . . I started doing a lot of thinking after I held Suzannah in my

445

arms for the first time. Without realizing it, I began planning the future—all the things I wanted Suzannah to have and all the things I wanted to do for her. I realized then that my parents must have experienced the same feelings . . . that same swelling of love and pride, and that same determination that their child would have the best they could offer. My parents carried that determination too far, but I think they've seen the error of their ways. At least, that's what their letter said. I . . . I want to give them another chance, darling. Somehow that's become very important to me. I want them to see Suzannah . . . to see our beautiful daughter. I know they'll love her . . . and they'll love you for giving her to me. She's their only grandchild."

A tremor more violent than the last shook William, and Carolina glanced up nervously toward Doc. She squeezed William's hand. "Let's not talk about this now, William."

"Will you think about it?" William's fevered gaze was intent. "Promise me you'll think about it."

"All right, I promise."

Carolina attempted to motion Doc toward them, only to have William grasp her hand more tightly than before. His voice was a ragged whisper.

"I love you, Carolina."

A new trembling beset Carolina as William continued without waiting for a reply, "You don't have to say anything. I . . . I love you enough for both of us right now. We'll build on that love. I promise you that, and so much more, darling."

William shuddered again and Carolina motioned Doc toward them. Her heart wrenching, she glanced toward Drake's pallet as Doc assumed her place at William's side. Her heart torn in two, Carolina closed her eyes.

Twenty-eight

Standing a few steps back, Doc wearily assessed the pallets stretched across his office floor in uneven rows. The heat of summer, intensified by the close quarters, increased the discomfort of his patients who lay in varying degrees of devastating illness. He had lost three in the past two days, and he knew he would lose more. Contrary to Miriam's belief, he had not yet become hardened against death. The calluses on the outside were carefully fixed, but on the inside his ineffectiveness against this disease that stole lives out from under him, rubbed him raw. Strangely, his only comfort in the ongoing ordeal was Miriam's steadfast presence beside him. Somewhere in the back of his mind a warning bell rang at that acknowledgment, but he was too tired to heed it.

Looking down at the pallet a few feet away, Doc heaved a silent sigh of relief. Markham was sleeping peacefully at last. As he had predicted, the young man's discomfort had worsened in the two days since he had been stricken. Fever, chills, violent cramping, and bodily purging had taken its toll. His youthful face was drawn and his eyes were darkly ringed, but his condition had stabilized.

As Doc watched, Carolina drew herself slowly to her feet from her husband's bedside. She swayed as she paused to look down at him, but Doc withheld useless protest as she turned and made her way across the floor toward Drake's pallet in the opposite corner of the room. She had crisscrossed the room in the same manner without sleep for the past forty-eight hours, and he knew she would continue to do so until she was no longer able to put one foot in front of the other.

Rising from Drake's bedside as Carolina approached, Rosie waited only until Carolina assumed her place there before walking wearily toward the door. Exhaustion was evident in Rosie's step and in her stance. He was grateful that he had at least been successful in convincing Rosie to take time out to eat, but he knew he had achieved that minor victory only because he had insisted she would need her strength to help Drake through recuperation.

Doc gave a short, hard laugh. It had been more difficult than he had believed to speak of Drake's recuperation when the hard truth was that he had little hope of Drake's lasting through the week.

Rosie's step faltered and Miriam appeared unexpectedly at her side. He noted unconsciously as Miriam took Rosie's arm that a single strand of hair had escaped the widow's tightly bound bun and that her spotless apron was no longer spotless. But the widow's posture was erect and her expression composed, and in her small eyes he saw the light of compassion as she patted Rosie's hand.

Miriam's unanticipated gesture raised an unwelcome thickness in Doc's throat. The subtle change on the outside of Miriam was indicative of the greater change that had taken place on the inside.

Doc gave a short, hard sniff. Damned if the stiff old biddy hadn't gone human on him. . . .

Movement at the corner of his eye turned Doc in time to see Carolina swaying weakly. Beside her in a moment, he grasped her arm, steadying her as he growled into her pale face, "You won't do anyone any good if you allow yourself to get sick, Carolina! You can't continue to push yourself this way! Splitting your days and nights between Drake and your husband and sandwiching moments in between for Suzannah. . . ." He shook his head with disapproval. "You have to sleep sometime!"

Carolina nodded without comment. She kneeled beside Drake the moment Doc released her arm. She stroked Drake's cheek, then turned unexpectedly to Doc as he crouched beside her. Her pale eyes pinned him.

"Drake looks better, doesn't he, Doc? He . . . he's quieter. He's cooler, too."

Unwilling to perpetuate a useless lie, Doc strengthened himself for the only response he could make.

"He's not doin' well."

"No, he's better."

"You're deceivin' yourself, Carolina." Doc paused. His courage momentarily deserting him, he took a steadying breath. "Drake won't be gettin' better, my dear."

Carolina went suddenly still. "Wh . . . what do you mean?"

"You know what I mean."

"No, Drake's going to be all right! He's strong!"

"He's weak and gettin' weaker. He hasn't been lucid for two days. He's stopped takin' fluids. . . ."

"He'll take water for me! Look!" Grasping the glass on a nearby stand, Carolina held it to Drake's lips and whispered pleadingly into his ear, "Drake, darling, drink for me. Please drink . . ."

Drake's lips moved spasmodically and Carolina forced a few drops of the tepid water between them. She watched as he swallowed, then turned victoriously back to Doc.

"See! I told you he'd drink. Drake's going to be all right."

Recognizing the futility of protest, Doc smiled sadly. "Yes, of course."

"I'll stay with him while William's sleeping and I'll talk to him. Then he'll drink some more." Carolina's eyes were bright with frenzied insistence. "I'll try to get him to eat something, too."

Doc drew himself to his feet and Carolina turned immediately back to Drake. Pausing, Doc observed her desperate attempt to call back Drake's life as it gradually slipped away and he was struck with a sense of helplessness that was so keen it was almost pain.

Raising a hand to his forehead, Doc rubbed at the persistent ache there. He was getting too old to watch the cruel machinations of fate . . . too old to see young people loving with all their hearts, and suffering because of their love. Hell, where was the sense or reason to it all? What lesson could a man possibly learn from a horrendously mixed-up affair that seemed destined for a dark ending except . . . except that he must grasp at happiness when he has the chance . . . except that he must take the opportunity for love before it's whisked away and he finds himself a lonely old man questioning the reason for life . . . except that he must accept—

"Doc! Come quickly!"

The panic on Mary McCullough's face moved Doc abruptly toward her and the patient she attended. One look at the young prospector's still form and he knew it was too late.

Taking a moment to draw the coverlet up over the fellow's wasted body, Doc walked wearily to the window and stared out onto the street.

Doc was wrong this time. He was wrong!

Silent protest reverberated in Carolina's mind as she moved closer to Drake. She could see the perspiration beading on his forehead and could feel his fragile breath against her cheek. Drake would get better. She knew he would. She was *determined* he would.

Rinsing out the cloth beside the bed, Carolina bathed Drake's face and smoothed back his dark hair. In a ritual she had continued through the long week, she bared his chest to the waist and lay cooling cloths against his heated skin. She bathed his neck, his powerful arms, her agitation mounting as he remained lax and lifeless, without response despite her continued efforts.

A slow panic invading her senses when the heat in Drake's body continued to burn, Carolina pulled the coverlet up over his chest with trembling hands. Moving closer, she stretched herself out beside him. She pressed her lips against his ear as she had so many times while lying in his arms. She clutched him close, her voice trembling as she spoke to him from the heart.

"Please don't slip away from me, Drake. I can face almost anything except that. I can't lose you that way. I have to know you're well and happy so I can remember how beautiful it was to be in your arms and know you're remembering the same thing. Somewhere in the back of my mind I have to keep the hope alive that we'll be together again someday . . . somehow. Oh, Drake, I have to be able to believe . . ."

Suddenly sobbing, Carolina pressed her cheek to Drake's. The coarse stubble there scratched her face, but she felt only pleasure in its contact as she whispered more urgently than before, "Please don't leave me . . . not this way. Please, Drake, I need you. . . ."

But there was no response . . . not a ripple of expression . . . not a whisper of sound . . . and Carolina's sobs began anew. She was still clutching Drake desperately close when Miriam's sympathetic voice filtered through her distraction.

"Carolina. Come, dear, you're exhausted. You mustn't waste the energy you have left on tears. Carolina, listen to me." Drawing her back gently, Miriam continued, "It's time for Suzannah's feeding, dear."

Reluctant to separate from Drake's fevered warmth, Carolina turned to the widow. "I can't go. Not now. Drake is—"

"Drake is sleeping. I'll stay with him while you're gone." At her hesitant expression, Miriam added earnestly, "I give you my word I won't budge from his side, but you must go now."

Carolina hesitated a moment longer. She glanced at William's pallet to see him sleeping peacefully, then looked down again at Drake. She stroked his beard-roughened cheek, the smooth line of his brow, and touched her fingertips to his lips. He did not react at all, and her heart sank. She loathed to leave him, but Miriam was right. The fullness in her breasts told her Suzannah was waiting.

Drawing herself slowly to her feet, Carolina took Miriam's hand. "You won't leave him. . . ."

"My dear . . ." The widow's small eyes filled. "I'll watch over him with my life."

Drawing the office door closed behind her moments later, Carolina started up the street. Unaware of the hot summer sun on her head, Carolina was conscious only of the steps that took her farther and farther from Drake's side. Her pace rapidly increasing until it was just short of a run, Carolina made her way up the hillside. Hearing Suzannah crying as she came within sight of the cabin, she ran faster. She stopped only to bathe her face and arms and to don the clean apron that was waiting before entering the cabin and taking her child into her arms.

Settled in a soft chair, Carolina closed her eyes as Suzannah nursed hungrily. Fragmented images swelled over her, inundating her with memories. She recalled the first, long trip to Deadwood from Drake's wilderness cabin and the uncertainties that ceased the moment Drake wrapped his arms around her. She remembered the misunderstandings that followed, and she remembered that even after Drake had gone back to the cabin alone, she had not truly doubted that he would come back for her. He did come back, just as she had known he would. He told her he loved her, and she had vowed to be his wife forever.

Carolina bit back a sob. Forever had been so painfully short.

William's image supplanted Drake's in her mind and Carolina was overwhelmed with guilt. She had vowed to love William all her life as well. Strangely, in her heart she knew she had not truly broken that vow for she still loved him in so many ways. She also knew that had William not deserted her in that one moment of weakness, had his betrayal and the Indian attack not wiped his memory from her mind, she would never have allowed Drake to enter her heart. But, tragically, what might have been was not, and what was, was almost too difficult to be endured.

Drake was dying. . . .

A sob bringing her back to the present with a start, Carolina realized that she had fallen asleep with Suzannah at her breast. Panicked, she looked up at Josie who stood silently nearby.

"D . . . did I sleep long?"

"Not long, dear." Josie's full face creased into warmly understanding lines. "Not more than an hour. I didn't want to wake you. You looked so exhausted."

"I . . . I must go." Her sense of panic growing, Carolina carefully separated her sleeping child from her breast and buttoned her dress. She was trembling when she lay the child down in her cradle and turned back to Josie. "Thank you for everything, Josie. I can never repay you for what you've done."

Not waiting for the older woman's reply, Carolina stripped off the apron and within moments was racing back down the hill. Taking a moment to regain her breath as she reached the street, Carolina smoothed back her hair and wiped the perspiration from her brow. Somehow unable to restrain her anxiety, she was trembling wildly when she turned the knob and pushed open the door of Doc's office.

A profound silence greeted her as Doc met her at the door and took her arm. He was clearly disturbed, as was Miriam who appeared suddenly beside him, blocking her view into the room. Fear froze Carolina into speechlessness as Doc hesitated, obviously struggling for the right words. When he spoke, his words were devastatingly direct.

"Carolina, my dear, I don't know how to tell you this except to say that the disease proved too much for him. His heart just stopped beating. I did my best, but it was too late."

"His heart stopped beating . . . ?"

"He died peacefully, without pain."

"He's dead . . . ?"

"Yes."

He's dead. . . . He's dead. . . .

The words reverberated in Carolina's ears, whirling into a swirling vortex as she looked at the corner of the room and saw the empty pallet there. A shocked cry of protest leapt to her lips but she did not hear the sound as the maelstrom swelled, drawing her in to consume the light and leave her in merciful darkness.

Twenty-nine

Doc gazed out through the window of his office onto Dead-wood's main street. A heavy, gray sky had replaced the relent-less sun and heat of the previous few weeks. The air had turned chill and a brisk wind whipped at passersby, promising more of the same heavy downpours that had turned the town into a quagmire of relentless mud.

Doc knew that some would say the weather reflected the general mood of the town, and he supposed that was partially true. Deadwood had sobered some under the pall of almost daily funeral processions to the cemetery on the hill, but the bastard town was resilient. It's sorrow was short-lived, with nightfall resuscitating its lagging spirits until the next day and the next procession lowered another temporary veil of gloom.

Drawing back from the window, Doc turned to the room be-hind him and the waning number under his care. More than three weeks had passed since the first patient had been deliv-ered to his office. In that length of time, the most grievously affected had succumbed to the disease, and he was all but cer-tain that those who remained would survive. No new cases had been reported in the past few days, signaling an end to the deadly affair . . . and not a moment too soon.

Doc allowed himself to count his remaining patients. Fif-teen in all, most in the latter stages of the dread disease, lay on the same pallets they had occupied for the duration of their confinement. The rows had thinned, but the dedication of his faithful volunteers had not. Most stalwart of all was Miriam, constant by his side, relieving him of bothersome details as well as the more odious work others avoided, so he might spend his time where it was most desperately needed. Rosie, loyal to the cause, had continued her abandonment of the barroom for the sickroom. Then there was Carolina. . . . Working in almost total silence since the day she had returned from the cemetery on the hill, she had not left the room except to tend to her child. Devoting herself entirely to the welfare of her remaining patient, she had hovered over him, lavishing him with care she could no longer give the one who had slipped from her grasp. But she had not grieved. It worried him that he had not seen her shed a tear. It wasn't natural, and he feared the day the tears would finally come.

Doc turned at a groan from a nearby pallet. His patients still suffered from the painful illness, but he knew the suffering was not confined to those afflicted with the disease. His gaze moving automatically to Carolina's sober face, Doc nodded. No, not only the afflicted suffered. . . .

On her knees, Carolina reached for the washbasin on a nearby stand. She squeezed out the cloth and rubbed the soap briskly to work up a lather. Feeling the weight of her patient's gaze, she looked up at the pallet beside her.

Alert green eyes met hers. . . .

Her hands freezing at their task, Carolina felt her throat thicken. Drake's eyes were clear and his gaze was steady. His color had almost returned to normal and the shadows under his eyes had lightened. He was terribly thin, but his temperature had been normal for almost a week. He was strong enough to insist upon being propped up in a seated position for a good portion of the day as he was now. He was on his way to complete recovery.

Carolina nodded unconsciously. Yes, there was no doubt that Drake would soon be well.

"Are you all right, Carolina?"

Carolina attempted a smile. "I should be asking you that question. I'm not the one who was sick, you know."

Drake did not smile in return. Instead, he took her hand and repeated more softly than before, "Are you all right, darlin'?"

Avoiding response, Carolina withdrew her hand and squeezed out the soapy cloth with a soft command.

"Close your eyes."

Waiting the moment until Drake complied, Carolina washed his face gently. The cloth dragged across his stubbled cheeks as she rinsed his face clean, then patted it dry almost as she would a child's. Not bothering to speak, she again moistened the cloth and continued her ministrations, bathing Drake's neck, then spreading the comforting warmth across his broad shoulders and chest. She washed his arms and hands, meticulously scrubbing between each long, lax finger. She paused when she was through, realizing that the lack of privacy prevented the more thorough ministrations which she had performed without hesitation while Drake was so ill.

Carolina sat back on her heels. Her lips trembled as she attempted to force another smile. "Now I'm going to shave you."

Silent, Drake nodded as she drew herself to her feet and walked toward the bucket a few feet away. She felt his gaze follow her as she dumped the water and refilled the basin from a nearby kettle. Back beside him a moment later, she worked up a lather with the shaving brush Doc had provided and applied the soap to Drake's face. His gaze intent, Drake did not speak as she glided the razor against his skin with more expertise than she realized she possessed. He remained quiet as she leaned closer to wipe his face clean of the remaining soap. He was so silent that she was unprepared when he grasped her wrist with surprising strength, holding her immobile as he forced her to meet his gaze.

"I love you, Carolina."

Drake's rasping words twisted a knife of pain in her heart. Carolina closed her eyes briefly as he continued more softly than before, "I'm sorry about Markham. I know his death was a shock. Doc said he still doesn't understand how it happened."

"H . . . his heart stopped."

"I know."

"It shouldn't have happened that way." Carolina could not seem to halt the flow of words. "He shouldn't have died. He was too young. He had so many plans."

"Things don't always work out the way we think they should."

"I know."

Drake's grip tightened almost to the point of pain. "Listen to me, Carolina. Markham loved you, and he loved Suzannah, but I love both of you, too."

"I know." A sob rising inside her, Carolina repeated, "I know."

"Carolina . . ."

"Please let me go, Drake."

Drake's gaze held hers. Carolina remembered when there had been only coldness in those eyes that now shone with love. She had once dreamed of seeing that same emotion glowing there, but that was before.

Carolina pleaded softly, "Please. . . ."

Drake released her and Carolina sat back on her heels. Sober, her voice solemn, she whispered, "I know you're sorry about William. I'm sorry, too. I'm glad you're getting well. I . . . I don't think I could've stood it if you . . ." Carolina paused, biting her lips against the words she could not make herself say. She continued a moment later, "I know you love me, Drake. I love you, too."

Carolina reached out unexpectedly and touched his heavy, unruly hair. "Y . . . you need a haircut. I suppose that'll have to come next . . . but not right now. Now I have to go."

Waiting a moment longer, Carolina studied the gaunt lines of Drake's face. As pale and drawn as he was, she could still see the power behind his temporary weakness. He was still Drake, and he would survive. That thought somehow stabilized her as she stood up and walked toward the door.

"Drake . . . ?"

Realizing he had been staring at the doorway through which Carolina had disappeared only moments earlier, Drake turned at the sound of Rosie's voice. It had not taken him long to discern that an unspoken agreement between the two women had guaranteed him constant care while he had been too sick to realize their devotion. He was grateful to Rosie, but his gratitude could not overcome his strange distraction.

"Are you feelin' all right, Drake?" Rosie's beautiful face was thinner and marked with concern. "You're not feelin' sick again, are you?"

"No, I'm fine."

Relief registered in Rosie's eyes. "That's good. Doc says you're goin' to be fine. He says you've got the constitution of an ox."

"That so?" Drake almost smiled. "Tell Doc I said thanks for the compliment. But you're lookin' thinner than you should be. Maybe it's time for you to start takin' some time for yourself instead of spendin' every minute watchin' over me."

"I'm all right."

"It's my bet there's somebody who's been missin' your company these past few weeks."

Rosie's smile grew forced. "Well, you know what they say. 'Absence makes the heart grow fonder' . . . or somethin'."

"Maybe that's what some say . . ." Drake paused, adding, "but what I'm sayin' is thanks, Rosie, for all you've done."

Rosie blinked and swallowed hard. "You don't have to thank me."

"I know I don't. You're a special person, Rosie. I hope that gambler of yours appreciates what he's got."

Rosie's smile twitched as she drew herself to her feet and took a step backward. "Yeah, Tag's a smart fella." She swallowed again. "Well, there're other fellas in this room that need me more than you do right now. Just call if you want somethin' and I'll come runnin'." She added softly, "Anytime. . . ."

Drake mumbled his appreciation, but his gaze was already drifting back to the doorway where he had last seen Carolina. His distraction becoming discomfort, he shifted uneasily. He could not seem to forget Carolina's peculiar expression the moment before she had turned away. It worried him, weighing heavily on his mind.

His agitation growing more intense with each passing moment, Drake cursed aloud. Somehow he could not shake the feeling that Carolina had just said goodbye.

* * *

458

A leaden sky hung threateningly over the denuded hillside as Carolina braced herself against the biting wind. The muddy ground tugged at the hem of her gown as she walked between the uneven rows of grave markers and finally dropped to her knees beside the one she sought. Tears blurred her vision as she stared at the roughly carved name.

Bittersweet memories swept over her. She remembered the first time William had held her in his arms. She recalled the tremor in his voice, the promise in his eyes, the taste of his lips. She remembered that he had trembled as much as she when their eager flesh had met, and that she had loved him for loving her.

The wind whipped harder, flaying her with loosened strands of pale hair. Covering her face with her hands, Carolina sobbed. Her memories of William were so keen at that moment that they were almost debilitating. But in her confusion, she could not recall the most crucial thing of all—that exact moment when everything had changed—that exact moment when the beginning had become the beginning of the end.

Black, ominous clouds moved rapidly above her, releasing their first icy drops of rain, but Carolina was oblivious to the impending storm. Life had turned itself around so many times that the whirlwind had left her strangely dazed and bereft. Another blast of chilling wind abraded her and Carolina clutched herself tightly. She was cold. . . .

"Carolina. . . ."

Her head snapping up at the sound of the familiar voice, Carolina gasped with disbelief to see Drake walking unsteadily toward her. At his side in a moment, she grasped his arm.

"Drake! What are you doing here?"

"I had to see you." His expression grim, Drake shook off her grasp to take her firmly by the shoulders. "Tell me . . . tell me you weren't going to leave me."

"You have to get back to bed, Drake! You're not well!"

Drake shook her hard. "Tell me!"

Tears suddenly flowing freely, Carolina rasped, "I can't tell you that, Drake, don't you see? William's dead!"

A slow rage rose in Drake's eyes. "William's dead, but you have to go on. *We* must go on!"

"No, I couldn't! I can never forgive myself for what I did."

"What you did?"

"William came to this wilderness for me, and this wilderness took his life, b . . . but I wasn't even thinking about him when he died. I didn't even bother to check his condition before I left Doc's office that day. I was too busy thinking about you . . . worrying about you. William was my husband! He was the father of my child! He gave up a brilliant future for someone who had no future of her own! He made a mistake . . . a bad mistake that he regretted with all his heart when he left me alone on that wagon train . . . but I had vowed him my fidelity. I owed him forgiveness. I owed him another chance."

"Carolina, he's dead."

"No."

"He's dead."

"No, I won't let him die! I won't let him slip away so easily . . . as if he had never lived . . . as if his life had no meaning at all! I made him a promise, and I'm going to keep it."

"A promise?" Drake swayed, his color paling. "What kind of a promise?"

"Drake, please. You have to go back to Doc's office before the rain starts. You're still weak."

"Tell me about your promise!"

"All right! William wanted to take Suzannah and me back East."

"No. . . ."

"He said he wanted to give his parents another chance. He said he wanted them to see their only grandchild."

"No. . . ."

"I have to do it, don't you see? I have to let his parents come to know Suzannah, to see her grow so they can see a part of their son lives on. I have to do that for them and for William . . . and for myself. If I don't, it'll be as if William never really existed at all!"

"No! I won't let you go back."

The falling raindrops thickened, and Carolina gasped at their chilling touch. Drake's pallor deepened. He staggered and her anxiety surged to fear. Suddenly as furious with Drake as she was with fate's cruel betrayals, Carolina rasped, "You

460

say you love me, but you don't love me at all, damn you!"

"What are you talkin' about?"

"Look at you! You're still sick but you refuse to listen. You have to get out of the rain or you could have a relapse. You could die! Then it would be my fault . . . just like William's death was my fault! If you loved me, you wouldn't do this to me." With a heartfelt sob, Carolina cried, "If you loved me you would let me go!"

The force of the wind rocked them as Carolina looked up into Drake's tormented expression. Her heart aching, she saw his eyes grow gradually colder until his hands dropped limply back to his sides.

"All right, you win."

Turning, Drake started unsteadily back in the direction he had come. Carolina watched his progress back down the hill for long seconds before catching up to him and slipping her arm around his waist as he walked. She supported him, hating herself and hating him for the victory she had won.

The downpour had begun in earnest as they reached Doc's office doorway at last. Pausing there, drenched to the skin, Carolina looked up into Drake's frozen expression. Wishing she could change this moment of parting but aware that she could not, she pushed the door open. She surrendered Drake to the frenzy of welcoming arms, angry reproach, and frantic care awaiting him, then turned around and drew the door closed behind her. She did not look back.

Displacing the violent storms of the past week, summer had returned with a vengeance. The endless stretch of blue above Carolina's head provided little respite from the brilliant morning sun that baked Deadwood's deeply rutted main street as the wagon train prepared to depart. Silent and composed, her few possessions packed in the carpetbag at her feet as Miriam stood beside her holding Suzannah, Carolina watched the familiar ritual of wagon positioning that backed up traffic the length of the street. The sounds of protesting cattle, cracking whips, and shouted commands grew to a din as the familiar wagon master walked to her side.

"It's time to leave, ma'am." Jim Thompson's face creased in a kindly smile. "Do you think we'll be makin' it to the end of the line together, this time?"

Carolina attempted a smile in return. The veteran wagon master had not forgotten the last time she had left Deadwood with his train. Nor had he forgotten the difficulty involved in returning her to Deadwood the following day.

"Yes, I think we will."

The moment of departure at hand, Carolina turned toward Miriam. Finding words difficult, she began hesitantly.

"I . . . I don't know how to thank you for all you've done, Miriam. You're one of the most generous women I've ever known. I'll never forget your kindness or your friendship."

"Generosity is easy when it has so many rewards." Miriam blinked back tears. "My dear, I hope you'll be happy with the decision you've made. I'll be depending upon you to write."

"I will."

"Soon."

"As soon as I can."

Not wishing to lengthen the difficult goodbye, Carolina accepted the hand Thompson extended and climbed up into the wagon. She settled back as his rolling call jerked the train into motion, unable to restrain a last glance toward Doc's office as the wagon moved slowly forward. She had not seen Drake since the day she had delivered him to Doc's door. She hoped desperately that he would be able to forgive her for what she felt she had to do, for she knew she would never be able to forgive herself.

Her hand on Suzannah's basket, Carolina strained her eyes through the grainy mist of the trail as the wagons rattled onward and Deadwood slipped out of sight. Allowing a sense of finality that she had kept at bay to settle in her mind, Carolina slowly closed her eyes.

Thirty

Three days on the trail were behind them as Jim Thompson signaled the wagons to halt with a rumbling shout. The sun was setting and his throat was parched from the ever-present dust as he guided his mount through the train. Issuing orders that had become second nature after eight years of wilderness crossings, he watched the careful circling of the wagons and nodded as guards assumed their positions. There had been no sign of Indians, but a second sense developed over the years somehow bedeviled him, and he was a careful man.

Thompson squinted in silent appraisal of the activity around him. It would soon be dark. They had pushed hard that day. Both men and beasts were tired. They had earned their rest.

Turning, the veteran wagon master observed the weariness with which his sole female passenger stepped down to the ground and began her nightly chores. He knew that despite her delicate stature and the willingness of his men to help her, she would ask no favors. He admired her for her independence, fortitude, and determination . . . but he wished she would smile.

Dismounting beside his wagon's water barrel, Thompson lifted the lid and dipped his cup. He drank long and deep, exhaling with satisfaction and wiping his full mustache with the back of his hand when he was done. His gaze drifted slowly back to follow Carolina Brand's slender, erect figure. Somehow saddened, he covered the barrel and returned to his work.

Darkness had fallen and the camp prepared to retire. The wagon train's nightly ritual had not been difficult for Carolina to master. The staples of the trail suited her well enough and she accepted the limited fare without a second thought, but she was restless.

Glancing across her fire, she saw Suzannah's daily linens, freshly washed, were drying well. She knew they would be ready for use again by morning when she would fold them and store them before another day of travel began.

Suzannah whimpered, and Carolina stood up and walked quickly back to the wagon. She lifted her child from her basket and looked down into the infant's perfect face, unable to smile despite the pleasure afforded. Aching inside with a silent conflict, she returned to the fire and put the babe to her breast. But her torment lingered. Strangely, the serenity with which she had begun her journey had deteriorated with each passing mile and the conflict within her had grown.

William . . . William. . . . She had been so fortunate to be loved by him. He had taken her away from a subservient existence where the demands of survival had subdued her dreams. He had freed her mind from the agitation of necessity, and in doing so, had opened up a new world to her. But he had paid an exorbitant price for the love he had given her. He had faltered under the pressures incurred, and he had erred. She had only now begun to realize that even in erring, he had forced her to grow.

Raising her head, Carolina stared into the darkness beyond the perimeter of her fire's light. In her mind's eye, she saw Drake's image there, and her throat tightened. The difficulty was that in growing, she had also learned what it was to *truly* love.

Oh, William. . . .

Her husband's name a sad lament in her mind that would not cease, Carolina closed her eyes. Why did he have to die? He was too young, and guilt was so difficult to bear.

The lights of Deadwood flickered to life as Doc stood at his office window. He ran his palm against his freshly-shaved chin, his sheer self-indulgence of the past hour amazing him. A hot bath at the bathhouse . . . a complete change of clothes . . . a haircut and a shave . . . and to top it off, the purchase of a new hat.

Well, he had earned some self-indulgence, hadn't he? It had been a damned long, hard pull until the last of his patients had walked out of his office under his own power that morning. It had taken him the rest of the day to clean the place up and he had done that chore with more pleasure than he had thought possible.

The epidemic had taken many lives, but, strangely, his stature in town had grown. Whether he liked it or not, he was now *respected* and *respectable* because of a dedication to his patients that many did not think he could muster, and because his long abstinence from the delights of establishments like the Nugget had seemed to shed new light on his character.

Doc's hairy brows knit into a frown. Despite that thinking, he had been certain the Nugget would be the first place he would choose to go when the epidemic was officially over. Instead, he had shocked even himself by choosing the *bathhouse* instead.

A shiver ran down Doc's spine. The effect of Miriam's pristine presence beside him all those long weeks was downright chilling.

An inexplicable knot tightened in Doc's stomach at the thought of Miriam. He had been curiously saddened when his last patient had been dismissed and Miriam had walked slowly back toward her cabin. He had experienced a sense of loss that was so keen that he had felt momentarily weak. Now clean, shaved, and more respectable than he had been in the past fifteen years, he was strangely empty.

The Nugget? No, he didn't want to go there. Rosie didn't spend much time there anymore, and the bottle had somehow lost its luster.

Doc was incredulous at that last thought, but so much had changed since that first patient had been carried into his office weeks earlier. His sense of the delicacy and value of human life had been renewed on a daily basis in the saddest of ways. He remembered the day he had stood looking at his patients, knowing many would not survive, and wondering at the cruel twists of life and love. He recalled questioning what a man could possibly learn from the horrendously mixed-up affairs under way, all of which seemed destined for dark endings. He had drawn the only conclusion possible, that a man must grasp at happiness when he had the chance, and that he must take the opportunity for love before it was whisked away and he found himself old and alone, questioning the reason for life. An emergency had aborted his thinking at that point, but he knew now that the most important part of that conclusion had gone unacknowledged — that man must accept change, however difficult it might be, simply because he had no choice, and he must also hope that if a second chance was served up to him, he'd be courageous enough to accept it.

Doc's brief sense of well-being slowly faded. He had spent years hiding behind old griefs and disillusionments. Would he spend the rest of his life doing more of the same . . . or was he man enough to take that second chance?

. Doc swallowed awkwardly. A soothing glass of red-eye gained appeal as he considered that difficult question. The thought entered the back of his mind that a short trip to the Nugget might not be so bad an idea. It just might clear his head, and if Rosie was there, he might —

The thud of running feet outside his door snapped Doc's mind from his disturbing meditation the moment before Bobbie Whalen thrust it open with a bang. The boy was breathless, his eyes wide as saucers as he gasped, "You gotta come, Doc! It's Mrs. Higgins! She called me to her door and told me to get you right away! She looked real funny, Doc. Somethin's wrong with her. You gotta hurry!"

Grabbing his bag, his heart thudding like a drum, Doc was out on the street in a minute. An early evening crowd jammed the boardwalk, but he pushed his way through, cursing his thoughtlessness in allowing Miriam to assume so heavy a load in the sickroom. She had slept little, eaten less, and worked as hard as he with never a word of complaint. She was only a woman, after all — and not a *young* woman, at that! If anything happened to her . . .

Night was again falling as Carolina's wagon plodded steadily onward, but she had little thought for the rigors of daily existence on the trail that had forced their train into extended hours of travel. Sleeping and eating little since the inception of their journey almost a week earlier, she had been unable to escape the past as memories of William and Drake vied, growing ever stronger.

I . . . I want to give my parents another chance, darling. Somehow, that's become very important to me. I want them to see Suzannah . . . to see our beautiful daughter. She's their only grandchild. Will you promise me you'll think about it? Promise me. . . .

All right, I promise. . . .

The torment continued.

I'm sorry about Markham, Carolina. Markham loved you and he loved Suzannah, but I love both of you, too. . . .

The recollections were so vivid that Carolina shuddered.

"Ma'am, are you all right back there? We'll be stoppin' for the night soon."

Carolina turned at the sound of her driver's voice. The fellow's sunburned face was creased into genuine lines of concern. Her regret sincere for the worry she caused him, Carolina forced a smile.

"I'm fine. I was just . . . dozing, that's all."

"Well . . ." The quiet fellow appeared unconvinced. "If you need anythin', just let me know."

"Thank you."

Carolina turned back to the road behind them. She knew she was turning back to the past as well and the torment which abounded.

Still running, Doc glanced behind him as Miriam's cabin came into view. He had lost Bobbie Whalen somewhere along the street, but he spared the boy little thought. The widow's cabin was dimly lit and he knew his fears were not unfounded. The only reason Miriam would not have lamps burning brightly as darkness fell would be if she were too weak to light them.

Pausing only long enough to catch his breath as he reached Miriam's door, Doc thrust it open. Two steps inside, he stopped cold. His mouth fell agape.

"M . . . Miriam?"

"Yes, it's Miriam. Come in, Jerome."

Doc watched with an eerie fascination as Miriam advanced slowly toward him. Her pink satin wrapper swished gently against her ankles as she paused to push the door closed behind him. The semilight imparted a strange allure as she smiled and tossed back her long, unbound hair in a way that was almost maidenly.

Doc swallowed hard. "B . . . Bobbie said you sent for me. He said that you said you were sick."

"That's not exactly right." Miriam's normally nasal twang appeared to have gone the way of her widow's weeds and her straitlaced manner. In its place was a husky whisper that matched the clinging wrapper and her seductive gaze as she continued, "I told Bobbie to tell you I *needed* you . . . because I do."

Taking his arm, Miriam drew him into the room. She unbuttoned his jacket and slipped it off his shoulders, then took his hat and tossed it onto a nearby chair.

"You look handsome . . . and so fresh and clean." Miriam drew her tongue along her narrow bottom lip. "You smell . . . delicious."

Doc gulped. "You . . . Bobbie said . . . ahh . . . what seems to be the problem? You don't look sick. I mean — "

"Oh, but I am sick, Jerome!" Stepping closer, Miriam pushed a wayward strand of hair back from her face. "I have a pain . . . right here." She placed her hand over her left, unbound breast. Her voice dropped a notch lower. "I think you should examine me. My heart's been aching so badly, that I'm afraid I might die."

Not waiting for his response, Miriam untied the sash from around her narrow waist and slid the wrapper to the floor. Holding herself proudly, she stood before him in a fine lace nightgown that was no more than a delicate shadow on her firm, thin body. Hesitating only a moment when Doc remained rigidly in place, she placed a hand on his shoulder and looked down at him, her expression soft and her voice warm.

"My heart started aching the moment I walked away from you this morning, and I realized that the closeness we had shared for the past month was at an end. The discomfort grew greater as the day wore on, until I was certain I was becoming sick from the distress of it. I knew I needed to do something to calm me, so I took a bath. Here. Smell . . ."

Miriam moved closer, cocking her head so Doc's lips were only inches from the fragrant skin of her neck. Obedient, he took an awkward sniff, and she drew back to look deeply into his eyes. "The bath soothed me, so then I washed my hair. I felt better for a while, but the ache returned. I was thinking of you, Jerome, and I knew I had to see you."

Miriam paused in her throaty explanation and Doc realized he was shaking. His breathing was rapid, almost as rapid as Miriam's. He started to perspire as she inched closer. Her seminakedness brushed him lightly as she took his hand and raised it to cover her breast.

"Can you feel how my heart is pounding? That isn't normal, is it?" Miriam's tongue darted out to lick her lips once more. "Isn't there something you can do?"

Doc choked. He blinked, then cleared his throat.

"Mir . . . Miriam . . ." His voice cracked and he tried once more. "Miriam, a . . . are you tryin' to seduce me?"

Miriam's lips trembled. Her voice dropping an octave lower, she replied, "My darling Jerome, I've never tried harder to do anything in my life."

Numb with shock, Doc went suddenly still. Snapping into motion a moment later, he threw his arms around Miriam and astounded even himself by sweeping her up into his arms. He heard Miriam's startled gasp as he carried her to the carefully scented bed awaiting them. In a moment he was lying beside her, his heart pounding against hers, his mustache caressing her cheek as he whispered against her lips, "Miriam, I want you to know that you have succeeded."

Hesitating, Doc astonished himself by continuing, "But before this goes any further, I have to ask you if you know for sure what you're doin' right now. And . . . and I need to know that you're not just lookin' at tonight as a lark that'll be over in the mornin'."

"Oh, Jerome." Unexpected tears filled Miriam's eyes. "I thought *I* was the one who was supposed to ask that question."

Feeling his own eyes fill as well, Doc responded, "Well, since you didn't, I figured I should, because I know damned well that once I have you, I won't be lettin' you go again. I want you to know right up front that you're goin' to have to pack away those widow's duds for the duration." He paused for a lecherous chuckle. "Because I sure as hell like you better the way you look now."

Miriam slipped her arms around his neck, her small eyes sincere. "Then I'll stay this way as long as you want me, because the truth is that I discovered somewhere between your office and my lonely walk back to this cabin that I loved you, and that I wouldn't be the woman I believed myself to be if I let you get away without a fight."

"Is that right?"

"That's right. But I must ask you . . ." Miriam bit her lips, then continued with soft determination, "Do you think you could love me someday?" At Doc's look of genuine confusion, she clarified quickly, "I mean, aside from . . . sex?"

"Miriam . . ."

His response a deep, seeking kiss that ended up rocking him to his toes, Doc drew back, assessing his former widow woman with new respect. Taking a breath, he whispered solemnly and formally, "Miriam Higgins, will you do me the honor of becoming my wife?"

"Jerome!"

Growling aloud as Miriam suddenly burst into sobs, Doc demanded a flat, unfeeling, "Answer me, woman!"

Under control within moments, a trace of the old Miriam returned as she responded as formally as he, "Yes, Jerome. I'm pleased to accept your proposal."

Doc searched the widow's plain, thin face. What he read

there raised a profound joy inside him that returned his lecherous grin.

"Then the honeymoon starts right *now!*"

And he'd be damned if they wouldn't usher in the mornin'. . . .

Morning came early on the trail. The camp had been on the move at the first light of dawn in order to make up for previous delays, but the effort had been to little avail. Standing a distance from her wagon in the unrelenting heat of late afternoon, Carolina attempted to placate her wailing child. After almost a week of traveling, she ached in both body and spirit. Her wagon's loss of a wheel was the most recent setback in their seemingly endless journey, but Carolina knew that the journey she had traveled in her mind had been more taxing than the ground physically covered.

Suzannah's wail continued.

"Seems like the little one doesn't like waitin' out here in the sun." At Carolina's shoulder as he was in most moments of difficulty, Jim Thompson attempted an encouraging smile. "Why don't you try singin' to her, ma'am? You might not get much appreciation out of the babe, but the rest of us fellas wouldn't mind hearin' the sound of a woman's voice in song right about now."

Carolina looked at the patient wagon master. Realizing he was serious, she looked down at her fretful daughter and surprised herself by beginning in a hesitant soprano, "Oh, Suzannah, don't you cry for me . . ."

But the words choked in her throat and Carolina was suddenly unable to go on. And she remembered. . . .

Another day and another departing wagon train jammed Deadwood's main street. In the furor of protesting beasts and angry drivers, Rosie adjusted her traveling clothes and turned to the portly bartender who stood beside her.

"You're sure you want to do this, Barney?" Realizing the question was unnecessary as he threw his carpetbag up into the wagon beside hers, she pressed, "You're throwin' away the chance of a lifetime, you know."

"I suppose you're right, Rosie." Barney's oversize mustache twitched. "It isn't every day that a bartender gets a saloon handed to him on a silver platter . . . and it isn't every day that he decides to walk away from it, either. But I'm not doin' anythin' that you didn't do."

"I suppose . . ."

"So, I'm sayin' I'm still goin' back to Cheyenne with you." Barney grinned and shrugged his beefy shoulders. "I've had enough of this place. I've got a need for some real civilization."

Barney's grin broadened but Rosie read the more tender truth behind her old friend's statement. She appreciated his concern for her and the need he felt to protect her. She knew nothing she could say would change things. Barney would deliver her to Cheyenne and see her safely settled . . . but she knew she didn't really need his help or anyone else's now. She was on the right track for the first time in more than seven years. Her mind was set and her sights were clear.

Drake loved Carolina and Carolina loved Drake. Whether they were together or apart, that would never change. Drake was her friend, and as a friend, they would always be a part of each other. She could accept that reality now and be content with it.

Doc loved Miriam and Miriam loved Doc. The pink satin wrapper and slinky lace nightgown she had lent Miriam a few days earlier had done the trick. She had seen the happy couple only once afterward, and as far as she knew, they hadn't gotten out of bed since.

So that left Tag and Rosie. . . .

Rosie's smile faded, because standing between them was Ella and all the wrong things she had said to Tag over the years. Worst of all, she knew that Tag knew, that at the time she had said them, she had meant every word.

Shouts from the head of the train snapped Rosie from her thoughts. Raising her chin, she took the hand Barney offered, stepped up onto the wagon, and assumed her seat. He hopped up beside her and she grasped her hat as the wagon jerked into motion.

Rosie's smile returned. She was wearin' a bright red traveling outfit, her color was high, and her hopes were right up there with it. The old Rosie was back, and she was unbeatable. She'd find Tag, all right . . . and when she did, she'd give Ella a run for her money.

Turning to Barney, Rosie winked boldly. After all, there wasn't a man who could take his eyes off her once she walked into sight, was there? And when she was really trying . . . well . . .

How long would it be before they reached Cheyenne?

The long difficult day had finally come to an end. Weary, Carolina sat by the fire, her babe at her breast. How long had they been on the trail? A week? Longer? She had almost lost track of time as one day had stretched into the next, but as time had slipped by, the inner turmoil she had suffered during the early part of her journey had gradually ceased.

Watching her daughter's flushed face as she nursed to satisfaction, Carolina marveled anew at the resemblance to William which emerged more clearly each day. She saw that resemblance in her daughter's high, patrician forehead, eyes that grew ever more blue, and the fleeting dimple in Suzannah's cheek that had been so much of William's charm. She was pleased at the resemblance. She had told William so during one of the many conversations she had had with him in her mind. She had told him that, and so much more. She had been unable to hear his response, but each time she had seen his face, his expression had been the same as it had been the last time they had spoken together. She would never forget the love there. That love had put her at peace with William's memory at last.

As for Drake, she knew now that her feelings for him would never change. She had come to terms with that realization and had put her guilts to rest. The process had been long and difficult, but the effect had worked a miraculous transformation inside her. She was finally ready for what was ahead of her.

A tremor shook Carolina as the shadows darkened and Suzannah's eyes fluttered closed. Her trembling increased as the sounds of camp slowly stilled, as she readied her daughter for the night and placed her back in the basket to sleep. It persisted as she poured water into a basin and carefully washed her hands and face. It swelled to an aching hunger, bringing tears to her eyes as she fought to quell it.

Carolina looked up at the starlit sky, seeking to communicate a last time with one she saw only in her mind's eye. An undetermined period of time passed before she finally lowered her gaze to the circle of darkness surrounding her. She studied it for a few moments before walking boldly forward.

Halting abruptly as the blackness enveloped her, Carolina attempted to still her shuddering. Finding that beyond her, she whispered, "It's no good, Drake. I know you're here. Please show yourself. I have to talk to you."

Silence was her only response. About to despair, Carolina heard the rustle of a step. She caught her breath as a shadow moved and Drake was suddenly beside her. His expression, hardly discernible, was cold.

"How did you know I was here?"

"I've known all along that you were following the train. No, I didn't see you. Nobody else saw you either, but I knew you were there. I was always able to tell when you were nearby. When we were in the cabin, I could feel you looking at me and the sensation made me feel safe. Later it made me feel comfortingly warm. Finally, it made me feel loved. That's when I started to realize that I loved you, too, Drake."

"*Do* you love me, Carolina?" Angry disbelief was in Drake's voice as he took a step closer. "I told myself you lied to me that day on the hillside when you said you loved me . . . that you had always lied. I told myself that love doesn't purposely inflict pain and that despite all you had said and done, you had never really loved me." Drake paused. She saw the convulsive working of his throat in the moment before he rasped, "I convinced myself of that, and then I realized that it didn't really make any difference, because I still loved you."

"Oh, Drake . . ."

"No, let me finish! I don't expect what I feel for you to

474

make any difference now. I don't suppose it ever really did. You were too caught up in guilts and denials. You wanted to punish yourself, and you didn't care who else suffered along with you."

"I did care, Drake!"

"Not enough!"

The truth in Drake's words shook Carolina, holding her silent. Finally able to respond, she whispered, "You're right. I didn't care enough. All I could think about was that William had died alone . . . that in those final moments before I walked away from him, I still hadn't been able to tell him I loved him. Oh, Drake," Carolina's voice caught on a sob, "it was such a simple thing to say, but I held the words back. It hurt him, but he told me he loved me enough for both of us and I'd grow to love him again. Still, I couldn't say the words. When he died, I couldn't forgive myself for that. I don't suppose I ever will."

"Carolina . . ."

"No, let me finish now, Drake. I couldn't think surrounded by things that reminded me of William . . . Miriam's cabin, Doc's office . . . even Deadwood. They all promoted my guilt. It wasn't until I was out here that I was able to start seeing things more clearly. When things began to straighten out in my mind, I did the only thing I could do. I spoke to William. I know he heard me. I told him that had he lived, I wouldn't have left him. I would've been faithful to him all my life and I would've fought to put you finally out of my mind . . . because I would've Drake! Tonight, when your presence around me was so strong, I explained to him that what could've been, could no longer be, and I had finally realized that in order to make the most of my life *and* Suzannah's, I couldn't continue serving my guilts. I told him that the only way for me to go forward would be with you, Drake . . . *with you*. I know William understood because . . . because he loved me, Drake. He really loved me, and love forgives. Love makes happiness, and love means —"

In a sudden blur of the moment, Drake's arms were around her. She felt his strength envelop her as he rasped against her lips, "Love means I'll never let you go again, Carolina, no matter what you say or what you do."

Drake's mouth covered hers, muffling her joyful cry. The warmth, the scent, the power of him . . . the love. It filled her. It made her whole as she returned his kiss with all the fervor of her bruised and aching heart.

Drake held her close, his loving words echoing within her. So much was yet unsaid, but Carolina was content. The long, painful road that Drake and she had traveled toward each other had come to an end. With Drake's arms finally around her, she knew . . . oh how clearly she knew . . . that it had been worth every step.

Epilogue

The hot weather had begun to wane as summer bowed to fall, but inside Drake's secluded cabin in the hills, time stood still. Carolina shifted in Drake's arms, knowing it was always that way after they made love, while the beauty lingered and the aura was still so strong. She tucked her face into the curve of his neck as Drake drew her closer, pressing her naked flesh against his. His warmth filled her and the happiness inside her swelled as she savored their moment of quiet intimacy.

Vibrant sparks of gold swirled in the green of Drake's eyes and Carolina's throat tightened. Love had softened those hard eyes, but the glory of the emotion between them did not stop there, nor in the bed where they lay despite the bright morning sunlight outside the window.

"What are you thinkin' about, Carolina?"

Carolina smiled. She had become accustomed to Drake's unconscious perusals, to his loving scrutiny and the sharp edges that remained, revealing that he did not yet quite believe that he would never again lose her. She responded with a smile.

"I was thinking that I've already gotten lazy, lying in bed in the middle of the morning without shame. The next step is to grow fat, I guess."

But Drake didn't smile. Turning on his side toward her, he cupped her chin with his palm, then trailed the flat of his hand down her neck in a slow sweep of her smooth flesh until it came to rest at her hip. "You're as thin as a girl. Your appearance deceived me when I found you on the mountain that

477

day. I thought I had discovered a helpless, wounded child."

"I was little more than that, at first."

"No, that's not true. Even when you were so close to death that I wasn't sure if your next breath would be your last, you fought for your life and Suzannah's. I've only now come to realize that I owe you more than I can ever repay for that."

Carolina was momentarily confused. "*You* owe *me*? You saved *my* life."

"No." Drake shook his head. Solemn, he lowered his mouth to hers. He drank long and deep from it, then drew back, caressing her cheek with soul-shattering tenderness as he whispered, "There wasn't much left of me when I found you. Then you gave me beautiful, precious gifts. You brought me Suzannah's life to bring into the world, and when I wasn't even sure I was worthy of that privilege, you gave me your trust."

"I always knew you were worthy, Drake. *Always*. . . ."

"But *I* wasn't sure, Carolina. Don't you see? You forced me to find out, step by step, a day at a time. You let me read in your eyes all that you could offer me, and you healed me, darlin'."

"And then I took it back." Sadness returning, Carolina whispered, "I'm so sorry, darling."

"For lovin' me?"

Carolina's throat tightened to the point of pain. "Never . . . never sorry for that."

Silently contemplative for long moments, his gaze searching her face, Drake finally whispered, "I've been thinkin' things over. We have almost enough gold dust accumulated to be able to leave here, soon." And at Carolina's look of sudden dismay, "Don't worry, darlin'. This territory will be opened up to settlement soon. It's real cattle country, and it'll be a new beginnin' for both of us. But first, there's somethin' I think we should do." Drake paused, watching her closely as he said, "I want to take you and Suzannah back East for a little while."

"Back East? Oh, Drake. . . ."

"You made a promise. I want you to keep it." A flash of the old Drake returned as his dark brows knit into a frown. "I've been thinkin' over what you said about owing it to Markham. I owe him that, too. He lost so much . . . the woman he loved, his daughter, his life. I don't know how fate singled me out to survive, but I know you were right when you said Markham's parents deserve to see their grandchild. I can do that much for him at least."

A whimper from the basket nearby turned Carolina and Drake simultaneously toward it. Drake stayed Carolina when she attempted to rise.

"She's not slept out, yet. I'll get her back to sleep."

Back beside her minutes later, Drake cupped Carolina's face with his hands. He read in her eyes the myriad feelings she could not manage to express. A world of promise beyond words in his voice, he whispered, "I love you, Carolina."

Her heart so full of love at that moment that she could not speak, Carolina raised her mouth to his. Drake had proved his love for her in so many ways. It was her turn to prove her love for him in return, and she would do it willingly . . . eagerly . . . joyfully . . . if it took the rest of their lives.